DANCING
from the
SHADOWS

a novel

D'Ann Renner

AMBASSADOR INTERNATIONAL
GREENVILLE, SOUTH CAROLINA & BELFAST, NORTHERN IRELAND

www.ambassador-international.com

Advance Praise for
DANCING FROM THE SHADOWS

"I intended to read just a chapter or two of D'Ann Renner's novel but the story sucked me in, compelling me to read long past the time I should have put it down. Renner portrays the heartaches and triumphs of raising a special needs child with humor and amazing accuracy. I found myself laughing and crying along with the St. John family as they dealt with the extreme stress experienced by families with disabilities. I would recommend *Dancing From The Shadows*, not just to the autism world, but to anyone interested in turning denial into dancing, adversity into adventure."

—*Jacline Moore*
Georgia TACA (Talk about Curing Autism) Coordinator
www.tacanow.org

"D'Ann Renner has given us a glimpse into the struggles of a family coping with raising an autistic child. Having worked with many families with such struggles, the story awakens not only the stark realities of the emotional rollercoaster that families go through but also a true sense of the hope that comes with understanding, patience, and love."

—*David S. Cantor, Ph.D.*
President, Psychological Sciences Institute, PC
www.psyscienceinst.com
President, Innovative Health Foundation, Inc.
www.innovativehealthfoundation.org

"I love It! *Dancing From the Shadows* is a compelling glimpse into the real world of parents who are raising children with special needs–the love, the fear, the struggles, the joy. Inspirational and delightful, a good read."

—*Lucy Cusick*
Co-founder & Executive Director
FOCUS, Families of Children Under Stress
www.Focus-ga.org

Dancing From the Shadows is dedicated to my mother, Barbara Holmes Worcester. Mom, always convinced I had a story to tell, encouraged, cajoled, and pushed until it was done. Thanks, Mom, I love you!

Dancing from the Shadows

This is a fictional work. Although incidents such as the ones portrayed do occur in the special needs world, the names, characters, places and incidents either are the product of the author's imagination or are used fictitiously. Any resemblance to actual persons, living or dead, or events is entirely coincidental. While certain places are real, the events that take place there are not.

© 2012 by D'Ann Renner

All rights reserved. Printed in the United States of America. Except as permitted under the United States Copyright Act of 1976, no part of this publication may be reproduced or distributed in any form or by any means, or stored in a data base or retrieval system, without the prior written permission of the publisher.

ISBN: 978-1-62020-112-1
eISBN: 978-1-62020-161-9

Unless otherwise indicated all Scripture quotations are taken from THE HOLY BIBLE, NEW INTERNATIONAL VERSION®, NIV® Copyright © 1973, 1978, 1984, 2011 by Biblica, Inc.™ Used by permission. All rights reserved worldwide.

Cover Design and Typesetting: Matthew Mulder
E-book conversion: Anna Riebe

AMBASSADOR INTERNATIONAL
Emerald House
427 Wade Hampton Blvd.
Greenville, SC 29609, USA
www.ambassador-international.com

AMBASSADOR BOOKS
The Mount
2 Woodstock Link
Belfast, BT6 8DD, Northern Ireland, UK
www.ambassador-international.com

The colophon is a trademark of Ambassador

Acknowledgements

Without the support of my number one fan, my wonderful husband Bruce, this novel would not have been possible. He urges me to write, offers loving suggestions, and mans the home front when I'm lost in the writing/speaking world.

I also appreciate the time, patience and input of the FORUM Writer's Group, who listened to my novel 1500 words at a time, and responded with constructive criticism and writing tips. These talented and dedicated writers were instrumental in showing me how to transform a raw story into a compelling narrative.

Finally, a grateful shout-out to the dedicated educators, therapists and doctors who staff the special needs world. Working alongside us, you empower our children's progress. While we don't always agree on specific tactics, we know your overall strategy is to help our kids be the very best they can be, and we appreciate you.

Contents

Chapter 1
Molar Nightmare 9
Chapter 2
It's Not Enough. 21
Chapter 3
Bone of My Bone 31
Chapter 4
Ready or Not 50
Chapter 5
Flight 68 from Purgatory. 72
Chapter 6
Home Strange Home. 85
Chapter 7
Daunting Diagnosis. 99
Chapter 8
Shouldering the Burden. 112
Chapter 9
Joys of Potty Training 120
Chapter 10
Intense Questions 131
Chapter 11
In Search of the Perfect Doctor 136
Chapter 12
Danger Zone. 145
Chapter 13
Sorting Through the Information Haystack 155
Chapter 14
A Support System Crashes 164

CHAPTER 15
  Denial, Danger, and Disrespect 181
CHAPTER 16
  Depression 189
CHAPTER 17
  Shaking a Fist at God 198
CHAPTER 18
  Conflict of Interest 211
CHAPTER 19
  Everyone Has Something. 218
CHAPTER 20
  Painful Transitions 229
CHAPTER 21
  Mounting Tensions 253
CHAPTER 22
  Two Sides of the Coin 269
CHAPTER 23
  Irrevocable Decision 279
CHAPTER 24
  The Storm Breaks 294
CHAPTER 25
  Accident 305
CHAPTER 26
  Limbo 319
CHAPTER 27
  The End 327
EPILOGUE
  Three Years Later 340

Chapter 1

Molar Nightmare

The Star Wars ring tone reverberated off the bathroom walls and ceiling, causing Tori to stand motionless; mascara wand midair. She flipped open her phone.

Over blood-curdling screams, which she recognized as her son's, Tori heard Sandi Walker, Gabe's teacher, say, "Something's wrong with Gabe. He keeps scratching his cheeks."

"I'm on my way."

Tori hopped into her car and sped to the school, hoping her five-year-old's ailment was something easy to diagnose and treat. Fortunately, the school was nearby.

While stopped at the red light in front of the school, she called her pediatrician.

The pediatrician's scheduler offered, "Dr. Jeffries can see you if you can come in the next fifteen minutes."

Tori checked her watch. It was tight, but with green lights and blind policemen, she could make it. She called the school and arranged to have Gabe waiting at the curb, and then left a quick message canceling brunch with her eccentric neighbor, Serena.

Mrs. Walker stood outside with Gabe. His little hands were tightly secured with heavy plastic gloves; his bloody face gave mute testimony to their necessity. Any optimism about Gabe's problem being something simple dissolved like sugar in the strong Irish

Breakfast tea she would not be drinking with Serena. Shaken, Tori shook off thoughts of strait jackets and orderlies in white suits.

While initialing the school sign-out sheet, Tori noticed blood oozing from a gash in Mrs. Walker's hand.

"What happened?"

"Gabe scratched me twice this morning; I don't know why."

Tori dropped the sign-out clipboard.

"Gabe did that?" Tori dropped her head to the steering wheel and fought for composure. She lifted her head. The scratch was nasty.

"Sandi, I'm so, so sorry! I can't believe—Gabe really likes you. . . ." Tori choked back a sob. "Should you see a doctor? We'll pay for it."

Not sure how.

Mrs. Walker bent and retrieved the clipboard.

"Don't worry about it, I've experienced much worse than this." She winked. "I keep my tetanus shots up-to-date."

Tori turned to Gabe. "Young man, what do you tell your teacher?"

"Sorry, Walker," Gabe responded through his tears.

"Mrs. Walker," Tori corrected.

The teacher gave an approving smile.

"I'm glad you're making him accept responsibility. Many parents don't." She leaned into the back seat window.

"Feel better soon, Gabe, but no more scratching. It's inappropriate even when we feel bad." Mrs. Walker smiled and went back into the school.

Tori's hands were shaking too badly to fasten her seatbelt. She turned off the car, took several deep breaths, and then turned to speak to her son.

"We're going to get you help, Darlin'. Just hang on. Mama needs to call Daddy real quick to tell him you're not feeling well."

She called Phillip to brief him about their son's odd behavior. Phillip was reassuring.

"Ok, sweet petite, settle down. Let's pray," he suggested. "Lord, we're worried about Gabe; we don't know what's wrong.

We almost never know what's wrong. Give us Your peace in the face of not knowing. Help us figure it out quickly. Amen."

Tori's hands steadied.

"Thanks; that helped. I'd better get going."

"Ok, munchkin. I'm packing up my computer; I'll work from home today."

"Thanks, and thanks for praying with me. Love you. Bye." She pulled away from the curb and headed out.

The light at the school exit was red. *Blast. No one's coming and Gabe's in agony.*

Tori ran the light and headed toward the doctor's office; her knuckles white on the steering wheel. She watched Gabe through the rearview mirror as she drove.

"You okay, little prince?"

"Gabe *hurting*!"

Gabe was pulling at his cheek. Tori grimaced in the mirror. *Ask a stupid question. . . .*

At the next light she pulled up the number of his dentist, wondering how parents had coped in the days before cell phones.

At the pediatrician's office, she and Gabe were immediately taken into an examination room—Gabe's screams were echoing off the waiting room walls.

"Gabe, can you show me what hurts?" Dr. Jeffries asked.

"He's crying," Gabe said.

He had stopped screaming, but gave an occasional hiccup of tears. The gloves he was wearing irritated him and he was no longer scratching himself, so Tori removed them.

"How long has he been this way?" Dr. Jeffries peered into Gabe's ears.

"Just today, I think," Tori said as she nervously tugged at an escaped curl from the elegant French twist she had created for her outing.

"Gabe's not exactly communicative. He didn't blow me his usual good morning raspberry." She curled her lower lip between her teeth. "His temperature was normal, but I should've picked up he wasn't feeling well. We have this game—one of the few he'll play—where he tries to steal my hot tea. We have fun with it, but he wasn't interested today."

"Gabe, lay back, please." Dr. Jeffries kneaded Gabe's stomach. "Does this hurt, son?"

Gabe rolled off the table and buried his face in Tori's lap, rubbing his mouth hard against her leg.

"Answer, Gabe." Tori stroked Gabe's hair.

A muffled "Gabe hurt!" emerged.

"Well, there you have it." The pediatrician sat down at his computer. "Gabe hurts. I can't find anything wrong medically."

He scrolled through Gabe's medical charts.

"The pain is centered at his face, but there's no apparent throat or sinus problem." He checked the screen. "Ahh, he's five . . . old enough to be cutting his six-year molars, but they shouldn't cause this much pain. Take him to a pediatric dentist right away."

"I have an appointment right after this with Dr. Wu."

Dr. Jeffries nodded. "She's good. If he's not cutting his molars, call me. We'll need to order tests."

An hour later, Tori and her son sat in Dr. Wu's waiting room. When worried, she tended to mess with her hair, so the remains of the morning's graceful up do hung limply around her face. She tried to distract Gabe, who alternated between chewing on a book, screaming, and trying to hit Tori.

"That boy's being naughty isn't he, Mommy?" a little girl said at the top of her clear, thin voice. "I'm being good, aren't I?"

"Yes, darling, but speak quietly," her mother said. "I'm sure he's usually a very nice boy."

Tori picked Gabe up.

"Hush, now. I know you hurt. I'm sorry. We're working on it."

She tried to rock Gabe. He hit her with his soggy book. Just then, Dr. Wu appeared.

She smiled and wagged her finger at Gabe. "Gabriel St. John! Why are you making all that noise? Come on back. Let's have a look at you."

In her office, she deftly managed to avoid being bitten while doing a quick exam.

"Gabe's cutting his six-year molars. How sensitive is he to pain?"

Tori shrugged. "Sometimes he's very sensitive, other times he hardly notices it."

Gabe screamed and hit himself in the face. He got in two good blows before Tori could restrain him.

"I'd say he's noticing it this time," Dr. Wu said.

She scribbled something on her prescription pad, tore off a sheet, and handed it to Tori.

"This is for Paregoric—a strong pain medication. It should ease Gabe's pain and make him sleepy. Don't worry, Mom, he's going to be fine."

By the time Tori reached the store, Gabe was punching himself in the mouth and trying to escape his car seat. She wrestled him into a shopping cart. After barely thwarting his third attempt to jump out, Tori laid her body over the cart and pushed it on her tip toes. Her ears rang from his shrill screams. The cart dug painfully into her ribs. Every few minutes, Gabe hit her.

An idle stock boy watched.

"Why are you walking like that? Does he want out?"

No, I'm a prima ballerina; I do this to exercise my toes. Tori nodded curtly.

An older gentleman approached her.

"That looks awkward, ma'am. May I push the cart while you try to calm your little man?"

Tori nodded gratefully. He helped them into the pharmacy, gave her a courtly bow, and disappeared.

Either he's an angel in disguise, or a really nice man.

Tori joined the back of the long line at the prescription drop-off counter. In front of her was a thin woman with bleached blonde, highly teased hair; a tight top; and low slung blue jeans. An idle compartment of Tori's brain wondered what made middle-aged women feel dressing like a teenager was a desirable trait.

Just then, Big Hair spoke to the woman in front of her in a penetrating whisper,

"Some mothers just can't control their children! If he were mine, I'd blister his bottom. No way would my child behave this way in public!" Tori chuckled. She knew she was on the verge on hysteria, but she could not help herself. A few people edged away.

Salvation came in the form of Carlee—a plump, black woman who was Tori's favorite pharmacy technician. Carlee came out to check on the commotion. She took the prescription and reassured Tori in her caramel sugar accent.

"Y'all go sit down in the waiting area, honey. I'll get this filled. Can Gabe have a lollipop?"

"Sure. Sugar and food coloring are the least of my worries at this point."

Gabe grabbed the lollipop, ripped off the paper, and bit down on it like a T-Rex crunching bones. Carlee supplied Tori with a handful of lollipops and hurried behind the counter.

"Well!" said Big Hair, hitching up her jeans. "If I had known all I need to do to get preferential treatment is bring in a badly behaved child and let him start screaming . . ."

Tori's arms strained against tired shoulder sockets as she tried to keep Gabe still. She twisted to look at Big Hair.

"My . . . son . . . has . . . autism. He's in . . . a lot . . . of pain. Leave him . . . alone."

Carlee hurried out then and handed Tori a plastic spoon and Gabe's prescription.

"Here, Darlin', you let Mama give you this. It'll make you'll feel better."

Carlee turned to Big Hair. "This 'lil baby is in a lot of pain, else he'd be his own sweet self."

Thankfully, Gabe had always taken medication easily. He swallowed obediently. Big Hair flushed, turned away, and began examining a display of laxatives.

Carlee turned to Tori.

"We have all your information on file, Ms. St. John. Just initial this and get this little love home."

Tori signed for the Paregoric, wrangled Gabe into his car seat, and headed home.

"Hold on a few minutes more, Little Prince. The medicine should make you feel better any minute now."

Please God, let it make him feel better.

Gabe chomped his way through four lollipops, pausing occasionally to wail. By the time they got home, even a fifth lollipop couldn't keep him calm. He acted like a cornered animal, lashing out at Tori and clawing his cheeks until they bled.

Where is Phillip?

As a last resort, Tori wrestled Gabe to the ground. Hovering over him, her arms pinned him to the floor. Tori wept; hot tears fell on her son's frantic face, mixing with those streaming down his bloody cheeks.

They stayed there for what seemed like hours; until Gabe finally stopped fighting. Tori saw through puffy lids that Gabe's eyelids were drooping. Within five minutes he fell asleep. She pulled herself to her knees, got an afghan off the couch, and covered him.

The garage door opened; a door slammed.

"Tori, Gabe, I'm home! Sorry I'm late. Traffic . . ." Phillip rounded the corner into the den and came to a halt; eyes wide, as he surveyed the scene.

"What . . .?" Phillip looked at Gabe's bloody face. "Is he okay? Are *you* okay?"

He pulled Tori to her feet. "I'll get the hydrogen peroxide and clean him up. Why don't you go lay down?"

"In a minute. I need to call Dr. Klein and ask her for an emergency teleconference. Gabe can't take much more of this; neither can I. There's got to be something we can do."

"Emergency teleconference? Are those the ones costing ninety-five dollars per ten minute increments?"

"Yes." Tori fixed him with a steely glare—her eyes narrowed. "Is that a problem?"

Phillip held up his hands, palms out. "Not at all . . . Absolutely not. I'll get the phone."

Eleanor Klein's receptionist was distressed.

"I'm so sorry, but she's out of the country. I'll leave an urgent message for her to call you."

Dr. Klein had not called two hours later when an ear-splitting scream announced Gabe had awakened. Tori gave him more medicine. His shrieks intensified.

Phillip held the sobbing preschooler while Tori sang Gabe's favorite songs. Tunes that had delighted and soothed in the past, failed to give solace today.

Lydia arrived home. She bounced into the room, full of restless energy.

"Mom, my homework's done. Let's go outside." She tossed a small football hand-to-hand.

"Sorry, Sweetheart, I can't right now. Your brother's sick."

"Oh." The eight-year-old cocked her head and studied Gabe. "Sure he's not faking it?"

She shrugged. "Daddy, will you throw the football with me?"

"Sorry, Cupcake. Mama and I are pretty busy with Gabe."

Lydia's jaw jutted.

"Both of you? Why are you holding him like that, anyway?"

"If we don't hold him still, he hurts himself or us." Phillip said. "See the scratches?"

"He hurt." Gabe looked bewildered, as if wondering why they wouldn't help him.

Lydia snorted.

"If I did that, I'd be in time out. Gabe never gets in trouble. I want to play football."

"Lydia, sweetheart, your brother is cutting his molars, and it's very painful. You know he has—"

"Special needs. Yeah, I know." The eight-year-old's shoulders slumped. "Try giving him crushed ice, he loves that; maybe it'll help him feel better. Guess I'll go rot my mind with TV."

Tori started to go after Lydia, and then stopped. "I hate that she feels this way, but we can't leave Gabe right now. I'll make it up to her later."

Gabe had stopped trying to escape. Tori took advantage of the lull in the storm to coax spoonfuls of crushed ice into his mouth. He ate like a little bird. He chewed for a few seconds, swallowed, and then tilted his head back, opening his mouth for the next bite.

"I wish he could talk to us," Tori mourned.

Two lone tears slid down the planes of Phillip's tan cheek. The tears were an anomaly on a face that seldom felt their touch.

"If he could express himself," Phillip said, "I'm afraid he'd ask why we didn't help him. I have a CD of Home Remedies in my car's glove compartment, want me to get it?"

Tori smiled through her concern. The contents of her analytical husband's glove box were legendary.

"I have the book. I dabbed Oil of Clove on his gums while he was asleep."

"Well, call his pediatrician. Maybe Dr. Jeffries can suggest something."

Tori called the doctor and left an emergency page. He called back right away and Tori explained what was going on.

"So," she concluded, pushing her hair out of her eyes, "I was wondering if we could take him to the emergency room."

Phillip's head jerked up.

Gabe's pediatrician spoke gently, "I understand your concern, but the hospital can't help. We know what's wrong; he's cutting his six year molars. He's already on the strongest pain medication he can take."

"I thought maybe they could put him under; a mild anesthesia . . . just until the worst has passed."

Dr. Jeffries exhaled loudly. "No reputable hospital, or doctor, would anesthetize a child because he's cutting molars."

"But you have no idea how much pain he's in!" Tori realized she was shouting. "I'm sorry. I didn't mean to yell at you."

She rubbed her temple. "I'm a little frazzled. A lot frazzled."

"No apology necessary. I'm a parent, too. Hold to the thought that cutting six year molars is not life-threatening; Gabe will be fine. Try soaking a washcloth in apple juice; ice it 'til it's really cold, and then rub it against his gums."

Tori hung up and slumped into a chair; her head in her hands.

Phillip cocked his head.

"Anesthesia? What were you thinking?"

"It's all I could come up with," Tori mumbled through her fingers.

Phillip rolled his eyes. "Anesthesia's a bit of an overkill."

Gabe gave a raspy scream through vocal cords that sounded painfully strained.

"Is he getting at all sleepy?" Tori said.

Phillip loosened his grip to look. Gabe twisted his head back and bit his father.

"No, he's wide awake," Phillip said.

It seemed like eons before Gabe fell asleep again. As Phillip carried him upstairs, the phone rang. Tori pounced on it. Dr. Klein was speaking over a dull roar of background voices. Phillip ran downstairs. Tori put the call on speakerphone.

"I hope this is important," the crusty doctor said. "I don't get many vacations."

Tori sketched a picture of Gabe with tusks protruding out of his mouth as she brought Dr. Klein up-to-date. Tori drew constantly. Before she finished the sketch or her story, Dr. Klein interrupted.

"Stop. What type of painkiller did his dentist prescribe? Something containing opiates?"

"Um . . . let me see . . . Paregoric. Is that—?"

"Yes, it's an opiate," Dr. Klein said. "I wish doctors wouldn't prescribe for special needs children without checking. You should always clear any medication with me before giving it to Gabe. Got it?"

"Yes." Tori said. She blew a lock of hair off her forehead.

"Opiates are disinhibitors," Dr. Klein said. "Disinhibitors lessen self-control. Children with autism often don't usually have a strong natural restraint system to begin with, so drugs like this can definitely cause the type reaction you're seeing, often without giving pain relief."

"But what can we give him? He's in agony!"

Dr. Klein's voice softened.

"I know. I've heard an adult with autism describe the pain as red hot needles being stuck up his gums. Sadly, effective pain meds will contain opiates or opiate derivatives. Hold on."

She spoke to someone in the background. "Save me a couple of those chocolate thingies."

She resumed instructions. "No school. Rub his gums with Anbesol. Whiskey may help, too."

"Are you saying massage his gums with alcohol?" Tori walked to the cabinet and pulled out a dusty bottle of cooking sherry.

"Or drink it yourselves, whatever helps most. Within reason, let him chew whatever he wants, but don't let him use your fingers as a chew-toy, ha, ha. Get the strongest freezable teething ring you can find. This is not going to be fun. Buy some smelling salts at the pharmacy. They could help center him a little when he's berserk with pain."

"We'll be praying," Tori said.

Phillip was making the wind it up motion. The doctor's meter was running.

Tori covered the phone.

"We have seven minutes left of the second ten minutes."

Phillip nodded, but took off his watch and put it in her hand.

"A correlation between coping skills and prayer *has* been documented."

Dr. Klein's tongue made a sucking sound against the roof of her mouth, a habit she had when thinking. Tori visualized her—mouth open, eyes contemplating some far away vision.

Dr. Klein, who was an atheist, spoke abruptly. "Prayer might cause a placebo effect. If it helps, who cares?"

"How long do molars take to cut?" Tori said.

"A week if you're lucky, three if you're not."

"Then I'll pray for them to cut fast."

"Huh?" The phone clicked. Dr. Klein never said good-bye.

Tori headed for the store, hoping they made mega-super-strength Anbesol.

Five days later, which felt like years, Tori woke at six o'clock in the morning. Something was not right. She checked Gabe's room; he was gone. She thundered downstairs and discovered Gabe on the couch, watching a video intently, even though he could quote the lines by heart.

He was quiet, so Tori went into the kitchen and made herself a cup of tea. Minutes later, Gabe came in, blew a raspberry in Tori's direction, and stole her hot tea.

"Gabe's." He giggled, fudgesicle eyes twinkling over the rim of the cup.

Tori recaptured her cup, blew on it, and gave him a sip.

"Looks like you're feeling better."

Gabe pointed to the cup.

"More."

"You've had enough, Snollygoster. How about school today?"

Gabe nodded, beaming.

"Phillip! Lydia!" she called up the stairs. "Gabe's cut his molars."

After everyone had left, Tori looked around. The house could star on a reality show for chaotic homes. Tori estimated she had a bazillion emails to answer, not to mention fifteen calls from her mother; since yesterday. She had no idea where to start; possibly with changing her sweats, which she had worn for three days.

As she trudged up the stairs, Tori happened to glance at one of the framed photographs lining the staircase wall. Gazing out at her was a poised, attractive career-woman, smiling as she accepted a trophy.

That was only three years ago. How did that successful, beautiful business-lady evolve into me? Tori sank down on a stair step and thought back to the day it all started.

CHAPTER 2

It's Not Enough

"Tori, a three hundred and twenty-five million dollar contract? Incredible!"

"Thanks, Bryan," Tori told her favorite co-worker. "It was a good team."

"Gorgeous, talented, and modest; I bet you get marketing VP when Herndon retires." Bryan grinned. "Gotta go; I have a meeting. Great sale, Maestro!"

Bryan bowed his way out of her office. Tori's smile faded as he left.

I'm not all that excited. That's odd.

She glanced at her watch. Six-thirty. Navigating Highway 285 would be like salmon swimming upstream. She called Phillip, her husband of twelve years.

"Hi, Love, want to have dinner while traffic dies down?"

Forty-five minutes later, Tori looked affectionately at Phillip as he stretched his tall frame out over a chair and relaxed at one of their favorite restaurants.

"Good day?"

"Okay. Better now," Phillip leaned in and brushed her lips with his.

The waiter glided up to their table and kissed his fingers to Tori.

"Ahh, Miss Tori . . . stunning as usual. Tonight we have the lobster risotto with pine nuts, yes?"

"Yes! Sounds wonderful, Carlo."

Phillip rolled his eyes.

"The heart attack special? I'm watching my figure."

He flexed his shoulders, making muscles ripple under his snug knit shirt.

Tori stuck her tongue out at him. She loved good food and constantly battled to stop her petite frame's tendency to morph from curvaceous to plump. Phillip, who loved exercise, vegetables and all things healthy, maintained his trim physique without effort.

Phillip had just ordered grilled tilapia when Tori's cell phone rang. She looked at caller ID.

"It's Mom. Let me tell her I'll call back."

"Hi, Mom?" Tori said, looking at the screen. "Fudgesicle, my battery's gone! Mom will spend the next hour imagining me in a horrible car wreck."

Phillip scooted his chair back.

"Let me have your phone."

"You don't have a battery for my phone in your glove compartment! Do you?"

Phillip smirked.

"Back in a second."

He left holding Tori's cell phone and was back minutes later. He presented Tori's phone with a flourish.

"Aladdin's Cave has nothing on my glove box. Your mother called again. I said you'd call later."

He draped himself over his chair, focused his sapphire gaze on her, and ruffled her thick curls.

"Why the sad face, my diminutive darling? You're SmithStone's heroine."

"Diminutive darling? That's a new one."

"You know I'm always looking for new ways to describe your elfin beauty. But what's up?"

"I feel . . . uneasy, like my success doesn't make a difference in the long run."

"As in tomorrow they'll be asking, 'What have you done for me lately?'"

"As in eternally. The poorest Americans live better than most of the world."

"You're having a mid-life crisis?" Phillip thrust out his lower lip. "Does that mean you want a Ferrari and a boy-toy? You're not budgeted for a new car anytime soon."

Tori stifled a laugh and pointed her finger at him.

"C'mon, I'm serious. There's a Bible verse that's always haunted me," she doodled on her napkin. "From whom much is given, much is required."

"Okay, seriously. Based on our tax returns, our charitable giving, by percentage of income, is 339.4 percent higher than the average American," Phillip said.

"Yes, but with two incomes and no kids, it's easy to give!"

Phillip glanced at the napkin. She had drawn two pigs—one with her face and one with his. He grimaced at her.

"Capitalist pigs? Aw, c'mon Little Red, that's not true." He tilted back on his chair legs. "Why this sudden introspection?"

"Lean back any further and you'll fall over. It's not sudden. I've been noticing for a while our lives are self-absorbed." Tori's eyes pleaded with Phillip. "I want . . . more."

"What does *more* look like? We volunteer often, we give a lot, and we sponsor children. We even considered adopting a third-world child and decided it was impractical." Phillip brought his chair back down. "Do you want to take a year off and concentrate on painting?"

"No." Tori sipped her tea. "Painting's a creative outlet, but I'm not good enough to go pro. I'd forgotten our adoption discussions. Hmm. Maybe that's an idea."

Tori saw an expression of dismay cross Phillip's face.

"Relax. Just a thought."

The next night, they ate on their deck, enjoying garlicky grilled shrimp accompanied by crisp salads and soft jazz.

"I've been thinking," Tori said.

"Uh oh."

Tori popped him with her napkin.

"We've considered adoption over the years. The discussions never went anywhere. Why is that?"

"When you wanted a child, I didn't." Phillip said. "By the time I came around, you had second thoughts. Why'd you hesitate?"

Tori pushed salad around her plate.

"Dad wanted a boy. He got me." She slipped a piece of shrimp under the table to Amber, their Siamese-Persian cat. "I needed to prove I could succeed."

"Stop spoiling her. That shrimp cost twelve dollars a pound."

"I'll always love you best, Sweetie." Tori popped a shrimp in Phillip's mouth then continued. "I'd rather hear squeaky Styrofoam than children whining. And I need plenty of alone time. Those aren't maternal traits."

She slipped Amber an anchovy. "Lately though, I've thought I could make a good mom. Maybe."

Before Phillip could reply, Amber launched herself onto Tori's lap.

"Ouch! I'm not a ladder! And *you* need a pedicure." Tori peeled Amber's claws off her legs. "Go maul Daddy; he's the one who says you can't have any more shrimp."

She looked at Phillip. "I've had the business success. I'm still . . ." Tori lifted a hand, and then let it fall. "There's an empty ache, sometimes. Why don't you want kids?"

"I like life neat and predictable. Children aren't."

Life is good now. The idea of sharing Tori, my money, or my time intimidates me. However, we are getting older. If Tori wants it—

"The idea's growing on me. Are you seriously considering parenthood?"

"I . . . I think I'm as ready as I'll ever be." Tori said.

Their eyes locked.

Tori's and Phillip's favorite neighbor was Serena D'Antonio, a Venezuelan lady who lived across the street. She was funny, outspoken, and thoughtful. She exuded an energy that belied her sixty plus years.

Her translation of English was picturesque and amusing, although the St. Johns suspected Serena's misquotes often contained a hidden message. She had been hinting it was time the St. Johns started their family. As soon as dinner was cleared, Tori ran to Serena's house.

"Hi, beautiful," Tori said, pecking Serena on the cheek. "Where's your guardian?"

Just then Scotch, Serena's fiercely protective dog, thundered into the house and skidded around the corner to the kitchen, nails clicking on the beautiful tile floor. Finding Tori already in place, he skipped his usual inspection, and settled for a sniff and cautionary growl.

"We've decided to look into adoption!"

Tori expected congratulations. Serena bent and scrubbed her already pristine counter. With a faint frown, she asked,

"So, you are ready, then, to quit your job?"

"Quit? We can't afford a baby if I don't work."

"Who then will raise the child?"

"We'll have a nanny or an au pair during the day. Phillip and I will spend quality time with it nights and weekends. The mom works in most families these days."

"You're such the career woman, Victoria. I think you'll need the break clean from your job."

Tori frowned.

"You speak of quality time," Serena straightened. "I see you often when you are first home. There is very little quality left at your day's end. All has been lavished on SoapStone. Your vessel is drained. By the next morning, your pitcher it is full again, but then you will be off to your office, while this nanny-pair raises your baby."

"SmithStone. And we'll plan for concentrated periods of quality time."

"I see. Be sure and notify the child of the schedule, so he can cooperate," Serena said. "What I recall with los niños is large *quantities* of time. It's hard to have one without the other."

"I'll cut back. I won't keep pouring my best into SmithStone."

"To cut back, Querida, is not your nature. Anything you choose to do, you will do it very well. It is your strength . . . and your weakness."

"My strength and weakness?"

"Most weaknesses are strengths, which have been taken too far, or in the wrong direction."

Tori stroked Scotch's glossy black fur and frowned.

"Are you saying my compulsion for excellence generates the weakness of being unable to multi-task? Not true. I'd never survive at SmithStone without the ability to juggle ninety-nine plates simultaneously."

"But the number of dishes at work will remain the same. Even a part-time baby raised by a nanny-pair will add 399 dishes to your load. When you juggle those together with your business plates, something will crash. God pray it won't be the baby."

Tori scooted her chair back. "I need to go, it's late."

Back at home, Tori stomped around on what her mother used to call angry feet.

"Serena told me my vessel is empty at the end of the day. Plus, I have too many plates."

"Empty vessels and an over-abundance of plates? You're not making sense," Phillip said. "Hard day at the office, Ma Petite? Have a Coke; maybe your caffeine/sugar reserves are low."

He slurped loudly from his bottled energy drink, turning it so Tori could see the ALL NATURAL label.

"Oh, stop patronizing me. In ten years they'll discover tofu causes cancer in laboratory animals. Here's what Serena said."

Tori reviewed their conversation. Phillip pursed his lips.

"She has a point. We're gone by six-thirty every morning and seldom make it home before seven o'clock in the evening. Full briefcases are the norm on weekends."

They talked to friends with children. Some couples had both continued working, several moms and one dad had quit their jobs. Phillip had fun drawing up a drastic budget for life on one salary.

"You make almost as much money as I do. This year, with your mega-sale commissions and bonuses, you'll make more than me. Maybe I should stay home."

A vase shattered in the sink.

"Oops," Tori said. "Do you want to stay home?"

"No, although I may like being a kept man. Could we still have the nanny?" Phillip waggled his eyebrows at Tori. "A young, buxom nanny, of course."

"Of course." Tori hugged Phillip from behind and rested her face on his back. "What did I do to deserve you?"

"Being who you are is enough. I'm glad we don't fight like other couples. Whether you decide to stay home or get a nanny, I'll back you."

"Thanks," Tori said. "Once we have a child, our lives will be perfect."

They decided Tori would take a one-year maternity leave, and then determine what to do next.

The adoption procedure killed thousands of trees. Every facet of their lives was documented, notarized, and sent away for embassy seals. As they worked, they considered the child they wanted.

"This report says the chance of being adopted after the age of eighteen months drops by 75 percent!" Phillip said one day. "And if a child reaches age four, its chances for adoption are virtually non-existent. Of course, to validate this, I should do a cross-analysis."

Tori rolled her eyes.

"We don't need a cross-analysis to confirm most people want to adopt babies. The older a child gets the less desirable they become."

"That stinks! How would you feel about adopting an older child?"

Tori tilted her head.

"Hmm. I've always found toddlers more interesting than babies."

"Hey, guess what? The odds of a special needs child being adopted are—"

"No." Tori's voice was implacable.

"We could really make a difference."

"Not interested."

"Are you sure? It'd be difficult, but I'm okay with a special needs child."

"You may be okay. I'm the one who'll stay home. I'm quitting my job, which slashes our income. We're getting a non-English speaking older child who's been institutionalized all his life. It's enough."

"I understand." Phillip's eyes caressed his graph. "It's just that the analysis shows—."

"Why," Tori asked sweetly, "don't you stick your analysis in your ear?"

Phillip backed away, palms out.

"Okay. No special needs; got it."

Tori flexed a cramped hand. No more paperwork today. She visited Serena instead.

She was met with the inviting smell of freshly baked cookies and Scotch's unwelcoming growls. His threat to rip her apart subsided upon Serena's invitation to come in, but he sniffed her thoroughly before padding away.

"Do you think he'll ever stop checking me out?"

"No. It is his job." Serena patted Scotch's head.

Tori grabbed a warm cookie.

"So, what's up?"

"You have met Jack, yes? He is taking me horseback riding," Serena said. "I am glad I know already how to ride. Don, he took me on roller-blades last week. I am sore still. You cannot teach an old kitten too many new tricks at once. Would you like tea?"

"I'd love tea. For a mature lady, you certainly have a lot of beaus," Tori teased. "Is Jack the one ten years younger than you?"

"Do you imply," Serena said frowning, "I am too elderly to ride the horses, or too old for a younger gentleman?"

She paused and held Tori's tea out of reach. "Let me see what you have drawn on the back of my Visa bill."

She snatched the envelope from Tori. The picture depicted Serena riding barebacked on the beach, arms flung wide. A smile spread over Serena's face.

"This is well-imagined. I look young."

Tori rescued her tea.

"You're ageless." She sank her teeth into her second cookie. "Yum! These cookies are heavenly. What are they?"

Tori reached for a third.

"Toffee oatmeal with dark chocolate. Very fattening, these cookies, with much butter and sugar. You should not eat more than two."

Tori pulled back her hand.

Serena grinned.

"Only two, that is, if you are serious about losing those ten pounds you keep talking about." She pushed the plate closer to Tori. "Me, I think men like curves."

She looked complacently at her own well-rounded figure. "How many niños are you getting? Us, we were a small family, only eight children."

"Oh, my gosh . . . eight children! How was that for your family? Didn't you have access to . . .?" Tori trailed off, realizing her question might be in bad taste.

"Birth control?" Serena smiled. "Oh, yes, we did have, but in my country, the more children, the more blessings. As for me, it was wonderful—always someone to play with, to talk to, to fight with. I remember once . . ."

Tori was an only child. Her chin rested on her hand as she listened to Serena recount tales of adventures and laughter, bumps and bruises.

Back at home, Tori was thoughtful.

"What do you think about only children?" she said.

"Not much. Growing up as the middle child of three was a pain sometimes, but we were family. What was it like, being an *only*?"

"Lonely," said Tori. "Do you think we should consider adopting two kids?"

Phillip looked surprised.

"I assumed we'd adopt another child later. Get two at the same time, you mean?"

"Yes. By the time we get finished, we may not want to do this process again."

"It may be more cost-effective to adopt them at the same time, too," Phillip said, nibbling on a mechanical pencil. "I'll get figures from ChildNet for two at once, and do a comparative analysis. Adjusting for inflation, I'll be surprised if two at once isn't less expensive. But won't that be a lot of work for you?"

"How much harder can two be than one? They can entertain each other."

Phillip looked doubtful.

"I'm not sure it works that way." He shrugged his shoulders. "Well, you're the one who'll be entertaining them on a day-to-day basis. Fine with me."

They continued the process. While they jumped through various paperwork hoops, Children's Hope scanned the globe, looking for orphans who met the St. John profile.

CHAPTER 3

Bone of My Bone

Today, she would see them for the first time. A daughter and son born half a world away in another woman's womb, fathered by a man she had never met—their children.

Tori whipped her red convertible in and out of traffic, negotiating the streets of Atlanta with a skill born of experience, not concentration. It was a beautiful spring day in March, with sunny skies and mild temperatures. The air was saturated with the intense scent of tiny white Bradford Pear blossoms. In the fall, the trees burst into flame, burning brilliant shades of gold, red, burgundy, and yellow.

I wonder if we'll have the kids by fall.

Her cell phone rang. She glanced at the caller ID and punched the receive button.

"I got your message. So, the video finally came," Phillip said. "Hang on. I've got Delia on the other line; let me get rid of her."

Tori smiled at a woman in the car next to her, trying to merge. She waved her in.

"Okay, I'm back. Sorry. Delia wants input on a project."

"Delia? Is she new on your team? I thought I'd met everyone."

"She's not on my team. She's a VP over in the sales division. She's been asking my advice lately because I know the market better than she does. Where are you?"

"Close to ChildNet. Can you get off and meet me at home?"

"It'll be about an hour before I can break away."

"Okay. I couldn't concentrate once they called; took a half day. I'll wait for you."

"You'd better! We've told the agency we wanted these children, completed tons of paperwork, and written a million checks, but we can still back off if we see Stolcha has buckteeth, or Stefano has dandruff." Phillip's voice was teasing.

"Nothing could make me back off. Unless, that is, we aren't allowed to change Stolcha's name to Lydia!" She giggled. "Did I tell you they suggested we use her middle name? Evidently the name Assenova doesn't carry the same connotation in Bulgaria as it does here. I asked if she had a nickname and they told me it was Slati. Can you imagine how kids would torment her? Besides, I love the name Gabriel for Stefano."

"I do, too, although I still prefer the name Horace." Phillip cleared his throat.

"Oh, Phillip! He'd be tormented with that name."

Her husband sighed. "You're probably right. I can't wait to see the video."

"Me, too. They've been good about sending pictures, but seeing them in video flesh is much more exciting than fuzzy internet pictures."

"And probably more informative than a two-page summary that says both kids are healthy and normal, except for Stefano's speech delay."

Tori's car shot past the ChildNet entrance.

"Oops. I need to pay attention. Bye."

Tori swung into a parking space and climbed the stairs to the ChildNet office.

Do stairs count as exercise?

She picked up her speed. Lorraine, the social worker, looked up from her desk as Tori burst in.

"Well, well, what brings you here this early in the day?" she asked with a sly grin. "Are you sure SmithStone will be able to stay in business without you?"

"SmithStone won't remember my name five minutes after I've left." Tori smiled and stuck her hand out. "We'd like to meet our children, please!"

Chapter 3 — Bone of My Bone

Laughing, Lorraine handed over a videotape.

"Your kids are adorable! You're going to have your hands full with Stolcha," Lorraine grinned, "she reminds me of what you must've been like as a child. Stefano's subdued, but he's younger. He's probably overwhelmed. And, wow, is he gorgeous! He's going to be a heartbreaker."

"Well, if Stefano's quiet, he'll soon grow out of it in self-defense." Tori dashed from the office clutching the precious video.

Tori paced in front of the television as if on a short leash. Phillip sat in a wing chair, a notebook on his lap, pen poised. The tape started; the camera focused on a cinderblock building, a little worn, but clean and neat. The lens zoomed past an entryway boasting a mural of happy children and into a bright, well-furnished playroom. Scanning the children, it came to rest on their daughter.

Stolcha's wavy dark hair stood out from her head in pigtails that resembled donkey's ears. She had worn pants in all the pictures they had received before, but today she wore a pretty pink dress, lacy socks, and white patent leather shoes. She appeared fascinated with her attire, switching her gaze from her dress to her bare legs and back again. As they watched, she lifted the frock and examined the frilly pink panties underneath.

An adult arm came into the picture and pulled the dress down with a soft admonition. Stolcha giggled and pulled it back up, fingering the lace on the panties. A wagging finger appeared on the screen, giving the universal no-no sign.

"That must be the mother arm," Tori said, laughing.

The dress was jerked down and instructions given in Slavic. Stolcha smiled brilliantly at the camera.

"Killer smile," Phillip said.

Tori smiled. "Nice panties."

Stolcha came nearer, giving them a close up of large, dark eyes, long lashes, a pug nose, beautiful olive skin, and a full mouth over a resolute chin. She reached out a curious hand. Slightly dirty fingers filled the picture for a second before Stolcha tired of the camera and moved away.

The camera bounced, doing its best to follow her. She moved like a dragonfly, darting here and there to explore, never stopping for long. The disembodied mother arm appeared often, directing Stolcha one way or another. Other children trailed her around the room.

"Wonder where Stefano is?" Tori scanned the crowd of children.

Stolcha climbed on a little plastic car sitting at the top of a short slide and gleefully rode it down.

"The Occupational Safety and Health Administration would have a heart attack," Phillip said.

Coming back for another ride, Stolcha encountered another child at the top of the slide. She elbowed him aside, jumped on, and raced down again. Phillip and Tori looked at each other, smiling and shook their heads.

"Let's hope she doesn't usually get away with stuff like that." Phillip frowned and jotted in his notebook.

On the third slide trip, the car sat slightly askew. The mother arm came into the picture again, trying to reposition the car, murmuring what was probably an instruction to wait. Stolcha brushed the arm aside, made a face at the off camera adult, leapt into the car, and took off. The car careened half-way down, and then went over the edge. Stolcha shrieked gleefully as she fell.

Concerned shouts rang out, but Stolcha jumped up unhurt. Her dress was up around her armpits, which gave her ample opportunity to check out the panties again before someone made her pull down the dress.

"Not a whiner," Phillip said approvingly.

The camera followed Stolcha for five minutes as she ran through the playroom, followed by a band of admirers. As Stolcha dove into a fabric tunnel, the camera cut back to the slide.

Stefano sat quietly in the car, looking like a miniature Greek God. Tori was smitten.

What a darling. He looks lonely, though, like he needs lots of hugs.

The camera stayed focused on Stefano. Thick black lashes swept his cheeks as he looked down at the car, exploring it cautiously with his fingers. His head and face looked as if a baby's pink rosebud mouth had been added to Michelangelo's sculpture of the young David. He had the same hair, fudge colored eyes, and high cheekbones as his sister.

Chapter 3 – Bone of My Bone

There was no resemblance beyond the physical. Where Stolcha shimmered with purpose, Stefano seemed lost. Everything about Stolcha shouted a zest for living. Stefano sat motionless, not looking at the toys or the children playing around him, seemingly content to let life flow by unacknowledged.

Tori's hands were shaking, but underneath her apprehension was a sense of recognition—bone of my bone, flesh of my flesh.

Having paid full tribute to Stefano's beauty, the camera cut from scene to scene. Here was Stolcha, looking dubiously at Stefano while listening to quiet instructions. Children's Hope had said the two lived in different parts of the orphanage, separated by age and unaware they were siblings.

The arm plucked Stefano from the car, put him in a wagon, and gave the handle to Stolcha. Stolcha shook her head and dropped the handle. Sharper instructions sounded in the background. Stolcha stomped her foot and began to cry. The scene cut abruptly.

It started again with a jerk, panning the group of playing children. Stolcha appeared, stomping her feet heavily, full lips pouting as she pulled Stefano in the wagon.

A tent filled with balls appeared. Both children sat inside. Stolcha flung balls gleefully. The hand gave Stefano a ball. He accepted it and turned it over, studying it.

Stolcha seemed resigned to Stefano now; she threw balls to him. He caught one. Briefly his lips twisted slightly upwards.

"Wait, was that a smile?" Phillip said.

Tori did not reply. Mind, body, and soul strained toward the screen. Phillip took her hand and she gripped it like a lifeline.

The camera moved outside. Stefano toddled unsteadily up a short incline, gripping the hand of another disembodied adult. Stolcha scampered alongside, chattering like a magpie.

"He's walking." Tori felt warmth flow through her body.

"Is he walking independently?" Phillip asked. "He's a small three-year-old."

The final clip showed the children in a field. Stolcha picked flowers while Stefano sat. Stolcha smiled at her brother and handed him a flower. He gazed at it, switching it from hand to hand as if the switching motion required concentration. The video ended.

"Something's wrong with Stefano." Tori rubbed her arms and looked at Phillip.

Phillip hugged her.

"We don't know how orphanage kids act. The referral said Stefano was speech delayed, but normal. Stolcha has enough energy for both of them!"

Tori laughed and relaxed a bit.

Stefano was probably shy, overwhelmed at being in a strange room with older, unfamiliar kids. That must be it. After all, I was very clear in the paperwork we submitted, wasn't I? No special needs kids.

They played the video again, stopping at clips of Stefano. Every emotion he did not show, every sound he did not make felt like a fist slamming into Tori's stomach.

One shot showed a pen full of squirming, yipping puppies. Stolcha was climbing the fence to get at them, pink panties shining. Stefano sat on his bottom waving his fingers in front of his eyes. In the background you could hear Stolcha's shrieks of joy as she cavorted with the rambunctious bundles of fur and evaded capture by a phantom adult.

Tori felt the chill in her heart solidify into ice. How could a child resist puppies? As icicles broke off in chunks and spread through her body, she realized she felt not only fear, but determination. She had been a warrior in the business world. She would fight for her son, if needed.

Tori sat close to the television screen and re-played the clip of Stefano in the ball pit. She froze it at the point where she thought he may have smiled.

Phillip followed the clips as intently as Tori.

"The most encouraging glimpse of Stefano is ten seconds out of a thirty-minute tape."

Tori felt her carefully-scripted world dissolving. There was no choice to be made. She spoke without hesitation.

"They're our children and we need to get them as fast as possible because it looks like our son needs us."

Phillip gazed at her solemnly over wire rim glasses, and then broke into a smile and nodded.

"I agree. We wouldn't reject a biological child because of a disability. We've prayed. These are our children. Whatever they need, we'll do it. They'll be fine."

Tori pushed at her cuticles.

"We were fairly specific, weren't we honey . . . about not wanting a special needs child?"

"Yes, you were consistent throughout the process."

The piles of paperwork had seemed never-ending. Phillip smiled as he remembered Tori's complaints:

"This process feels like sitting in a traffic jam. Every time I move an inch forward, I catch glimpses of never-ending miles of cars in front of me. Write an essay on child discipline, sign, notarize, and seal eight copies of this document agreeing you won't sell your child's organs; and send your fingerprints to the FBI, the Georgia Bureau of Investigation, Interpol, and the government of Bulgaria, so they can do four separate criminal background checks. The requirements stretched endlessly into the distance."

Every three months or so, the process was infiltrated by bursts of sunshine as fuzzy Internet images gave impending family-hood a sense of reality. Stolcha continued to look like high-voltage energy while Stefano stared off into the distance at something only he could see. One set of pictures in particular thrilled them: Stefano, smiling with downcast eyes as Stolcha kissed his cheek.

Phillip came back to the present.

"I tried to be clear," Tori was saying as she nibbled at her bottom lip.

"Oh, you were. No question, my vertically-challenged darling."

"ChildNet is a reputable agency. They vouch for this orphanage. They wouldn't send us a special needs child, unless they misunderstood. Was I plain enough?"

"You included a three-page essay titled "Building the Successful St. John Family" and mentioned no special needs several times. No, I don't think there's any chance they could've misunderstood."

Phillip patted her shoulder.

Tori sighed in relief.

"Good. Oh, Phillip, I want to be a great mom, but I know me. I'm not self-sacrificing enough for a special needs child. I feel guilty, but it's not something I want to do. Do you think I'm awful? Does God think I'm awful?"

Phillip hugged her.

"No, Shortest of Heroines. We're going international, taking two older kids at once. ChildNet told me we're one of the most option-open couples they've ever worked with. So, don't stress. God knows your heart."

"*That* doesn't make me feel better. It's a pretty self-centered heart."

"You don't want a child with special needs. Not many people do. Let it go."

Family and close friends were dubious when they saw the video. Cassie Gunderson, a staunch ally since college, was Tori's best friend. Cassie was Catholic turned agnostic. Over the years, scintillating and sometimes heated arguments on faith had arisen, but their respect for each other had grown. After her husband died, Cassie returned to her career as a special needs instructor. They were meeting for breakfast to discuss the video. Tori knew Cassie would ask hard questions.

Tori watched, amused, as heads turned to follow Cassie's progression. Easily six feet tall, with eyes that looked like they had been chipped from the ice of a Nordic fjord, Cassie looked as if scarcely a generation had passed since a voluptuous, flaxen-haired ancestress jumped off her Viking dragon-ship and waded ashore. A huge purse was slung over one shoulder, and a short dress displayed shapely legs.

Cassie folded her long body into the chair and summoned the waitress.

"I'll have a Super Grande White Mocha Frappuccino, soy with triple shots, two everything bagels slathered with lox and cream cheese, and a banana.

The waitress brought the drink quickly. Cassie took a deep gulp.

"Ahh, caffeine coursing through my veins. I needed that. I'm bushed."

Tori hoisted Cassie's purse.

"I'd be exhausted, too, carrying around this suitcase. A gift from your chiropractor?"

"Ha, ha."

Cassie pulled the video from her purse. "Can I be straight with you?"

Tori eyed her across a tall glass of sweet tea, with lemon, naturally.

"I wouldn't have asked otherwise." Tori grinned and crossed her heart. "Doesn't mean I'll accept your opinion, but I won't get mad. What bothers you?"

"Duh! Did we watch the same video?"

"Gabe." Tori nibbled on a cranberry-orange scone.

"Among other things—how long did it take you to do your hair this morning?"

Bewildered, Tori ran her fingers over her head. Today her hair was interspersed with tiny braids, held back by two thick braids on each side.

"This? About an hour."

"An hour a day for hair? Yours is not a mama existence, my friend."

Tori shifted in her seat.

"I don't have to spend—"

Cassie held up a finger.

"Hear me out. From what your mother says, you started calling the shots the day you entered the world two months early."

Tori grinned, poured sugar on the table, and used her straw to carve out geometric shapes.

"Tsk. And here I always thought independence was a good thing," Tori quipped.

"Independence and parenthood are diametrically opposed. Children's needs dominate their parent's lives . . . and that's with normal children, if such creatures exist. Odds are strong Gabe has special needs. You've always said that was the last thing you wanted."

She looked at the shapes Tori made. "Waitresses must love you."

"I leave nice tips." Tori wiped out the figures and started over.

"It's not just Gabe," Cassie said, touching Tori's arm. "Lydia's an earthquake waiting to happen. You can tell from the jut of her chin, she's accustomed to getting her way."

"Other people deal with strong-willed and special needs children." Tori scowled.

"Sure they do. Most don't transform themselves, overnight, from a well-heeled, no kids-couple to the financially-strapped parents of a five-year-old cyclone and a two-year-old with issues."

Tori swept the sugar into a napkin and crumbled it up.

"It'll be an adjustment."

"An adjustment? More like a train-wreck. You're almost forty. You've developed a successful career. You live the good life. Aren't you afraid you'll regret losing all that?"

"Do I come across as that shallow of a person? Too superficial to handle the same sacrifices other moms have made since Eve let Cain have the best cut of meat?"

Cassie rubbed her temples. "Most of us start when we're younger, more flexible."

Tori fixed her eyes on Cassie's face and pleaded, "C'mon, I can do this."

"I have no doubt you're capable of being a great mom," Cassie admitted. "Not your standard issue mom, but a first-class one."

Tori blew her a kiss.

"Thanks . . . I think. Was that a compliment?"

"Hush. I'm not finished." Cassie rested her elbows on the table and leaned in. "I'll support whatever decision you make. But you need to go in with your eyes open."

Tori studied the salt shaker. When she looked up, her face was sober.

"I hear you. It does sound insane. I'm scared. The thing is: I really feel it's God's plan for us."

Cassie threw up her hands.

"God's plan? Try your biological clock running in overdrive!"

Tori thought for a moment. She sucked her lip in, and then popped it back out.

"That's not it. Here's why. This whole idea is way out of the box for Phillip and me. We enjoy our life. I like to be in control and know exactly how things are going to work, especially when it comes to money." Tori's hands beat a quick tattoo on the table. "So, here's the plan: exhaust our liquid reserves with adoption costs, cut our income in half, and double our expenses. Does that sound like a roadmap Phillip or I would develop?"

"No," Cassie said, with a quick grin. "And by the way, your expenses will more than double. Children require lots more money than adults."

Tori's eyebrows rose, but she decided to ignore Cassie's disturbing prediction.

"Okay, whatever. So, we're planning to live by a financial plan I'd never design in order to do something I've never wanted to do, for which most people think I'm woefully unequipped. Yet, I'm determined to do it. It isn't raging hormones. It's God."

"But I don't believe in God," Cassie reminded her, "so I attribute it to lunacy."

Tori didn't laugh.

"Faith is lunacy to those who don't believe, but now's not the time to rehash old arguments."

Tori crossed her hands behind her head and stared at her friend.

Cassie nodded slowly. "Put away the laser scalpel eyes. I've got your back."

Tori didn't tell Cassie or anyone else that while she never wavered in her determination to adopt Gabe and Lydia, a small black cloud had floated onto the pleasant landscape etched in her head. Over the next months, she threw herself into parenthood preparations with an energy friends dubbed as: Super-Tori mode.

Behind her upbeat façade, a minuscule grain of fear burrowed deep into her brain. Assuring herself about what the Sovereign Lord surely would or would not do did not help. Life had taught Tori that while God was always good, He was seldom predictable.

To complicate matters, His good was often impossible to detect with the human eye; it had to be taken by faith. Based on her observations, God's ways were often not only mysterious, but uncomfortable. This awareness provided fertile ground for the insidious kernel of doubt. A sprig of depression sprouted; unremarkable, but tenacious. It grew slowly and quietly, feeding on pain and disappointments never fully recognized or resolved. Tori wondered, sometimes, why she wasn't happier. When those feelings surfaced, she stuffed them and gave extra energy to whatever she was doing at the time.

She didn't talk much to Phillip about her fears. When she did, he brushed them off, seemingly unconcerned.

"God will take care of us," he would say, patting her shoulder.

The only problem with that is neither God nor Phillip will be doing the physical and emotional day-to-day work—I will.

Tori and Phillip had always been honest with each other, but Tori didn't know how to reveal feelings she scarcely acknowledged. As they waited for the adoption to go through, uneasy thoughts insisted on elbowing their way to the surface. Thinking of explaining them to Phillip, Tori ended up shaking her head.

After all, what could I say? "I love these children. I accept they're God's plan for us, but they're not what I expected?" No.

It did not help that it had been her idea in the first place. No one was forcing her. She could back out at any time. She would consider backing out, but she already loved them.

In addition, there was the awkward bit about believing it was God's plan. Historically, a child of God who deliberately defied His will ended up doing it, anyway, after God explained it to them differently. Tori had no desire to experience the modern version of spending three days wallowing inside the belly of a whale.

Tori did not want anyone to see the selfishness and lack of faith she had discovered in her soul. In preparation for the woman she intended to be, she fitted herself into a Madonna mold. Any thought that did not fit her blissful mother-in-waiting persona was ruthlessly drowned in a sea of denial, until such thoughts sank deep into the murky floor of her subconscious and lay there unacknowledged.

Tori was surprised at the sense of weariness and mental fatigue she felt as she drove into the neighborhood, home early after a relatively easy day. Serena waved and called out from her front porch.

Chapter 3 — Bone of My Bone

Tori pulled to the curb. The aroma of sharp, buttery cheese blended with bold spices tangoed its way through the open windows of her convertible.

"Hola! Come have a glass of tea with an old woman. Possibly you will give me your opinion. The cheese straws I have baked are maybe too spicy."

Tori's taste buds did a somersault. Neighborhood lore said a fight had once broken out at a party over the last of Serena's cheese straws. And she poured a nice glass of iced tea. Tori vaulted from her car and ran up Serena's steps.

Serena lived in one of the smaller homes in the neighborhood. A few years after her husband's death, she had scandalized the neighborhood standards committee by ditching the traditional lawn. Instead, she created a gorgeous, eco-friendly rock garden, complete with waterfall and koi pond. When warned the committee was searching for a covenant violation, Serena laughed.

"They will not find that needle in my wood stack!" Serena, an expert paralegal before her retirement, was one of the few homeowners who had actually read the covenants from cover to cover. After the yard was featured by the Atlanta Garden Society, even the sternest proponents of look-alike landscaping conceded it was appealing.

Amber and the neighborhood hawk loved the charming pond and waterfall. They ate so many of the expensive Koi that even the indefatigable Serena was forced to give up and stock the pond with lily pads instead.

"Come in, come in," Serena welcomed. "Let us sit on the deck."

Plopping into an oversized deck chair, Tori extended a placating hand to Scotch, who had positioned himself and his bared teeth in front of her.

"It's okay, boy, it's just me!"

The dog sniffed Tori, and then wagged his tail. Tori scratched behind his ear and crooned, "Who's really a big baby? Where's my favorite puppy dog?"

Scotch gave a short bark of approval, as if to say, "I'm here! Your favorite puppy's right here."

He settled at her feet, knowing Tori would slip him a forbidden tidbit when Serena was not looking.

"Mmm, these are delectable," Tori said, savoring a cheese straw.

"So, why are you unhappy?" Serena handed Tori a thick blue glass of fresh brewed sweet tea with lemon.

Tori was too tired to put up a façade and Serena was too sharp to be fooled.

"More depressed than unhappy." Stealthily, she dropped a cheese straw under the table.

"Stop! Bad dog, bad Tori!"

Scotch slunk away, looking back with longing at the pastry he had dropped at Serena's command. He whimpered as Serena picked up the treat and dropped it in the trashcan.

"Do not give him any unless you want to do clean up," Serena said. "Cayenne is bad for dogs."

She sat down across from Tori.

"It is Gabriel, I think, who causes this frown. Relax your face," she instructed, smoothing Tori's forehead. "You are never too young to think of wrinkles. Now, tell me."

Tori ran her finger around the edge of her tea glass.

"Everyone who looks at the video is doubtful of my ability to handle these kids. I'm not particularly patient . . ."

"You, Chiquita, are not patient at all!" interrupted Serena.

"Yes, right, thanks for the encouragement. So, we agree I'm not good mother material to begin with, but—"

"I have not said you lack good mother skills. God grows in His children what is needed. His is not the cookie-cutter mentality. You will not be the Betty Crocker, no." Serena shook her head. "Instead, you will be the mother your children need."

"I suppose . . . but how does He expect me to cope with a special need? Especially, if it's autism!" Tori took a large gulp of tea, choked, and spilled some on her blouse.

"At home you must soak her with cold water; the stain will go. Let us assume it is autism. Why is that so terrible?" Serena met Tori's incredulous look with a placid smile.

"Why is that so terrible? What do you mean? Autism is horrible." Tori shuddered and drained her remaining tea. "They don't look at you. They aren't affectionate. They sit around and bang their heads on the floor. They—"

Serena slapped her hand on the table.

"They, they, they. I grow impatient with these *theys*. You have gathered much information on this subject: autism?"

"Well, not exactly," Tori sputtered, "but I've heard—"

"Shame on you, Victoria! You are creating your own monster, is this not so?"

"I am not!"

"Si, you are. By failing to learn of the thing you fear, you give it powers far beyond any it may have. You allow this maybe to terrorize you with things that may or may not be true. Me, I am sixty-one, I know. I quote the philosopher Michel de Montaigne:

'My life has been full of terrible misfortunes, most of which never happened.'

"While you focus on impending doom, the mind is too busy wallowing in despair to conjure up the good that might be. Here, let us take a look."

Serena got her laptop, logged in and clicked keys. Tori marveled at Serena's comfort with technology. Her own mother barely acknowledged cell phones.

"There. I have Googled: autism facts. Observe—thousands of hits! This one looks good: Autism: Facts and Fables."

She put on a pair of multicolored cat-eye reading glasses and read:

> "Autistic people are incapable of feeling love or even affection: fable. People with autism have emotions, but often show them in different ways.
>
> "Autism is a medical condition: fact. Autism is a neurological disorder recognized by the American Medical Association . . . the brain develops differently in people with autism.
>
> "One in every eighty-eight children is now being diagnosed on the autistic spectrum: fact. The incidence is four times higher in boys.

"All people with autism have an extraordinary special gift of some sort: fable, No two people with autism are different. Their abilities and gifts cover a huge range, just as do the gifts and abilities of neuro-typical people."

Serena removed her glasses and turned to Tori.

"There is much more. If you are worried about autism, research it. Or," she smiled mischievously, "you could wait and see."

She waved her index finger at Tori. "But you have not the wait and see wiring."

She put her hand on Tori's wrist.

"At work, you anticipate the problems and meet them head on. Why do you not do so now? You have a son who may have a significant medical condition. What will be needed for his care? I know you, Muchacha. A contingency plan, it will make you feel better. If you never need it, it will be good. If you do need such a plan, you will not waste precious time developing it. Speaking of precious time, you will not have so much once los niños get here. How long has it been since you and Phillip took a vacation?"

"A while. We've been busy with the paperwork and all."

"Do you know what is the best thing you can do for any child—special needs or no?"

Tori walked over to the refrigerator, opened it, and poured a glass of cold water.

"Um, give them love, discipline, and spend time with and enjoy them; give them a good education, nutritious food, plenty of exercise, and a moral example. Am I getting warm?"

"No. All that, certainly, but, the most important thing you can do for any children is to have a strong relationship with their father. Many women do not have that option. You do. So, while you still have the ability, take some with your children's papa."

"That's an awesome idea. Gabe could be fine once he's out of the orphanage," Tori protested. "With love and care and—"

"Correct, but this idea that maybe Gabriel he will be fine, this is not what is creating your frown. Stop building the personal . . ." she snapped her fingers impatiently. "It is that I am getting old; the proper word rests in my mouth, but come out it will not. Ahh. Here he is. Stop building a personal demon in the basement of your mind. Bring him out; expose him to light, to the truth."

Tori stared at her.

"How'd you get so wise?"

Serena turned away.

"By making mistakes. For me it was shutting the barn window after the donkey escaped."

She brushed her eyes with the back of her hand, her voice choked with tears.

"I refused to acknowledge, often, that even flaws have beauty. My husband, he died as I was beginning to recognize how unique he was, how very much I loved him." She pulled herself to her feet.

"As the Amish say, 'We get too soon old and too late wise.' Do not let my pain be wasted. And now, go home. Scotch and I, we need our walk."

Phillip came in as she cooked dinner. He kissed Tori's cheek and headed for the refrigerator.

"Ooh, you made mint tea. Want a glass? How was your day?"

"I'd love a glass. My day was okay. I got home early and had cheese straws with Serena."

Phillip's head popped out of the refrigerator.

"Cheese straws? Serena's jalapeño-cayenne cheese straws; did you save me any?"

Tori chuckled.

"Stop drooling. She sent over a dozen, but I ate them to protect you from yourself. They're loaded with pure, salted butter."

Phillip grabbed her and started tickling her ribs.

"Where are they, wench?"

"Stop!" Tori shrieked, gasping with laughter. "In the cookie jar."

Phillip released her and swatted her bottom. He plunged his hand into the jar, brought out a fistful and munched with gusto.

"The woman has a gift. What'd you talk about?"

"Autism. She wants me research it; thinks I'd feel better with a contingency plan."

"Prepare for the worst, so you'll be able to handle anything? Couldn't hurt."

He took a long swallow of the mint tea, and then pulled Tori into his lap.

"Why do you need something to make you feel better, Sweet-n-Low? Are you still worried about Gabe? I think the kids will be fine, but you're the one who's staying home. You'll feel the brunt of any problems. It's not too late to back out."

They spoke simultaneously.

"Well it's just that I—"

"If you're not sure, I don't want—"

They laughed.

"Ladies first," Phillip said, tweaking a red curl.

She should open up. Tori hesitated.

"It's a huge leap of faith. God's taken care of us so far, though. So, there's no reason to think He'll fail us now."

Phillip subjected her to an intense scrutiny.

"Do you believe that here," he tapped her chest, "as well as here?" He tapped her forehead.

"The distance between our heads and hearts have been described as the longest thirty point five centimeters in existence."

Tori laughed.

"Thirty point five centimeters? I thought it was the longest twelve inches."

"World's gone metric, Munchkin. Time to catch up."

Tori shook her head, pasted on a bright smile, and let the moment slip away into the realm of communications that should have been.

"I'm looking forward to being a mom, really. I'm just tired."

"Okay, if you're sure. I can see how you'd be exhausted. I'm bushed and I haven't struggled through as much paperwork as you have. Why don't we take a vacation? Before the kids get here."

"Sounds good to me. We still have plane tickets from being bumped. Don't we need to use them this year?"

"By October 23. What say we fly out to California, rent a convertible, and drive down the coast, like we did five years ago? That was a great vacation. We could stay at that bed and breakfast we liked so much—the one in Mendocino—and take day trips from there."

"Mmm, good idea," Tori said. There may not be a lot of B and B vacations once the kids get here. We'll want to go to Disney."

CHAPTER 4

Ready or Not

Tori's cell phone warbled the tune to "Somewhere Over the Rainbow," ChildNet's ringtone. Tori got calls from them often, asking for just one more piece of information.

"Yes, what do they want now, blood tests? Or have the urine samples expired?" Tori held her phone between shoulder and ear, idly playing with her hair, which she had blown straight that day.

Lorraine, their ChildNet Caseworker, laughed.

"No. They want you to come get your children."

"You mean they want us to make actual travel plans?" Tori yelped. "When?"

She dropped the phone, and then grabbed it as co-workers, hearing the commotion, came running over.

"As soon as you can get there. Everything's done."

"Woo hoo!" Tori ended the call, forgetting to say goodbye.

She called Phillip while she updated her co-workers and received their congratulations.

"They're ours! I can't wait—"

"Hi, Runt. What's up?"

"The kids! We're done!"

"What do you mean?" Phillip sounded confused.

"We're parents! Finally! Make tracks for Bulgaria!"

"You mean *really* bring them home? I thought they'd be in middle school before we got them."

Chapter 4 — Ready or Not

"No! Can you stand it? We fly to Bulgaria and get them. I'm taking off early to look at flights. Come home as soon as you can."

"Absolutely. I'm not working late. I can hardly believe this."

"Believe it. I'm so glad you're excited. Sometimes I wondered."

"I'll admit this is the first time it's seemed totally real. I was afraid it'd fall through. ChildNet is sure?"

"Absolutely . . . positively . . . I've got to run. I need to wrap up a few things before I can leave."

"Me, too. I'll be home as soon as I can get there."

That night Tori greeted Phillip before he closed his car door.

"I have flights for next week on hold until six o'clock tonight," she told him, following him into the house.

"So soon? Isn't that expensive?" he asked with a puckered brow. "What does CheapFlight say? Let's check. Which airline?"

"British Air. They have the most direct flights."

"Let me see; weren't the cheapest flights offered by Aeroflot?"

He peered over his bifocals at the screen.

"Hmm. We could save—" he waved his glasses at her. "The two of us could save $685.43 on Aeroflot. We're parents now; we need to be fiscally responsible. I looked at college costs today." He shuddered. "If we put $685.43 in a 529 account, in thirteen years, depending on the interest rate—"

He busily punched keys on his calculator. Tori took the calculator away gently and set it on the desk.

"Aeroflot's first available flight is in three weeks," she interjected. "British Air goes from Atlanta to London to Sofia. Aeroflot's route is Atlanta to Detroit to London to Moscow to St. Petersburg to Sofia. With layovers that's fifteen hours more each way. That's four extra vacation days for you, and we'd have to wait an extra three weeks to bring our children home."

"I hadn't thought of that. Guess I need some practice at thinking like a daddy." Phillip brightened. "British Air is a Delta partner, so we'll get frequent flyer points."

They had a long, but uneventful series of flights into Bulgaria. Ivan their guide and translator picked them up for the drive to their four star hotel. Entering their room, which was tiny, they were enveloped in a blanket of moist heat.

"Did we come to the sauna by accident?" Tori quipped.

Ivan earnestly explained the situation. It turned out the difference between a four- and five-star hotel in Bulgaria was air conditioning.

"Normally," Ivan said "to pay for air conditioning is unnecessary. But at this moment, Bulgaria is experiencing a heat wave. It has been 34–36 Celsius all month."

"But we paid an upgrade fee for a spacious gold level room." Phillip said.

They looked around. A double bed was jammed against the one little window, leaving just enough space for an undersized dresser. Crossing the room in two steps, Phillip opened the bathroom door to display a toilet, a utilitarian sink, and a miniscule shower.

"This won't work," he said.

Ivan sighed.

The front desk was staffed by a man whose big ears, droopy cheeks, and forlorn expression reminded Tori of a Bassett Hound. Phillip pulled out their hotel confirmation and pointed to it.

"We reserved a gold-level room. Our room is iron, at best, and extremely hot."

The clerk's jowls sank lower as he sighed.

"Big official is come; beautiful room gone," he mourned. "Manager tells me say sorry, manager leave. I regret." He looked ready to cry.

Tori stifled the urge to pat him on the head.

"I'm sure," she said persuasively, "that you can think of something. Do you have a nicer room available? Anything?"

The clerk perked up.

"Not room, but we have suite." He stretched out his arms "Nice, big suite, with two beds, couch, even bathtub. No ready tonight, but tomorrow . . ."

"That sounds fine—" started Phillip, but Bassett Hound was still talking.

"Is forty-five dollars American extra per night, that suite," the clerk said.

"But we already paid!" Phillip protested.

Tori put her hand on his arm.

"And has overhead fan!" Bassett Hound beamed triumphantly, index finger twirling in the air. "Whhrrr! Most cool!"

He beamed. Tori felt sure his tail was wagging. He handed them a six-inch circular fan.

"For tonight . . . will help," he said, with more hope than conviction.

"Fine."

Tori dredged up a smile as she wiped mascara off her cheeks with a shirt sleeve. Phillip grumbled something unintelligible.

"We're exhausted," Tori said, "and he's not in charge. Let's take it up with the manager later."

Ivan left, promising, "Tomorrow at nine o'clock we go get children."

Phillip and Tori took the fan back and positioned it. Phillip had a knack for falling asleep. Once he was horizontal, he was gone. He fell asleep immediately.

Tori stared at the ceiling. *Tomorrow we meet our children!*

"In twenty-four hours you'll have more responsibility than you've ever held before, in a field for which you have no training," her worry imp slyly reminded her.

Tori turned and looked at her husband. Phillip snored peacefully, apparently unconcerned their lives were about to change irrevocably. She virtuously resisted the urge to wake him and ask how he could sleep at a time like this.

A family—two lives counting on me. Am I ready for this?

The imp answered, "Ready or not, here they come!"

Tori rolled to the edge of the bed and sat up, soaking in the fan's feeble puffs of tepid air.

"One life may have a special need," the imp said.

I refuse to think that way! God is good; He knows I can't handle special needs.

The imp fell silent.

So Gabe may be behind developmentally. We can work with that. It'll be okay.

"Loving care can't cure neurological problems," the imp hissed.

Giving up on natural rest, Tori took a sleeping pill her doctor had prescribed for jetlag. She drifted into an uneasy sleep, her last thought a prayer.

Please let it be okay.

The next day's sunshine contrasted with Tori's cloudy brain. She ordered strong hot tea at breakfast, hoping for a caffeine boost, and then spilled the sugar bowl trying to sweeten it. Phillip didn't comment.

Tori remembered a book on the agency's required reading list entitled: <u>Adopting the Older Child</u>. She had wanted to rename it: <u>Abandon All Hope, Ye Who Enter Into Older Child Adoption.</u>

Its Table of Contents was bleak:
1. Torture: Your Child and the Family Pet
2. Right and Wrong Ways to Handle Your Child's Sexual Advances
3. The Compliant Child

Evidently an amiable adoptee was cause for alarm. Interventions should be undertaken at once to bring out their natural, God-given gift of insubordination.

Tori knew the agency was right to prepare parents thoroughly. She had heard horror stories about adoptive parents who cancelled on the orphanage steps with the flimsiest of excuses. All the information Tori and Phillip received stressed bonding with adoptive children takes time.

One speaker showed a clip of happy children as they ran with outstretched arms into their parent's embrace, laughing as they were swung up into the air. The clip had come to an abrupt halt with the words: IT DOES NOT HAPPEN THIS WAY.

The speaker was passionate.

> "These children have been abandoned, betrayed, maybe worse. A few weeks with a loving family won't change that. They left the only world they've ever known;

they're scared and confused. Earning their love and trust will be a slow process. Expect a period of time at least equivalent to your child's age at adoption for true bonding to occur."

He closed by saying:

"Love is an act of the will."

Tori remembered this the next morning as they drove up to the orphanage. The home was a big, concrete building in a poor residential area. It was plain, but as clean and cheerful as a few yards of colorful fabric and cans of paint could make it. They were taken immediately to the director's office.

The director was a striking woman. They had been told she held several degrees and was highly regarded. She welcomed them in excellent, lightly-accented English.

"I am Dr. Velakova. It is good to meet you."

She was cordial, but Tori's antenna—honed by years of reading customers' body language—sensed reserve.

She doesn't like us. That's silly. It's a different culture.

They had brought two suitcases, pastel and primary colored; monogrammed LYDIA and GABE. They had been told to bring everything the kids needed for the trip home, from the skin out. Tori had done her best with the sketchy size information provided, stuffing the bags with several sizes of each item. The cases were taken away at once.

Stolcha/Lydia came in with her caregiver first. They were accompanied by an imposing woman introduced as Matron. Stolcha pulled her suitcase proudly, not seeming at all intimidated by her new parents.

Matron brought her forward, announcing formally, "Stolcha/Lydia St. John."

Lydia was even cuter in person than her pictures had shown, with an engaging personality. Thick hair fell in waves to her shoulders. Her olive skin glowed as if freshly scrubbed and her big brown eyes were alive with intelligence and curiosity.

The Matron introduced Tori and Phillip to Lydia as Mama and Papa. Lydia gave them hugs and a curtsey before eagerly exploring the room. She was adorable in a little dress with matching pantaloons, hair ribbon, and cute sandals. The worker held out two identical pairs of sandals and an identical outfit, and said something to Ivan.

"These do not fit," he translated.

"We weren't sure about the sizes," Tori said. "Can you use the clothes and shoes that don't fit?"

"Yes, thank you," Dr. Velakova answered.

She told the caregiver, who lit up like she had won the lottery. She took the suitcase contents out and held them up one-by-one, eyeing Lydia. She put the ones that looked like they'd fit back in the suitcase and put the rest aside.

Lydia was bouncing around the room, grabbing treasures from a small toy chest, chattering constantly, when she saw things being taken out of her suitcase. Her little face scrunched in outrage. She shrieked and ran over, trying to shut the bag while pushing the caregiver away.

Matron came over, hugged Lydia, and spoke soothingly. After a while, with a suspicious look at the caregiver, Lydia nodded, bottom lip poking out. Ivan told the St. Johns Lydia had agreed to leave the things that did not fit for her friends. Mama and Papa would buy her new ones at home.

Lydia went to Phillip, grabbed his hand, and pointed insistently at his watch. She tried to pull it off. The caregiver smiled and spoke to Matron, who laughed. Ivan translated.

Lydia had seen a watch on Phillip's arm in one of his pictures. She wanted one and had been bugging the caregiver non-stop. Lydia jumped up and down, beaming and prattling.

The caregiver licked her lips nervously, avoiding the director's eyes, and added something in a low voice. Matron stopped laughing and addressed Phillip. The caregiver had placated Lydia with the promise her new Papa would buy her a watch.

The director frowned, but Phillip smiled. Picking Lydia up, he pointed to his watch, circled her thin wrist with his fingers, pointed to her, and grinned. A huge smile stretched across Lydia's face.

Chapter 4 – Ready or Not

Finally. Gabe.

He came in, small, vulnerable, and as emotionless as a painting. Tori gazed at him and was lost. Matron made the introduction, and then tenderly pushed him into Tori's arms. He went without resistance or interest. Tori was struck by how light and tiny he was for a forty-two month old child. She hoisted him onto her hip, and spoke to the director.

"He seems small, almost frail for a child his age." Out of the corner of her eye, Tori saw the director and Matron exchange a quick glance.

"Eastern European children are smaller than Americans," Dr. Velakova said coldly.

Tori glanced at Lydia, and then at Gabe, then back at the director.

"But he seems so much smaller for his age than Lydia."

Tori had turned away from Dr. Velakova to look at Lydia, but she had a direct view of the Matron, who looked scared. Tori looked quickly at the director. Behind Dr. Velakova's impassive face, Tori sensed uneasiness. The director stepped to the window and looked out.

"Sadly, the food our children get often doesn't have a good nutritional value and they never get enough. Stolcha is strong and aggressive, no one steals her food. We try to protect little ones like Stefano, but it is not always possible." She turned and spoke to Phillip. "Here is the schedule the children usually follow. It would be wisest not to vary from it too much at first. Routine will help allay anxiety for the first few days."

Tori wondered at the undercurrents between Matron and the doctor, but dismissed it. Gabe was much more interesting. He seemed unaware of the new people, sounds, and sights around him. Lydia's caregiver spoke to Gabe's nurse, who immediately started pulling items out of his suitcase. Gabe didn't object.

Tori began gently swaying back and forth. Looking down, she thought his face became slightly animated. She picked up the pace of her movements. What may have been a smile flickered across his passive face. Tori bounced and the sighting was confirmed: Gabe was smiling.

Phillip took him and gently tossed him in the air. The smile widened. Phillip tossed Gabe again, then, at Tori's nod toward Lydia, began throwing their delighted daughter into the air.

Tori cuddled Gabe, who seemed less stiff. Fierce, protective sensations worked their way from her heart outward, fervent emotions she had been warned not to expect. She would slay dragons for this child. He may be flawed; but he was theirs. They would live love and show him he was safe. Her thoughts darted like hummingbirds, considering ways to coax Gabe into their world.

Phillip began handing out small gifts they had brought for the director and her staff: lotions, chocolates, and Bulgarian language bibles. Tori smiled absently, but her thoughts were focused on a book she had been reading, *What to Expect the Toddler Years.* She was pretty sure Gabe should have a mouthful of baby teeth. She looked into his mouth again. Gabe had teeth, but not as many as she expected. She caught an uneasy exchange of glances between Matron and the director.

"You have perhaps questions, madam?" Dr. Velakova asked.

"Yes, of course." She patted Gabe's little behind and directed him toward Phillip, who flung his arms wide and waited, a besotted grin on his face. Gabe took a few uncertain steps and tottered, clearly off balance.

"Hey, careful, Little Buddy."

Phillip caught Gabe before he could fall. He looked at Tori, puzzled.

"At three and a half years old, shouldn't he be steadier on his feet?"

"He is a late walker," the director explained, crossing her arms "Now he is walking, he will improve rapidly."

She tapped her foot.

"Your questions, please?"

Tori scrambled for her notebook. She skimmed over food, routines, and a brief medical history. Other questions were more important to her.

"Has Lydia bonded with someone here?"

Dr. Velakova smiled broadly and directed the question to Lydia's caregiver, who still knelt by the suitcase.

"Olga?"

Olga giggled, stood up, and spoke with animation, mimicking a thrusting gesture with her hand.

"Stolcha wants go everywhere Olga goes. She follows Olga to the bathroom and sticks her hand under the door," the director said. "She cries when Olga's shift ends. She wanted to bring Olga to the US."

A look of panic crossed Phillip's face.

"Olga said her husband would be too lonely. Stolcha also has a special friend, Louka, who was adopted by an American couple. She misses Louka and talks about seeing him in the United States. We had to tell her your country is bigger than ours, so she may not see him. She sulked until Olga promised her the watch."

"Ahh," Tori said, "bribery; the universal childcare language. What about Gabe?"

"He is a lovely boy, is he not?" the doctor asked. "We will be sad to see him go."

"Yes, he's adorable; I've already lost my heart to him. I was wondering, though, did he also bond with someone?"

The doctor's face was emotionless as she asked the caregivers. They shrugged, and shook their heads.

"No, they say he is just a baby still."

"But he's three and a half years old," Phillip said. Dr. Velakova shifted in her chair, folded her arms and did not reply.

"No one special at all?" Tori persisted.

"No one, but it will come. I, who see so many children, know this."

Her eyes met Tori's with a look half defiant and half appeal. "This boy has much potential, but I have done all I can here."

Tori searched the doctor's eyes, and then slowly nodded. "Gabe will be given every opportunity."

Phillip nodded. He started to say more, but Ivan interrupted. He had been fidgeting since Gabe came in.

"You are pleased with these children? You will take them?"

Phillip and Tori looked at each other and simultaneously answered.

"Yes!"

The doctor pursed her lips. She seemed uncertain. She turned abruptly to Matron.

"Matron, I am sure the children would like to show their Papa around."

Matron, who had listened intently throughout the whole conversation said, "I have some English. Very pleased show you this orphanage; our home."

"I'd like that," Phillip said. He turned and raised his eyebrows. "Tori?"

"I need to review some details with Dr. Velakova. I'll catch up later."

Matron, Phillip, and the kids left the room. The director looked pointedly from Ivan to the door. He pretended not to notice. She frowned, but shut the door; firmly.

"You have asked many questions. You will be asked at your embassy if these children are satisfactory, if they are as you were promised. You must decide if this is so." The director's gaze speared Tori.

Ivan began protesting.

"Ivan," Tori said, "please join the tour."

Ivan left after a glance at her stern expression. Tori returned the director's stare and waited. The minutes passed. The doctor spoke first.

"Never before has a woman met me look for look. Your eyes are persuasive. They demand."

"People have said that before. I only want you to speak plainly."

Dr. Velakova nodded. "I also dislike elephants in the room, but . . . this is my life's work. I do not know you."

Help, Lord! If I ever needed diplomacy, I need it now.

Tori sank onto the couch and gestured to it.

"Will you sit with me, director?"

Dr. Velakova paused, and then sat at the far end of the couch, perched stiffly on its edge.

"I can see you love children, doctor. You have a reputation as a great leader, passionate advocate, and champion for orphanages in Eastern Europe."

Dr. Velakova inclined her head.

"Yes? I thank you for your kind words. I hope them to be true, but what has that to do with Stolcha and Stefano today?"

Tori leaned in to her.

"Were I in your shoes, I'd be frustrated when regulations blocked me from placing my children where I felt they could thrive. I would be tempted to bend a rule or two."

"The end justifies the means, you are saying?"

"More like 'it's easier to ask for forgiveness than to get permission.' Doctor, you are safe with me and my husband, but to help my children, I need information."

Dr. Velakova had the laser scalpel now. She fastened Tori with a searing look that seemed to probe Tori's deepest hopes and anxieties. Finally, she took a deep breath.

"I speak with bluntness, then. If you have doubts, leave the children here. There are concerns, I do not know how large. I want so much for Stefano and Stolcha to have the life you can offer them, but it is better you leave them now than for them to be traumatized later if the problems grow too big."

"We love and accept *both* of our children as they are."

Once more they locked onto each other's faces, searching. Tori concentrated on communicating trustworthiness. Again, it was the director who spoke first.

"After all, to live is to risk; your questions then, Madam."

"Gabe can't be forty-two months old."

"There, you are wrong. Bulgarian law says he must be at least thirty-six months old before adoption."

"I see." Tori spoke carefully. "As you say, he must be older than he appears. He seems to live in his own world. Do you think it could be simply because he's been in an orphanage all his life? Could he want connection once he's in a good home?"

"I do not know," the doctor said. "It is a question that has often plagued me. Is it a question of desire or ability, or a combination of the two?"

She massaged her temples. "I have tried to make this a good place, but an orphanage, no matter how good, is not a beneficial place for children who need extra help."

She frowned. "Bulgaria has little to offer, even outside the orphanage system. In the U.S.; though . . ."

Tori smiled.

"I understand. It's critical to get Gabe where he can get what he needs. Do you think he'll *need* more than basic help?"

"Time only will tell you. I cannot. He doesn't fit a usual mode, our Stefano."

Her lips twisted as she stood up. She rested her hands on her hips.

"I wish I could provide you with the assurance you crave."

She pruned dead leaves off a sickly-looking spathicillium and spoke with what appeared to be only casual interest; her attention focused on the greenery.

"Can Stefano be your son, madam, if you can't have the answers you need?"

She ripped off a healthy green leaf. Tori stood and stepped in close, forcing her to make eye contact.

"You're right. I like answers, like to be in control, but I'm also a woman of faith. Weak faith, often, but I have no doubt these kids are meant to be mine; ours. It's true I am uneasy about Gabe. It doesn't matter. I already love him, love them both—as an act of will."

"And your husband? Does he also love as an act of the will?"

"Yes. He's actually a nicer person than I am. He was willing to consider special needs from the beginning. I wasn't. I felt I couldn't handle it. God changed my heart."

Tori mentally slapped her forehead in disgust.

Great, now I've blown it. She won't want to have her Stefano raised by a hard-hearted woman who only wanted easy children.

The director surprised her.

"That is good. A course agreed to with reluctance because of love and because God calls is sturdier, better-grounded, than a path driven by emotions."

Tori was comforted by her words.

"Dr. Velakova, I'll tell you something strange. I've already bonded with Gabe."

Dr. Velakova's hands stilled on the plant she had been absently shredding. Her lips curved upward.

"Most unusual. God is good."

"All the time," Tori responded.

Apparently satisfied, the director opened up a little.

"You realize, even if Gabe's issues turn out to be small, your road will not be smooth." She grinned.

She tapped a pencil against her teeth thoughtfully.

"Stolcha, too, will not be easy. She is . . . an armload? Do I use the idiom correctly?"

Tori returned her grin.

"I think the phrase you want is that Lydia is a handful."

The director's laugh was a pleasant surprise: throaty and exuberant.

"Once more, you are wrong. Stolcha is definitely an armload rather than a handful."

This struck both women as hysterically funny and broke the tension. They started laughing, then howling, loud enough for Matron, in the hallway, to hear and smile.

Tori took a tissue from a box on the director's desk and wiped her streaming eyes.

"Dr. Velakova, I'm a woman with many faults." She looked down. "Most of my life has been me-centered, but to the best of my ability, I'll make sure both of my children reach the full potential God has given them."

For the first time, the director's smile was warm and genuine. "That is enough. So, you will want to join the tour."

She hesitated. "You are a strong woman. I think you will become stronger. I pray God's blessings on you and your family."

She left the room. Tori quickly found her group, who appeared to be enjoying their tour.

"I have shown the husband we have fine orphanage, most good in Bulgaria. Come, I show you more." Lydia pranced between them proudly, holding their hands. The orphanage was clean and neat. Obvious efforts had been made to create a safe, cheerful environment.

In one room, lunch was being served by a lady in overalls who ladled out bowls of a thin soup made of noodles and carrots. Each child received two saltine crackers. Gabe started whining and struggling in Phillip's arms, straining toward the food.

"Is it his lunchtime?" Phillip asked Matron.

"No. They ate earlier, since you were coming . . ." she added matter-of-factly, "but our children are always hungry."

Tori had noticed how thin the children were. The workers were thin also. She looked down at the trim figure she worked so hard to maintain and caught Phillip's eye. She searched in her purse for crackers, anything, and found nothing.

She pulled Phillip aside and whispered, "I feel awful."

"Me, too." Phillip grimaced. "These poor kids."

Impulsively, he reached under his shirt and pulled out the money pouch he wore next to his chest.

"We're carrying a lot of cash in case we had to pay bribes. No demands so far. I have about four thousand. You?"

They had been told quite often organized crime surfaced during foreign adoptions, wanting a cut. They had brought money they had saved for granite countertops, hoping they wouldn't need it. Tori pulled out the money pouch snapped inside her bra.

"I've got about five thousand."

"You don't mind about the countertops, do you?"

"No, of course not."

Not much, anyway.

"I'm going to keep about two thousand; do you think that'll be enough?"

"If we get in trouble, we can always use our credit cards."

"Tori," Phillip said with a grin, "I know we're talking organized crime here, but do you really think the Mafia takes credit cards?"

"Idiot."

Tori slapped his arm. Phillip handed her a sheaf of bills.

"Here. Give them as much as you like."

Tori left the tour once more and went in search of Dr. Velakova's office. After a few wrong turns and directions given in pantomime, she found it.

Chapter 4 – Ready or Not

"You changed your mind." Dr. Velakova looked stricken, but not surprised.

Tori smiled reassuringly and shook her head.

"No. I told you we love them. It's just that, well, we have so much and these children have so little, and . . . here, take it. Buy whatever you need most."

Tori pushed a wad of bills into her hand. Surprised, the director took them. She gasped as she saw the crisp fifty and one hundred dollar bills. Her eyes widened.

"There must be thousands here; in American dollars!"

As she spoke, Matron rushed in and gave Tori a beseeching glance.

"Please, madam, reconsider. You are their only hope. No one will want to adopt a girl so old as Stolcha, already almost five. My Stefano, he will die in that other home and—"

"No, Sveta," the director said. She spoke rapidly in Bulgarian and displayed the pile of money.

"Today angels walked among us." Matron grabbed Tori's hands, kissing them repeatedly. Tori pulled away, embarrassed. Wryly she wondered how her former co-workers would react to the idea of her as an angel.

Who needs granite countertops?

"No, please don't. It's about seven thousand. We thought you could put it to good use."

"Madam, you have little idea of what we can accomplish with this money. We will get a new central heater, which will work better and cost less to run. We will buy better food and more of it. I can even hire a few more workers, so the children will get more attention." Dr. Velakova smiled. "Oh, yes, this money will be stretched and multiplied many times. On behalf of the children, we thank you."

She paused. "My name is Tatiana."

"And I'm Tori."

Impulsively, Tori stepped toward her, and then stopped, uncertain how to proceed. Tatiana smiled, met her in the middle, and clasped her shoulder. Tori returned the grip. Watching them, Matron shook her head, and enveloped both women in a motherly hug.

An overhead fan stirred the tepid air in their new suite. Phillip, holding Gabe on one hip, opened the door to their balcony.

"Tori, look!" A cool breeze wafted in, caressing her sweaty skin. "We face the Black Sea!"

At the hotel's rocky beach a short time later, Lydia was quick to master the fine art of sand-castle building. Phillip helped her, obeying her imperious gestures with a meekness that would have surprised his co-workers. Gabe plopped down a couple of feet away from Tori.

Absently, Tori scooped up a handful of sand and let it trickle through her fingers. She noticed Gabe watching. She scooted next to him. Gabe moved and turned his head.

Tori trickled the sand through her fingers repeatedly. Gabe peered at her out of the corner of his eyes. Trickle, scoop, trickle; he turned his head to watch. Scoop, trickle, scoop. Holding his fingers in a loose fist, Gabe inched toward her. Trickle, scoop; he moved closer.

Tori held her breath, inched over, and trickled a few grains of sand over his fist. Gabe's lips curved up. He was hesitant, but finally allowed Tori to fill his hand with sand. He closed his hand, shook it, and frowned. With slow movements, Tori spread his fingers allowing the sand to sift through. Gabe's frown vanished.

He studied the trickling sand intently. Satisfied, he then dug his hand into the beach. Scoop, trickle . . . A few scoop-trickles later Tori heard a hushed sound. She leaned in and listened to the soft, baby sound of Gabe chuckling. Soon fat, merry giggles erupted.

Scoop, trickle; laugh. Scoop, trickle; giggle.

Teary-eyed, Tori looked toward the sky and whispered, "Thank you."

The advent of the children inspired housekeeping to produce a large, free-standing fan. Tori glanced up from her guide book to see Gabe reaching little fingers through its grill. With a yelp, she dropped the book and snatched him away from the spinning blades.

"We need to keep our eyes on him every second," Phillip said.

Tori, shaken by visions of bloody, severed fingers, snapped, "By *we* you mean *me*. I'm not the only parent in the room, Phillip!"

Lydia, interested in this new tone glanced, birdlike, from one to the other. Gabe whined.

"I know that." Phillip crossed his arms. "Although, you'll be the main caregiver."

Tori collapsed on the couch, holding Gabe, who struggled to escape.

"Cut me some slack! I locked the balcony, blocked the electric outlets, put medicines and sharp objects out of reach . . . who knew he'd want to stick his fingers in the fan?"

Phillip looked stricken and kissed the top of her head.

"Sorry, Lil' Darlin', you're right. Maybe he's hot. Let's give them a bath."

He filled the huge tub. As the kids splashed around, Gabe slipped on the slick porcelain surface and went under water. Tori pulled him up. He choked a little and screwed his fists into his eyes, but he didn't seem scared.

"Tough kid," Phillip said with an approving nod as Gabe pulled away from Tori's supporting arm. He re-submerged and lay stretched out on the bottom of the tub, smiling a Mona Lisa smile.

Lydia splashed Tori with an impish grin. Tori splashed vigorously in return. Quirking one eyebrow in Lydia's direction, Tori looked at Phillip, splashed him, and then beckoned Lydia with a *your turn* bow and wave.

Lydia was delighted to be recruited and was soon drenching Phillip. Surfacing for air, Gabe sputtered as Lydia doused him. He then grinned and kicked his feet, soaking them all. In moments they were a sodden, soapy, and hysterically happy mess.

Mealtime was disturbing. Lydia jabbed her forefinger at a picture of macaroni and cheese. Their waiter agreed.

"Is good for children, yes? For Sir and Madam, we has local especialty—salad of goat cheese and vegetables, all fresh."

Tori and Phillip agreed. The waiter brought a basket of hot breadsticks.

"Like fire," he warned.

Tori used a napkin to put one on her plate and passed the basket to Lydia, but Gabe intercepted. Oblivious to the heat, he stuffed the remaining three breadsticks into his mouth at once. Lydia howled and tried without success to snatch one from his furiously chewing jaws. Phillip rescued one breadstick and gave it to Lydia.

In the meantime, Lydia had stolen Tori's. With one breadstick in each hand, Lydia glared malevolently at Gabe while she took large alternating bites of bread. With fortunate timing, the waiter appeared right then, bearing two huge, steaming platters of macaroni and cheese.

"I'm glad he turned up with their meals when he did. They're really fixated on food, aren't they?" Phillip murmured to Tori. "Didn't I order *small* plates?"

"I don't think the size will be a problem," Tori said, watching her children eat.

Lydia worked steadily through the gooey mound of noodles, one arm wrapped around her plate, protecting it, while her wary eyes watched for further assaults. Gabe attacked the macaroni with a fork in each hand, gobbling as fast as he could.

"They handle utensils well," Phillip observed.

A big glob of pasta sailed off Gabe's fork, landed on Phillip's shoulder and slid greasily down into his shirt pocket.

"Sort of," he amended.

Tori's laughter was diverted by a glance at Gabe, who was swallowing each huge bite in quick succession while shoveling more food into his mouth. His thin cheeks were as full as an overfed chipmunks.

"He'll choke!"

Tori tried to pry some macaroni out of his mouth. Gabe did not appreciate her interference and sank razor sharp teeth into her thumb.

"Hey, that hurt!"

She shook her fingers, and then narrowed her eyes.

"I'm not up on the Heimlich Maneuver, little man, so let's do this my way, okay?"

She captured Gabe's right hand, being careful not to get any extremities close to his mouth. Despite this handicap, he finished in record time. Scanning the table, his eyes locked onto Tori's salad, sitting beyond his reach. He swiveled and looked straight at Tori with an imploring glance.

"Look, Phillip. He makes eye contact when he really wants something."

"Yeah, I think our boy's going to be fine," Phillip said as Tori handed Gabe her salad. "He's already learned how to manipulate his mama."

In the meantime, Lydia had been studying the menu and noticed a picture of ice cream, slathered in chocolate and piled high with whipped cream. She tugged on Tori's sleeve, showed her the treat and gave her a beguiling smile. Tori beckoned the waiter.

"Our girl, also, knows how to get what she wants; just ask Mama," Phillip teased.

Tori stuck her tongue out and ordered two dishes of ice cream.

"Aren't we spoiling these kids by giving them our food and ordering them whatever they want?" Phillip asked.

"I don't think so," said Tori. "It seems natural for them to want food and lots of it. They're petrified they won't get enough to eat, especially Gabe. Let's get them home and demonstrate there's plenty of food. I think the behavior will fade."

Lydia, who was picking up English much quicker than they had expected, asked, "Go McDonals?"

Tori and Phillip exchanged glances. They seldom ate fast food.

"How does she know about McDonald's? I didn't expect them to have it here."

"I'll go down to the front desk and check." Phillip said.

"Ride them up and down in the elevator for fifteen minutes first. I crave quiet."

"Already? What happens when they're both talking and having friends over?"

"Hush and go away."

Tori walked to the mirror and swept all her hair to one side.
Does Lydia ever slow down?

She had just finished braiding her hair into a side ponytail when she heard the hotel key grinding in the door.

They're back already.

"Bulgaria does indeed have a McDonald's," Phillip announced, "It's downtown, but we don't want to start them on junk food, do we? Especially not McDonald's!"

Every so often, overcome by the urge for a bacon cheeseburger on a highly processed soft white bun, accompanied by salty, crisp fries, Tori indulged in McDonald's; most of the time she opted not to distress Phillip by mentioning these little sorties. Such openness was likely to produce a loving lecture on calories, hydrogenated fat, and excess sodium.

Lydia jumped up and down chanting "Mcdonals, Mcdonals!" while Gabe played with a spoon he had stolen from the restaurant the night before.

"Come on, Phillip, we need to ease up every so often," Tori coaxed, her mouth watering. "Everything in moderation. Besides, it'd be a treat for them."

Marveling at Lydia's intuition, she finished by saying, "How can you resist those eyes?"

Lydia, sensing her new father's objection to McDonald's had turned a battery of pleading eyes and a wistful mouth full force onto Phillip. Glancing down into the molten pools of chocolate beseeching him to agree, Phillip relented.

"Obviously, she hasn't seen *Super Size Me*," he muttered, holding his stomach as if already nauseated, "but okay."

Tori gave Lydia the thumbs up gesture.

It was a warm, pretty morning, so they decided to walk. It was a nice, but humid hike to the Golden Arches, so the adults thankfully welcomed the restaurant's air conditioned embrace. The kids were delighted with their Happy Meals, which came complete with tiny replicas of Tweety Bird and Sylvester.

Lydia traded Gabe a French fry for his Sylvester. In short order, she was amusing herself with the figures while Gabe contentedly spun his drink lid. They stopped their play only to munch on more fries, with ketchup, of course.

The kids loved the taste of ketchup, as was clearly indicated by the red goo all over their faces, hair, and clothing.

"Ketchup has as much sugar as ice cream," Phillip grumbled.

He seemed to forget his irritation as he played Sylvester to Lydia's Tweety and showed Gabe how to rip open ketchup packets with his teeth.

Tori, rescuing Gabe's drink lid from the floor for the fifth time, decided not to worry about germs. That is, until they returned to the states.

Thank you, Father, for my family.

Sated, they strolled out into a sun-drenched afternoon.

CHAPTER 5

Flight 68 from Purgatory

The journey home began well enough with a short flight to London. By the time Lydia became restless, the plane was landing. They moved through immigration to the desk of a red-haired official who welcomed them to London with a thick Scottish burr.

He gave their American passports a cursory glance, but stiffened when he saw Gabe's and Lydia's Bulgarian passports.

"These are not your real children, then?"

"Yes," Phillip said in a sharp tone, holding Gabe a little tighter.

Tori put her hand on Lydia's shoulder.

"They *are* our *real* children, newly adopted. We're taking them home from Bulgaria. Is there a problem?"

"Well now," said the official, "that would depend. Going straight to the gate, are you? Your children have visas for the U.S., not England."

"We have hotel reservations tonight. We leave at 10:15 a.m., in twenty-three hours. We were told they didn't need English visas unless we stayed over twenty-four hours."

"True enough by the old rule, but with heightened security, it's questionable. If the children's stay is over twenty hours, *technically* they should have visas."

Tori groaned.

The man glanced at the children. He looked sympathetic.

"Might I see your hotel booking, then?"

Phillip showed him.

"Alright, so," the official said, "I'm able to give you a mite bit of leeway because you're staying at the airport. Your wee ones don't look any more a threat than an average toddler. I'm going to let you pass."

"Thank you!" Tori said.

He smiled and waved them on.

The airport hotel was basic, but nice. Tori stretched out luxuriously on the bed, feeling her back crack.

"Ahh, that feels good."

Lydia collapsed onto the bed beside her and extended her arms high over her head.

"Ahh," she parroted, looking at Tori.

Tori smiled and pulled Lydia next to her. Lydia didn't resist.

"Do you want some music?" Phillip asked.

At Tori's nod, he turned on the radio. A grin split Gabe's face. He danced on his tip toes, eyes closed, rocking back and forth and swaying. Tori was pleased he was having fun, but was a little puzzled. Most toddlers enjoyed music, but why was he dancing on his toes with his eyes shut?

"He looks a little like Ray Charles," Phillip said, ruffling Gabe's hair.

"Or Stevie Wonder 'en Pointe'," Tori said.

She fell asleep quickly, lulled by the hum of the air conditioning, wondering about her little man.

At the British Air check-in desk the next morning, a matronly lady, wearing a name tag that read: Mrs. Smythe, took their travel documents. Her eyes traveled thoughtfully from Gabe, who was spewing crumbs in a wide radius as he munched on a cookie, to Lydia.

Lydia had won a battle with Phillip and sat triumphantly enthroned atop the suitcases piled onto a luggage cart. Phillip had one hand on the cart and one on Lydia's shoulder. He studiously ignored the No Children on Luggage Trolleys signs scattered around the terminal.

"It's a long flight," the pleasant-faced Mrs. Smythe murmured. "Twelve or more hours, depending on headwinds."

She took the documents and reviewed them.

"These are your new children, I see. Look an adorable handful, they do. Congratulations."

"Thank you," Tori said.

She reached out to stop Lydia from climbing onto the ticket counter while keeping hold of Gabe with the other hand.

"Stay there, honey, you'll fall!"

Lydia tilted a stubborn chin in Tori's direction and continued to climb. Phillip plucked her off the cart and tossed her in the air. She giggled and he tossed her again. Gabe pulled free from Tori and held his arms up to Phillip.

"And he tells *me* I'm spoiling them," Tori told Mrs. Smythe.

The lady smiled. "Would you mind waiting just a moment while I check something?" Tori nodded.

Please, Lord, don't let there be anything wrong.

Mrs. Smythe's fingers moved efficiently over her keyboard. Occasionally, she stopped to examine the tiny numbers and letters on their tickets.

Meanwhile, Tori inspected Gabe's diaper.

He had had diarrhea the past few days. It was getting worse.

Mrs. Smythe peered at her screen, clicked a few more keys, and talked to herself.

"Yes, that will do quite well." She beamed at Tori and Phillip. "I've upgraded you to business class. It'll make the flight easier."

"You're kidding! Thank you, thank you!" Tori said.

"You're quite welcome," Mrs. Smythe said. "Think of it as a baby gift. I'm adopted myself. It's wonderful, what you've done."

"We really appreciate it," Phillip said. "I suspect before this trip is over, we'll be thinking of you very fondly."

The lady laughed and gave them their tickets.

"It's almost nine o'clock. Since you're in business class, you can board straight away. The plane is scheduled to depart at 9:45 a.m."

Chapter 5 — Flight 68 from Purgatory

They sat four in a row in large, comfortable seats.

Tori mused *Business class is a good thing. Twelve hours seems like infinity.*

A hefty woman in orange and black stiletto heels tottered pass. She wore a tight orange sweater with a mini-skirt that did not quite match and black fishnet stockings. She collapsed into a seat three rows behind them.

"Tangelo's friends really shouldn't allow her to wear that," Tori whispered to Phillip.

Their amusement was short-lived.

"They ought not to let children ride in business class," Tori heard Tangelo say in a whiny voice to her seatmate. "I'm paying premium for peace and quiet, aren't I?"

Tori felt slightly guilty, but not enough to sit in coach.

At first, Lydia was intrigued by everything, but she did not like wearing the seatbelt and was squirming before the flight took off.

"You'll need to keep that tightly buckled around her at all times," said one flight attendant, whose mouth seemed to be set in a perpetually sour expression.

Tori named her Lemon Lips. She had explained their situation to Celeste, the head flight attendant. Celeste, who was immediately sympathetic, said she would inform her crew. She then assured Tori they would help in any way they could. Fortunately, Lemon Lips seemed to spend most of her time in another cabin.

The attendants for business class, Michael and Leslie, were solicitous and warm. They presented Gabe and Lydia with little British Air carry-on bags stuffed with fun things for children. Gabe preferred an empty china coffee cup. He turned it over in his small hands, carefully examining it from every angle, as if he were a tiny archaeologist and the cup a fossil of a hitherto unknown species.

9:59 a.m. The plane's engines started. Lydia squealed and pressed her button nose against the window. Gabe rocked back and forth, eyes tightly closed and hands pressed firmly against his ears. Tori squeezed a pillow around his head to help cover his ears. As the plane leveled and the noise subsided, he cautiously uncovered his ears and stopped rocking.

10:43 a.m. A malodorous miasma rose from Gabe's seat.

Leaning over, Phillip said, "He reeks. When did you last change him?"

"Before we boarded the plane," she answered.

She checked Gabe and wrinkled her nose.

"He's dirty all the way through."

Holding him underneath one arm, Tori went forward to the small bathroom. The stench was overwhelming in the small cubicle. Tori gagged, but then realized Gabe's rear end was red. Sympathy overtook her revulsion.

Okay, Victoria, stop the prima donna act. You're a mother.

Stripping Gabe, she dropped his nasty clothes on the floor, bathed him in the tiny sink, and changed him. As she fastened the Velcro, she banged her elbow on the wall. Holding Gabe on one arm, she bent down to retrieve his clothes, and smacked her forehead against the toilet.

Words unfit to be thought—much less spoken—raced through her head. She contorted her body to reach Gabe's clothes; holding her breath, she rinsed them and sealed them in a plastic bag.

I brought six changes of clothes and more than a dozen diapers; should be enough. I'd guess we've been in the air several hours now.

Tori checked her watch. Her shoulders slumped. Only an hour had passed.

11:03 a.m. Gabe slept.

11:15 a.m. Returning from the bathroom, Lydia pinched Gabe hard on his cheek. He woke with a jerk and started crying. Phillip swatted Lydia's bottom. She responded with a pathetic, keening wail, which resounded through the airplane.

Passengers craned their necks around, trying to see what was happening. Lydia howled and struggled like she was being beaten as Phillip fastened her into her seat. The man directly in front of Tori stood up, swept them with a contemptuous glare and made a show of putting on the bulky earphones before he sat back down.

A few fellow passengers looked sympathetic. Yet, a man in a pinstriped business suit asked a flight attendant to move him. Phillip's ears turned red.

"If she were mine, I'd give her something to cry about!" Tangelo said in a loud, shrill voice.

Chapter 5 – Flight 68 from Purgatory

Celeste came by.

"Would you like some Benadryl?" she whispered.

Tori was tempted.

Phillip's brow creased.

"In 21.8 percent of cases, Benadryl makes children *more* active, instead of less."

"I've heard that, too," Tori said. "We can't risk a reaction at 35,000 feet. Thanks Celeste, but I guess we'll pass."

Celeste squeezed her shoulder and left.

12:14 p.m. A nice lunch was served. Gabe had two risotto dinners. Michael would have brought him a third, but since everything he had eaten had traveled rapidly through his digestive system, Tori nixed more food and asked for milk instead.

Lemon Lips happened to be passing.

"You know," she said, "he really should have pre-ordered from the child's menu."

She sniffed. "Giving him so many adult dinners may make us run short for others."

Michael smiled at Lemon Lips with bared lips.

"Not your cabin, Dearie, is it? I'll handle this."

Lunch continued. Lydia's bottom lip poked out, but Leslie turned Lydia's sulky lips into a smile by bringing her a luridly colored fruit punch topped with a little umbrella. Tori was pleased when Lydia said thank you in English without prompting.

Leslie brought tea for Tori and Phillip, along with crayons and coloring books for the kids. Gabe polished off a tasty purple crayon before Tori realized he had it. Lydia finished coloring everything in twenty minutes, and then spent another fifteen playing with the toys Tori had packed. Both children started whining.

Gabe was on his third outfit. Tori mulled over how she and Gabe could have been crawling over tightly packed people in coach to reach the restroom and shuddered.

1:17 p.m. Gabe lay on Phillip's chest, whimpering. Tori and Lydia made circuits of the airplane. It was monotonous, but it beat listening to Lydia gripe loudly in Bulgarian at anyone within earshot. Tori wondered what Lydia was thinking.

Lydia passed through the attendant's galley and glanced out the window. A look of fear crossed her face. Tori felt a stab of empathy. It must be scary, being this high up.

Lydia continued through the aisles, slapping alternating seat backs. She stopped abruptly and Tori ran into her. Lydia was looking up at her as if she wanted something. Tori opened her hands, shrugged her shoulders, and shook her head. She mimicked drinking.

"Are you thirsty, honey or do you need to use the bathroom?"

Lydia shook her head, said something and stomped her foot. A tear rolled down her cheek. Tori tried to hug her, but Lydia jerked away and glared at her.

Tori bit her cheek. Thrusting her lip out, Lydia turned and walked on. Tori followed, feeling helpless.

2:30 p.m. As they walked by Phillip and Gabe, Lydia smacked Gabe on the arm, and then ran ahead. Tori restrained herself from running Lydia down and giving her a thorough spanking.

They told us orphanage kids experience sensory overload when they leave. She acts defiant and brave, but that's undoubtedly a façade. She has no control in a scary situation. I'd be angry and confused, too, if I were in her shoes.

Tori resolved to give her daughter the benefit of doubt.

She rubbed tired eyes, and then went in pursuit of her Lydia, who was escaping down the aisle. An elderly man in a beret, several seats ahead stretched his arm across the aisle, blocking Lydia.

He smiled at her pleasantly, and said, "Wait for your mama."

Lydia opened her mouth to howl, but the man twisted his features into a goggle-eyed frog face and flicked his tongue as if he saw a fly. Lydia studied him with eyes and mouth wide open, and then opted to laugh. Tori caught up and gave him an appreciative look.

"Thanks. You're quite the frog."

"Years of practice as a child psychologist. Humor breaks down walls." He reached out and shook her hand. "John Stark. Are your children newly adopted?'

"Tori St. John. Nice to meet you. Yes, we've only had them a few days."

"I thought so. Don't worry. You'll need to wipe several hundred dripping noses, make gallons of Kool-Aid, and sit through lots of Barney before they accept you, but it'll happen. Give them structure, be consistent, and wait. You're doing a good job, Mom. Don't doubt yourself."

He patted Lydia's cheek and made another face. Lemon Lips pushed a drink cart down the aisle and frowned.

"Excuse me, please, you're blocking the aisle."

Dr. Stark scooted over to the empty window seat. Tori sat down in his seat and pulled Lydia into her lap, letting the cart pass. Dr. Stark wanted to hear their story. Eventually, Lydia became restless. Tori gave the doctor a grateful smile. Lydia gave him a little wave and they resumed their march around the plane.

3:15 p.m. Michael came by offering drinks. Tori considered ordering a scotch, straight up, and slipping it into Lydia's juice. Regretfully, she decided good mothers probably wouldn't even consider it.

Gabe was down to his last set of clothes and one diaper. Celeste assured Tori they had diapers in assorted sizes and varieties. Unfortunately, they had no clothes to fit.

Lydia amused herself by drawing over the in-flight magazines. Nearby passengers passed her new magazines as soon as she finished one.

Michael came by and quietly slipped Tori a small box of Godiva chocolate.

"Don't tell anyone, love. It's technically only for our VIP level frequent flyers," he whispered, "but I thought since you aren't having another drink, you need the chocolate worse."

"I think I love you," Tori mouthed.

Michael winked and moved on.

4:00 p.m. Tangelo decided to give child-rearing advice. She stood up and fixed an irate stare on the St. Johns.

"Look, lady," she said in a huffy voice. "You're too lenient with those kids."

Phillip shook his head at Tori, put a restraining arm on her shoulder, and placed a finger on her lips.

"Let it pass, Little Bit," he whispered. "There's not much we can say."

Tangelo waved a fat, ring-laden hand toward them. "I think I speak for all of us when I say you've obviously let that girl run wild for too long."

Most of the other passengers pretended to be absorbed elsewhere.

Dr. Stark stood up.

"You don't speak for me, Ma'am."

Tangelo glared at him, hands on her hips, outsized chest heaving. Tori wished one of her buttons would pop off. Everyone was listening now, either openly or surreptitiously.

Dr. Stark spoke with an air of calm authority.

"These children have been in an institution from birth. They have just been adopted. They're adapting to more change than most of us will experience in a lifetime. Do you have children, Ma'am?"

"Well, no, but—"

"Then you've no right to judge the parenting skills of a couple going through the child-rearing equivalent of jungle combat."

"Humph!" Tangelo snorted. "Well, what right do *you* have—"

He gave a courtly little bow.

"Dr. John Stark, practicing child psychologist. Thirty-five years with Harvard Medical Center."

Tangelo's face fell. One hand nervously played with a bright orange, plastic earring.

"Yeah, so shut yer trap!" an anonymous voice called out.

A bright red blush stained Tangelo's face, making her resemble a bowl of orange Jell-O topped with a fat red cherry. She sat and slipped down in her seat.

A few passengers applauded. Several sent abashed smiles in the St. John's direction. One lady pulled a package of M&M'S out of her carry-on and asked permission to give them to the children.

6:30 p.m. Tori and Lydia circled the plane. A man in coach was asleep with his legs stretched across the aisle. Lydia gave Tori an insolent look, as if to say: "What are you going to do about *this*, huh?" She deliberately kicked him.

Tori had enough. Apologizing to the startled man, she whisked Lydia into the bathroom and paddled her bottom. Lydia yelped once, and then began sobbing tearful bursts of salty emotion.

Leslie knocked on the door.

"Is everything alright, then?" she asked.

Tori hugged Lydia and used gentle fingers to wipe her tears.

"Yes, we just needed to establish a few guidelines. Scared and tired do not excuse rude and undisciplined."

Leslie laughed softly.

"I can tape that, can I, to pass on to future passengers?"

Lemon Lips looked down her nose at Tori as they left the restroom.

"I don't hold with beating a child," Tori overheard her say loudly.

"There's a big difference between a beating and a spanking. Proper monsters, some children become, when their parents don't take a hand," Michael said.

Head held high, Tori brushed by them and carried her tear-streaked daughter back to their seats.

"What happened?" Phillip asked.

Tori told him. Phillip raised an eyebrow.

"Are you sure that was a good idea?"

Was it? I had all these ideas about loving discipline, calm discussions, and natural consequences, yet we don't even make it to U.S. soil before I spank her.

Tori straightened her shoulders.

"I considered it necessary," she said, "given what Lydia did. That poor man will probably have a huge bruise. Reasoning with her doesn't help. We've distracted, scolded, and bribed. Nothing worked."

She stroked one of Lydia's curls away from her face and kissed her forehead. "Several of the books I read say children need boundaries to make them feel loved and secure."

Leslie came by.

"Only four more hours," she said, with the bright smile of a cheerleader. "That is, if the wind doesn't keep slowing us down."

Tori turned to Phillip.

"Lydia was testing me. Had I let her behavior pass, she would have been a little hellion the rest of the trip."

Phillip looked at Lydia, now quietly snuggled into Tori's lap.

"You appear to have made the right choice."

8:10 p.m. Tori grabbed another blanket, scooped Gabe up, and went forward to the bathroom. It smelled like a state fair Porta-Potty at the end of a hot summer day. Tears sprang to Tori's eyes.

Lord, what have I gotten us into?

She remembered the Bible verse when Christ promised, "I will never leave you or forsake you."

So, God's here in the stink with me. Just keep going, one diaper wipe after another. Phillip was attempting damage control with sanitary hand wipes. Michael came by.

"Anything I can do to help?"

Their eyes met over the grimy blanket.

Phillip said, "It's going to be hard to wash this out."

"Throw it away," Michael said without hesitation. "I'll get you another stack."

"Great. You guys have been awesome. I'm going to write a letter."

"I'll bring you a comment card."

"Absolutely. Get me your names, and a whole stack of cards."

"Righto."

8:55 p.m. Gabe was flushed and his lips were dry.

"Phillip, I'm worried about dehydration."

Phillip caught Michael's arm as he passed and explained their concern.

Michael got on the intercom and asked if there was a doctor on board. An internist came forward right away. After examining Gabe, she seemed puzzled.

"He's under-nourished, but he seems healthy. There's no fever, his lungs are clear. Has he been exposed to a virus or eaten anything out of the norm?"

Tori and Phillip looked at each other, mouths dropping open. Phillip explained their circumstance. The doctor chuckled.

"It's no wonder his system's upset. I'll give you some anti-diarrhea medicine, said the doctor. "They should have told you to increase his intake gradually and to restrict him to bland foods. He'll be fine."

"Keep pumping liquids into him, but not milk. Water or Gatorade," she said with a twinkle in her eyes. "Follow the BRAT diet: bananas, rice, applesauce, and toast."

She winked. "Rice does *not* include risotto."

10:40 p.m. "I think we've walked the equivalent of a marathon," Phillip moaned to Tori as he and Lydia walked past.

"Well," said Tori, getting up to change Gabe's diaper for only the second time since the medicine, "just think, it could've been cattle car instead of business class. Ugly."

"At least you can still laugh about it," commented a lady who had watched with fascinated horror as the trip unfolded. "I've aged five years just watching you."

"Without God and a sense of humor," said Tori, "I'd have jumped off the plane myself by now."

"Not without taking the kids," Phillip warned.

In the little bathroom mirror, Tori saw a wraith with deep pits under her eyes, bitten lips, and the paleness of fatigue. The braids she had efficiently coiled around her head twelve hours earlier hung limply over her back. She decided to ignore her appearance and changed Gabe into a diaper with pink kittens cavorting all over it.

The Brit Air supply was running low. Other passengers were studiously avoiding what the St. John family had come to consider their personal bathroom.

11:30 p.m. Survival may be possible. Customs forms and glowing comment cards were filled out They tried to return Gabe's coffee cup, but he became so upset Leslie gifted him with it. Now that the plane was circling Atlanta airspace, Lydia had fallen into an exhausted sleep. She breathed quietly and rhythmically, looking angelic.

5:00 p.m. local time Flight 68 from purgatory was officially over. Gabe met their welcoming committee wearing a Minnie Mouse pull-up and the last clean British Air blanket. Lydia's dress was wrinkled and dirty. Her hair formed a tangled cloud around her face, but she had recovered her normal vivacity and was beautiful.

They were home. Battered, bruised, exhausted, and—in Gabe's case—aromatic, but they were home.

Chapter 6
Home Strange Home

As they drove home, Tori braided a strand of hair, pulled her fingers through to loose it, and then started again.

Will the kids like their new home?

They pulled into their driveway. Phillip rescued the beleaguered hair from Tori's fingers and tucked it behind her ear.

"It's going to be fine, mini-Mom."

Across the street, Scotch trotted back and forth in his front yard, confined to Serena's property by invisible fencing. His wagging tail bespoke welcome, but his fierce, bared teeth and low-throated grumble warned them he was not a dog to be trifled with. Gabe, content with his coffee mug, did not notice.

Lydia noticed.

"Coaga, Coaga!" she wailed, climbing like a little monkey rapidly up Phillip's legs.

He swung her up in his arms. Lydia scrambled until she was crouched on Phillip's shoulders, one arm wrapped tightly around his neck. Serena hurried to quiet her dog.

"Come on, Princessa," Phillip said, hoping to distract the frightened toddler, "I have something to show you."

A look of horror crossed Lydia's face. Tori turned to see Scotch loping toward Serena, tongue bouncing as he ran.

She probably thinks Scotch is going to eat Serena.

"It's okay, Darlin'," she said, touching Lydia's cheek. "That's just Scotch. He's a good dog. Good Coaga."

Phillip plucked Lydia off his shoulders and carried her inside to the foyer, followed by Tori holding Gabe. Lydia stared up the staircase, her eyes as big as doughnuts. Phillip started up the stairs, but Lydia wriggled and spoke rapidly.

Tori heard the meaning in her daughter's unintelligible words.

"Put her down, honey. She wants to do it herself."

Phillip put his daughter down. The intrepid toddler flashed them a brief smile, and then set her chin and began scaling the high steps on all fours. Her slender legs propelled her upward as her family followed. Reaching the wide hallway at the top, Lydia paused, not sure where to go next. Tori took Lydia's hand and led the way into the children's bedroom.

Each child would eventually have his and her own room, but Tori thought Lydia and Gabe would draw comfort from each other initially, so they had created a room for the kids to share. Three sides were painted a soothing sky blue. A whimsical Noah's Ark mural finished the last wall of what they hoped was a welcoming haven for their children.

Lydia, her face glowing, ran around the room, stopping now and then to touch something. She gave the olive-skinned doll nestled against colorful pillows on the bottom mattress of blue bunk beds a cursory glance. A stuffed tiger with a benevolent smile earned a quick hug, but Lydia gravitated to the toy shelves as if pulled by an invisible string. Face intent, she rummaged through them like a pirate queen inspecting her treasures.

Tori sat Gabe on the floor, wondering what he would go for. For the moment, he sat and watched Lydia. Tori and Phillip had packed away many of the toys they had received for later, fearing the kids would be overwhelmed. Although there were still more toys than an average Christmas morning, Lydia had soon examined each one and emptied the shelves.

"Why don't we straighten our room now?" Phillip asked.

He picked up a toy, put it away, took another, gave it to Lydia, and pointed at the colorful shelving. Obediently, she put it away.

"Good job, Lydia," Phillip said.

He looked from Lydia to the pile of toys and waited. Lydia gave him a charming smile, jumped up to check out the rest of the room and left him standing by the mound of playthings. Tori giggled, earning a scowl from Phillip.

"Oh, honey, they're too excited to be neat today. Let them play. We'll practice cleaning up our mess tomorrow."

"Begin in the way you mean to go on," retorted Phillip, but Tori had turned to Gabe and tried to interest him in a ball.

Finding no support in his quest for tidiness, Phillip walked over to stand beside Lydia, who was studying the mural, her forehead creased as if trying to interpret the meaning of the big boat and all those animals.

She pointed to the dark, swollen clouds and said, "Ploaie."

"It's going to rain." Phillip fluttered his fingers downward. "Rain."

"Ploaie, rain," Lydia said.

She ran to the dresser. Her fingers stroked the wood, feeling it as if its texture imparted a meaning to her fingers. She opened the drawers with care, her eyes wide with anticipation. Her mouth turned down at the socks, underwear, and pajamas she found.

Tori held Gabe up to the large window, which framed a view of the leafy backyard. His eyes flickered and brightened when he saw the swing set. Lydia looked over, saw it, and clapped her hands.

She pulled at Tori's arm and pointed outside at the swing set, bouncing on her toes.

Before Tori could respond, Lydia's fleeting attention was captured by the closed closet door. She approached it, looking back at Tori as if to be assured this mysterious portal was safe. Her hand reached out to open it. She paused. Her eyes darted to Phillip. He grinned and made a shooing motion. Lydia turned the knob.

"Oh!" Lydia's mouth formed a perfect circle.

She flung the door wide open revealing a walk-in closet. One side was hung with dozens of girls' outfits, the other with boys. Shoes lined each side, and a shelf at the back was filled with belts, hats, and other accessories. Lydia ran her hands reverently over each outfit, her eyes caressing the garments.

In less than a minute, Lydia had stripped and re-dressed herself in hot pink overalls and a purple-flowered shirt, complete with pink-spangled cowgirl boots and a tiara.

"Beautiful!" Phillip gave a wolf-whistle.

Tori applauded, and then turned Lydia to face the full-length mirror on the closet door. Lydia's face was solemn as she studied her reflection, turning to view every angle. Breaking into a huge smile, Lydia turned to her parents and spoke with great concentration.

"Tank. Tan-ku."

Phillip grabbed Lydia and swung her in circles before putting her down.

"You're welcome, sweet girl!"

Tori watched; her heart swelling with joy.

Lydia dragged Gabe into the closet, pointing at his clothes and babbling. Gabe seemed unimpressed. Lydia cocked her head to one side, considering. She pulled down a navy blue polo shirt, and draped it over Gabe's chest. Gabe shrugged it off and left the closet.

Lydia shrugged, sweeping her slight arms wide. She tried to hold all her clothes at once, and then turned to her parents.

"My?" the toddler questioned. "My?"

Blinking away tears, Tori nodded. She took Lydia's hand and placed it on the little girl's chest.

"Mine," she prompted, and spread Lydia's arms to indicate the girls clothes. She put Lydia's hand on her chest again.

"Mine."

"Mine!" Lydia chortled. "Mine!"

Behind her, Gabe giggled. Tori and Phillip turned eagerly to see what aspect of his new room had engaged their son's attention.

Gabe's head was tilted back, his Hershey bar eyes fixed on the ceiling, a rapt expression on his face. Tori and Phillip followed his gaze upward.

A ceiling fan, its blades painted in soft primary colors, spun in lazy circles. Gabe was mesmerized.

"Well, Little Prince," said Tori, "who knew you'd be happier with a coffee mug and a ceiling fan than a room full of toys and stuffed animals?"

"There's a fan in just about every room in the house, so he should be delighted," Phillip said.

He walked over to the switch and turned the fan on high. Gabe chortled and waved his arms. Phillip gave Tori a hug, and then looked around the bedroom with approval.

"I think they like it. It's cheerful and welcoming, worth every hour we spent getting it ready."

"*And* every penny?" Tori asked with a mischievous grin.

Phillip, who had grumbled over the money Tori spent on the room, said, "Oh, fine, rub it in. Okay, worth every penny, too!"

Phillip kissed the top of Tori's head. "We're parents, Little Bit!"

Lydia rolled a fire engine around the room, turning the siren's urgent wail on and off. Gabe crouched in the corner and covered his ears with his hands. Phillip leaned over and disabled the sound.

"That's enough for now, Sweetie. It hurts your brother's ears."

"And mine!" Tori mouthed at Phillip.

Phillip grinned, and mouthed back, "Get used to it."

Lydia pursed her lips as if to complain, but decided to content herself with ringing the bell hanging outside the cab of the bright red truck. As she raced it around the room yanking the bell, it broke off the chain. Lydia rocked back on her heels, the truck in one hand, the bell in the other, a look of dismay on her face.

"Mama," she called, looking at Tori. "Mama, Daddy!"

Phillip re-attached the bell, using his teeth to close the ring that had come loose. Lydia beamed and returned to her play.

Tori bumped fists with Phillip.

"Good work, Papa. No award or bonus I ever got felt as good to me as hearing 'Mama, Daddy' just now. I'm home."

Phillip only nodded, but Tori noticed his eyes were full of tears.

Phillip took off from work the following week. The family spent much of their time in the large fenced backyard. Gabe especially loved the swing set. He seemed happier and more alert after swinging.

The only thing Gabe liked more than swinging was eating. After he choked a couple of times, Phillip stood behind him while he ate, grasping his arms, so he could not shove food in faster than he could swallow it.

They learned the hard way if the kids ate the amount they wanted at the speed they preferred: they became sick. On the other hand, if their plates became empty before they were full, each child would immediately grab for someone else's plate.

Tori served small portions, but replaced food as the children ate. As the week went on, Lydia seemed to realize there was plenty of food and relaxed a bit. Gabe remained fiercely protective of his food, tensing if anyone approached his side of the table while he was eating.

The children had full medical work-ups two days after they arrived home. Dr. Paul Jeffries and his wife had adopted two children from Lithuania; he had extensive experience with third world children.

After giving both kids thorough examinations, Dr. Jeffries frowned as he consulted his growth chart. "Gabe is supposed to be three and a half years old?"

"We think there was a mix-up in the records." Tori said. "He's probably around two years old."

"That makes more sense. I'm ordering a bone age x-ray for him, and we'll see what the dentist says. If the bone age and his dental development show him to be around two, I'd suggest you change his age legally when you file your U.S. adoption papers."

Tori nodded.

"Overall, I'd say you have two healthy children. Gabe's behind developmentally, even for age two, but that's not abnormal considering his background. They have a parasite, but medicine will clear that up. They aren't malnourished, but they are undernourished. I'd like to see them again in six months."

"What's the difference between *mal*nourished and *under*nourished?"

"Undernourished children are behind the normal growth curves and thinner than is healthy. With good nutrition, they usually recover quickly. In malnourishment, the body starts digesting itself."

Chapter 6 – Home Strange Home

The Chick-fil-A biscuit Tori had for breakfast rose in her throat.

Dr. Jeffries noticed her reaction.

"I know," he said. "Since we adopted, my wife and I have become regular supporters of a missionary group that works directly with Lithuanian orphanages."

"That's a great idea! I think we'll try to find a similar group in Bulgaria."

Dr. Jeffries' smile was warm.

"It'll feel good to give something back to the countries that gave you your children."

Bone and dental x-rays indicated Gabe was 16–24 months old. The St. Johns decided to establish his age as twenty-four months.

Tori and Phillip attended First Unity Christian Church, where they were active members. During their second weekend at home, they attended. They arrived for second service as streams of early service worshipers exited the sanctuary.

Someone spotted them and came running, calling back over her shoulder, "The St. Johns are home with the kids!"

Tori, Phillip and the children were soon enveloped by a mob of admirers. Questions and comments blended in a cacophony of voices.

"Adorable . . . long eyelashes . . . can I bring . . . kiss Aunt Susie . . . homemade mac and cheese . . ."

Gabe wriggled into Phillip's shoulder as if he were trying to burrow a hiding place. Lydia enjoyed the attention at first, but as the numbers multiplied and the noise level rose, her pleased smile faded away. She grabbed two fistfuls of Tori's dress and buried her face against her mother's leg.

A red-headed boy about Lydia's age ran over and spoke to Lydia's back.

His freckled face was earnest as he asked, "Are you the orp'n? I'm Jake. Mommy says we hafta be friends."

He put a hand on Lydia's shoulder and tried to draw her away from Tori.

"Come on! Don't be a 'fraidy cat!"

The harder he pulled, the tighter Lydia clutched her mother's dress. Tori's outfit strained against the pressure. A button unfastened, revealing the lace of Tori's black bra and more cleavage than was considered seemly at First Unity.

"Stop!" Tori refastened her top and bent to push Jake away.

Her movement popped the button loose again. The tug-of-war continued and a second button started working free. Phillip, surrounded by well-wishers, couldn't see what was happening. Sweeping a frantic eye over the crowd, Tori saw Donna Brown, Unity's director of education.

"Donna!" Tori hissed to the stylish, plump woman.

Donna had the ability to assess and control even the stickiest situations with grace. She glided through the crowd to Tori's side without apparent effort, buttoned Tori's dress and winked.

"Nice bra. Victoria's Secret?" she asked in an undertone.

"Jacob," Donna said, freeing the boy's grip, "you're scaring Lydia."

She gave him a gentle push, and then turned and spoke to the adults.

"I think the children are overwhelmed. Let's give them some space. Maggie Burke is coordinating meals in the foyer."

Good-naturedly, the crowd dispersed. Many of them headed to the foyer with Reverend Maggie Burke, Unity's assistant pastor. Tori smoothed her dress.

"Thanks, Donna."

"Always glad to help," Donna said, bowing her head of elegantly cropped silver blonde hair. "Are the kids going to Sunday school?"

"We're not quite sure," said Tori

At the same time Phillip said, "Yes."

All three laughed.

"I'm uneasy about leaving the kids in childcare so soon," Tori explained, "but Phillip thinks they'll be fine."

Tori hoped Donna would agree with her, but she was disappointed.

Chapter 6 – Home Strange Home

"It's normal for mothers to have separation anxiety," Donna said. "The kids will be with some of our most seasoned teachers. Try it."

Their first stop was the Cherub room, home of the two-year-olds. The Cherub room was under the benevolent rule of Ms. Jasmine Sinclair, who always looked as if she had just stepped from the cover of *Vogue* magazine.

She pulled a pager out of the box, and turned it on; nothing happened. She thumped it on the counter—nothing. Jasmine shook her head.

"Drat! The batteries are dead again. They're supposed to be the long-lasting kind. Hold on," she told Tori.

She opened a supply closet door, pulled out a step-ladder, and climbed agilely to the top, unhindered by her form-fitting turquoise dress. She retrieved a package of batteries from a shelf above her head and descended the ladder, tiny feet pattering quickly down the steps in three-inch black heels.

Out of the corner of her eye, Tori saw Phillip was having trouble keeping his mouth shut at the sight of the elegant Ms. Sinclair scrambling up and down the ladder. Tori smiled.

Church lore held that Ms. Sinclair, clad in a red silk pants suit with matching accessories, once used a garden hose to douse a raging house fire without disturbing a single braid of her intricately-woven coiffure.

Jasmine replaced the battery, tested the pager, and then handed it to Tori.

"Now, give me this handsome young man."

A smile broke out over her attractive face, enhancing her high ebony cheekbones as Gabe was handed to her. She waved away the assistant who came to get him.

"I'll take him," she said, giving Gabe a hug.

"I'm so glad you're home, Gabriel," she said, and then led him to the toys. Gabe examined his fingers as if making sure he still had ten.

"Don't worry; they're often shy at first," Jasmine said.

She held out a blue truck jacked up on huge wheels. Gabe stooped to look under it and study the wheels. He straightened, took the truck, and walked away.

Somewhat reassured, Tori and Phillip took Lydia to the five-year-old Seraph classroom, two doors down the hall.

Abby Mitchell was a pleasant lady with a daughter Lydia's age. Abby met them with a welcoming smile, her daughter Sara at her elbow. She then turned and clapped her hands for attention.

"Children," she said to her group, "this is our new friend, Lydia. She doesn't speak English yet, so be sure to help her have a good time."

The children stared at Lydia, who after a brief glance held up her arms to Phillip. He stooped to pick her up, but Abby shook her head.

"You two go on," she told the St. Johns. "Sara and I will make sure she's comfortable."

"I don't have a good feeling about this," Tori told Phillip as they walked toward their Sunday school class.

"She'll be class president by the time we get back," he responded, squeezing her hand.

They heard a scream and turned around. Lydia raced down the hall away from them, Abby in hot pursuit. Tori started after them, but Phillip caught her arm and pulled her back.

"Wait and see what happens," he said. "Let them try to handle it."

Tori chewed the inside of her lip, pushed her hair back, and wondered how Phillip could be so calm.

Lydia could be in the parking lot by now!"

An Ice Age passed before they saw Abby return, alone. She stopped when she saw them.

"Lydia prefers to be in Gabe's room today. That's probably a good idea for now." She paused. "If it's okay with you, Sara and I will come over later this week. Lydia may be more comfortable next Sunday if she spends time with us in her own home."

"That's a great idea. Thanks," Tori said. "I know how busy you are. It's really considerate of you to spend the extra time with her. I'll call you tomorrow."

They arrived at their classroom in time for prayer requests. Phillip shared they were concerned about Gabe's development. After class, the teacher asked if they had heard of Babies Can't Wait

(BCW). When they shook their heads, he leaned against the doorframe and explained.

"It's a government program for delayed children. They send therapists into the home, at no cost to the family. My neighbor loves the program; her daughter has received speech therapy since she was eighteen months old."

"I'll check it out tomorrow," Tori promised. "Thanks!"

Tori tried to listen to the service. At one point, Phillip gently took the bulletin away from her. He tapped the sketch Tori had made of Lydia behind bars, crying, and raised his eyebrows. Tori kept her hands tightly clasped the rest of the service.

After worship, they returned to the Cherub room. Gabe was snuggled into Ms. Sinclair's lap, his face encrusted with juice and cookie crumbs, his thin fingers lazily spinning the truck wheels. It was hard to tell who was more content, Gabe or her.

Lydia rode a large, black rocking horse with red spots. She looked happy galloping in place, but ran to Tori as soon as she saw her, clutching Tori's leg and whimpering.

"Now, Sweetheart, none of that, you've been just fine until now," Ms. Sinclair said briskly. "Here, Darlin', Aunt Jasmine's got something for you."

She handed Lydia a unicorn sticker. Lydia stopped whining.

"Gabe was just adorable. He likes me! He didn't want anything to do with anybody at first, just wanted his truck. He warmed up by snack time, though!"

She stroked Gabe's head with a dainty hand.

"He sat and ate animal crackers until I thought he'd explode! I offered to put him down, but he wanted to stay with his Aunt Jasmine!"

Tori gave Ms. Sinclair a weak smile as she boosted Lydia onto her hip. No need to tell her Gabe would sit in Darth Vader's lap if Vader had a steady supply of animal crackers.

Phillip lifted Gabe.

"Let's leave the truck here, buddy."

Phillip wrestled the pickup from Gabe's death grip. A piercing wail shattered the peace.

"Oh, let him keep it," Jasmine said. "I assure you it won't be missed. Bring it back when he gets tired of it."

Not waiting for an answer, she gave the truck to Gabe. Phillip sighed and raked his fingers through his hair.

"Doesn't look like I have much choice. Thank you."

Lydia wriggled off Tori's hip, ran to the rocking horse, clutched its reins and dragged it toward the door.

"Oh, no baby, that's too big to take home," Phillip laughed. "It needs to live here."

He took the rocking horse from Lydia.

"Mine!" Lydia said, thumping her chest and pulling at the toy.

Phillip returned the horse to its spot, put his hand on Lydia's shoulder, and walked her out of the room as she protested.

Tori groaned. She had a diaper bag on one arm, Gabe and his truck on the other, and a sulking daughter. Tori tried to console Lydia, but Lydia ignored her and fastened a basilisk glare on Gabe.

"Phillip!" Tori said as she fastened Lydia into her car seat. "I bet she thinks we're playing favorites."

Phillip fished around in his ubiquitous glove compartment and pulled out a small plastic pony with bright pink hair.

"Here, Sweetie," he told Lydia.

Lydia took the pony, but continued to frown. Phillip shrugged and started the car.

"The truck is small. That rocking horse is the size of a Shetland pony. It's not the same thing."

"I know," Tori pleaded, "but she doesn't understand that. We could give her the rocking horse your parents bought for her, the one we stored in the attic."

"You're spoiling her." Phillip threw up his arms.

"I'm just trying to be fair. I don't want her to resent Gabe."

"I think you're setting a precedent we'll regret later," Phillip grumbled.

As soon as lunch was over, though, he climbed the stairs to the attic and brought down the rocking horse. When Lydia squealed and kissed him, Phillip's face softened and he gave her an affectionate spank on the bottom.

Chapter 6 – Home Strange Home

"You're wrapping Daddy around your little finger, Minx," he said ruefully as he lifted her onto the horse.

They spent the rest of the day playing with Lydia and her horse, while Gabe played with his truck. Phillip got another truck and tried to play with him, but Gabe ignored him.

The next day, Phillip went back to work. Tori and the kids played non-stop throughout the morning, and then enjoyed a late picnic lunch outside in the fort of the swing set. It was long past nap time, but the only one willing to lie down was Tori, so they ended up in the den.

Lydia collapsed on the couch and was soon fast asleep. Gabe rolled his truck back and forth, watching the wheels, ignoring Tori.

Remembering how Gabe had danced in the London hotel room, Tori, who had taken ballet for years, started a classical CD. Though her steps were not as light, her middle-aged muscles remembered movements etched long ago and responded instinctively with glissades and pirouettes in a supple ode to life and hope.

Arms and legs outstretched, Tori executed a jete, which propelled her into Gabe's personal space. He moved away. Tori kicked her toes and whirled across the polished wooden floor until she faced him again. Gabe turned his back. With arms raised like the wings of a swan, Tori fluttered in front of him.

Her son registered a protest, which Tori ignored. Everywhere Gabe went Tori pursued him with dance, compelling him with eyes, heart, and movement to accept her into his world.

After numerous revolutions of point and counterpoint, Gabe retreating while Tori advanced, a slow half-smile curved Gabe's lips. He swiveled away, but peeked back over his shoulder to see if Tori would follow. When she did, he scrambled to his feet. Tori danced in place on her toes and held out her arms.

Gabe's molten chocolate eyes locked directly with Tori's green ones for a heartbeat. After a few seconds, he shifted his eyes away, but lifted his arms. Tori picked him up, hugged him tight to her chest, and danced.

Sunlight through the windowpanes illuminated their pas de deux, bathing the oak floor with rainbow-hued spotlights. Outside the light breeze danced with their two Weeping Willow trees, swaying leafy branches in a sultry tango. After a few minutes, Gabe wriggled down and returned to his truck, but the song in Tori's soul danced on long after the music faded into the afternoon sunshine.

CHAPTER 7

Daunting Diagnosis

"Just like that ol' time rock-n-roll!" Phillip sang along with Bob Seger and the Silver Bullet Band. Tori turned up the radio and beat time on the dashboard, joining her soprano warble to Phillip's bass. They were driving to Gabe's third appointment with Dr. Lani Shriva. Nine months had passed since Gabe's last visit with the prestigious child psychologist.

Gabe had come a long way. He smiled often. He repeated words and sounds endlessly, popping them out when least expected. He had bonded with his family, constantly requesting hugs or to be tossed in the air.

A year ago, Dr. Shriva had met the whole family at their first appointment. Her office had an oak desk to one side, fronted by a small conversation area. The rest of the spacious room was given over to a well-equipped play area.

Dr. Shriva asked questions and did a few simple tests while the children played. After forty-five minutes, she pronounced Lydia fine and scheduled Gabe's second visit.

During the second visit, Dr. Shriva concentrated on Gabe. At the end of an hour she announced Gabe had significant developmental delay.

"Orphanage life could account for his delays," she said. "His gross motor skills are good, and he seems to have recovered from the apathy you described earlier. Let's give him some time. I'll redo the tests in nine months."

Driving to the doctor's office now, Tori remembered how hopeful she had been as they left Shriva's office nine months ago.

"That's good news. Gabe could be normal for an orphan, just a little behind."

Phillip had shaken his head.

"That's not what the doctor said, Half-Pint."

"Well, okay, so he's a lot behind, but time is on our side. We're not in a race."

Phillip's brow furrowed, then relaxed.

"I never thought of it that way, but you're right. Eventually, he'll catch up."

At the next light, Phillip had kissed her.

"God chose you to be Gabe's mom."

"*And* chose you as his father. Between us, we can make up for Gabe's time in the orphanage. If it takes a decade, so be it."

The orphanage background doesn't seem to affect Lydia much.

Tori had dismissed the renegade thought.

After the second appointment, they had started speech therapy right away. Jenny, Gabe's therapist, was knowledgeable in many aspects of developmental delay, and had done volunteer work in orphanages. After the first week, she suggested further testing.

"Gabe dislikes noise, hates random textures, and focuses better after swinging motions. Those are symptoms of sensory integration dysfunction."

"Sensory dis-what?" Tori asked.

"Sensory integration dysfunction, SID, occurs when the sensory systems don't develop properly. It's common in institutionalized children."

Jenny's voice was unsteady as she continued, "The orphanages I've seen weren't able to provide much by way of positive physical input."

"But Lydia was in the orphanage even longer."

Chapter 7 – Daunting Diagnosis

"You said Lydia was popular. She probably got cuddled more. There's an excellent book you should read, *The Out-of-Sync Child*, by Carol Stock Kranowitz. M. A."

The book explained a lot. Gabe's picture could have illustrated several chapters. Tori scheduled tests for both children. Lydia scored within the low normal range. The therapist suggested some exercises, but was not overly concerned.

Gabe's evaluation showed his sensory system to be significantly underdeveloped. SID therapy yielded immediate improvements. He talked more, made peace with the vacuum cleaner, and no longer objected to wearing socks.

Tori sketched smiley faces, sunbursts, and happy, plump caterpillars everywhere. Phillip stocked his glove compartment with various sensory tools such as tactile brushes. Now, nine months later, they were happy as they prepared to show Dr. Shriva how Gabe had thrived.

A giggle erupted from the back seat. Phillip glanced in the rearview mirror while Tori turned to look back. Gabe lounged in his car seat chortling at a private joke, white teeth flashing. Phillip waved to him in the mirror.

"Gabe's come a long way. He's not the same child we brought home from the orphanage."

"No." Tori agreed. "He's a butterfly, out of his cocoon and flying high."

"Ahh. That would explain the drawing of a butterfly with Gabe's face, which I found this morning, drawn in *ink* on my monthly report." Phillip gave Tori a mock frown. "Which road do we turn on?"

"Um, here!" Tori pointed. "Turn right! Darn, you missed it! We'll be late!"

"A little warning would be nice. Turning then would've required us to jump over a rather large SUV," Phillip said dryly as he cut up a side street. "Besides, I think this road goes through."

He swung the SUV into Dr. Shriva's parking lot.

"Ta da! Three minutes, twenty-nine seconds to spare!"

Dr. Shriva asked them about Gabe's progress, and then played with him and repeated the previous tests. An hour later she called the St. Johns back into her office.

"Isn't he doing great?" Tori couldn't keep the smile off her face.

Dr. Shriva studied her notes with a slight frown, tapping her pen on tight lips.

She looked at them, and then returned her gaze to her papers, as if something profound was hidden in her notes. Finally she came around her desk and sat in a chair next to them. Her eyes mourned.

"I'm sorry. Gabe has made little progress. He's not developing normally."

Dr. Shriva's words sucked the oxygen out of Tori's lungs. Black swirls fogged her vision. From a distance, she heard Phillip protesting.

"That's ridiculous. He's a different child entirely!"

Gabe chose this moment to scramble into Phillip's lap, take the lid off Phillip's Starbucks cup, and start playing with it.

"See! He's bonded."

Phillip bent, rummaged in Gabe's diaper bag, and pulled out a clear folder.

"Here's a bar graph detailing his new word usage. I have another chart, which clearly shows—"

"Mr. St. John," Dr. Shriva interrupted, "I didn't say he hasn't learned anything, or that he's unhappy. Physically he's flourishing. Developmentally, however, none of the anomalies I observed last time have changed."

In her mind Tori saw Gabe, banging his head against the floor of a murky, vermin-infested cell. The mist thickened; oblivion beckoned. A Bible verse surfaced: *I know the plans I have for you . . . plans for good, not evil . . . to give you a future and a hope . . .*

Tori's brain grabbed the lifeline, stiffening her knees just in time to prevent her body from sliding like an amoeba onto the floor. She gulped air and resurfaced.

Phillip thrust out his jaw.

"So he's behind." He clasped a protective arm around Gabe. "He's getting therapy. He'll catch up."

Chapter 7 — Daunting Diagnosis

Dr. Shriva put down her pencil and leaned toward them.

"I know you'll do everything possible for Gabe." She paused and waited until she had Tori's and Phillip's attention. "Even so, please hear what I'm about to say. This isn't as simple as Gabe lagging behind on a normal development chart. Gabe's mind is developing differently from neuro-typical children. He's moving along his own, separate curve."

Tori furrowed her brow.

"I don't understand. He's bright."

"Yes, but his neurological processing issues may make it difficult for him to learn."

"Processing issues? Are you saying Gabe has sensory integration dysfunction?" Phillip asked hopefully. "We knew that."

"Certainly he has SID, but it's more complicated than that."

"Tell us what you think is wrong." Tori leaned forward, gripping the arms of her chair.

"Only a medical doctor can give a formal diagnosis, and they usually wait until a child is over four years of age. Gabe's only three."

"But, you're thinking something," Phillip said. "Please be frank with us."

Dr. Shriva sighed.

"Gabe's symptoms and behaviors are most often seen in children with autism." She picked up a pamphlet. "The Autism Speaks organization has a *100 Day Kit for Parents of Children Newly Diagnosed with Autism*.1 You may want to go to the organization's website."

Tori jumped to her feet.

"My son is *not* autistic!" She pointed to Gabe and Phillip with a shaking finger. "Look! See how he's cuddling with Phillip?"

Dr. Shriva took her glasses off and polished them before answering in quiet, measured tones.

"Sadly, Gabe may be sitting with Mr. St. John because he wants to play with the lid, or because he likes the pressure of your husband's arm, or both."

---

1 Go to www.autismspeaks.org for a free copy of the *100 Day Kit for Parents of Children Newly Diagnosed with Autism*.

"But he likes to be near us. He looks at us, sometimes." Tori heard a shrill voice and realized it was hers. "Autistic people don't *do* that!"

"The autistic spectrum is broad," Dr. Shriva said. "One cannot say that all people with autism do or don't do *anything*. The questionnaires you and his therapists filled out confirm my observations and indicate Gabe has pervasive development disorder, PDD, which is on the autistic spectrum."

"What, exactly, is PDD?" Phillip spat out the acronym.

Dr. Shriva went back behind her desk.

"A simple definition of PDD is higher functioning autism. It's an umbrella diagnosis on the DSM-III . . ."

The medical jargon flowed meaninglessly around Tori. Her world had tilted.

"Mrs. St. John? Are you ill?" Dr. Shriva asked.

Her hand hovered over her intercom button. "Would you like some cold water?"

Tori's stomach churned. She wouldn't mind throwing up over Gabe's folder. Filled with unknown words and impersonal numbers, the documents in that folder judged Gabe incomplete, and defective.

The future they projected sentenced her son to a barren wasteland. Tori's nausea turned to fury. She slammed her hand down on Dr. Shriva's polished oak desk.

"These measurements aren't Gabe! All this process does is calculate results and grind out a label that doesn't represent Gabe or what he can be."

In the background, Phillip nodded approval. Tori burned green laser-eyes into Dr. Shriva's dark ones.

"Your data doesn't even begin to explain the true Gabe." Tori whirled and left the office, slamming the door behind her.

Phillip nodded curtly and turned to leave.

The doctor called him back.

"Although your wife is unaware of it, she has grasped the essential reality about Gabe's autism. When you can both acknowledge and internalize that truth, Gabe and your family will be fine."

Phillip scowled. "I don't know what you mean."

Dr. Shriva shrugged a slender brown shoulder and said nothing more.

Determined to prove Dr. Shriva wrong, Tori set up her laptop at the kitchen table, where she could look out the window every few seconds. The kids seemed well-occupied and content, but yesterday, during forty-five unsupervised seconds, Gabe had dismantled the remote control and tried to eat the batteries. Tori had to call poison control.

Tori Googled: traits of autism in children. Halfway through the first article, Tori had a throbbing headache.

A paper copy may be easier to read.

She hit the *Print* button, stood up, rolled her neck from side-to-side, and then retrieved the document. She sat and read phrases such as:

> Children with autism often choose odd things as toys, or play with toys atypically. They often fixate on patterns and seek constant repetition, possibly as a way to restore order to sensory overload.

Tori looked out the kitchen window. Lydia gathered pine cones for some mysterious project. Gabe sat in the sandbox, filled his beloved silver mixing bowl with sand, dumped it, and then refilled it. Lydia chattered something at him, waving a pine cone. Gabe ignored her. Lydia kicked a pine cone into the sand box. Gabe tossed it over his shoulder and concentrated on his bowl.

"Mama!" Lydia stood at the back door, frowning. "Gabe wasn't playing wif me!"

Tori corrected her, "Gabe *isn't* playing *with me,* Sweetheart."

Lydia turned her palms up and shrugged. Her thick, curved eyebrow lifted.

"But you not trying play wif him." Lydia's faced brightened. "Mama, *I* play wif you!"

She tugged at Tori's hand. Tori smiled.

"Okay, give me five minutes. Run on outside, and I'll be—"

Lydia plunked down on the floor by Tori's chair.

"My wait for you. 'Cuz sometimes the five minuteses is longer."

Tori leaned over, took Lydia's face in her hands, and pressed a kiss to her daughter's forehead, savoring the salty taste of childish adventures.

"Okay, Princessa, thanks."

She continued to read:

> A child with autism often desires to be with someone he or she trusts, but may ignore the person.

Gabe came in the back door carrying his bowl and sat down in the far corner of the kitchen, his back to Tori. Before she realized what he was doing, he had dumped sand onto the floor and was trying to scoop it back into the bowl.

When Lydia tried to help, he pushed her away. A shudder rippled up Tori's spine. She needed a nice, soothing glass of lemon-mint iced tea.

"Okay, kids, let's fix a drink and we'll go outside. Lydia, you know those plants in the green container outside, the ones I said were mint?"

Lydia puffed out her little chest, "I knows, Mama! The ones for your tea."

"Yes. Would you bring me a couple of leaves, please?"

Lydia ran out, slamming the deck door, her pigtails bouncing. Tori cut lemon, but abandoned the idea of citrus the second time she sliced her finger.

"Look, Mama, I gots you mints!"

Lydia stood in the kitchen, beaming from ear-to-ear, displaying several uprooted mint plants for Tori's inspection.

"I said *a couple* of leaves!" Tori snapped.

Lydia's smile vanished. Tori could have kicked herself.

"But that's fine, honey, in fact, that's even better. Now, we'll have enough mint for tea at supper. Good thinking!"

She was relieved to see Lydia's face brighten. Lydia was volatile, but thank God, she didn't appear to hold grudges.

Tori decided she had read enough for now. Gabe's evaluation for special needs pre-school would clarify matters.

"Mama! Know what I wanna be when I grow up?"

"What, Sweetheart?"

"A dragonfly!"

Tori had expected princess, astronaut, or cowboy.

"Why a dragonfly?"

"'Cause they fly, they're beautiful, ever'one smiles when they see one, and . . ." Lydia looked thoughtful.

"And . . .?" Tori prompted.

"Since they're called a *dragon*-fly, maybe if they need to they can shoot fire. Like maybe if someone was mean to Gabe, I could scare them away."

She's a deep thinker.

"Those are good reasons. I think you're three-quarters dragonfly already," Tori said.

A wondering smile bloomed on her daughter's face.

"Really? How?"

"You're beyond beautiful; you're iridescent. Daddy and I smile when we see you, and you're smart enough to think of a way to protect Gabe without toasting people. So, we just need to get you some flying lessons."

Lydia spun in circles, singing: "I'm three-corters dragonfly!"

She stumbled breathlessly into Tori, who caught her and ruffled her hair.

"Tell you what, kids, why don't we have a snack?"

"Snack!"

Gabe nodded his head, and then looked hopeful.

"Choc . . . Choc snack?"

He pointed to the top of the refrigerator, where Tori kept what she believed was a secret stash. Tori wiped a smudge of dirt off Gabe's forehead. She recalled the fresh, nutritious apples she had bought the day before, and the autism research she had planned to finish today.

"Dark Chocolate!" Lydia said.

No secret stashes with these two around.

Tori pulled out a stool to retrieve the dark chocolate-covered raisins she had been hoarding.

The apples will keep, and so will the research. I need to savor my dragonfly moments.

Gabe's testing was complete. Tori knelt on the floor, dealing with his shoes. He liked his shoes to fit as tightly as an anaconda's embrace. If someone didn't tie his shoes for him, he would sit on the floor for hours, trying.

"He has *autism*?" one psychologist asked, rifling through Gabe's file.

The evaluator's dubious question caused Tori to look up from her task of yanking Gabe's laces into their customary tourniquet.

"Yes, PDD. Why?"

"Hmm. Gabe doesn't fit the autistic profile we're used to. He's compliant, and although he's speech-delayed, he tries to communicate. It's obvious he'll be verbal. Plus, you gave me nice eye contact when you wanted my doughnut, didn't you?" she asked Gabe.

She ruffled his hair. Gabe jerked away.

A delicious shiver ran down Tori's arms.

"Are you saying he could handle regular pre-school?"

The Ledo County assessor backtracked.

"Oh, no. Definitely not. Gabe has significant developmental delays. Special needs Pre-K is strongly indicated."

"Oh. Would you recommend something different if you thought he had autism?"

"No. At his age, the protocol for autism and developmental delay are the same."

Then, it doesn't really matter what we call it, does it?

"Okay, then, what next?" asked Tori.

"We'll schedule an individualized education plan, IEP, meeting with you, the school, and county staff. The IEP sets goals and measurements for Gabe."

She hefted a large file.

"Before you go, there are several forms to complete."

She handed Tori document after document, naming them in a monotonous voice.

"Medical release . . . immunization history . . . parental rights . . . consent for further testing . . ."

Tori's brain, numbed by bureaucratic overload, ceased functioning. Working on autopilot, she accepted the forms.

"Mrs. St. John?"

Tori started.

"Sorry," she said, blinking dazed eyes. "That's all?"

"Yes. Would you like to fill these out now."

Tori pulled out a form at random—proof of residency. She scanned the requirements.

"No. I don't have a copy of my mortgage with me," she said, pulling Gabe's head out of her purse, where he was prospecting for candy.

The first time Tori took Gabe to school was one of the saddest days of her life. She and Phillip had prayed, investigated, and decided pre-school was the best thing for him. Gabe was taking the first steps forward into normality. Tori was determined to be positive. The scene that welcomed them supported her optimism.

The roomy special needs classroom was painted in calm pastel shades, sounds muffled by a white noise machine. Gabe's name was displayed in cheery letters above a wooden storage cubicle.

A rocker rested on a colorful hooked rug, surrounded by a snug circle of bean bag chairs and flanked by bookcases. The lead teacher, Ms. Floyd, was young, pretty, and intuitive. She suggested Tori stay for a while, and then quietly leave.

When she left an hour later, Gabe didn't seem upset. Tori smiled as she got into her car.

Well, that wasn't so bad.

She called Phillip to bring him up-to-date.

"Hi, Less Than Tall. How'd it go?"

Tori burst into tears. Phillip let the torrent subside, and then spoke in a kind voice.

"Come on, Honey, settle down and tell me what happened."

Tori wiped her eyes and took a large gulp of the iced tea she had bought on the way in. Even warm and watered down, sweet tea with lemon had the power to soothe her.

"I don't know. I feel like Gabe just boarded the last train to Siberia, leaving me alone in an empty rail station."

"That's illogical. We agreed in order for Gabe to catch up, he needs more help than he can get in a regular school." Phillip's voice became worried. "We never did take a look at the classroom because it was being repainted. Is it depressing? They *said* it was equipped to meet his sensory needs. I *knew* we should have insisted on a tour."

"The classroom's sensory heaven; equipped with the latest technology."

"Oh. Well, you checked out every teacher, aide, and therapist online, and then insisted on meeting each one. They seemed great. I was impressed by their listening skills at the IEP meeting."

"Yeah. Me, too. And Mrs. Floyd won Georgia Teacher of the Year award last year." Tori slid down in the car seat. "I don't know . . ."

Phillip sounded impatient.

"It sounds great. Is it that time of the month? I hate to run, but I've got a meeting in five minutes."

"Go. I'm fine. First day blues, I guess. I'll see you tonight."

Tori disconnected. What *did* bother her? She considered the children in Gabe's class.

One plucky girl, Allison, housed a cheerful spirit in her twisted body. She introduced herself to Gabe in a mangled voice. Another child—a cute, happy-go-lucky boy with Down's syndrome—chattered non-stop, jumping between subjects like a grasshopper. A mentally-challenged girl painstakingly traced the letters of her name.

The fourth child glared at the teachers' attempts to engage him and struck out at one aide, who tried to turn him to face the rest of the class. He sat in silence; his hostile face closed while he meticulously adjusted and re-adjusted wooden blocks to create a precise square.

A quick, hard thrust of his arm destroyed the pattern, and then he began again. The reason for her misery struck like an incoming missile. Tori realized she was projecting Gabe's future from these precious, broken children in his class.

Gabe's classmates represented shattered expectations. Many of the normal milestones families take for granted hovered beyond reach. Everyday accomplishments such as talking, toilet training, and dressing formed stark mountains in a landscape that usually consisted of gently rolling green hills.

Marriage, meaningful jobs, even friendships were not a given. Dreams such as independence were irrevocably gone, vaporized in the nuclear blast of an unforgiving disability.

Tori had taken up residence in a shadow universe. Unlike the business world, she now inhabited a realm where she could not control parameters, drive resources to a desired outcome, and insist upon an acceptable solution. She loved Gabe with an intensity that hurt, but he was a complex package; instructions not included.

She cried for herself and Gabe, mourning faded possibilities. People passed, faces averted from her pain. Still she wept. Finally, it was enough. She lifted her head, threw back her shoulders, and stiffened her mental spine.

Grief is healthy, but it's time to move on.

New technology existed; fresh theories, innovative treatments.

This is my career now: the care, nurturing, and protection of Gabe . . . and Lydia, of course.

Tori sighed. She decided a chocolate frosted, angel-cream filled Krispy Kreme doughnut, or maybe six of them, would make her feel better. At least for the moment; until the next time she got on the scales.

CHAPTER 8

Shouldering the Burden

Tori walked a series of greased high-wires, balancing typical family demands with Gabe's needs. In her spare time, she plunged deep into the world of research and networking. She slept little, living on nerves and caffeine.

Tori found her muse could not adjust to constant chaos and was unable to be creative in fifteen-minute snatches. She turned her most recent painting to the wall, uncompleted, and locked the door to her tiny attic studio.

Someday soon, when there's time . . .

Gabe turned four years old. As he became more confident, his quirky behavior confirmed his atypical thought process. Although Phillip was ready to accept the diagnosis of autism, Tori was not. She did not use the A-word and kept researching, hoping to find a diagnosis, which fit Gabe better; a diagnosis with an established cure. Gabe's behaviors made that increasingly difficult.

If something was not being used, Gabe wanted it put away properly. That would have been a good thing were it not for Gabe's definition of putting things away properly: Amber's dried cat food belonged in the vegetable bin while the ideal place for a cut flower arrangement was in the shower.

Gabe didn't sleep much, preferring to sneak out of his room at night to roam around the house, stealthily taking things apart. They installed child locks against Houdini, Jr. to no avail. After he dismantled the toaster oven with a toy screwdriver, they started locking his bedroom at night and prayed they'd never have a house-fire.

Gabe had no use for purely ornamental objects. Tori first recognized his minimalist decorating preferences when she discovered Gabe stuffing accent pillows into the trash. She scolded him thoroughly and thought she had made her point.

After a long weekend away, Tori arrived home to the impression the house was looking a bit Spartan. She couldn't see anything amiss and she'd never been a slave to perfect decor, so she shrugged and went on.

A few days later, though, while Gabe was supposed to be watching a video, Tori saw him leave her office, carrying an ornately carved wooden stallion. She crept behind him up the stairs, ducked behind her bedroom door, and peered out.

Gabe entered his room, then quickly left empty-handed and went back downstairs.

Tori tiptoed into his room. The lid to Gabe's wooden toy box was ajar. It had once been filled with playthings designed to delight a boy's heart, but as it became apparent his heart wasn't even mildly interested—much less delighted—the toys were donated. Tori lifted the lid.

The decorative steed had joined an august company of decorative items the St. Johns had collected during their childless years: antique perfume bottles, native art . . . stuff. Evidently, Gabe had been stealthily removing superfluous items, one at a time.

Phillip thought it was hilarious. "I don't understand why you're frustrated, babe," he smirked. "After all, you didn't realize the gewgaws were missing until you opened his toy box."

Understanding dawned for Phillip the day he could not find his cherished graphing calculator.

"It was here on my desk last night," he told Tori.

"Weren't you and Gabe playing in your office last night?"

"Yes, but not with my favorite calculator."

"Did you leave Gabe alone?"

"No . . . wait. Lydia hollered from upstairs wanting me to spell something. I walked to the landing and told her to get a dictionary. It couldn't have taken more than thirty seconds. Gabe was gone when I got back."

"He was probably putting your calculator away. Have you looked in your glove compartment?"

"Yes. I've looked everywhere it could logically be."

"Logic is relative with our boy. Have you checked the kitchen trash can?"

"The trash?"

"If Gabe dislikes something or doesn't see a need for it, he throws it away or hides it. I found a fresh bunch of bananas in the trash yesterday. Gabe hates bananas."

Phillip stomped to the kitchen and began sifting through the trash, nose wrinkled. Tori fought to look appropriately somber at the thought of Phillip's missing calculator.

"Could you bring me a pair of gloves? I cannot *believe* I'm looking in the trash for my five hundred dollar calculator. Why didn't you tell me Gabe's been doing this?"

"I did; several times. I said he was driving me crazy trashing or stashing things where most mortals wouldn't think to look." Tori's hands went to her hips. "You found it amusing when he hid my *gewgaws* in his toy box, remember?"

"Humph, but this is my *calculator*. It's different."

"My flat iron's been missing for ages. I guess you didn't notice I've been curly since January."

Phillip had once said Tori's sexy hair was the second thing that attracted him, after her smile. He used to savor her experiments with hair fashion.

Have I become more mommy than lover?

"Not here," Phillip said, slamming the trashcan lid.

He wiped his hands with antiseptic and yelled for Gabe.

When his son appeared, he asked, "Gabe, did you put away Daddy's calculator?"

Gabe grinned and strutted. "Away!"

"G-r-reat son. Good job. Where?"

Gabe seemed puzzled.

"My calculator. Show me."

Phillip's tone was ominous.

Gabe sidled over to Tori and hid behind her.

"Gabriel Winston St. John, I want my calculator *now!*"

"Stop yelling at him! He can't help it."

Tori wrapped her arms around Gabe. He buried his face against her leg. Phillip rolled his eyes, turned, and threw up his arms as if to implore an imaginary audience.

"He's playing you!"

Gabe whimpered. Tori shot Phillip a dirty look and pushed Gabe's hair out of his eyes.

"It's okay, Sweetheart, but Daddy wants his toy. Wait." Tori got her calculator and showed it to Gabe. "Like this, but bigger, with a lot more buttons. Did you move it?"

Gabe sighed and led them to his room. He checked the toy box. Empty. Gabe sat back on his haunches.

"Not."

He gazed at his fingers. A low grumble vibrated in Phillip's throat. Tori put her hand on his arm.

"He's remembering *something*. It takes longer to process."

She squatted in front of Gabe and patted his leg.

"It's okay, Sweetheart. Think about it."

Gabe thought; Phillip paced. After several minutes, Gabe brightened. He pointed to his closet and mimicked throwing something. Phillip looked, and then reached to the back of the top shelf. He pulled out two hair bows, Gabe's house shoes, Tori's flat iron, and a decaying carrot. No calculator.

Tori repossessed her flat iron.

"Thanks! I hope you find our juice glasses. Evidently, Gabe thinks ice tea glasses are adequate for juice."

She was answered with a growl. Phillip searched the house thoroughly, muttering under his breath. His calculator was finally located under his shoe rack. The glasses never surfaced.

One doctor, Dr. David Wyatts, tentatively disagreed with Dr. Shriva.

"Gabe has major developmental issues with a strong neurological component, but whether or not it develops into autism is largely up to you. How's his behavior? Is Gabe aggressive?"

Phillip shrugged.

"Gabe wants his own way, just like most kids, but he's learned about consequences: timeout, losing privileges, and skipping dessert. Aggression is Gabe's default mode. He wants to attack when he's really frustrated. Usually, he doesn't."

"Most children aggress at some point," Dr. Wyatts said. "Spectrum children carry more frustration than typical children. There's so much they can't do. I advise against punitive consequences. Ignoring inappropriate behavior usually extinguishes it. Timeouts reward autistic children by allowing them to withdraw. Spanking is not only inappropriate, but ineffective. Even most neuro-typical children don't respond to beatings."

Phillip felt his face heat up. He took a deep breath.

"We never beat Gabe. We sometimes give him a pop on the rear. Gabe hates timeouts, losing privileges, and spankings. All three consequences cause him to stop misbehaving."

Dr. Wyatts waved his hand in dismissal of their disciplinary techniques.

"The most recent studies don't bear you out. The best idea is to distract the child."

Phillip pictured Tori waving Gabe's silver bowl in his face, trying to distract him into removing his teeth from her arm.

Looking at them over steepled fingers, Dr. Wyatts continued.

"With the right intervention, Gabe could attain near-normalcy. I'm concerned Gabe hasn't developed a meaningful relationship with you."

Dr. Wyatts waited while Tori and Phillip simultaneously cited instances of Gabe's meaningful relationships with them. When they spluttered to a stop, his face was grave.

"The relationships appear pragmatic on Gabe's part. He reveals a need, you meet it. No matter how charming he is in the process of getting what he wants, it's not an adequate basis for a relationship."

He leaned back in his chair and clasped his hands on his rotund stomach.

"Gabe is at risk of talking without caring if anyone's listening, memorizing lists of unimportant information, rehashing events long past, repeating things totally out of context, and making no attempt to participate in true communication."

He sat up.

"Gabe's only chance of normalcy is in immediately beginning neuro trans-differential therapy, NTD."[2]

He spun his chair around to his bookshelf and selected a large book.

"This book is the NTD handbook; a groundbreaking work."

He explained NDT at length and concluded, "Instead of therapies designed to pull Gabe into *your* world, you'll use symbols to enter *his* world, implement structured routines to gradually enlarge it, and then employ play techniques to coax him into the neurotypical world. Do you see what I'm saying?"

Phillip thought even Tori, who knew more about autism than he did, looked dumbfounded. No help there.

Einstein probably couldn't see what you're saying, but at four hundred and fifty dollars an hour, I'm sure you'll make it clear to us.

Fortunately, Dr. Wyatts did not really want an answer. He stared at Phillip, and then focused on Tori.

"Recovery is possible. You're Gabe's main caregiver. *You* are the most critical component of Gabe's future. Sign up for next month's training class. The most effective parents do NDT at least four hours a day."

Tori's eyes widened.

"How can we fit four hours into all his current therapies? What about the rest of our family?"

Good question, Tori. You already don't have time for much besides Gabe.

"NDT is the optimal use of Gabe's time. Consider stopping other therapies for now. I'm not even sure school is a good idea; you may consider homeschooling instead. Most schools practice only traditional therapies. As for your family, NDT should become

---

2   Neuro trans-differential therapy (NTD) exists only in the author's mind. It is not an actual therapy, nor is it intended to represent a particular therapy.

your family's way of life. Everyone should participate. Grandparents, aunts, uncles, cousins, your nanny—"

"We don't have a nanny and both sets of family are out-of-state," Tori said.

Phillip thought she looked shell-shocked. Dr. Wyatts placed his palms on Gabe's file.

"It's not easy. It is, though, crucial to his prognosis. Gabe's future is in your hands."

They were subdued on the ride home.

"We're hemorrhaging money. Does insurance cover things like this?" Phillip asked.

"You wish! They won't even cover speech therapy unless he has a stroke."

Phillip wondered how his paycheck could stand the strain. However, Tori's research said many considered NDT to be the most effective intervention for autism.

We can't take the chance of missing something that could help our son.

They read the books, took the training, and hired someone to help them do four hours of NDT daily. They did not pull Gabe out of school or stop his other therapies.

"We've always believed in balance and moderation," Phillip told Tori. "Let's not put all Gabe's therapy eggs in the NDT basket."

"I agree. NDT is highly acclaimed right now, but so are other therapies," Tori said.

Her green eyes were strained. "I'm constantly checking out the therapy du jour. No one really knows."

"From what you've told me, it seems like most advocates of a particular therapy discount other methods." Phillip's jaw worked. "How do we know we're not missing the right one?"

They stared at each other.

"We pray, we track results; we pray, we ask questions; we pray," Tori said. "Dr. Jeffries recommends we find a developmental pediatrician who can oversee all Gabe's therapies and give us guidance. I'll start looking."

"Thank God I married a bulldog." Phillip said.

Tori frowned, "Not the most flattering pet name you've ever given me."

Phillip ruffled her hair. "What I mean is, I know I can count on you to find the best."

"Ruff, ruff, woof," Tori replied, sticking her tongue out and panting.

As time and therapies passed, they conceded Gabe had autism. Tori would not, could not, accept it was permanent. Somehow, some way, Gabe was going to get better.

CHAPTER 9

Joys of Potty Training

The hit documentary, *Everybody Pees*, was rolling its ending credits.

"Agin, agin evbuddy pees!" Gabe chortled.

Tori sighed. She was at her wits end. She had begun the week with high hopes and firm resolve. It was past time; they'd been working on this for months.

Gabe was almost seven years old and Tori was tired of changing diapers. Tired of being excluded from the few programs available for special needs kids because he was not toilet trained. Tired of hearing Phillip's father talk about how Phillip had been fully trained at eighteen months; tired of pretending to not hear her mother wistfully talk about cloth diapers.

To her surprise, Gabe had trained himself for bowel movements over a year ago. One day at a restaurant, he tugged her to the bathroom, plopped his rear on the toilet, and had a bowel movement.

Tori knew she was blessed. Tori sighed. She had tried every potty training method recommended, short of the two thousand dollar toilet training boot camp some parents tried as a last resort.

Knowing all this, Tori offered up a fervent prayer of thanksgiving when Gabe pooped on his own. She mentally started to spend the time and money she would save. She could join a Jazzercise class, or, maybe, it would be better to set the money aside as date money for her and Phillip or . . .

Later, Serena said Tori had counted her eggs before the chicken peed. Gabe seemed quite content to ace bowel movement, but was totally uninterested in mastering the pee.

Tori tried everything: shooting Cheerios, wearing big boy character pants, keeping Gabe on his potty seat until he peed, applause and praise for even accidental successes, letting him run around bare-bottomed, and offering his favorite yogurt covered pretzels as a reward.

Every method recommended had been tried and found wanting. Gabe proudly wore his Spiderman big boy pants, but showed no remorse at soaking Spidey. Regardless of the level of celebration that occurred when he trickled a few drops into the toilet, Gabe did not feel motivated to repeat the action on his own.

Gabe cooperated with shooting cereal when Tori insisted, but seemed incredulous that she considered this to be a desirable activity. He tried to make it more interesting by widening the target area and shooting up at the hand towel. He was hurt when Tori did not appreciate his efforts.

He would happily consume any treat offered, but did not seem to connect it with actions on his part.

Gabe appeared to enjoy going around with a bare derriere. He simply went wherever he was when the need hit. Lydia shrieked like a train whistle when he peed on her bedroom floor.

Phillip helped by demonstrating. Gabe watched with apparent boredom. Phillip found the whole process hysterically funny. The more amused he became, the grouchier Tori got.

Gabe watched the *Everybody Pees* video tirelessly as a parade of cartoon animals talked, danced, and sang about the joys of appropriate toileting. He really appreciated the soundtrack. Tori had to stop him from singing the theme song at the top of his lungs in public.

She really could not blame him; it was a catchy little tune. Tori often caught herself humming it.

While Tori tried to convince Gabe that seven times was enough in one afternoon to watch the same video, the doorbell rang. Grateful for the interruption, Tori ran to open it.

It was Serena, holding a large box of gourmet chocolates in one hand.

"Hello, Gabriel!" she said, taking Gabe's hand.

He promptly snatched it away.

"Gabe, say hello to Miss Serena."

"He-lo Miss Se-re-na," Gabe murmured in his sing-song voice, hopping up and down like a pogo stick.

Serena smiled and mussed his hair affectionately. Gabe promptly tousled her hairdo.

"Oops. Gabe! Leave her hair alone!" Tori waved Serena to the couch and sat beside her. "Sorry, Serena . . . forgot to tell you he's mirroring physical actions. For heaven's sake, don't pat him on the back, he'll knock the breath out of you!"

Gabe turned an umbrella into an airplane and flew it out of the room.

"I know dollars are tight, but can you not buy the child a real airplane?" Serena asked.

Tori walked over to an armoire and opened a cabinet door. Airplanes of every model, size, and color tumbled out. She threw up her hands and collapsed back onto the couch.

Serena handed Tori the box of chocolate.

"For you."

"Thank-you, but to what do I owe the pleasure? It's not my birthday, or Valentine's Day, or anything like that."

"It is Everybody Pees Day. Do you not celebrate it in your country?"

Serena hummed the tune. Tori threw a pillow at her. Serena giggled.

"It is for to cheer you up, Pobrecita. Lydia answered the phone last night—"

"Wait, you called last night? Lydia never told me! Was I supposed to call you back? If that child doesn't stop forgetting—"

"She said you could not come to the phone; you were busy scrubbing the bathroom walls. Apparently your face was mean and you were singing "Everybody Pees" under your breath. I deduced Gabe is not peeing well. In my country, that calls for chocolate."

"I think I'd like Venezuela. I may eat the entire box by myself, tonight. Gabe just will not cooperate!"

"That's because," Lydia said, coming down the stairs and into the den, "he knows he can get away with just about anything. Hi, Miss Serena."

"Wassup, goat?" Serena said, putting out her fist in greeting.

Lydia grinned and tapped her fist to Serena's.

"I think you mean wassup, dawg."

"Humph. Dog, goat, cat, what does matter? Matters only that I am speaking teen jargon. I am very hip-hop, is it not true?"

"Um, it is not . . ."

Tori gave Lydia a slight shake of her head and speared her with laser-beam eyes.

". . . true that you act like an old lady, that's for sure."

Lydia sauntered past them and went upstairs.

"Are you not afraid that look will blind her?" Serena smiled.

"Ha! She's already developing a resistance to it."

Tori opened the box of chocolates, offered it to Serena, and then chose one for herself. As if by magic, Gabe appeared.

"Chocolate, Gabe?" he asked.

"No. Do you need to go to the bathroom?" Tori asked, noting an hour had passed since the last accident.

"No," he answered, eyes riveted on the candy.

"He wants chocolate."

"This is Mama's chocolate!" Tori snapped.

Noting Serena's lifted eyebrow, she defended herself.

"I don't want to spoil him. No seven year old needs fine chocolate. He should be satisfied with Hershey's, but Gabe's got epicurean tastes. If he gets one bite of this chocolate, he'll make my life miserable until he's finagled the entire box."

"It is well you do not indulge him," Serena said dryly.

"What? I don't spoil him!"

"Do too!" Lydia's voice wafted from upstairs.

"If you do not rot him, how is it he will be able to eat all the chocolates away from you?"

Tori did not answer. Gabe had crawled into her lap. He snuggled close to Tori, and put one hand on either side of her face.

"Look at me, look at me!" he demanded, using exactly the same inflection Phillip used when he wanted Gabe's attention.

Tori could not help smiling. Obediently, she looked at him. Gabe looked up at her through his long black lashes, making eye contact. He chose his words carefully.

"I," he poked his finger into his chest, "want . . . chocolate . . . please, Mama!"

"Nothing wrong with his speech when he wants something, is there?" Serena said.

Tori rolled her eyes.

"No, at least not with expressing his needs."

A thought struck. *The yogurt covered pretzels hadn't worked, but—*

"Gabe, you want chocolate?" she demanded.

"This," he said, pointing at the box of chocolate.

"Okay. Pee in the toilet, you get chocolate; pee in your pants, no chocolate. Understand?" Tori asked.

Gabe jumped out of her lap and trotted out of the room toward the adjacent bathroom. Tori heard the door open, and then the sound of pee hitting water, followed by the flush of a toilet. Gabe immediately strutted back in, naked, holding a wad of damp toilet paper.

"Gabe peed," he announced, reaching for the chocolate.

Tori sat speechless.

"Before chocolate, let us talk of dressing, flushing the toilet paper, and washing our hands," Serena told Gabe, leading him back to the bathroom.

He came back clothed, and stuck out a clean hand. Tori presented him with a chocolate. Gabe inhaled it.

"Again chocolate."

"Chocolate when you pee in the toilet."

Gabe ran from the room once more. They heard a flush. He returned moments later, this time in his Spiderman underwear.

"Gabe peed, dressed." He stuck out his hand.

"You get chocolate if you pee when you need to pee, not every time you dribble a couple of drops," Tori explained.

Dear Lord, please don't let this be another dead end.

But Gabe went to the toilet by himself an hour later, presented himself for chocolate, and went on with life. To everyone's amazement, he never had another accident, even at naptime and bedtime.

He consumed the majority of Tori's fine chocolates, but she did not care, even sending See's chocolate to school with him lest he regress. After a week, she began tapering down the chocolate. By the end of two weeks he no longer asked for rewards.

After two accident-free weeks, Tori tied a congratulatory balloon onto Gabe's chair at the dinner table and prepared a meal featuring his favorite dishes.

Lydia didn't say much and ate hardly anything.

"Are you feeling okay, Princessa?" Tori asked her at bedtime.

"My throat's a little scratchy, but I feel okay."

Tori felt Lydia's head.

"No fever. Are you congested?"

"No. I said I'm fine. Go check on the crown prince of pottydom; he's probably sick. If the little pig isn't, he should be. He ate so much."

"Honey! Why're you being so nasty? Gabe being toilet-trained is a major accomplishment."

"Hmph. What'll you do if he ever learns his phone number and address? Have a parade with dancing elephants? I'm over having a party every time he figures something out. No one acted like it was a big deal when I learned where to pee and poop *and* I wasn't bribed with chocolate."

Tori stroked Lydia's hair.

"Sweetheart, you know we're proud of you. It's just that with Gabe's challenges, things are hard for him. He doesn't understand things the way you do."

"Challenges, huh? I think he understands a lot more than you give him credit for."

Lydia released a theatrical yawn.

"Actually, my throat is getting sorer. I don't think I should talk anymore."

She turned over on her side. Tori kissed her cheek.

"We love you lots, you know."

"Yeah. Turn the light out as you leave, would you?"

Downstairs, Phillip leaned against the kitchen counter with his hands in his pant pockets, collar unbuttoned.

"You're gloomy all of a sudden. What's up?" he asked. "I loaded the dishwasher for you; thought we could turn in early."

Tori stifled a groan. Her mood definitely didn't match the gleam in Phillip's eye.

"It's Lydia. Another case of the green-eyed-monster. According to her, we rejoice every time Gabe succeeds at something and ignore the fact she does the same things sooner and better."

Phillip straightened up and put his hands on his hips.

"We celebrate her achievements. Didn't we just let her give a drum recital, and then take her and her friends out to dinner at Chucky Cheese afterwards? My head is still pounding."

Tori sighed.

"I know, but we do make a big deal of everything Gabe accomplishes, no matter how small. That's what she sees. She doesn't get how hard things are for him."

Phillip flung his hands up.

"We've explained it to her countless times! She's almost ten years old. When is she going to figure it out?"

"Keep in mind she didn't even know she had a brother until four years ago. She hasn't fully come to grips with being part of a family."

Tori touched Phillip's arm.

"Lydia's insecure, Honey. Emotionally, she's a needy, bottomless pit. We have to be patient. Only God can fill that void. She's too young to understand that yet."

Phillip's eyes softened.

"You're right. I was headed upstairs to say good-night. I'll bathe my littlest princess with affirmation."

He leered. "I'm looking forward to affirming my big princess, too."

Tori was exhausted, but she pulled a smile out of somewhere.

"Great. I have to clean Amber's box first, though, or she'll start leaving us indications of her displeasure."

"The cat box? Again?" Phillip moaned. "I'll do it. Not my idea of romance, though."

Tori clawed her hand, ran her fingernails gently down Phillip's cheek and spoke in her best Cat Woman purr.

"You have no idea how sexy you are when you're cleaning the litter box for me. Rowwwr."

The next morning, Lydia's voice sounded like a hinge in dire need of oiling.

"I'm not sick, Mom, honest. I just sound like it," she rasped. "Can you make pancakes? I'm starving."

Lydia's forehead was cool to the touch. Tori checked her eyes. They looked clear.

"Maybe you should stay home from school today, just in case."

"Mu-thur! I'm fine."

"Well, laryngitis isn't usually serious. I suppose you can go, if you promise to call me the second you start feeling ill."

When Lydia dragged into the kitchen that afternoon, her face was glum.

"What's wrong, Princessa?" Tori asked. "You were supposed to call me if you felt bad!"

Lydia shook her head, pulled a pad and pen out of her backpack, and wrote:

> Not sick, but when I talk, no one can understand. Kids made fun of me all day.

Tori set a glass of apple juice and a plate of cookies on the counter beside Lydia and gave her a hug.

"Sounds like a no-good, rotten day. Want to lie down for a few minutes?"

"Aagh knott sikt!"

The garbled reply was accompanied by a hostile glare. Lydia grabbed the juice and cookies, stomped to the kitchen table, and started doing her homework.

Tori regarded her daughter's bent head thoughtfully.

"Honey, I have an idea."

Lydia lifted her head and gave Tori a baleful look. She tried to speak, pulled out her pad, scribbled, ripped the page out, and thrust the note at Tori:

> *Can it wait? My homework is hard. I couldn't ask questions like usual when I didn't understand.*

"No. Daddy and I are concerned. We don't think you understand what Gabe goes through," Tori replied. "Not being able to communicate is part of what he experiences every day. As long as you have laryngitis, there are a couple of other things we can do to give you a better feel for Gabe's life."

Lydia's wavy black hair swirled in all directions as she emphatically shook her head.

"I'll pay you twenty dollars," Tori said.

Lydia's eyes lit up. She wrote:

> *For how long?*

"Just until bedtime," Tori said.

Lydia cocked her head on one side and pursed her lips, pretending to consider the offer. The avaricious gleam in her eye gave Lydia away before she scribbled her acceptance.

> *Fine, I guess.*

Tori punched Lydia's shoulder lightly.

"Okay. I'll be right back."

In the living room, Tori rummaged through her music collection until she found a CD of alternative violin music that a friend had given her. She went into the kitchen, turned the volume up on her portable CD player, and popped in the disc.

High-pitched, rhythmic screeching pounded against Tori's eardrums. She carried the player to the table and put the headset over Lydia's ears.

Lydia's eyes widened and her mouth dropped open. She flicked the CD player off and scrawled furiously:

I can't concentrate with that on! It's worse than when Amber got stuck in the laundry chute.

Tori turned the CD player back on.

"That's the type of input Gabe's sensory system feeds his brain. He has to try to learn in spite of it."

Lydia rolled her eyes and wrote:

That is so bogus. You can't know that's how Gabe feels.

Tori smiled.

"Actually, I can. I attended a talk a couple of months ago by an adult man who has pretty much overcome his autism."

Tori paused as hope fluttered in her heart.

If he can beat autism, so can Gabe, she considered.

"So?" Lydia croaked.

"So, he said regular, everyday noises often sounded like a loud racket to him. I figure this CD qualifies."

Tori got a pair of leather gardening gloves from under the sink and handed them to Lydia.

"Put these on. He said his fingers felt clumsy and fat, like sausages."

Lydia put the gloves on, tried working a math problem, and threw her pen down in disgust. She pulled off the right glove, waved her math paper in Tori's face, and then wrote a note:

Look at this writing! My teachers will kill me.

Tori picked up the glove and handed it back to Lydia.

"No gloves, no pay. I'll write a note for your teachers. Anyway, you only have to do it today. Your brother lives with it all the time."

Lydia started another note, but Tori plucked the pad from her hands.

"Sorry. Gabe can't communicate via pad, so you can't either."

At 5:45 p.m., Lydia gave up on her homework. At six-thirty, she left the dinner table in tears and retreated to the den after she dropped several spoonfuls of mashed potatoes into her lap. At eight o'clock, frustrated by her inability to communicate via gestures, she ripped off the gloves and yanked off her headset.

Snatching pen and paper, she resigned from Gabe's world:

> *I'm done! I wouldn't do this another minute even if you paid me fifty dollars!*

At that moment, Gabe came downstairs in his pajamas, beaming.

"Ready for bed, all by self, Mama."

"Did you brush your teeth?" Tori asked.

Gabe's face fell.

"No."

Shoulders slumped, he turned and trudged upstairs.

Lydia watched him, her face a mixture of frustration and confusion. A few minutes later, she rasped she was going to bed. Tori wondered if Lydia was re-thinking her oft-expressed opinion about Gabe having an easy life.

The next morning, Lydia grabbed Gabe as he and Tori headed outside to wait for the bus.

She gave him a fierce hug.

"Have a good day, Bro. Love you," she ground out.

CHAPTER 10

Intense Questions

Serena called.
"Would my Gabriel like to help an old lady make cookies?"
"Gabe, do you want to help Miss Serena bake cookies?"
Gabe's eyes lit up. "Yes!"
"He just eats the dough and chocolate," Lydia muttered.
"It's called quality control, Sweetheart. Anyway, Serena knew I wanted time for you and me to go have a hot chocolate."
Anticipation sparkled in Lydia's eyes.
"Starbucks hot chocolate with whipped cream and salted caramel?"
Tori raised her eyebrows. She had let Lydia take a sip of her favorite hot chocolate the last time they had been at Starbucks. *Looks like the specially-priced kids' hot chocolate is a thing of the past for my girl.*
"Hmm, I think that could be arranged," Tori said.
"I'm almost ten. Does that mean I'm too old to ride the carousel at the mall?"
"Absolutely not. I'm planning to ride, too. I claim the tiger!"
Laughing and swinging hands, they walked Gabe over to Serena's, and then drove toward the mall. Lydia, usually a chatterbox, was quiet for a few moments.
"Mama?"
"Yes, Princessa?"

"How come that woman didn't like me?"

"What woman?"

"That woman whose tummy Gabe and I were in. How come she didn't let us stay with her?"

Dread wrung Tori's stomach. She had known the topic would come up eventually. She hadn't expected it so soon. Tori bit her lip and said a quick prayer for wisdom.

"It wasn't she didn't like you. You were very sick and they thought you may die. So, they took you to the hospital. After you got better, the doctors told them you needed good food for a while and medicine. They didn't have money to buy food and medicine, so they gave you to the orphanage to take care of you."

"But, if she loved me, wouldn't she keep me, anyway? And Gabe, too?"

"Ahh, no, Sweetheart. When you really love someone, you want what's best for them. It's called sacrificial love."

"Sa-cri-*fi*-cial."

Lydia rolled the word around on her tongue, savoring it.

"Were they still poor when they sacrificed Gabe?"

"I think so, yes."

Tori thought furiously and made a decision.

"Your family left Bulgaria right before we came and got you, looking for jobs. Before they left, your big sister wrote you a letter. The orphanage gave it to us for you to read someday. I had it translated. We were going to wait till you were older to have you read it."

"I'm old enough now. Let's go home; I want to read it."

Praying she was doing the right thing, Tori turned the car around, went home, pulled the letter out of the bottom of her jewelry box, and gave it to Lydia. She went upstairs and shut the door to her room while Tori sat at the kitchen table, staring into her Vanilla Zero.

She had read the letter so often over the past five years, she had memorized it:

My Sister, My Brother:

You will be asking: why did we give you away? I can write, so I speak for family. Remains eight of us since you left. We love you, but we are too poor. Before you, was a baby who died. With you came joy, Stolcha, but you got sick, we fear to death. We took you to orphanage for food, medicine, warmth. There was then another baby, also she died.

The next year Mama lost a baby before born, then again the next year came Stefano. My brother, you were fine, beautiful, but from beginning very sick. My feet were heavy, dragging, when I took you to orphanage. Almost I turn back, but you start the deep cough again, you turn blue, and I run fast as the wind to orphanage clinic.

We thought always that when you were older, stronger, we would have work, we would bring you home. Can you remember, we visited you every month? Never did we think you were gone forever. Now, they tell how Stefano is needing special helps. They come from orphanage, saying Americans, good people, wants you for own children. They offer better than you can ever have with us. Full bellies, doctors, new clothes. But most important you can go to school. Me, I leave after fifth year. Teacher and I both cry. I was smart, but I must leave and work.

Hopes and fears exhaust our family as we talk, pray, and weep; try to think of best. Finally, it is decided. We give you to Americans.

Your leaving rips wound that cannot heal, but we must let you go. Grandfather has said it, "Sometimes real love walks away."

Never doubt your memory possesses us. We are going to Romania to find work. Our loving prayers follow you forever.

Isabel Assenova Passenavich

It was an hour before Lydia came downstairs. Her eyes were puffy. Tori tried to hug her. Lydia glared and pushed her backwards. Tori stumbled, and then regained her balance.

"Why'd you do that?" Tori asked gently, knowing Lydia must be feeling distraught.

"I want to know my real family."

Her words gut-punched Tori, even though she had known it might happen.

Stay calm, Victoria. She's not quite ten and has just had a shock.

Tori forced her daughter's chin up.

"It must be hard; I'm sorry. The letter shows how much they loved you." Tori took a deep breath. "But, Daddy, Gabe, and I are your family now."

"It's not fair! Couldn't they keep me and give Gabe away?" Lydia said, putting her hands on her hips and giving Tori a defiant look.

Tori jerked Lydia's hands off her hips and gripped her wrists.

"Whether you like it or not, I'm your mother. You will treat me with respect, understand?"

Lydia nodded. Her eyes filled with tears. When Tori released her wrists, she rubbed them repeatedly, as if she had rope burns. Her brown eyes brimmed with reproach.

Tori did not apologize.

"They're your biological parents. Real parents are the ones who love, feed, and clothe you; who give you what you need when it'd be easier to give you what you want. We've sacrificed a lot in order to give you the best life possible—" Tori stopped.

She did not want to lay on a guilt trip.

"Can we find them, my bio-family?"

That could spell heartache for all of us.

"Someday, when you're older."

"When I'm twelve, maybe?"

"No, when you're twenty-one."

"Twenty-one? I could be dead by then. Why?"
"No, Stolcha . . ."
Lydia's eyes widened at the use of her old name.
"You won't be dead at twenty-one, God willing. If you'd stayed with your bio-family you'd probably have been dead by now."
Lydia gasped and put her hand over her mouth.
Tori realized her hurt was speaking.
Lydia's a child. I'm the adult here, the mature one, supposedly.
"Besides, it's private information. They can't legally tell you until you're an adult."
That may not be true in Bulgaria. I don't know what the law is there.
Tori did not care.
It's too soon. It hasn't even been five years. I'm afraid to add birth parents into our family mix. I can't believe she still doesn't understand I'm her real mother.
"Hey, Princessa! This was supposed to be our day. How about we go on to the mall now, get some hot chocolate; ride the carousel?"
"I guess."
"Come on. We can take another look at that Kids Bop CD you wanted."
"You said I didn't need it."
Lydia sniffled, and then wiped her nose with her sleeve.
"You don't, but sometimes shopping makes us girls feel better. Besides, I got a coupon."
Lydia gave a half-smile.
"Okay. Let's go."
The cheery face Tori put on hid her deep hurt.
I'm trying to buy my daughter's love. Dad wanted a boy. Lydia wants her real mother. Phillip seems distant. Does anyone want me, just the way I am? Only Gabe.

CHAPTER 11

In Search of the Perfect Doctor

Putrid, boggy ground sucked at her feet. Phillip was somewhere behind her, but she couldn't see him. Pterodactyl-sized mosquitoes attacked her with huge syringes while gibbering wraiths capered at the edge of her vision.

"Up to you," they mocked, "Gabe's future is up to you."

Tori jerked as needles sliced her skin.

"Hmm?" Phillip stirred.

"Bad dream."

A shudder rippled down Tori's spine.

Phillip opened groggy eyes and pulled her close.

"You're soaked. You dreamed about Gabe?" He yawned. "He's fine."

"I know. Sorry to wake you. Go back to sleep."

"Okay."

Phillip turned over and was asleep in seconds.

Tori turned the shower on high, hoping the pounding heat would relax her mind. Instead of cooperating, her brain replayed her futile search for Gabe's developmental pediatrician.

Chapter 11 — In Search of the Perfect Doctor

Tori ran into Monica Mechling shortly after she started asking for recommendations. She and Monica had met the year before and kept in touch. Monica's acerbic personality could be irritating, but Tori admired how tenderly Monica cared for her daughter, Song, who had moderate to severe autism. Tori related to Monica's quest to help eight year old Song recover from her autism. Monica, a loner, had bonded with Tori the day Tori nicknamed her ex-husband's girlfriend Pop-Tart.

Monica was outside a therapist's office, smoking.
"Hi, Monica! Good to see you. How's Song?"
"Rough. She's entering puberty."
"What's happening?" Tori asked sympathetically.
"I don't feel like analyzing Song today."
"Just trying to help."
Spanx too tight today, Monica?
Monica looked a little abashed.
"Sorry. Tough day," she admitted. "I hear you're looking for a developmental pediatrician. Heard of Dr. Eleanor Klein?"
Tori responded, "Her name has come up several times."
"Not surprising. She's the hottest DevPed in the Southeast; deservedly so."
Tori raised an eyebrow. For Monica, this was lavish praise.
"But in order to pay her," Monica said, "you'll have to rob a bank. She charges five hundred dollars an hour, takes no insurance, and still has a mammoth waiting list. Song saw her for a while; Dr. Klein was awesome. Then Harold left me for Pop-Tart."
Monica took a deep drag from her cigarette, filling her lungs with smoke.
"Ahh, that's good."
"You do realize you're killing yourself?"
"It's stress release. Want one?"
"No thanks."
Tori coughed in Monica's face. Monica grinned.

"Drama queen. Klein has twin brothers with severe autism. She holds degrees in developmental pediatrics, psychiatry, and neurology. With adults, her bedside manner is one degree worse than a porcupine with a hangover. With kids, she's the best there is."

Monica stubbed out her cigarette.

"I'll drive the getaway car for 30 percent of the take."

Dr. Klein was not accepting new patients. Tori kept looking. Most doctors did not have that extra something Tori and Phillip wanted. Some were ludicrous.

Dr. Xpediente said there was not much to be done about autism; he suggested Gabe was disrupting their lives, and recommended sending him away. Dr. Druggup prescribed enough medicine to create a Gabe-Zombie.

Dr. Zen's doctorate turned out to be in philosophy. His recommendation was that Gabe's life forces needed to be revitalized. Dr. Gunberick required thousands of dollars worth of testing before he would even talk to them.

So the days went, dragging huge chunks of time with them. The previous night at dinner, Lydia had stunned them.

"Know what I want to be when I grow up?" Lydia fiercely stabbed a green bean with her fork.

"What, Cupcake?" Phillip asked.

"Special needs. Then Mama will be taking me out of school for appointments, getting me frappés on the way home, and worrying about me all the time."

They had rushed to assure Lydia of her importance, but Tori was dismayed because her precocious twelve-year-old had a point. Tori spent a lot more time with Gabe than she did with Lydia.

It's no wonder I had a nightmare last night.

Gabe's developmental clock is ticking, Lydia is falling through the cracks, and I've blown six months looking for a doctor. I'm not wasting anymore time trying to find someone as good as Dr. Klein. We're getting her.

With that decision, Tori felt thirty pounds lighter. She would find a way to work around the infamous waiting list. If need be, she'd sell her jewelry to pay the fees. As far as Klein's personality, some of Tori's former co-workers made irate grizzlies look cuddly.

Chapter 11 – In Search of the Perfect Doctor

That night, Tori told Phillip she wanted Eleanor Klein.

"The expensive, grouchy one with a waiting list thicker than the Yellow Pages?"

"She's the best."

"You've activated laser scalpel eyes. God help anyone who tries to stop you," Phillip said with a faint smile. "Let me know when the appointment is scheduled."

"Dr. Klein's office, Mrs. Gatti speaking."

"Hello, this is Tori St. John. We'd like our son, Gabe, who has autism, to see Dr. Klein."

Tori held the cordless phone between her ear and shoulder while she loaded the dishwasher.

"Sorry; she isn't taking new patients. I can recommend several doctors."

"Thank-you, but I'm not interested in anyone else. Please put Gabe on her waiting list."

"It goes six years out. Dr. Rosenbloom, a fine pediatrician, has only an eight-month wait. His number—"

Tori interrupted. "I'm sure Dr. Rosenbloom is wonderful. We want Dr. Klein."

The receptionist sighed.

"Ma'am, Dr. Klein feels adamantly that developmental concerns must be addressed immediately, rather than waiting on a particular doctor."

"We agree," Tori said pleasantly. "Gabe sees two doctors and several therapists. We'd like Dr. Klein to oversee his various interventions."

She put Gabe's mixing bowl in the dishwasher, smiling at the grubby handprints on its surface.

She repeated, "Please put him on the list."

Mrs. Gatti snorted.

"Gabe may be shaving before he sees her. The only time a patient leaves is if they move or die."

"All I can do is try."

Tori relayed Gabe's information, and then asked, "What happens when there's a cancellation?"

"*If* someone cancels, I call down the list until I reach someone with a current intake package."

"Intake package?"

"At new patient appointments, parents submit a detailed, up-to-date history on their child. No packet, no appointment."

"Sounds reasonable. Could you fax it to me? I'll complete it, and then update periodically. So we'll be ready to seize the moment when it comes."

Mrs. Gatti laughed.

"Gabe's lucky you're in his corner. I'll send the packet."

"Thanks. Would you mind if I called occasionally for a status update?"

"Would it matter if I did mind?"

"Not much," Tori answered sweetly.

A year passed. Tori called Dr. Klein's office monthly. Mrs. Gatti was friendly, but implacable.

"Hi, this is—"

"Hi, Tori. Gabe is number three hundred and twenty-five," Mrs. Gatti said.

"I update his intake package monthly. We'll be ready when you call," Tori said.

"If people on the waiting list start dying under mysterious circumstances, I'm calling the feds."

Atlanta had experienced a sudden, fierce ice storm when Mrs. Gatti called four months later.

"All today's patients have cancelled. I've called twelve deep into the waiting list with no takers. We're stuck for three hours, until Dr. Klein's husband can rescue us with his truck. If Gabe can be here in an hour, Dr. Klein will see him. She won't wait."

"We'll be there."

"Good. Please fax the intake report."
"It's on its way."

As a northerner, Phillip scoffed at ice. He was home ten minutes after Tori's call. They were twenty minutes early for their appointment.

"Hello, Gabe," Dr. Klein said, holding out her hand. "I'm Dr. Eleanor."

Gabe turned his head away.

"What toys do you like?"

Ignoring her well-stocked toy box, Gabe pivoted toward her desk and reached for a leather encased kaleidoscope.

"That *is* a cool toy. You may play with it, but if you break it I'll bill your parents."

She gave a bark of laughter, and then addressed Tori and Phillip.

"I read your package." She drummed her fingernails on her desk. "You're already trying everything. I'm expensive; I'm busy. Why are you here?"

"We need help understanding Gabe's world," Phillip said, shifting in his chair. "What causes autism?"

"Nobody knows. Write your congressman. Demand more research."

Tori sat forward with her hands clasped between her knees.

"I'm more interested in how to fix it."

"I can't 'fix' autism. If you're looking for the miracle cure—"

"I'm not. May I finish?"

Dr. Klein smiled for the first time.

"Go on."

"There's no cure for autism, yet. Some interventions may help, but there's not enough time or money to try everything. We don't want to make the wrong choice and miss something that may help Gabe."

Dr. Klein nodded.

"I can work with that, if you understand *you're* Gabe's subject matter experts. Autism isn't one-size-fits-all. Discover what helps *Gabe*. Keep looking, run ideas past me. I'll warn you away from the snake oil, suggest anything you miss, and keep an eye on his progress."

She snapped Gabe's folder shut.

"I'll see Gabe in three months."

She ruffled Gabe's hair, and then left without saying goodbye.

They developed a sense of what worked and what did not. When something looked hopeful, they ran it by Dr. Klein. If she approved, they tried it. If it seemed beneficial, they added it to Gabe's routine. It was an expensive mix.

After observing Gabe for nine months, Klein recommended they put Gabe on Sitextra.[3] The medication calmed neurotransmitters, regulating emotional responses; thus stabilizing his moods.

"Gabe's sensory system has him in a constant state of heightened emotions, which produces anxiety and a tendency to aggression. It's like mega-PMS, all the time. This medication will give him an even playing field."

"What about side effects?" Tori asked.

"The biggest is increased hunger."

Tori and Phillip looked at each other ruefully. Gabe already accounted for half their grocery bill.

"The other potential side effects sound scary, but their chances of happening are miniscule. Check it out and let me know."

Tori did internet research and had an interview with their pharmacist, who said if he had a son like Gabe he would not hesitate. They put Gabe on the medication and noticed an immediate improvement. Not only was Gabe calmer and less anxious, but he was able to control his aggressive tendencies.

Tori re-read the email with its thinly veiled demand that parents with delinquent soccer fees pay up. She groaned and raked her fingers through her hair. Phillip made good money, but their

---

3   Fictitious medication

expenses outpaced the national debt. Lydia, who needed help to catch up, was in private school. Everyday expenses were high in today's economy.

The killer expenditure, though, was therapy. Their formerly plump savings account was emaciated. Tori could not handle a part-time job; she stayed busy from six o'clock in the morning until eleven o'clock at night, and Lydia and Phillip still felt short-changed.

She may be able to get advice from Families of Children Under Stress (FOCUS), a great nonprofit organization, which supported special needs children and their families.

"This is Kristi at FOCUS. How can I help?"

"Hi, Kristi. This is Tori St. John, Gabe's mother. Can you tell me what parents do when Babies Can't Wait, BCW, doesn't cover therapy, anymore?"

Tori slid a sheet of cookies into the oven. Not good for her diet, but the kids would turn somersaults when they saw them.

"We're rapidly running out of money."

"Been there. You make too much to qualify for government aid, but not enough to pay one hundred and twenty-five dollars an hour for therapy, right?"

"Right. Any advice?"

"Have you heard of the Deeming Waiver?"

"Our BCW social worker mentioned something called a *demon* waiver, but she got an urgent phone call before she explained. Gabe aged out of the program soon after. I'd forgotten about it."

Kristi chuckled. "*Deeming*, not demon. A while back, a middle-income family with a special needs daughter depleted their financial resources on therapy. At that time, the only option for them to get government help was to legally abandon their child, so she could live at a state nursing home and receive therapy there."

Kristi loudly slurped a drink.

"They sued the government on grounds they could take better care of her at home, for less cost, if they could get help with therapies and other costs. The courts agreed and the Deeming

Waiver—based on the need of the child, not the income of the parents—was born.

"Fabulous! Oops, hold on."

The aroma of oatmeal chocolate chip cookies told Tori she needed to pull her cookies from the oven before they burned.

"Sorry 'bout that. How do I start?"

"Contact the Department of Children's Services. Don't stop with the Deeming Waiver. Keep networking, looking for things. Many parents are hesitant to accept government aid, but the more a child can develop now, the less of a burden they are on the state later."

"I agree. Plus, we've paid taxes for a long time. It's better for money to be spent on special needs than on studying the mating habits of cockroaches," Tori said.

Tori was turned down initially, but before long, Gabe was approved.

CHAPTER 12
Danger Zone

"Break time."

Delia Minton—a tall, slender platinum blonde—stood in the doorway of Phillip's office.

"Organic green tea with raw honey."

"Mmm. My favorite."

"I know."

Phillip wondered how she knew, but decided not to look a gift Starbucks in the mouth. Phillip was known to have marketing flair as well as software expertise, so it was not unusual for other departments to run problems by him. It was unusual, however, for someone Delia's level to be here. Phillip took the tea and indicated a chair.

"Thanks. How's Racoby going?"

"Not well."

Delia, the sales vice president, was a rising star in Jameston & Sons. She had been promoted several times in three years. The golden girl was lagging significantly behind her year-to-date objective, though. She needed to bring in some big numbers before year end.

Racoby Hotels was a conglomerate of hotels, restaurants, two cruise lines, and a national car rental agency. Recently, they had put their reservations system out to bid. Ten million dollars were on the line.

"I've skimmed over the bid. It's a tough one." Phillip said, looking at her over the rim of his cup. "I've worked with the consultant, Sniderleigh. He's a snake."

"That's one of the reasons I'm here," she added lightly, "not that I need a reason to visit my favorite co-worker."

Phillip laughed. "I'm hardly a co-worker. You're what, two levels above me?"

"The thought occurs to me, and to some of my peers," Delia said, lifting her forefinger, "that you'd be an even better fit if you were at least three levels up. You're so much more than software and technical issues. We need you higher up to help with big picture thinking."

She smiled lazily, crossed her long legs, and stretched out, balancing the coffee on her flat stomach with one finger.

"I can facilitate that movement," she offered. "Interested?"

There was a time Tori's belly was flat.

Phillip rebuked the traitorous thought.

"I'm listening."

"Racoby merged with Rycorp," Delia explained. "That more than triples the potential revenue."

Phillip whistled. "Whoa! Serious bucks."

A slight frown creased Delia's forehead.

"Racoby has pulled the bid. If it hadn't been withdrawn, we would have lost it. A new, combined bid will be issued next month."

"Why were we losing?"

Delia shrugged graceful shoulders.

"Several reasons." She replied, ticking the reasons off on long, elegant fingers. "Price: we're high. Product: the bid asks for features we can't provide. Person: Dick Sniderleigh—he's pond scum. Sniderleigh dislikes Jameston & Sons, but he loathes me. I'm not sure why."

Phillip centered his calendar on his desk.

"Sniderleigh hates Jameston & Sons because we fired him five years ago. Did he make a pass at you?"

"Yes. I shut him down."

Chapter 12 – Danger Zone

"And you wonder why he doesn't like you?" He gave Delia a mocking smile. "I don't suppose you have friends in the Mafia?"

Delia shook her head.

"Sadly, no."

"Then you're stuck with Sniderleigh. Have you contacted headquarters?"

"Yes. That's why I'm here." Delia leaned forward and he caught a faint whiff of musky perfume. "Phillip, I need help. I'm in over my head."

"I'm sure Bill will—"

Delia interrupted him.

"Bill may be my area vice president, but he's sub-par and he knows it. He feels threatened by me. He tried to block my last promotion, and then I ended up working for him. He'd love to see me fall on my face."

Delia's nose wrinkled in distaste.

"I don't know that Bill would appreciate my involvement."

Delia's smile was smug. "No worries. I'm reporting directly to Ron Pierce on this."

Phillip whistled. Ron Pierce was the company's vice president.

"Together, Racoby and Rycorp represent thirty million dollars in revenue. Jameston wants the business; badly. Gina says—"

"Gina Ballante?" Phillip asked.

Delia nodded, surprised he had to ask.

Now, Phillip was really intrigued. Gina Ballante, Jameston & Son's president, reported directly to the chief executive officer.

"You run with the big dogs," he said, half-standing to give a mock bow.

Delia smirked.

"Gina was my sorority big sister at Wheaton. If we win, she's promised to create another vice president position for me, or . . ."

Delia smiled.

For a brief moment Phillip got an impression of pointed, predatory teeth.

". . . or get rid of one of the others. But I can't win without a design engineer who knows our systems inside out; someone with marketing savvy."

Phillip pursed his lips. "It'll be tough, and time-consuming. To win, we'll need to break new ground."

"Gina, Ron, and I have talked. In order to start winning more of these technical bids, we need a vice president of technical marketing. We agree you're the obvious choice."

Phillip's heart-rate increased. He hadn't expected a shot at a vice presidency for at least another five years.

"Interesting," he said.

He took a sip of coffee.

"So?" Delia touched his arm. "When can you start?"

"Not so fast. I need to talk it over with Stuart. He's not my biggest fan."

Delia's full lips pouted.

"Gina and Ron have approved it; your boss isn't likely to object."

"Probably not, but I like to think things through. I'm already swamped between here and home."

Plus, you're known around the office as Machiavelli in stilettos. How closely do I want to work with you?

"Talk it over with Stuart and that cute little wife of yours. Neither of them will want to hold you back."

Phillip's cell phone was on his desk. She picked it up and punched buttons.

"There, I've entered all three of my numbers." She rose and sauntered to the door. "I've had my eye on you for a while; we'll be a good team. Let me know tonight."

She flashed a movie star smile.

"If you hurry, you can catch Stuart before he leaves."

Stuart made his dislike of Phillip apparent at every opportunity; Phillip was not anxious to talk to him. His boss was jealous of Phillip's progression at Jameston.

Stuart had held the same position for fifteen years; he was not likely to go any higher. Especially since several female employees had complained about him. Phillip groaned.

May as well get it over with.

As Delia had projected, Stuart did not object, but he scowled as he gave grudging approval.

"You always get the breaks. Delia's smart, well-connected," he winked, "and very easy on the eyes."

Other than raising his eyebrows, Phillip ignored Stuart's comment.

"The project would take up most of my time."

"So, you'll be tied at the hip to a babe. What red blooded male *wouldn't* want to be tied to those hips?" Stuart leered.

"Your comment is demeaning both to me *and* Ms. Minton."

"Oh, so it's *Ms. Minton* now, church boy? Don't be a hypocrite. You'll enjoy working with her, all right."

"Certainly. I hope to have a pleasant, productive, and professional working relationship with her," retorted Phillip. "I would remind you I am happily married, and will talk to Tori before making a decision."

He left Stuart's office, ignoring the clucking sounds that followed him. Phillip called Tori right away.

"Hello, my vertically-challenged vixen."

"Vertically-challenged vixen? You're reaching."

"How's your day been?"

"Pretty much as usual. We went to the library to choose a book for Lydia's book report, which is due in two days. She got *Babe: The Gallant Pig* by Dick King-Smith, because it was the shortest on the reading list. The elderly librarian who helped us was not impressed. What about your day?"

"An interesting opportunity has come up—"

"Gabe, no ice cream! And shut the freezer door."

Gabe persisted with requests for various foods. Poor Tori. Phillip was glad he was the bread-winner, not the stay-at-home parent. He fiddled with a pencil while Tori dealt with their son.

"You may have carrots, that's it. Sorry, Hon, you were saying?"

"Delia Minton, the assistant vice president over sales—"

"Mom, can I sleep over at Morgan's?" Lydia asked.

"No, you've been practically living together."

"Well, then, can she come here?"

"No."

"But, Mom—"

'Lydia, I am trying to talk to your father. Hush, please."

"Why can't I—"

"I'm on the phone! Be quiet."

"Ignore her!" Phillip urged.

"I know. Sorry. Is Delia the gorgeous, snooty girl I met at the Christmas party?"

"Yes . . . I mean, no. She's not snooty, but you did meet her. I suppose she's attractive enough, if you care for that type. The point is—"

The doorbell rang.

"Lydia, get the door!" Tori yelled. "What about her?"

"She's requested I work with her on a special project. It's quite a nice opportunity. I'll probably be promoted if we're successful. However, it'll take time away from home, so I wanted to check—"

"Mom, Serena's here!"

"To be sure you didn't mind before I committed—"

"It's fine, Honey; whatever you think. Gotta go," Tori said. "See you tonight. Stop and pick up the cleaning, would you?"

She hung up.

I guess she doesn't mind.

Despite an uneasy feeling, he decided to tell Delia before he left for the day.

At least, with her, I can have an uninterrupted conversation.

As usual, he ignored the elevator. He ran four flights of stairs up to Delia's office.

She was on the phone and held up one finger. Phillip had not been in her office before. Looking around, he was surprised to see a bulletin board filled with newspaper articles about animals. He strolled over to look. To his surprise, the captions indicated Delia was actively involved with animal rescue and People for the Ethical Treatment of Animals (PETA).

Delia hung up.

"The answer is yes?"

"It appears there are no obstacles to our working together." He indicated the bulletin board. "I see you're fond of animals."

"Dogs. You can relax and be yourself with them; you never have to wonder about their underlying motive. They just love you, pure and simple. Hang on a second."

She punched an extension.

"Ms. Minton here. Transfer Mr. St. John into the office across from mine." She paused. "Tomorrow morning."

At the burst of protest on the other end, her already cold voice dropped a few degrees.

"We discussed this yesterday. I expect it to be done. Prioritize."

She hung up. Her haughty expression melted into an inviting smile.

"It'll be easier to work together once we're on the same floor."

Phillip crossed his arms over his chest. He hadn't realized Delia was so controlling.

"I'm not sure. I'll want to check with my department regularly. They need access to me."

"If they can't get to you easily, you won't be bothered with trivialities. You can stop by every morning. At the moment, I need you worse than they do."

Phillip's face must have reflected his irritation. Delia smiled apologetically.

"I'm sorry; I should have checked with you first. I'm used to identifying and removing obstacles. I'll try not to be so overbearing."

That was a handsome apology. Working with her should be fine. After all, anyone who loves animals can't be too bad.

"Apology accepted. I guess I can move."

Delia shifted into work mode.

"HQ just emailed this spreadsheet." She turned to her computer. "It shows the pricing corporate is offering. If we compare it to the prices our competition is likely to offer, we're 13 percent high. I need you to find a way to lower our prices."

"Not necessarily," Phillip said, pulling a chair up beside her. "We have better systems and a better reputation. No one can currently meet all the system requirements, correct?"

"Right. They're asking for features nobody offers yet."

"That's one of Sniderleigh's favorite tricks. He writes requirements to include next generation features, and then wants vendors to lower prices because they're non-compliant."

Phillip rocked back and forth in his chair a couple of times.

"When I heard Sniderleigh had written the bid, I read it. For once, the features he's asking for are reasonable. It was just a matter of time before someone requested them."

Delia's eyes brightened.

"Could the features he wants be developed quickly?"

A huge smile spread across Phillip's face.

"It just so happens my team and I have almost finished a system with the features Racoby wants. With a little work, we should be able to prove we're the only ones who can meet the bid's specifications." He sat back, steepling his fingers. "We may be able to justify *raising* prices. Let's review the bid goals and objectives."

They worked steadily, trading ideas back and forth. Phillip was startled to realize it was eight-thirty in the evening and he had not called home.

At home, Tori was a little irritated Phillip had not called, but she was busy with emails. These days the melodious tone she heard when she received new mail pealed like wind chimes in a thunderstorm.

It was usually a parent whose child had just been diagnosed with a special need, one who had hit the wall with the school system or therapy, or someone who had run out of money and was desperately searching for some grant or waiver to continue therapy. Tori helped as best she could.

She was on the computer hours every day when the kids were gone. Often, though, there just *were not* any easy answers. While Phillip and Delia worked on technology projections, Tori answered an email from a good friend, Kellie, whose three-year-old son had cerebral palsy.

From: Kellie
Subject: Robin surgery
> Robin has to have hip surgery; his muscles are pulling apart. It'll be extremely painful. He'll be in a full body cast, with a catheter, for six months. I can't stop crying.

From: Tori
> I'm so sorry. How can I help?

From: Kellie
> A kick in the butt, maybe? Robin's normal mentally; I have so much to be thankful for, but I constantly look at what I don't have.

From: Tori
> I'm the wrong one to dispense butt kicks. I watch normal kids and wonder if there's something wrong with me. Why did God give other children a healthy, typical life, while Gabe has life's odds stacked against him? Am I being punished?

From: Tori
> Hey, Kellie! I came across some verses last night that booted me smack in my derrière:
>> Oh, the depths of the riches of the wisdom and knowledge of God! How unsearchable his judgments, and His paths beyond tracing out!
>> —Romans 11:33, NIV
>
> I've been asking God too many whys lately. I've suggested ways He could care for Gabe, Robin, and several others a bit better than He has been doing; like I had a better option God hadn't thought of yet! When I read those verses I realized I needed to pray one of my most frequent prayers:
>> I believe in Your goodness, Lord, help Thou my unbelief.

From: Kellie
My rear's a little sore, but thanks, I needed that!

From: Tori
God doesn't expect you to be happy Robin needs an awful surgery. He wants us to trust He will make all things work out for good in the end. That doesn't mean you'll enjoy it. His peace is an overall thing, too. We have long-term peace because we know God has already written the happy ending. Oops, looks like I got carried away. Thus endeth the sermon.

From: Kellie
Thank you, Mother Tori! Seriously, though, I appreciate it.

CHAPTER 13

Sorting Through the Information Haystack

Tori felt like she was flying full throttle through a fog. Often on her computer until the early morning hours, she sought information on the nebulous foe that had taken her son captive.

Tori the businesswoman had charged into battle fully-armed, making decisions based on available data and taking calculated risks. She shrugged off defeat. After all, she could recoup her losses in the next round.

Tori the mother made decisions in a nobody really knows environment and agonized over the risk, knowing each failure stole time, which could never be recaptured. The medical field had almost no information, so Tori relied on email, internet articles, and online support groups.

From: Becky

You said Gabe had sucked the well dry with neuro transdifferential therapy. Alene connected better with NTD, but couldn't count to twenty or recognize letters. We switched to Freedom to Choose Between Parameters Therapy (FTCBPT), forty hours a week. We call it **fit-c-bipped**. We're going broke, but she's starting to read!

To: Becky
> *I'd rather Gabe be able to hold a conversation than say his multiplication tables.*

Tori paused, fingers resting lightly on the keyboard. Becky was sensitive about Alene's inability to exchange social greetings. She hit the delete key.

To: Becky
> *We've considered FTCBPT, but Dr. Klein says "intense FTCBPT can hinder a child's ability to think and act dynamically."*

Tori tasted blood as she hit the send button.
I've got to stop biting my lip, my thought process, and my decisions . . .

From: Becky
> *Whatever. FTCBPT works for us.*

From: Tori:
> *You're right. Every spectrum child is different.*

Tori researched FTCBPT. It seemed ubiquitous. Some schools were even starting to fund it.
Am I missing the boat?
Tori explained FTCBPT to her family at dinner.
"So, Phillip, what do you think?"
"I dislike it."
"Why?"
Tori passed Lydia a napkin. "Honey, napkins absorb better than sleeves."
"If we're not going to follow Dr. Klein's advice, for what are we paying her?" Phillip sipped his acai juice, "Additionally, you seem to be unable to pronounce the acronym for this therapy without spitting."
He wrinkled his nose. "Distasteful."
"Fit-c-bipped!" Lydia said, spewing bread crumbs.

Gabe giggled and tried to repeat it. What emerged were garbled consonants and bits of pork loin.

"Stop saying fit-c-bipped!"

Tori tried not to spit or to laugh, and failed miserably. Phillip chuckled. Soon, they were all expelling FTCBPTs and food across the table.

Holistic and bio-medical treatments were another consideration. Stories proliferated about the improvements people experienced when they changed what they ate, absorbed, and eliminated. Removing steroids, preservatives, food colorings, and processed foods was recommended.

Gluten—wheat and grains and casein dairy products—were accused of causing or worsening autism. The gluten-free/casein-free diet (GFCF) ruled the world of autism.

Support Group Posting:

> *Our naturopath, Karl Midford, put Timmy on a regimen of GFCF and an organic lifestyle. He says it allows the body to fight off pathogens. After six months with Karl, we've been able to stop all Timmy's medications.*

Dr. Klein warned Tori GFCF did not work for many kids, but she said it could do no harm and might do a lot of good.

So, the St. Johns hired Karl and went organic GFCF. Their grocery bill rose as Tori's popularity in the family plummeted. After a few meals like pizza made with soy cheese, organic tomato paste, and a rice flour crust, Lydia and Phillip revolted.

"It tastes like cardboard smeared with axle grease." Phillip pushed his plate away.

"Does even our food have to be about Gabe?" Lydia asked.

So, Tori prepared two meals. Gabe's meals were cooked in a stringent atmosphere: special foods, separate sets of cookware, a stringent preparation regime. They installed expensive water and air purifiers, purged Gabe's system, and started a regiment of vitamins and minerals.

It didn't seem to make a difference. Tori expressed solidarity with Gabe by eating GFCF and lost a few pounds. Gabe started to look like an underfed Greyhound.

Medication was controversial. Some considered it a pacifier for lazy adults. Others lauded it as a blessed elixir of peace and a semblance of normality. Gabe took Sitextra to address frustration and anxiety. It worked well, but the St. Johns' foray into bio-meds meant they took him off it.

To: Karl
It's been eighteen months. Gabe's worse. I've been doing my own blind study with Gabe's teachers and GFCF doesn't appear to make a difference. As you instructed, we weaned Gabe off Sitextra. He's been medication-free six months. In the past three weeks, Gabe's pediatrician, the school nurse, and his teacher all told me they were alarmed by Gabe's regression. I don't know what to do!

From: Karl
Drugs are tourniquets applied to hemorrhaging arteries. Regressions happen. Work it through.

Tori read Karl's email and slammed her fists on the keyboard. *Work it through? Gabe's a hurting child, not an algebra problem!*

Tori worried her bottom lip between her teeth.

Should we hold out longer? Karl said it took time. How much time is enough?

The GFCF diet helped so many children. Anytime anyone found out about Gabe's autism, they would ask, "Is he on the diet?"

Tori reviewed Gabe's diet time and again, wondered what she was doing wrong.

"Phillip," she said one night, "maybe I'm not following the diet correctly."

"You keep GFCF Kosher in our kitchen, you've read five GFCF books cover to cover, and have a large index file of notes. How could you be doing it wrong? Email Dr. Klein."

Tori did, and received a reply within an hour:

Chapter 13 — Sorting Through the Information Haystack

From: Dr. Klein
You have done due diligence to enable Gabe to live drug-free. It is apparent he doesn't function well without medication. Restart. Regarding GFCF, Gabe appears to be one of the children who show no improvement on the diet.

Still Tori waffled, unwilling to give up on the dream. A few days later, she was cooking when Gabe wandered in wearing the sad and hungry look he usually wore these days. He eyed the normal food, and then turned a beseeching look on Tori.

"Gabe wants food, Gabe be *good* boy."

The poor child thinks we're punishing him!

Tori slumped against the cabinet, caught Gabe in a hug, and offered him a piece of fried chicken. Gabe's eyes widened. He grabbed the drumstick and gobbled it so fast it reminded Tori of the early, post-orphanage days. She ended the GFCF diet and reinstated his medicine.

Gabe rejoiced and the St. Johns rejoiced with him. She did not tell Gabe's teachers what had changed; she just kept having them rank him in the blind study. His scores improved dramatically.

One support group Tori sporadically attended reacted to her decision as if she had announced Gabe's new diet would consist of lead shavings imported from Sarevjo. She stopped attending. Still, bio-meds seemed to offer hope.

To: Monica
I heard you're trying new supplements with Song. How's that working?

From: Monica
Expensively. People get rich off our desperation. I try not to expect anything, so I won't be disappointed, but I can't help hoping TruNutrients will really help Song. They're sold by a lady whose grand-niece has shown significant progress with them.

From: Seth
> *Karl found all kinds of junk during Dean's detox: aluminum, parasites, vaccine poisoning, etc. Hair analysis showed he doesn't absorb nutrients well. We're ready to rebuild his system. I'm wondering about TruNutrients. I'm almost out of money; we used Karla's income for therapies. Still, anything that will help Dean is worth it.*

To: Seth
> *Even Karl admitted that Gabe's detox showed nothing. We've gone to a diet of mostly natural foods, low in sugar and dyes. TruNutrients didn't make a noticeable difference for Gabe or Song. Monica's furious; she's demanded a full refund. We buy our supplements from the health-food store. I admire you. It can't have been easy since Karla left, but you're doing a superb job.*

From: Seth
> *Monica's over-the-top. Appreciate the input and the kudos. I still can't believe Karla abandoned Dean. Me, I understand, but her son? She doesn't even take him on weekends.*

Tori's eyes watered. Karla had always been blunt about her frustration with being a special needs mom. She tended to assume Dean's lack of speech meant he didn't understand.

Tori shuddered to think what Dean might have heard. He was around seven years old when Karla left, old enough to know he was being rejected.

To: Seth
> *You know there's financial aid Dean can qualify for, right? Do you have the Deeming Waiver?*

From: Seth
I don't think we qualify for anything. I make over fifty thousand dollars a year.

To: Seth
It's based on the child's need, not the parent's income, so Dean should qualify. Information attached.

To: Tori
Thanks. Could we meet for lunch to go over the forms?

To: Seth
Sure. I'll find a BOGO coupon. I'll bring my calendar to the next support group meeting.

To: Tori
I haven't gone much since Karla left. Everyone's a couple.

To: Seth
*Everyone is **not** a couple, and they're too absorbed in their own problems to pay attention to you. You need the support now more than ever. Come next time, we can sit together. Phillip works most nights, anyway.*

To: Tori
I may just do that. Thanks.

Tori pushed away from her computer and shook her hands to get the circulation back. She felt sorry for Seth and Dean; Karla, too. Karla would eventually regret her son's loss; maybe Seth's, too. How many good-looking, kind, and personable men did Karla think there were in the world?

From: MaryLynne Stevenson
Hey there, Ms. Tori. How's Gabe doing? It's time to submit another request for MOG. Is there anything new that would further our cause?

Gabe qualified for the More Options Grant (MOG), which augmented the Deeming Waiver, but there was limited funding. MaryLynne, a social worker, toiled over her caseload with the tenacity of an ant. She had been trying for five years to get Gabe the MOG—Tori knew of families still on the waiting list after ten years.

To: MaryLynne Stevenson
Gabe went ballistic on his sixth day at Creekside Elementary. We were trying to go without meds. He's back on medication and having no problems, but our stress level has ramped up.

From: MaryLynne Stevenson
Please fax a copy of Gabe's most recent evaluation to update our request for funding. How is your family functioning under the additional pressure?

Tori grimaced.

She jumped every time the phone rang, afraid it was Gabe's school. Although she was doing better, Lydia still envied the extra attention Gabe got. Phillip resented no-longer being the center of Tori's world. She felt hurt that Phillip seemed to view her as just a homemaker these days.

To: MaryLynne Stevenson
Badly—we see a family counselor.

From: MaryLynne Stevenson
Would your counselor send me a letter about the pressure on your family?

The counselor gladly sent a letter, including a recent business article, which ranked stress by professions. According to the article, special needs mothers and combat soldiers experienced identical levels of tension.

Stress rode them like a leech. The divorce rate among special needs families was twice as high as normal. In fact, she was worried now about one of the couples in their support group.

The man had told Phillip his wife was "not the woman I married. I don't love her anymore." His wife complained bitterly to anyone who would listen about what a rotten husband and father he was.

Despite his faults, Phillip's a wonderful husband and father. If something happened to our marriage, I think I'd crawl into a corner and shatter.

She decided to call Phillip, tell him how much she appreciated him. Maybe he could take a long lunch. She would do her hair and makeup; put on her skinny jeans.

Phillip's secretary answered her call.

"Hi, Marion, is Phillip there?"

"You just missed him; he was headed out to lunch."

"I'll call his cell. Maybe I can meet him."

There was a split second of silence.

"I think he and Delia are having a working lunch. Delia said they'd be back by two."

Tori frowned at her watch; it was eleven-thirty in the morning. She vaguely remembered Phillip complaining about the Racoby consultant. She hadn't been paying much attention last night.

"Probably Racoby," Tori said. "No problem."

She hung up.

Hmm.

Tori raked her fingers through her hair and considered Delia. Tall, beautiful, disdainful of stay-at-home-moms . . . Delia always looked like she had just stepped out of the day spa. Tori felt twenty pounds heavier just thinking about her.

It was not that she didn't trust Phillip—he was naïve. She had heard Delia's MBA stood for *morally bankrupt aggressor*. Maybe she would make Phillip's favorite turkey loaf and put the kids to bed early. However, first, there was one last email she had to handle.

CHAPTER 14

A Support System Crashes

"Swim? Swim? Swim?"

Gabe's words plopped onto Tori's eardrums like Chinese water torture. He had spent yesterday repeating lines from *Shrek*. The repetition had lasted three weeks so far. Smothering an impulse to gag him, Tori locked herself in her closet and let out a primal scream. It felt good.

Lord, grant me patience . . . or deafness.

"Swim? Swim? Swim?"

This type repetition, called perseveration, was typical in children with autism. What had been a minor, controllable issue for Gabe in the past was now relentless. It was still going on when Tori pulled into the church parking lot, three weeks later, praying for semi-normal behavior. Reverend Maggie Burke, assistant pastor, was dropping off her daughter Missy when they arrived.

"Hello, Tori. I'm surprised to see Gabe."

Tori had noticed Maggie, who'd always seemed friendly before, had been cooler to her lately.

"Really? We're here every Sunday."

"Were you aware a couple of the deacons had to chase Gabe when he ran away from class last week? Missy was quite distressed."

Chapter 14 – A Support System Crashes

Tori's eyes narrowed.

"Gabe isn't deaf. Please don't speak as if he isn't here." She turned Gabe over to his teacher, Bridgette Wimberley, which gave her a few seconds to compose herself. Still, she knew her tone was hostile. She didn't care.

"Gabe's terrified of thunderstorms. Lightning struck a tree and Gabe panicked. Every child has fears. Bridgette mentioned Missy locks herself in the supply closet every time she sees a bug."

Maggie glared. "That's different!"

Tori infused her voice with milk and honey.

"You're right, it's not the same. Gabe has autism, which causes him to act differently sometimes. Remember, Christ's commandment is 'Let the children come to Me,' not 'Bring Me the normal kids.'"

"But Gabe even pinched Brigette, which shows a total lack of respect for his teacher! Spare the rod and spoil the child, the Good Book says; looks like Gabe needs more rod!"

Tori stepped closer to Maggie, who stepped back. Tori stepped closer. Maggie's second step put her against the wall.

"Gabe apologized," Tori said; her voice low and intense. "Everyone understood. Do you spank Missy when she locks herself in the closet, or is an apology to the custodian sufficient? You did have Missy apologize, right?"

If I hit her over the head with her Bible, would some of it penetrate?

Maggie compressed thin lips into her receding chin and stalked away.

Phillip frowned when Tori told him about the encounter.

"We talked to Brigette, the educational director, and Father Dave after Gabe pinched Brigette. They don't appear worried. Ignore Maggie."

Tori tried to follow Phillip's advice, but halfway through the sermon, her pager went off. Hurrying down the hall, she heard Gabe wailing from an unused classroom.

"What happened?" Tori asked Mrs. Wimberly.

Gabe was really too big for Tori to hold now. However, when he was distressed, he let her cuddle him, so she held him, anyway.

"Gabe was repeating," Bridgette said. "Some kids yelled at him. We made them apologize, but I caught Missy later making ugly faces at him."

Tori closed her eyes. Humankind's young were mindlessly cruel. They seemed unaware careless words and laughter could poison the self-esteem of their victims.

"Thirty minutes later," Bridgette continued, "Gabe started crying. Some kids made fun of him, so I brought him here. I'm so sorry. I'll talk to their parents."

Tori's throat ached. She stroked Gabe's head and murmured soothing words.

"Should he stay home for a while?" Tori mouthed.

"No!" Bridgette's cheeks flamed crimson. "Don't let Maggie put stupid ideas into your head. We'll work through this."

Bridgette whispered in Tori's ear so Gabe couldn't hear. "We told Reverend Burke we didn't want Gabe to stay home. Donna agreed with us."

Tori felt like she had butterflies swarming in her stomach. Most of First Unity had been thrilled to be assigned a female pastor for the first time. Maggie was an influential woman. Would Donna, who paired vision with practicality, hold firm?

Donna was in her office, pouring coffee into a huge mug. When she saw Tori she smiled.

"The coffee's just the way I like it, strong as super-glue. Want some?"

"No thanks." Tori sat. "Reverend Burke greeted me this morning by saying she was surprised to see Gabe. It appeared to be an unpleasant surprise."

Donna's smile faded.

"For an intelligent woman, Maggie's ignorant. She wants Gabe to stay home for a while."

Tori threw up her hands.

"Autism isn't a phase. Gabe's always going to act differently."

"Everyone, including Gabe, is welcome in Sunday school. I told Maggie that."

Tori chewed on her lip, and then forced herself to stop.

"Have other parents complained?"

"Only two."

Donna held her hand up as Tori surged out of her seat, ready to protest.

"Wait. Those parents are usually yakking about *something*." Donna winked.

"But what did they say?" Tori pleated the skirt of her dress.

"One parent said he danced too wildly during last month's praise dance and another complained he was repeating everything. I don't put much credence in what they say."

Donna took a sip of coffee.

"Lyndon says Gabe is tainting Missy's learning environment."

Missy Burke had been born years after her father, Lyndon, Donna's assistant education director, had given up on having children. Missy was the unexpected jewel crowning his middle age.

"That's not good. Lyndon exists to erase the slightest frown from Missy's face."

Donna took another sip of coffee.

"True, but I wouldn't worry. I'm sure this will blow over."

Tori got up.

"Not unless Gabe's autism blows over."

The butterflies in her stomach had turned into locusts.

I'm used to fighting for Gabe, but I never expected fellow church members to be the opposing force.

The conference room felt like a sauna. Droplets trickled like tears down the sides of a pitcher of ice water, which sat perspiring on the table. Tori traced geometric patterns in the condensation as she analyzed the people in the small room.

The Burkes: foes. They had been outspoken around church, rallying friends to their cause. Father Dave: he had been fair and impartial, but he would grasp at any solution to minimize conflict. Glenda: Father Dave's assistant, was only there to record the proceedings. She preferred computers to people and seldom spoke.

Brigette Wimberley: ally. Despite the pinching incident, she would crawl over broken glass for Gabe. Donna: an ally so far, but she would do what was best for everyone. The Burkes would try to convince her best would be for Gabe to go home. Tori and Phillip needed to solidify Donna's belief that Gabe belonged, differences and all.

Father Dave opened with prayer.

Then he said, "Phillip, why don't you start."

"Everyone here, but Tori and me seems to know exactly what's to be discussed today. Rumors are running wild. I must insist we be included in further staff discussions regarding our son."

Maggie glared at Bridgette and Donna.

"Sharing staff discussions out of context causes misunderstandings."

"We have been told you don't want Gabe here whilst he is exhibiting different behaviors. Put that into context for us," Phillip said in a level voice.

"Context?" Maggie floundered.

The room was silent save for the clicking of Glenda's nails against her keyboard. Maggie cleared her throat.

"Yes, well. The context is that while Gabe is disrupting class, he should stay home. We'll pray that his difficulty passes quickly. Many children stay home until they grow out of the biting and pinching stage."

"Unless God chooses to intervene, Gabe's not going to grow out of autism." Tori said.

Brigette's ample chest heaved.

"Hold on! Gabe sometimes causes a momentary blip. Everyone, but you," she said, gazing at the Burkes, "accepts it."

Maggie frowned.

"I'm not picking on Gabe. I want what's best for *all* the children."

"A class of nine and ten year olds is semi-organized chaos anyway," Bridgette said. "Most kids hardly notice Gabe."

"Missy says she can't concentrate with Gabe talking all the time!" Lyndon protested causing his Adam's apple to bob up and down.

"If anyone's disrupting the class, it's Missy. She chatters non-stop." Bridgette retorted.

Tori smothered a smile, sketched Missy as a magpie, and then hurriedly scribbled over the drawing. She expected Lyndon to refute the teacher's statement, but Maggie shook her head at him.

Interesting. It would appear Maggie's not as oblivious to Missy's shortcomings as Lyndon. Could she be swayed?

Tori rested her arms on the table and spoke to Maggie.

"Look. I know you refused the doctors' advice to abort Missy, even though they said she'd be severely malformed. Praise God, she was fine. Gabe wasn't. Can't you talk to Missy, help her understand that Gabe's not wrong, just different?"

Maggie looked uncertain for a moment, but then her eyes hardened.

"I'm sorry for your pain, but this isn't about Missy. The fact is, Gabe's odd behaviors irritate the normal children."

Mentally, Tori stripped off her gloves. This was war.

Father Dave spoke, "Donna, as education director, what's your opinion?"

"Yes," Maggie said.

Looking at her face, Tori imagined Maggie licking her chops.

"Tell us how concerned other parents are!"

Donna raised an eyebrow.

"I never mentioned other parents."

"Why, Maggie," Tori said. "Surely, as assistant pastor, you're not spreading rumors?"

Maggie looked flustered.

"Well, I . . . no . . . but . . . parents discuss—"

"In the future," Father Dave interjected, "Let's remember, scripture says if you have a problem with a believer, talk to him or her, not others. Understood?"

His eyes swept the room, lingering for a moment on the Burkes' sulky faces.

"Fine," he said, thumping his hand on the table. "Donna? Are other parents worried?"

"Two other families expressed concern. These particular parents are . . . ahh . . . not hesitant to complain. The issue here is the well-being of our church members. Parents of disabled children need Christian nurturing and support."

Donna made eye contact with each person before continuing.

"More importantly, Gabe needs spiritual training. Special needs children often comprehend far more than we think. Gabe needs the opportunity to absorb what he can."

"Let's be frank," Tori said, yanking at a curl. "Gabe's autism causes disruptive behaviors. We don't know when or if these behaviors will stop, or what may replace them. We want to worship as a family. What's the solution?"

"Our Missy responds to consistent discipline," Lyndon said smugly.

Bridgette choked. Glenda lifted her eyes from her keyboard. Everyone else looked stunned. Missy was generally acknowledged as the most spoiled child at Unity.

"What punishment does Gabe experience for bad behavior?" Lyndon asked.

"If he's aggressive: time out, loss of privileges, spankings, if appropriate," Phillip said. "However, Gabe usually displays autistic symptoms, not misbehavior. For those, we redirect him."

"But surely he knows he's annoying others," Lyndon said. "Perhaps an escalation of consequences . . ."

The man's a certified idiot. Why in heaven is he assistant director of anything?

"What do you recommend?" Tori asked with a saccharine smile. "A TASER gun, perhaps?"

Phillip sat a glass of water in front of her, his signal Tori needed to stay calm and focused. She drained the glass, wishing it was an Oreo milkshake.

"Regardless of the cause, we need to consider the overall good of the church," Maggie said, speaking in her let's-all-be-reasonable voice.

"If you won't keep Gabe home, you need to commit to having one of you with him anytime he's on church property. Staying home is a better solution. Can't you get a babysitter?"

"Babysitters for disabled children are scarce and expensive," Tori answered. "But have you been listening to us *at all*? We need a resolution that takes into account the fact autism is for life. What you're proposing are short-term solutions."

Phillip's chair screeched against the tile as he stood up.

"We have been members of First Unity for fifteen years. We've given generously of our time and money. Now, when we need the church's understanding, you," he jabbed a finger at the Burkes, "are saying 'Take your problem home where it doesn't affect us. We'll pray that your trouble is short-lived.'"

"That's not what I'm saying." Maggie's face shone with a light sheen of sweat.

"It's hard to interpret any other way," Tori said. "What, exactly, *are* you saying?"

"Well . . . I'm saying until Gabe stops . . . that is, while he's . . . um . . ." Maggie stuttered to a stop.

"Phillip is correct that the grapevine has been active," Donna said. "Six people have volunteered to be with Gabe in the classroom, while Tori and Phillip worship. How does that sound?"

Phillip sat back down.

"That could work."

"But the distraction . . ." Maggie seemed genuinely distressed.

"We'll move Missy into another classroom," Donna said.

Lyndon's eyes bulged. "*Missy's* not the problem!"

"Missy's the only child who is consistently irritated, so she's the one we'll move," Donna replied.

Lyndon started to protest. Donna swiveled her chair and looked at him.

"Lyndon, do you have a problem with my decision?"

"Um, no."

"Well," Father Dave said. "We seem to have a solution that meets everyone's needs."

Everyone, but the Burkes, seemed relieved. Tori had reservations. They had won the first skirmish. They could probably win the war, but at what cost? At the center of the battle was a child bound to be damaged by the bullets fired.

"We'll touch base in a few weeks. Let's pray, and then we can all get home before traffic gets *really* bad," Father Dave quipped.

"Too late," Tori said, looking out the window. "The traffic's already backed up to downtown. Let's order Chinese! Phillip probably has a menu in his glove compartment."

Groans and laughter greeted her statement. The tension diffused a little as the group broke up.

Although a compromise had been reached, from that day on Tori felt she never let her full weight sink into the pew. The phone rang like the St. Johns held swing votes in an election year.

"Have you really been asked to leave?"

"Did Donna ask for Maggie's resignation?"

"I heard Gabe bit Missy. Hope he bit hard."

One friend pulled Tori aside.

"You should know," she said, patting Tori's hand, "there's a core group who agree with the Burkes. In a vote, though, Gabe will probably win."

Ice pierced Tori's bones.

Gabe the subject of a church vote?

One beautiful Sunday, classes met on the playground. Tori lingered to watch Gabe. When he climbed on a swing, the girl beside him got off and ran away. The boy on Gabe's other side did the same. Tori's mouth went dry. She went to Donna immediately.

Donna waved a doughnut at her.

"Fresh Krispy Kreme, yes?"

"I couldn't swallow. Other than the one time Gabe pinched Missy, Gabe's never hurt another child, but kids are frightened of him. Why?"

Donna licked her fingers and scowled.

"Rumors. Earlier I overheard a mom tell her daughter 'be careful around Gabe.' She backed down when I confronted her, but Gabe having assistants with him all the time has caused speculation."

Tori's jaw hardened.

"It's been a month since the meeting. Time to follow-up."

"Okay, but please don't worry. The position of our home board is to unequivocally support special needs. This will blow over."

Chapter 14 – A Support System Crashes

Tori left encouraged. However as she tucked him in that night, Gabe asked, "Jesus love?"

"Absolutely, Little Prince. We do, too. Was someone ugly to you?"

Gabe pulled the covers over his head and turned away.

When Tori told Phillip, his eyes narrowed.

"Time to find a new church."

Lydia protested. "But, I don't—"

Tori cut her off in mid-squeal.

"Hush, Sweet Pea. We don't want to leave, either, but some people don't want Gabe." She explained what had been happening.

"*That's* un-churchy! I'll kick anyone who's ugly to Gabe." Lydia smirked. "I kick hard."

Tori sympathized.

I'd like to kick Reverend Burke, right in her scrawny. . .

Tori banished the un-Christian thought.

"Lydia, Jesus says turn the other cheek."

"Jesus is perfect; I'm not. Since He made me this way, I'm fine. If we change churches, I get to help choose."

Lydia flounced out of the room. At twelve years old, she had elevated the flounce to an art form.

Phillip grinned.

"Well, we have Princessa's conditional permission. Why don't you call some other churches?"

Tears blurred Tori's eyes. She cried easily these days; often with rage, sometimes with hurt, sometimes with fear.

"I can't believe we're having this conversation. After fifteen years of total commitment, they're ready to throw us out like a dirty rag, just because Gabe's disrupting the smooth flow of a Sunday school class."

"We're pretty heavily invested in time and relationships at Unity. We've stayed with the church through some pretty rough times. I don't think she's trying to throw us out. Maggie's egotistical. I doubt she's considered the possibility we may leave rather than bend to her analysis of what's best," Phillip said.

"I don't *want* to leave Unity, but I won't allow Gabe to be hurt."

"I think his mama's more hurt than he is," Phillip said, gathering her into a bear hug. "But he does know something's wrong."

When someone hit her child, Tori bruised. Maggie's suggestion felt like a blanket rejection. As Tori called churches and asked about special needs programs, her world turned to monochrome. The one church she found with a special needs program was forty minutes away in good traffic, too distant to be practical.

Every dead end loosened her tenuous grip on hope. She periodically hid in her closet for relief, hoping no one would notice the swollen aftermath of her crying jags.

Although the Burkes acted as if everything was normal, Phillip thought they seemed uneasy.

"Maggie may be wishing she hadn't kicked this hornet's nest," he commented to Tori after he saw Maggie snubbed one Sunday.

"Maggie organized meals for us when we first got back with the kids. If there was a treatment for autism, she'd be the first to take up a collection, but it's different when she feels her child is being threatened. Churches are putting in wheelchair ramps, but they're unprepared for disabilities with a behavioral element."

"We may need to start our own church," Phillip said.

His dry comment was a joke, but it was not funny because Tori knew he might be right.

A month after she started calling, Tori had not located a suitable church. At noon, she still wore her sleep shirt. Tori considered heating her lukewarm tea, but decided it was too much effort. She'd already called the likely churches.

Tori wondered about the humongous church on the corner, the one often mistaken for a private college. Phillip and Tori had visited Grace Fellowship two years ago. While it was good, they preferred smaller churches. However, Grace was a stone Tori could not leave unturned.

She and Phillip had decided to be very specific with the churches they called. Hopefully, if they had to move their membership, they would not face the same situation again at the new church. Tori left a blunt message for Grace Church's Children's Department.

This will spare us both an uncomfortable conversation.

Grace's director of education called back within fifteen minutes.

"Hi, this is Joe Bloomberg, from Grace Fellowship Church. We have some options that may work well for Gabe. We'd love for you to visit."

"Um, you listened to the whole message, right? Gabe's behavior can be . . . irritating."

Joe laughed.

"He won't bother us. We have a fun class. The leaders have been trained by special needs therapists. Or Gabe can go to a typical class and we'll train the teacher."

A tenuous, warm breeze caressed Tori's soul, like spring beckoning to a heart resigned to endless winter.

Joe Bloomberg met them Sunday and took them to Gabe's class. The room was spacious and bright. Praise music played softly. When Gabe ignored the toys, a teacher led him into an adjoining room. Following, Phillip and Tori saw Gabe, his grin as big as a slice of watermelon, jumping on a mini-trampoline. They left.

The church was huge.

"How do you find your way?" Tori quipped. "Strew breadcrumbs?"

Joe grinned.

"I prefer a ball of string. But if you decide this is a good fit for you, Grace has many small communities of interest to make it cozy. Lydia," he said, smiling down at her, "it's black light Sunday in KidRealm. Want to look? I think you'll really like our youth pastor, Kiki."

Lydia dragged her feet until she saw Mari, a friend from school. Within moments, Lydia had melted into a group of babbling girls.

"The children seem content," Phillip told Joe. "Thank you."

"No problem." Joe pointed at some doors. "The worship service is right there in the main auditorium. I have to run. I'll call you tomorrow."

The auditorium was so large Tori expected to hear echoes. They were glancing through the jam-packed bulletin when they heard their names. They looked up and saw Charlotte and Paul Green, a couple they had lost touch with several years back.

"Hello! Are you members here?"

"For three years now."

"It seems nice," said Tori, "but so large—"

"The size takes some getting used to, but it meets a lot of needs," Paul said.

The couple sat down. "Grace Fellowship has problems, naturally, because we're all flawed. Overall, though, we love it."

A band walked onstage, and the music began.

After church they went to Gabe's classroom and found him drawing airplanes. He leapt up and ran to them.

"*Good* boy!" he announced, beaming. "He did not run away, pinch or repeat, or dance loud or . . ."

"Good job, Buddy." Phillip swung Gabe up and spun him around.

"How did it go?" Tori asked the head teacher.

"Great, we love him. He 'peated some . . ." she and Tori shared a smile ". . . but that's normal. Please bring him again. He's a delightful child. If you like, we'll work on planned ignoring and redirection strategies. I know how frustrating perseveration can be for moms."

Her words soaked like warm balm into Tori's lacerated heart.

Lydia was pumped.

"This church is way cool!" she said, flinging a small Frisbee into the air. "I'd be okay with it. In fact, maybe when I grow up, I'll be a youth pastor like Kiki."

Tori looked at Phillip and raised an eyebrow.

"I liked it. Did you?" Phillip asked.

"Way cool."

"Yes. Grace seems like a logical choice, but we shouldn't jump to conclusions."

"I agree," Tori said. "Let's decide after the Unity meeting."

Three weeks later, they drove to Unity for the meeting. Tori had her notebook with her and sketched a courthouse scene, showing Gabe as the accused. Phillip glanced over at it.

"Good drawing, but don't you think you should leave the notebook in the car? You've drawn Maggie with a heavy mustache and given Lyndon a humped nose and fangs."

"It's stress release. I'll keep it hidden. I won't draw anything I wouldn't say to their faces."

The same group as before crowded into the conference room. Greetings were perfunctory. Tori imagined she caught an acrid whiff of emotion, a mixture of nervousness, fear, and anger.

Donna opened the meeting, speaking briskly.

"Our denomination's executive mandate is to make every possible adaptation for special needs," she said. "There's a model for a class . . ."

"Which we don't have resources to staff," interrupted Lyndon, chewing on a fingernail.

Donna tapped her pencil.

"Actually, I already have two volunteers."

"It'll be expensive to train them." Lyndon frowned.

"We'll work it out," Father Dave said, blowing on his glasses and polishing them.

As assistant pastor, Maggie oversaw finances. She pursed her lips and started to speak. Father Dave glanced at her, his expression formidable. Maggie subsided.

"Have you taken the pulse of the church?" Phillip asked.

His eyelid fluttered slightly, a sure sign he was holding strong emotions in check.

"The majority of the deacons voted to form the class," Donna said. "So, now—"

"Excuse me," Phillip said. "Precisely how big a majority?"

"Seventy-six percent," Maggie said. "One-fourth . . ." She drummed her fingers on the table and answered, "Twenty-four percent of the deacons said no."

"According to church bylaws, 51 percent constitutes a majority." Father Dave eyed Maggie and cleared his throat. "The staff has *all* agreed to support it."

Heads nodded. After a slight pause, Maggie dipped her chin.

Tori poured some water, took a sip, and studied Maggie over the rim of the glass. She did not doubt Maggie would re-open the battle at another time.

"Really, Maggie?" Tori asked conversationally.

"I'll support the decision."

Maggie stared with apparent fascination at a stain on the wood-grained table.

"But what's your honest opinion?" Phillip asked. "Please speak as freely as you've been speaking around church."

Maggie glowered at him, leaned forward, arms on the table then hesitated.

Phillip waved his hand, indicating she should speak.

"Gabe is disruptive." Maggie said. "I'm sorry he's autistic, but Gabe's disability shouldn't take precedence over the needs of other children. It's not good stewardship to start a class for one child. The deacons thinking with their brains, instead of their emotions, agree."

Father Dave slapped his hand on the table.

"That comment was uncalled for and incorrect, Reverend Burke."

Maggie's face suffused with red.

"Sorry." She resumed her study of the stain.

Phillip looked at Tori and cocked his head. She nodded.

"Tori and I have talked and prayed about this at length," Phillip said. "Given our discussion today, the best thing for Gabe and . . . the unity of First Unity," he gave a wry smile, "is for us to leave."

Protests broke out.

"That's a retaliatory response!" Lyndon said. "Leaving is unnecessary."

"No, it isn't," Tori said, gripping her chair arms. "We feel like lepers."

"We've visited Grace Fellowship," Phillip said. "They have an established special needs class, which interacts with other classes. The kids and their parents have been friendly. Gabe seems happier."

"But we can start a class like that," Father Dave objected, throwing out a hand.

"We appreciate your willingness to work with us." Phillip spoke gently to Father Dave, but then his voice became harsh. "Twenty-four percent of the church is not willing. It's too big a number. Statistically speaking, when 24 percent of a group oppose a policy then that policy is usually doomed to fail."

Father Dave cast a look of acute dislike at Maggie.

"This wasn't my intent," Maggie said. A vein pulsed at the side of her neck.

Is the unhappy look on her face because we're leaving, because Father Dave is angry at her, or because we'll take our offerings with us?

Tori's voice was raw with tears shed and unshed.

"I need to say something. The population around us is increasing, but membership is flat. I think that's partly because we aren't open to diversity. We'd prefer our membership be typical, middle-class Caucasians with a few minorities sprinkled in for effect. Atlanta doesn't look like that."

"That's not true. We just want a calm environment in which to teach Christian values," Maggie said piously. "An atmosphere where Christian virtues flourish.

Fury propelled Tori to her feet.

"Which virtue was Missy practicing by openly inviting everyone in the class, except Gabe, to her party?"

"He understood that?" Lyndon wiped his mouth. He and Maggie exchanged a guilty look.

"Gabe is not stupid." Tori clenched her fists. "On the way home from church that Sunday, he said 'Gabe no party?'"

Maggie winced and protested, "But autistic kids don't want to be around other people."

"Half an hour of research would have debunked that myth. You could have called me and asked. Gabe loves parties." Tori sat down, breathing heavily.

Phillip took over.

"This isn't just us. One child in eighty-eight is now being diagnosed with autism. Add other childhood disabilities such as Down's syndrome, ADHD, and cerebral palsy, then one in every fifty children, at least, has a disability.[4] You need to get ready."

"Grace Church is big, cold, all about programs," Maggie said.

"Define cold," Tori said. "Grace doesn't know if we're givers or takers. They do know we're bringing a high-maintenance child who's unwelcome at his current church. We were welcomed

---

4 http://www.ageofautism.com/2012/03/cdc-announces-1-in-88-autism-numbers-safeminds-responds-with-autism-crisis-2012.html

without hesitation. Christ spent His time among the outcasts of His day and said He came to serve. Grace has lots of programs because they're attempting to love like He does."

Silence fell. After a minute, Maggie stirred.

"I'm sorry. I'll support the class."

Phillip gave her a withering look.

"Thanks, but no. We're tired of fighting. We'll stay until you find volunteers to replace us." He stood. "Come on, Tori, we're done here."

Father Dave rose, looking old.

"The rest of you stay; we have much to discuss. Phillip, Tori, we'll learn from this. Speaking on behalf of First Unity, I deeply regret your family has been hurt."

Bowing his head he blessed them.

To Tori, leaving First Unity after fifteen years felt like a divorce. After a few months, she stopped feeling unfaithful, but the split rankled like a paper cut.

A few months later, Tori noticed a new child, who looked and acted normal, being checked into Gabe's class. Suddenly, she went berserk. She kicked, hit, and then broke free and ran.

She was brought back spitting and screaming. Her father was furious; her mother looked ready to cry. Startled, Tori realized the child was spewing profanity.

I don't want Gabe exposed to this!

"Is this how the Burkes felt?" a still, small voice whispered. "Did you judge the Burkes too harshly?"

Tori introduced herself to the girl's parents and vowed silently to learn about behavior disorders.

CHAPTER 15

Denial, Danger, and Disrespect

Phillip usually enjoyed services at Grace Fellowship. Today's sermon made him uncomfortable.

"We're living in a culture that takes commitments lightly," the pastor said, "even marriage commitments."

Phillip thought the pastor looked straight at him.

"Sexual affairs are common in the workplace."

Phillip winced. He and Delia had been working together on the Racoby bid for over a year now, but he had not *touched* her.

"Avoid compromising positions . . . intimate business lunches . . ."

Delia and I need to have lunch together just about every day, Phillip assured himself, *it's business.*

Sniderleigh kept changing and adding to the bid requirements, almost as if the irascible consultant sensed Jacobson was close to meeting the technical requirements.

Hmm. Wonder if there's a leak in my department.

It could take another six months for Racoby to close, and then up to another six months
  dedicated to implementation.

No working lunches? Ludicrous.

"Business travel fraught with temptations . . ."

Delia, emerging from the pool during the annual convention, dripping wet in a bathing suit that revealed more than it concealed.

Phillip shook his head impatiently.

"Are you okay?" Tori whispered.

"Allergies."

He tapped his nose and grimaced. Tori frowned. She scribbled a note on her bulletin.

Allergies? Since when?

Phillip shrugged, and then gazed at the pastor, giving the appearance of a man totally immersed in the sermon. Out of the corner of his eye, he saw Tori scrutinize him before she tuned back into the service.

He was not even seriously considering an affair. If he and Delia enjoyed each other's company, it was a bonus they deserved; nothing more.

He was a family man.

The next morning, Phillip made Tori a cup of hot tea and carried it in to her, something he had not done in a while.

"Morning, Sweet-n-Low."

He gave her a kiss. Tori yawned and stretched.

"Mmm, tea. Thanks. What's the occasion?"

"Do I need a reason?"

He rumpled her hair and left.

"How are your allergies this morning?" she called after him.

He did not reply.

Five o'clock came so very early in the morning. Tori stood in the driveway with Gabe, waiting for the bus and craving another half hour of sleep. She dragged Gabe out of bed at six o'clock. By the time he dressed, brushed his teeth, and gobbled a cheese stick, he was wide awake.

In her career days, Tori got up by five-thirty, dressed, and drove to work on autopilot. She was awake by the time she got to the office at six-thirty.

Chapter 15 – Denial, Danger, and Disrespect

As a mother, she needed to have full brain cell function by the time her kids were awake, so she got up early enough to wake up fully before the kids. Otherwise, they outsmarted her.

It was sweet of Phillip to bring me tea this morning.

She savored the warmth of the ceramic against her cupped hands and sipped. Perfect. She was glad she had stopped trying to fit in twenty minutes of therapy before the bus came.

The bus was running late. Tori and Gabe strolled along the cul-de-sac hand-in-hand, looping back to their driveway. On the second lap, Gabe saw a bird hopping along the ground, broke away from Tori, and trotted toward it and the road.

"Hey, come back here! You can't catch that bird."

The bird flew a few feet, landed, cocked its head as if inviting a game of chase, and resumed hopping. Gabe broke into a trot.

"Gabriel Winston St. John, get your fanny back here. Now!"

The bird flew away, but Gabe kept running. Tori's tea went flying as she ran after him, but Gabe was quick and her soft moccasins were not made for pursuit. She kicked them off and ran barefoot, hardly noticing glass and rocks biting into her feet.

Bushes blocked Gabe from view, but she heard horns sounding. Terror shuddered through Tori. Gabe must have reached Danvers Avenue, the busy cross street at the end of their road.

Fueled by adrenalin, Tori raced to the thoroughfare and looked wildly in both directions. It had been less than two minutes, but Danvers curved. She could not see him.

Dear Christ, which way did he go?

A car crawled along Danvers. The driver searched out her windows, whipping her head back and forth. When she saw Tori, she pointed to the right.

"Thanks!" Tori gasped and sprinted right.

She heard the screech of tires and smelled burning rubber.

Oh, God, please, no!

As she rounded the curve, Tori saw Gabe. He cowered in the middle of the road, hands over his ears, looking bewildered.

Cars crept past him. Some people spoke into their cell phones. A few honked their horns. Gabe saw Tori and stepped toward her.

"Don't move!" Tori screeched.

A man stopped his car, put on his flashers, leapt out, and held up a hand to stop traffic. With a burst of speed, Tori reached Gabe and pulled him close. She felt his heart pounding wildly against hers.

Thank you, Lord Jesus!

She thanked the man profusely, and then escorted Gabe to the side of the road. She sank to the curb, still clutching him tightly, and burst into tears.

The school bus lumbered up behind her and came to a stop with a grinding of gears. With a hydraulic swoosh, the door opened. Tori heard the familiar, kind voice of the bus driver.

"Tori! What happened? You're white as a sheet. Get in, quick!"

Tori staggered onto the bus, pulling Gabe with her. Her trembling legs would not support her any further. She sank down on the sticky bus floor, shaking in time to the engine, which vibrated beneath her.

"Mama's crying," Gabe said.

He went to his accustomed seat, sat down and gazed out the window, his face tranquil. The driver shut the door, drove to Tori's house, and pulled up beside her driveway. She glanced in her rearview mirror.

"There's a policeman behind me."

Tori looked up at the mirror and saw flashing blue lights.

"Gabe ran after a bird . . . got away from me . . . I couldn't . . ."

"Gabe's fine," the driver soothed. "Have the officer call someone for you, okay? You look like you may pass out any minute."

"I'll be all right. Thanks for the ride."

The doors swooshed open. Tori grabbed a seat and pulled herself to her feet, wincing at the cuts and bruises.

"Sorry. I'm bleeding on your bus."

"I'm not worried about the bus, but you need to take care of those feet."

Tori nodded and stepped off the bus, careful to avoid the shards of ceramic, which littered the driveway.

"Thanks again!"

The driver waved and drove away. Tori turned her attention to the policeman.

"Hello, officer."

The policeman stooped down, picked up a moccasin, and handed it to her.

"Good morning, ma'am. I was patrolling Danvers and saw you rescue a child from the middle of the street."

"Yes, sir. My son has autism. I was holding his hand, but he broke away to chase a bird—"

"My nephew has autism; he has trouble controlling his impulses, too. I'm glad your son is safe. A young man with autism was killed in traffic last year. You'll want to keep a really firm grip on him from now on."

"Believe me, I will."

"Hope the rest of your day goes better."

He smiled, got in his patrol car, and left. Tori went inside, trembling and called Serena. It was afternoon and the kids were home before Tori could make a dent in her to-do list.

The kids are my priority, not the to-do list she reminded herself.

She taxied Lydia to tennis practice, sat in an outer office reading a five-year-old magazine while Gabe had neuro-feedback, picked Lydia up from practice, ran to the drugstore to buy poster board for a project Lydia had due the next day, and then dashed home to fix dinner.

As she pulled into the driveway, her cell phone played the opening bars of "Hot-Blooded," signaling a text message from Phillip.

Wkng lte, eatng out. B hm Asap.

Lte agn? Was gng 2 mk ur fvrite ckn.

Tori punched the send button harder than necessary. Guess it'd be frozen pizza and Lean Cuisine for dinner tonight.

Homework and Gabe's bedtime passed without incident. Tori dug into the bottom of her pajama drawer and pulled a big T-shirt from underneath the sexy negligees she had recently purchased in hopes of rekindling Phillip's flame. No sparks would fly tonight.

Tori cleansed her face while Lydia leaned against the bathroom counter and talked. Tori told herself how blessed she was Lydia was so open, but wished she hadn't slept an extra half hour that morning instead of having quiet time.

Lydia jumped from topic to topic, chattering with an enthusiasm that made Tori smile. Tori endured the discussion about whether or not Daddy might let Gabe get his ear pierced someday, declined to buy Lydia a Saint Bernard puppy, and nixed the idea twelve years old was old enough to stay home alone.

"Mom, I wish I could grow up to be a boy."

"Why, honey?"

"Boys get to do cooler things, like wear awesome clothes."

Tori glanced at her daughter. Lydia was dressed in baggy black shorts and a sloppy T-shirt.

"Sweetheart, you wear the same type of clothes boys do."

"Not to church! I hafta wear dresses—"

"Or nice pants, or a skirt."

"I hate skirts and nice pants! How come God made me a girl?"

"Princessa. Would you agree God is smarter than you?"

"I guess."

"Okay, then. He made you a wonderful, special girl who's growing into an exceptional young lady. The possibilities are endless."

"Did you ever want to be a boy?"

"For a while. As I matured, I liked being a girl more."

"Mom, how come I hafta make my bed and unload the dishwasher? Edie doesn't have chores. And why do I hafta make my own lunch?"

"You asked to make it yourself." Tori applied face cream.

Was that an age spot?

"Yeah, but you still make me pack nutritious stuff. I hate my lunches. They're boring. Edie—"

Tori gritted her teeth and wished Edie and her family would move to Tahiti. She made a mental note to call her mother and apologize for being an obnoxious twelve-year-old.

Tori forced herself to speak in a calm, pleasant voice.

"Okay, enough griping. Is there anything you're happy with that you'd like to talk about?"

"My birthday's only six months away. Can I have a slumber party?"

"Sure."

"How many kids can I invite?"

"Well, the girls in your class, I guess, plus a couple more."

"How many boys?"

"You can't have boys at a sleepover."

Lydia eyes narrowed.

"Why not? I'll be thirteen! Having just girls is boring."

"Boys and girls don't spend the night together. Especially, when they're thirteen."

"What if I only invite two or three boys? Dean has spent the night here." Lydia thrust out her bottom lip. "And I've spent the night at Andrew's house."

"Andrew is your cousin. Relatives are different."

"But Dean—"

"Dean was only eight, and he spent the night with Gabe, not you. Besides, he only spent the night because Mr. Seth went out of town and needed someone to keep him. You can have boys over for cake and stuff, but they can't stay for the slumber party."

"Then I don't want a slumber party!"

Lydia scowled at Tori, hands on her hips. Tori raised her voice.

"Fine, but I'm done with your attitude. Be respectful and pleasant or leave."

"Mu-Thur!" Lydia smacked her gum. "It's not disrespectful to express myself. It's *my* birthday party. All my friends get to do what *they* want. Edie—"

"Yes, I know. Edie had her party at Six Flags. I'm happy for her. Too bad you weren't adopted by a rich family. We're not spending five hundred dollars on a birthday party."

"I never get to do *anything*!" Lydia wailed. "Gabe gets everything he wants. You went online and bought circus tickets today, just because he pointed to the picture in the paper and jumped up and down. It's not fair."

"We got you a ticket, too. Honey, Gabe very seldom wants anything, so when he does, we tend to get it for him. He doesn't get half the things you get, or do a third of the things you do."

"Yeah, whatever."

"That's it. Go to your room and write a paragraph counting your blessings."

"Mo-om! What did I do? All I said was—"

"Young lady, we don't have to have a party at all. Add a paragraph on not arguing."

Tori caught a glimpse of herself in the mirror. The tense-faced woman reflected there was not one her former co-workers would have chosen to push. Lydia was undaunted.

"That's ridiculous! Give me another chance! The Bible says you have to show me grace."

"*And* a paragraph on respect. That's three paragraphs. Want to go for three pages?"

"Oh, you are . . ."

Glancing at her mother's face, Lydia opted not to finish. She whirled and stalked out. At the door, she turned.

Standing tall and throwing her shoulders back, Lydia said in a dignified voice, "Mother. I will be so glad when I am a teenager girl, so we don't have these disagreements, anymore."

Tossing her hair, Lydia marched from the room, head high, and closed the door with what was not quite a slam. Staring at the door, Tori laughed hysterically.

"From your lips to God's ears, Sweetheart!"

CHAPTER 16

Depression

Phillip called a team meeting, ostensibly to review progress on the Racoby bid. As each member presented his or her status, Phillip sipped coffee, watching them closely over the top of his brightly painted WE LOVE DADDY! mug.

The Racoby bid was dragging on. The consultant, Dick Sniderleigh, had laced the original bid requirements with features not currently offered by any of the vendors, including Phillip's company, Jacoby & Sons.

Phillip knew one of Sniderleigh's favorite tactics was to claim he had located an overseas company that could fulfill the bid. He then demanded price concessions from companies who could not. Phillip suspected the practice garnered Sniderleigh substantial bonuses.

Unknown to the rest of the industry, Phillip's department was testing a proprietary software package, which met the bid specifications. Yet, Sniderleigh's numerous bid modifications made Phillip wonder if the consultant had learned of their new capabilities.

Is one of my hand-picked, trusted design engineers leaking information?

When the updates were finished, he distributed Sniderleigh's latest bid modifications. There were murmurs of dismay as his team read the document.

"*More* changes? It's almost as if the old buzzard suspects we can meet his original feature requirements," Janet, his lead engineer said, slapping down the handout.

Phillip scanned the faces around the table. He saw only dismay, no guilt.

"Does anyone know how he could be getting inside information?"

Phillip thought he caught a flicker of awareness in Janet's eyes. Everyone else looked blank. There was a chorus of no, so Phillip dismissed the meeting.

Janet stayed behind. Shutting the door, she said, "About our suspected leak—"

"Yes? Have a seat."

"You know Stuart claims he practices hands off management with us."

Phillip nodded. His boss preached the benefits of giving his employees "freedom to excel." Stuart did as little as possible then appeared when it was time to get credit.

"Since Racoby, he's around all the time, asking questions."

Phillip gave a low whistle.

"Interesting." He took off his glasses and twirled them. "Hard to deny Stuart information."

"Not really." Janet smirked. "I'll suggest the team emphasize problems, rather than successes."

She gave a pert grin.

"And I can think of a red herring or two."

"You know I can't condone lying to Stuart."

"Ahh, but what is truth? Gotta go, boss."

Janet winked and left.

Tori sat in Grace Fellowship's auditorium, waiting for the Camp SuperStar end of summer presentation to begin. Lydia had a part in the fun, upbeat program. Tori and Gabe had come straight from a therapy appointment, so they were early. Gabe sat beside Tori, smiling as he piloted a small metal plane in the airspace above his seat.

I would've brought the forms I need to fill out for Gabe's aqua-therapy if I'd known we would be early. Oh, well; can't be helped.

Tori relaxed into her seat. The pulled curtains turned the quiet, air conditioned auditorium into a deep forest glade. Tori closed her

Chapter 16 – Depression

eyes, savoring a moment of relaxation. To her surprise, warm liquid trickled down her face and into her mouth. She tasted salt and opened her eyes. Gabe stared at her and giggled. Perplexed, Tori reached a hand to her face and wiped away the tears.

She had been so weepy lately. Just last week, Tori had burst into tears when she opened the milk carton and smelled the sour tang that reminded her she should have gone to the grocery store. She had taken to slipping away when she could; sneaking into her closet to have a good cry over nothing in particular.

Maybe it was time for her annual physical. She hadn't had one in five years. She probably had a vitamin deficiency of some sort.

"Lydia, I've got a doctor's appointment this afternoon, so I'll be late. Serena will be here to get you and Gabe off the bus."

"I'm too old for a babysitter. Serena will bake cookies though, so that's cool. Why're you going to the doctor?"

"Just a check-up. I haven't been feeling well lately; no energy, a little emotional."

"I've noticed." Lydia took a bite of egg-roll, about the only food Tori could get her to eat before school. "Maybe you're pregnant."

Tori spewed tea. "There's no way I'm pregnant."

Lydia raised an eyebrow, "Really?"

"I mean, there's a way, but . . . there's your bus, Honey."

As she ran out Lydia yelled, "A baby would be way cool!"

Tori shuddered.

"Although I'll wait for the lab results to give you a clean bill of health," Dr. Rosemund said, "you appear healthy . . . and you aren't pregnant."

Tori heaved a sigh of relief.

"The St. John family just avoided an unparalleled disaster."

"Your heart rate is somewhat elevated. Are you still exercising?"

"Does running up and down the stairs a bazillion times a day count?"

"It doesn't appear to be working. I'm mildly concerned about your blood pressure, too. It's still low, but it's elevated beyond normal for you," he said sternly. "That could be because you've gained ten pounds since I saw you last. I want you to lose those pounds."

Tori grimaced. She knew she needed to lose weight. Chocolate was so soothing, though. She jerked her attention back to what Dr. Rosemund was saying.

"However, I find nothing to explain your unexpected crying. How's your stress level?"

"No significant problems., but my day-to-day stress level is probably up there."

"What's causing the daily stress?"

"A ten-year-old son with autism. He's adorable, but he has low social skills, verbal aggression, perseveration, and Obsessive Compulsive Disorder. His sister is a strong-willed thirteen-year-old daughter with a knockout figure, who knows everything about everything and feels it's her responsibility to instruct lesser mortals."

Tori could have, should have stopped there, but under Dr. Rosemund's sympathetic eyes, she kept talking.

"You know my husband, Phillip; he's your patient, too. He doesn't relish coming home to the situation I've just described. He works all the time, usually with a gorgeous blonde."

Tori put her hand over her mouth.

What possessed me to say that? He'll think our marriage is in trouble.

Dr. Rosemund raised an eyebrow.

"There's nothing going on, of course."

Doctor Rosemund said nothing, just waited with that quirked eyebrow. Words tumbled out of Tori's mouth, seemingly of their own volition.

"It's just that Delia's extremely attractive and since I'm not so much, anymore, I feel like I've let Phillip down."

Dr. Rosemund shook his head. "You're still an attractive woman."

To her horror, Tori's traitorous eyes spurted tears. She dashed them away and rushed on.

"Phillip's an awesome guy. Despite their little quirks, the kids are great. Our family is healthy, overall. We can usually pay all our bills, no one in our immediate family is significantly ill, and I have close friends. God is Sovereign; God is good. That's my mantra."

"Do you believe your mantra?" Dr. Rosemund asked with a sudden sparkle to his professional demeanor.

"Most of the time; when I don't feel it, somewhere deep down I still know it's true."

"That helps. What you've described is an intensely stressful life. Your symptoms track with clinical depression. I'd like you to take a short quiz that measures depression."

"I'm not depressed." Tori put one hand on her hip. "I'm an upbeat person. Friends enjoy my sense of humor. Plus, the tears happen sporadically, when nothing bad has happened."

"Depression manifests itself in many ways. It's often a result of chemicals released by stressors. You may *not* be depressed. Why guess? Take the test; we'll talk more."

Tori filled out the test and turned it in to Dr. Rosemund's nurse.

What a waste of time.

Half an hour later, Dr. Rosemund returned.

"Your self-test indicates depression. I'm going to prescribe an anti-depressant—"

Tori jumped off the examining bed.

"But I'm a Christian! I can handle this without medication. I—"

The doctor raised a hand.

"You're too intelligent to believe that. It's akin to saying a Christian diabetic doesn't need insulin. Let me explain chemical depression."

Tori sat on the edge of the table. Dr. Rosemund leaned back on his stool and crossed his legs.

"When you experience stress, chemicals travel toward an appropriate part of the brain, causing emotions like depression or anxiety. That's normal. Adrenalin prepares you to face danger, chemical neurotransmitters help you deal with tension."

He tapped a pen on his clipboard.

"When you have a lot of stress over an extended period of time, the neurotransmitters carve a path directly to the emotional centers. Even a minor stress can now cause depression or anxiety you wouldn't normally feel. If nothing is done to stop it, it becomes what we call chemical depression."

Tori slumped back against the examining table. She had not noticed the antiseptic smell of the office before. Now, it made her nauseous.

"I don't believe this."

"I recommend counseling to help you develop coping strategies."

"I'll get some counseling, but no meds. They're a cop-out."

Dr. Rosemund waved his finger back and forth.

"Often a patient needs medication in order for counseling to be effective. Medication counters the release of chemicals and blocks stress paths in your brain. I feel you're too far down the path to make progress without an anti-depressant."

Tori tilted her chin stubbornly. Dr. Rosemund pointed his pen at her.

"You wouldn't refuse a blood transfusion or an antibiotic. You're headed for a crash if you don't take better care of yourself."

Tori imagined suffering from a nervous breakdown, lying helplessly in bed while the kids ran amok. Her tomboy princess thought Tori ignorant to say boys were more interested in Lydia's curves than her curve ball. She would be planning co-ed sleepovers while Gabe sat on the floor chasing platters of nachos with gallons of ice cream.

"Phillip doesn't like medication."

"Phillip isn't the one suffering from depression. If he has a problem with it, have him call me." Dr. Rosemund's face was grim. "I can recommend several good psychologists."

Tori left the doctor's office with a prescription and a sheaf of doctors' names. Finding one of the doctors took their insurance, she made an appointment. She did not fill the prescription.

Dr. Helene Merriam was intelligent and personable. Tori felt comfortable talking to her, but balked at the doctor's suggestion she come weekly for a few months.

Dr. Merriam was firm.

"From the brief history you've given me, you followed a high stress career with a high maintenance family and a personal quest to defeat autism. Many in your situation would've had some sort of a breakdown by now, but the years of stress are catching up with you emotionally and physically. I recommend you start taking antidepressants and we meet regularly."

"But—"

"Think of it this way. You're the control center of the massive Battle Star St. John. The control center needs reprogramming, but it'll take time. In the meantime, you need daily software patches. Without them the control center will crash; the battle star will cease functioning."

Phillip was home before dinner that night. He leaned against the counter while Tori chopped vegetables and relayed his suspicion someone was leaking information on the Racoby bid.

"Janet thinks Stuart's our mole."

"Stuart!" Tori thwacked a piece of celery in half. "What a swine."

"Unfortunately, there's no way to prove it. All we can do is damage control."

"Hmm." Tori put the knife down. "There *is* a way to partially prove it."

"How?"

"Plant some false information . . . Say, for example, you're worried one of your contractors is going bankrupt and won't be able to finish his part of the code."

"I'm not using subcontractors on this bid."

Tori's eyes twinkled.

"*You* and *your team* know that. Is Stuart likely to know?"

Phillip smiled.

"No. Stuart has no idea who does what. So, we plant the false info. If Stuart's our spy, he'll pass it on to Sniderleigh, who will . . . what?"

"My guess is he'll demand proof of financial viability on all subcontractors involved with his bid. It won't be solid evidence, but if you take it to Ron Pierce, it should help."

Phillip yanked at one of Tori's curls. "I'd forgotten how business-savvy you are, Tiny Terror."

Tori chuckled. "You haven't called me that in years."

"It was a business nickname someone coined after you uncovered a supplier cheating your customers and chopped him off at the knees. I was so proud of you."

"Are you still proud of me, Phillip, now that I'm not making waves in the business world and knocking down a six-figure income?"

"Well, I . . . of course, I am. You're good with the kids, you . . . why do you ask?"

Tori took a deep breath and told Phillip about her visits to Dr. Rosemund and Dr. Merriam.

"So," she concluded, "they both think I need counseling and medication. What do you think?"

She spoke softly, as Lydia and Gabe had wandered into the kitchen. Phillip seemed startled by her revelations.

"I hate you have so much stress in your life you're depressed. Is there anything I can do to help?"

"Do you *have* to work so much? Delia sees more of you than I do."

Phillip's eyes shifted.

"You know what getting the Racoby bid would mean to us."

"Is that all Delia is; someone to help you win the bid?"

"Naturally. Remember, I told you it'd be a lot of work; asked if it was okay. You said it was fine."

"I never expected it to last so long. It's been over a year."

"We think Snierleigh is trying to insure we *don't* get the business, so he's stretching things out. Delia doesn't like the delay any more than I do."

"Somehow, I doubt that."

Phillip shook his head warningly at Tori and cut his eyes towards the kids.

"Pas devant les infants."[5]

"Is Delia the lady who wore the really short shorts to Daddy's company picnic?" Lydia asked with interest. "She picked up Daddy's hamburger and took a bite of it without asking. Is that polite?"

"Gabe picnic?" Gabe asked.

Phillip picked the newspaper off the counter and found refuge behind it.

"I don't like drugs, but if you need medication to function, take it."

Guess that ends that discussion.

"I don't think I'll need it, since I'll be seeing the psychologist."

---

5   FRENCH: "Not in front of the children."

CHAPTER 17

Shaking a Fist at God

Looking out the kitchen window, Tori was delighted to see a few tentative rays of light break though the gloomy mist that had shrouded the neighborhood all week. After days of torrential rain, the weak beams of radiance seemed like goodwill ambassadors direct from heaven.

Tori pulled back the mini-blinds on the French doors leading out to the deck. Sitting her laundry basket on the floor beside the kitchen table, she started folding underwear. She was holding up a pair of Lydia's bikini panties, wondering how much they could possibly cover when the phone rang. Tori glanced at the caller ID.

Monica. Good!

Folding clothes was less monotonous when she could talk to someone.

"Hey, girl, what's up? Hang on, let me get my headset."

Monica, who had been divorced for two years now, had begun dating a little. Tori couldn't wait to hear about the blind date LaTonya, a mutual friend, had arranged.

"That's better. Now I can keep doing laundry while I talk."

"That's good," Monica said wryly "Heaven forbid you should single-task."

"I am woman, see me juggle. Hey, how was the date? Did you hit it off?"

"Not so much! What a jerk! I'm going to kill LaTonya."

"Uh oh. I had high hopes for this one. LaTonya has good taste. She felt sure what's his name would be a good match. What happened?"

"His name is Bart. He's good-looking, but a total waste, otherwise. To start with, he was forty-five minutes late. Then it turned out he had already made reservations at an expensive sushi place—I hate sushi. I would've said no if he'd bothered to ask. So, I just got a salad."

"And I know how fond you are of a nice, expensive salad," Tori murmured facetiously.

Monica was frugal; as a single mother, she had to be. One of her pet peeves was paying what she claimed was a 600 percent mark-up on restaurant salads.

"It was an $11.95 bowl of iceberg lettuce tossed with a few exhausted-looking chicken strips, swimming in generic ranch dressing," Monica said bitterly.

Tori knew Monica would not appreciate the giggles threatening to erupt from her throat. She looked around frantically for something to smother her mirth.

Aha!

Gentle wafts of aromatic Irish Breakfast from her favorite mug beckoned her. The strong, steaming liquid scalded her tongue and burned her throat, but effectively quenched her inappropriate laughter.

Monica continued, "We had agreed to go Dutch. After ordering the most expensive thing on the menu, along with three double scotches, the parasite told the waitress to 'just split the bill down the middle.' Mr. Generosity only left a 7 percent tip on his half, so I felt I needed to leave 30 percent on my half."

"Oh, Monica." Tori murmured sympathetically.

"Yeah. Are you beginning to get the picture? Bart spent the entire meal talking about Bart. One of those *enough about me, let's talk about what you think about me* type conversations."

"Oh, those are my personal favorites," Tori enthused.

"I couldn't wait for the night to be over. I told him I was tired, but he invited himself in. I had to fight him off for half an hour before I convinced him I wasn't playing hard to get. Lover Boy winked, said he 'liked a challenge' and 'would be calling me.' I'm changing all my numbers *and* my email."

It was no use. Laughter welled up and spilled over.

"Oh, Monica, that's horrible, but how funny! I told you to let me take you to the singles group at church."

"It's funny because it happened to me, not you," Monica said quietly. "And please don't talk to me about church. I believe in God. I used to go to church sometimes. I'm a pretty decent person. If God cares about me, He's certainly not doing a great job of showing it."

"I'm sorry." Tori said repentantly. "Sounds like the date from Hades."

"Last night's date is just another symptom of my pathetic life. I'm sick of trying to laugh it off as I bounce from catastrophe to calamity, depressed at being alone, tired of working my butt off to provide for my special needs child, alone. Did I mention alone?"

Tori tried to think of something encouraging to say, but came up empty. It didn't really matter. Monica was on a roll. Tori continued to enlarge the mountain of folded laundry building up on the kitchen table.

"I sink deeper into a debt quagmire every month, and I'm simply buying necessities."

Monica was quieter now, her soft words as desperate as her hysterics had been.

"My job is a pressure-cooker that's always about to blow. I come home drained from the tension, and then try to pull out energy for Song.

"I'm so sorry."

"Not your fault, just don't mention God. I'm ticked at Him. I'm tired of no being the answer to all my prayers. I'm too exhausted to keep doing this."

Tori stood helpless to address the morass of problems Monica faced. She dropped the towel she was folding and sank into a chair.

"Is there anything I can do?"

"Do you have any Mafia contacts who'd be willing to do a quick hit on Harold?"

"What's the irresponsible lowlife done now?"

"The slug is taking me back to court to get his child support lowered. He says he's 'suffered reversals in the market' and he can't afford to keep paying five hundred dollars per month for Song. Yet, when Pop-Tart—"

"May her wrinkles develop wrinkles," Tori intoned solemnly; a curse invoked when Harold's girlfriend was mentioned.

Monica usually laughed. Not today.

"Was promoted from bimbo to fiancée, he bought her a two-carat diamond."

Tori exploded, "There's not a decent bone in his rotund body. Surely, the courts won't overturn your divorce settlement. Harold's got plenty of money."

"Oh, my attorney says he'll lose. He also says the costs to defend the original decree will be prohibitive, and the judge might not rule Harold has to pay my legal fees. He thinks I'd probably save money by settling. Harold knows that, of course. He's offered two hundred and fifty dollars a month."

"For a special needs child!"

Tori was pacing now.

"I know; pathetic. But, with unpaid time off work and attorney costs of four hundred and seventy-five dollars an hour—I'll probably have to take it. Jerk."

"Wow. What can I say? I'll pray."

Tori mentally slapped herself.

Great. She's dealing with major problems and you offer her a platitude.

"I wish I could fix it," Tori said, feeling lame.

"You can't. This God you're praying to could, but He won't. Why have I become God's favorite punching bag?"

Tori measured possible responses. She took a sip of tea to fortify her.

"Monica, if you need to vent, go ahead. I can be supportive and fold clothes simultaneously." She folded the last of the whites and moved on to the colored pile. "But if you want an answer—"

"I should shut up and listen?" Monica was sarcastic.

"Well, yeah. If I'm going to re-direct my intellect from the absorbing task of matching socks . . ."

Tori shook her head as she realized the dryer had once again eaten one of her favorites.

". . . I don't want to be wasting my time."

"I have fifteen plus minutes of drive time left. I guess I'll listen."

Tori abandoned the socks.

God, give me words.

A memory surfaced. Tori turned her face up and mouthed, *Thank you.*

"This happened right before I met you. Gabe didn't talk much, except about food."

Monica chuckled. "I'm amazed the kid isn't fat."

"I know. He eats five times as much as me, but he's thin and I'm . . . um . . . voluptuous. I must absorb his extra calories. Anyway, he'd been irritable for days. The pediatrician couldn't find anything, and Gabe couldn't tell us what was wrong."

Tori's eyes grew distant.

"I remember that day clearly. It was naptime. I lay Gabe on the bed and realized he was hot. When I pulled his diaper off, there was a lump the size of a cherry on his groin. I rushed him to Dr. Jeffries, who said it was a hernia. He called an ambulance and had Gabe taken to Scottish Rite emergency room."

"Scary," Monica interjected. "From what you've said, Dr. Jeffries is pretty laid back."

"Yes." Tori bit her lip, remembering her fear. "Gabe's fever was rising and Dr. Jeffries was afraid the hernia was about to strangulate."

She continued to recall.

"At Scottish Rite, the ER staff did x-rays and tests, and then put us in a room to wait for results. I held Gabe and counted tiles in the acoustic ceiling. Finally, this young doctor, who looked like he'd been working 24/7 for three days walked in. Dr. Hernandez. He said Gabe had a hernia with infection in the surrounding tissue. He'd scheduled surgery for seven-thirty the next day because he wanted Gabe to fast before the procedure."

Tori sighed.

"As we were about to leave the house at five o'clock the next morning, the hospital called. They'd had two major emergencies and bumped Gabe's arrival time to one o'clock. He hadn't had anything to eat or drink since the night before. The nurse told me he still couldn't have anything."

"Oh, no!" Monica cried out. "What was the new surgery time?"

"Eleven o'clock."

Tori paused. She remembered the clock face after the nurse's call. The big hand pointed to twelve, the little hand rested uncompromisingly at five.

"Where was Phillip?" Monica asked.

"Out-of-town attending a seminar. He was mildly concerned, but not inclined to come home for the surgery. He said it sounded like it wasn't a huge deal, since they hadn't operated immediately and weren't planning on keeping him overnight."

"I'd have flipped out."

"I did. I told him Gabe was going under anesthesia, which was dangerous and his son having surgery is more important than picking up information. It went downhill from there."

"I can imagine. Men are slime."

"After I finished talking with the nurse, Gabe wandered in, located the mint chocolate chip ice cream, and pointed at it."

"You give him ice cream for breakfast?" Monica said incredulously.

"Of course not, but that doesn't stop the kid from asking. I explained we were going to the doctor, and the doctor said don't eat or drink until after the appointment. He shrugged and went down a notch on his food desirability hierarchy and asked for Doritos. I suggested we go out and swing."

"What did the neighbors think of you outside before daybreak, swinging?"

"I wouldn't have cared, but Gabe didn't go for it. He asked for nachos, which I usually go for."

"Nachos," Monica sounded intrigued, "for breakfast?"

"They're more nutritious than most cereals. Next he asked for leftover mac-n-cheese, and then plain cereal. I said he could have food later. He growled at me!"

Tori stretched, and then continued her narrative.

"I had an inspiration. I told him 'ice cream later . . . lots of ice cream with whipped cream and chocolate sauce.' That semi-pacified him, but he was back in fifteen minutes asking for water."

Tears spurted as Tori remembered the disbelief on Gabe's face when she told him he could not have water.

"Oh, no, what'd you do?"

> *In her mind, Tori saw Gabe scrunching his face up, really making an effort to pull out the correct, magic words.*

"May I have water, please?"

> *He'd strutted around the kitchen, proud of himself for retrieving the correct words.*

Tori winced at the memory, and continued. At least Monica was listening.

"I wanted to give in, but the nurse was clear. Something in his stomach might cause him to choke. I said no. Gabe threw himself to the floor: screamed, cried, yelled," she remembered. "When the tantrum didn't work he got up, walked over, and kicked my shin with all the strength his little Ked-shod foot could muster. Then he bit me."

Tori rubbed her arm. She could still remember the feeling, as if his teeth went clear to her bone.

"All Gabe saw was me denying him a basic necessity of life. He didn't trust me enough to know I'd never deny him something truly best for him in the long run."

Tori took a deep breath. Monica wasn't going to like this next part.

"Later it hit me—this is what God experiences. He knows what's best for us, overall, but we often can't accept that. We think He's denying us essential, good things; not realizing what we want could harm us. We lash out and throw tantrums. He loves us, anyway, and does what He knows needs to be done for our greater good."

Monica was silent for a long time.

"Oka-a-ay." Monica sighed. "I envy your faith, but I've become agnostic. This life stinks. God isn't doing anything to change it.

Hey, have to run, I'm at the office. Thanks for the pep talk. I'll think about it."

Monica clicked off. Tori returned to the abandoned mound of laundry.

Unfortunately, in a few days Tori had forgotten all her good advice to Monica.

She had just left the home of a friend who had invited Lydia to go roller skating with her son, Wyatt, and a group of friends. Tori had mentioned Gabe loved roller skating and asked if she and Gabe could come.

"It'll give him the illusion he's going on an outing with his sister and her friends, which would be really good for him. Of course, we'd pay our own way and wouldn't barge in . . ."

Sandy had looked embarrassed. An awkward pause followed.

"Well, I don't think that would work out very well this time. Wyatt adores Lydia, but . . . well . . . he's . . . well . . . uncomfortable around Gabe. Quite honestly, I think he'd pitch a fit if Gabe was included. You understand."

Tori lied and said she did. Yet, later that week, as she drove Lydia to Wyatt's house for the party, Gabe said, "Gabe skate?"

"No, honey, I'm sorry. Maybe next time; this is Wyatt's party—for Lydia and other friends his age."

"Wyatt and Gabe and Lydia and Mama?"

"The party's not for you!" Lydia snapped.

"You might try to be a little more sympathetic," Tori said as she dropped Lydia off.

"I'm sorry, Mom, but you always try to include Gabe in everything. I want my own friends. Gabe, I'll take you skating next week, okay?"

"Lydia and Wyatt and Gabe next week?"

"No! Just us!" Lydia whirled and went into the house.

Tori's fists clenched on the steering wheel; she wanted to do something to protect Gabe from his heart. Instead, she drove him to speech therapy. As she watched him walk away with his therapist, head down, her heart blistered.

Gabe wanted friends so badly, but kids thought he was strange. Parents didn't usually try to correct their perspective.

There was a small lake across from the speech center, circled by a walking path. Tori put on the shoes she usually carried in her car and loped across the street. As she walked, she mentally chastised various people, telling them all the things she had thought of saying once the moment was past.

There was Stephanie, who had justified her daughter, Ariane's, rudeness at Gabe's abortive attempt to play with her.

"Well, Tori, I'm sorry Gabe's feelings were hurt. I'm sure Ariane didn't mean to imply she didn't want to play with Gabe."

"'Go away, you're weird, I don't like you, and I don't want to play with you' doesn't exactly lend itself to misinterpretation."

That's what Tori should have said.

"Tommy's a sensitive child, you know. He's not comfortable with taking risks. I need to respect that boundary for him; don't you think so?" Becka had asked.

Tori had the perfect reply—now.

"Actually, Becka, I *don't* understand how excusing one child's rudeness to another is productive. Gabe risked asking Tommy to play. He didn't ask very well—taking Tommy by the arm and dragging him to the swing set isn't exactly smooth, but Tommy's eleven. He's old enough to make allowances for differences. How about teaching him respect for Gabe's vulnerability?"

Yes, that would've been the perfect comeback.

Tori's brain was a gerbil, running increasingly faster on the wheel of remembered slights. Their perpetrators were censured, their ugliness and hypocrisy annihilated in retrospect, with pithy, scathing phrases. On a roll with posthumous wrath, she turned her resentment on God Himself.

It crossed her mind she ought to hold back, but God already knew what she was thinking.

Look, God, we could use a break. Haven't we been through enough? You put this let's create a family idea into my head. I gave up a comfortable, easy lifestyle and a flourishing career to adopt these children. We're approaching middle-age. When we decided I'd stop working, we knew we were kissing early retirement goodbye.

Tori's mouth felt dry. She paused for a moment, and took a big swig of Vanilla Zero.

Yum, good stuff, even lukewarm.

She ignored the quiet voice that suggested her mouth was dry because she was trekking though dangerous, arid territory. The path was becoming crowded, so Tori got into her car, and continued her conversation with God.

You said adopt so we didn't try fertility drugs or invitro. You led us to go international—we signed up with a global adoption agency. You said get older kids, so we forgot babies. You said take two instead of one; we started on the Noah track, bought two of everything.

The quiet voice was almost indistinguishable now, though she thought she heard the faint reprimand: *ingratitude.*

*Father, we **do** love them, thank You very much, really. I mean that. But don't You think You went a little overboard with the complications? Going overnight from being DINKs to one-income parents of toddlers wasn't easy. Having kids with no idea of who we were or what a family was would have been challenging even without other issues. We expected learning difficulties and developmental delays, and we got them. Surely, all together that was enough. Did You need to throw autism into the pot, and give my son longings for friendships no one wants to have with him?*

No answer. Tori's palms began to sweat. She went on, anyway.

You and I both know You could heal Gabe—why won't You?

God spoke in an internal tornado, the roar more felt than heard; a quiet, ominous, *Are you finished?*

Usually, when Tori felt God speak it was with love and understanding; sometimes gently chiding, but always patient and affirming. This time though, she felt a minute fraction of the wrath of Holy God. The huge presence seared her mind with clearly realized words, filling her to the exclusion of anything, but listening. Emotionally, she stretched out on her face, unable to move.

What exactly have you given up that I did not first give you?

The beautiful, terrible voice sliced through her complaints like a well-honed blade.

Who blessed you with everything you're whining about losing? You've had a good education, a comfortable lifestyle, affirming friends, a successful career, and fifteen carefree years for you and your husband to lavish on each other.

*You had a good childhood, with enough trouble mixed in to make you strong. I **chose** you before the beginning of time to be Mine. Do you **dare** to tell me I have not arranged your life to your satisfaction?*

Tori's teeth began to chatter. Her soul mourned, *I'm sorry.*

God responded gently as Tori scrunched into a ball, wishing she could melt into the car's leather.

There is no need to hide from me, child, and no way to do so. I've given you the opportunity to make a radical difference in the lives of two of my precious children. The delight of their love will be yours eternally. The pain of parenting them will chisel away your flaws and carve you into the beautiful, perfect creature I designed.

You've asked me to help you grow. I'm giving you far above the best you could have imagined when you asked.

A hot, dry wind whipped Tori's hair about her face, even though the car was shut off, and the windows were closed. The volume of His message rose.

Have I made a mistake? Are the children I entrusted to you unsuitable? Are their needs inconvenient and disruptive to the life I've given you, or will you carry them with you to new heights?

"My life is Yours; their needs are my privilege," Tori whispered, "please forgive me."

Instantly the hot wind was gone. A fresh breeze dried the sweat on her face. Tori sensed soft, melodious music, which caressed her arms, wrapped itself around her, lifted her back into a sitting position, and spoke with dancing tones and crystal notes.

*I know you hurt for Gabe. Remember, he is under My care. The path you walk isn't easy, but from those to whom much is given, much is required. I will equip you and Phillip to be My instruments as **I** raise your children.*

There was a long silence. Tori thought it was over, but then she sensed a final bit of affectionate advice.

Negative emotions such as self-pity and anger form black holes, which suck away perspective. They drain you of the ability to be aware of My provisions. They deplete you of thankfulness. Ingratitude erases My peace.

Then His voice was gone.

Tori picked Gabe up from therapy and drove home thinking. There were people who were insensitive and uninformed about special needs, but there were also people who cared deeply and people who were willing to learn.

She applauded the neighbor who invited Gabe to her son's birthday party and asked what foods he could eat. She thought of her sister, who, although she was older than Tori—and long finished with child rearing—had given up several days of vacation, so Tori and Phillip could go to the beach for a long weekend without the children.

Soberly, Tori thought of the burden carried by single parents and thanked God she could be a stay at home mother.

Finally, she remembered with horror the words spoken by Hannah Winter, an acquaintance from Grace Fellowship's special needs support group.

"There's no future. Someday, I'll have the courage to kill my son, and then kill myself. That's the only way this hopelessness and pain will end."

Overcome, Hannah got up, nodded to the room, and left. Soberly, the moderator, Angelique, had spoken.

"Sadly, what Hannah has expressed is not uncommon. According to studies, the percentage of parents who contemplate suicide is higher among parents of children with autism than it is for parents with terminally-ill children."

She paused and looked searchingly around the room.

"I'll encourage Hannah to get professional help. If *anyone* here feels the same way, please let us know. We're here to help each other, and to remind each other there is hope."

Remembering the incident, Tori spoke to herself.

"I don't always understand God, but His ways and thoughts are higher than my ways and thoughts. I *do* believe in an afterlife; one where Gabe will be perfect. I've been desperate, but **never** as desperate as Hannah."

Tori continued to mull over the things for which she was grateful. By the time she pulled into the garage she realized, once again, God was right. Releasing anger and counting blessings gave one an accurate perspective on life.

The minute she pulled into the garage, Gabe dashed out and tugged her toward the kitchen.

"You didn't lose dessert, Mama!" he said anxiously.

"No, Gabe, you didn't lose dessert."

"Gabe gets mint chocolate chip ice cream."

"Mom," Lydia screeched. "The mint chocolate chip is mine! Remember, he got Chocolate Cherries Jubilee, an' he ate it all an' now he wants to eat mine. It's not *fair*!"

"Gabe gets mint chocolate chip ice cream!"

"He does not! I mean, *you* do not!" Lydia said indignantly. "Oh, Mom, I forgot to tell you, Amber yakked up a hairball on the new sweater Daddy had lying flat on the guest room bed."

"How long has it been there?"

"A week or two, I guess."

"Why didn't you clean it up, or at least tell me? Daddy's going to have a *fit*!"

"Ooh, gross; *I'm* not cleaning it up! She's your cat."

Tori sighed deeply.

It's good. It's all good.

CHAPTER 18

Conflict of Interest

Wednesday morning, after one of Gabe's long, sleepless nights, the phone rang as Tori, exhausted, staggered downstairs with an overflowing laundry basket. She dropped the basket at the foot of the stairs, leapt over Amber, who was stretched across the doorway of her office, and grabbed the phone.

"Hi, Tori, Susan Anderson."

"Hi, Susan, what's up?"

Tori twiddled with her hair as Susan explained she was the co-ordinator of a state-wide support group Parents of Special Families, PSF. The support group wanted Tori to speak from a layman's point-of-view about dealing with insurance companies. Tori loved speaking. Feedback forms indicated the audiences loved her informative, yet humorous style.

Hmm, split ends. My hair's long past needing a trim.

To her surprise, she got a lump in her throat, remembering how she used to entrust her curly mane to none, but the best salons.

Phillip used to love my hair. I need to make some money. This'll be the third time I've spoken this year. Unpaid. Hmm. Maybe I can do something with that.

"I'd like to develop a *paid* speaking career."

"We don't have the money to pay you, but we'll recommend you as a speaker," Susan said, coaxing, "Besides, we'll give you double respite spots this year. Guaranteed, no waiting list, you pick the date."

Tori drummed her fingers on the low-tech desk calendar she preferred to use. Most of the blocks were jam-packed. Phillip complained the house was messy and unorganized. She had set aside the weekend of the seminar for long-overdue spring cleaning. When would she prepare a talk? Still. Each PSF family was given three five-hour block blocks of qualified child-care per year.

Three extra respite slots? Priceless.

She would make it work; somehow.

"You're pandering to my weak spot," Tori grumbled. "Okay."

Tori crossed out spring-cleaning, scribbled in the seminar dates, and ran her fingers through her hair. Phillip was not going to be pleased.

"But how can I not do this?"

Tori paced back and forth, arms crossed, rehearsing her upcoming discussion with Phillip.

"God put us on this path for a reason. Can we refuse to help parents struggling up the road a few miles behind us?"

She flung her arms out passionately.

"How much would it have meant if someone had given *us* the benefit of their experience? Besides, it's a creative outlet for me."

Sure Phillip would have to agree, Tori ended her one-sided debate and walked into the foyer to retrieve the laundry.

Besides, who's he to complain about my workload?

"Really, though, Tori," she said, scolding her reflection in the entryway mirror, "you need to pay more attention to your family, the house, and yourself."

Her reflection nodded, abashed. Resolved to do better on the homemaker front, Tori headed for the laundry room.

"I'll call the gym today," she informed Amber, stepping over the sleeping cat. "No, wait. Better to start at the beginning of the month. I'll take brisk walks until then."

Humming, Tori set her basket down by the washing machine, opened the freezer door, and pulled out a package of shredded rotisserie chicken. She would make chicken tortilla casserole, one of Phillip's favorites.

She went to the kitchen and opened the refrigerator door. *Hmm. Out of lite cheddar. No problem. Normal cheddar will work if I blot the oil.*

Tori checked the pantry.

Uh oh. No cream of chicken soup, either high- or low-fat. There was cream of mushroom. Tori was the only one in the family who appreciated the tasty fungi, so she would have to pick out the mushrooms.

I really need to get to the store.

Gabe loved to grocery shop, but taking Gabe felt like taking a ravenous goat, without a rope. On a good day, when she had time to contain and re-direct Gabe, they both enjoyed it. If she waited until Gabe got home from school though, there would not be time to slow cook the casserole. She bent and pulled tortillas from the lower bin of the refrigerator.

Ugh. They aren't supposed to be green. I wonder if they could pass for spinach tortillas.

Tori's effort to spread the mold evenly for an overall green effect was a dismal failure.

"Three strikes and I'm out," she told Amber, who sat on the counter observing her mistress with unblinking eyes. "I'll make tortilla casserole tomorrow. Tonight, we're having . . ."

Amber jumped to the floor and wound in and out of Tori's legs, meowing insistently.

"*Not* tuna casserole," Tori scolded. "You know Daddy doesn't like canned tuna."

Amber's answering mewl sounded sarcastic. "I agree, he doesn't deserve it, but I've decided to take the high road, meet him more than half-way."

Tori rummaged through the freezer and found a container of homemade bison chili.

"Aha! Add a salad, and voila, dinner. Life is good," she mused as she headed back to her PC, leaving the basket of dirty clothes abandoned on the laundry room floor. "I don't need anti-depressants."

At Phillip's office, the bid was going well. He looked with approval at Delia's concise analysis.

"These are awesome!" He pumped his fist.

Delia flashed him a brilliant smile.

"Thanks, boss," she said teasingly.

She turned back to the flow-chart she had been studying, bending over the desk to examine a diagram. Her low cut silk shirt revealed smooth, perky breasts, scantily contained by a wisp of lace. Phillip tore his eyes away.

Great with numbers and gorgeous with it!

His eyes strayed.

Delia looked up and caught him staring. She smiled slowly at him, tossed back her mane of blonde-silvery hair, and stood, arching her back.

"I've been sitting too long."

She turned and stretched, showing him a firm little rear.

She's wearing a thong, if she's wearing anything.

Phillip swallowed.

"Hey, it's dinner-time," Delia said, looking at her slim gold watch.

Phillip looked at his watch and groaned. Eight forty-five. He had promised to be home early.

"Ahh, man! By the time I get home, I'll have missed dinner."

"Yeah, it's late for the little lady and kids. Let's grab a bite at Galiano's."

"Um, better not."

He left, taking the stairs. When he reached the parking lot he called Tori.

"Hi, Munchkin. I'm leaving."

"You're just now leaving? It'll be at least an hour before you're home! I made a nice dinner: bison chili with salad fresh from Serena's garden."

"I'm sorry. I completely lost track of time. Are the kids still up?"

"You know Gabe didn't sleep last night. He was gone an hour ago. Lydia's sleeping over at Susan's. I'd planned for us to have some alone time."

"I'm sorry."

Chapter 18 – Conflict of Interest

"Oh, never mind!" Tori snapped. "Dinner's on the stove."

"Not the salad, I hope?" Phillip joked, hoping to lighten the mood.

"In the fridge with your favorite homemade vinaigrette." Tori disconnected, not quite slamming the phone. Phillip thought wistfully about the lobster lasagna at Galiano's as he headed home to a cold dinner and, he feared, an even colder wife.

Tori rubbed the back of her neck. She had run to the market for fresh raspberries and made corn muffins from scratch. She followed the sound of sultry jazz to the dining room. Unlit vanilla candles waited to release their seductive smell and cast soft light on her best china and crystal. Tori snatched up a shimmering goblet and threw it across the room. It shattered with a satisfying crash.

No more trying to please the man.

Crystal crunched under delicate strappy heels as Tori swept glass into a dust-pan. The table could wait until tomorrow. She trudged upstairs and changed out of her low-cut, clingy red dress.

Phillip arrived home to a dark house. As he headed upstairs, he felt something crunch under his feet. Puzzled, he turned on the light in the foyer. It looked like a piece of crystal. He glanced over at the dining room and saw the romantically set table. He frowned.

Looks like I blew a romantic evening. It seems I'm not picking up on Tori's signals anymore.

"Maybe," a quiet voice said, "it's because you're too busy imagining what Delia is wearing under her business suits."

Any red-blooded male would notice Delia. I haven't done anything about it, that's what counts.

"How long will that last?" the voice responded.

Phillip ignored it.

The next morning when her alarm went off, Tori slapped the snooze button and missed, knocking the clock off the bedside table. She burrowed back under the covers, but the drone of the buzzing alarm penetrated the snug haven, whining insistently that a new day expected her to rise and work.

Tori dragged herself to her feet. Phillip was long gone, of course. As she stretched, she caught the stench of burnt sugar. Seconds later the fire alarm went off. Thundering down the stairs, Tori saw Lydia poking a smoking mound in the microwave.

Jumping onto a stool to wave a dish cloth in front of the screeching alarm, Tori let loose a torrent of invective.

"Lydia! How many times have I told you to take the cinnamon rolls out of the foil pan *before* you nuke it? I have enough problems without your carelessness!"

"I'm sorry, I forgot. I was trying to get my own breakfast because—"

"Mama?" Gabe stood in the doorway, rubbing sleep from his eyes.

Tori snarled, "Go back to bed!"

She turned on Lydia.

"Now, look what you've done! The stupid fire alarm woke your brother an hour early! Go to your room immediately!"

"But I need to be to school early for a mid-term review."

"Then why aren't you getting ready? Go! Leave!"

"I was trying . . , oh, never mind. And by the way, Gabe's upstairs crying. I think you scared him. *He's* not used to being yelled at."

Lydia slunk toward the door. Looking at her daughter's slumped shoulders, Tori was overcome with remorse. She ran after Lydia and hugged her.

"I'm sorry, Sweetheart; I didn't mean to scream."

Lydia pulled away.

"You're acting weird lately. Are you sick or something?"

She stomped to the door. Tori burst into tears. Lydia hesitated, came back, and patted Tori's shoulder.

"It's okay, Mom. Maybe you're hormonal. I'll turn on the teakettle. Make yourself some tea. I've gotta go or I'll be late."

Phillip called a few minutes later.

"Hi, Hon. Listen, I'm really sorry about last night. Delia brought good news just as I was about to leave. Then she had a question. We started working on it, and . . . you know how it goes. I *was* intending to be home for dinner. I miss seeing you and the kids."

Tori was slightly mollified. How many times in her business career had she got caught up in a work issue and ended up working until all hours?

"Okay. What was the good news?"

"Delia got rid of Stuart. He's been transferred to another department."

"What happened?"

"We planted some fake information with Stuart, to see if it'd show up next with Sniderleigh. It did, which gives us a pretty good indication Stuart passed it to him. Delia took the facts to Gina Ballante. It wasn't concrete enough to fire him, but Delia made sure he got put somewhere he couldn't do us any more harm." Phillip's voice was filled with admiration. "You don't mess with Delia. She handles things."

"A new Tiny Terror, huh?"

"What?"

Phillip sounded confused. It was obvious he didn't remember it had been Tori's idea to catch Stuart by planting fake information.

"Never mind. Glad Delia's so sharp."

Later that day, Tori filled her anti-depressant prescription.

CHAPTER 19

Everyone Has Something

Frustration fueled Phillip's steps as he jogged. Before he knew it, he had burned three miles of sidewalk without relieving his irritation.

Phillip had gone to lunch with a close friend, Rick. They were in a Bible study together, although Phillip had not attended in months. He scowled, feet hammering the pavement as he recalled their discussion.

The smell of grease and onions coated the air with comfort. Laughter and jukebox tunes complemented the robust aroma of the barbeque sauce that made Smokin' Ribs an Atlanta landmark and Rick's favorite restaurant. Last time Phillip had chosen a vegetarian deli called the Roasted Couscous.

Their booth was quiet despite the surrounding hubbub. Rick gnawed his last rib and dragged a fry through ketchup.

"Good to see you. You haven't been around much."

Phillip forked up a mouthful of baked sweet potato. "Mm, this, at least, is edible. My napkin probably has more flavor than this fish."

"What do you expect when you order baked fish in a barbeque joint? So, anything special happening these days?"

"Nothing much. I'm working a big bid with an executive from marketing. It's a huge opportunity. Stiff competition, a lot of custom work, late hours. You know the drill."

Rick chewed on a toothpick and considered Phillip.

"Your exec wouldn't happen to be a sexy blonde, would she?" He raised an eyebrow.

"I suppose Delia's reasonably attractive, yes," Phillip hedged. "But it's business."

Rick works nearby; should have known he was bound to see us.

"Give me a break! I've seen you with your reasonably attractive co-worker a few times lately. She's hot. People are talking."

Phillip pushed his plate aside.

"You're listening to gossip now?"

"I wouldn't give it much credence," Rick replied, "if I hadn't seen you yesterday at Daley's, tucked away in a cozy back booth. Didn't look much like *my* business meetings. You're playing with fire, buddy."

"It's legit; back off. I haven't done and don't plan to do anything wrong."

Rick held out placating palms.

"Fine."

"Good."

Phillip waved his water glass at a passing waitress.

"I'm just sayin' . . . Tori wouldn't have liked what I saw yesterday."

"You saw nothing!" Phillip retorted.

Rick had dropped it then, but the conversation had left Phillip feeling angry and uneasy.

People are talking?

The anti-depressants helped Tori. She no longer burst into tears at the slightest provocation. She was also able to be amused, rather than be despairing, about Gabe's apparent logic: I'm supposed to clean up my messes. So, if I spill milkshake on Amber and she starts cleaning herself, I should help her lick it off.

Despite the medicine, though, she remained prone to negative emotions that zeroed in like stealth bombers, blasting her peace without warning. Ugly, green-eyed envy slammed her when she saw a mother and son bantering back and forth. The thought

Gabe might never attend college dyed her world black when she saw an email announcing a new company scholarship plan for employees' children.

Hot blue kaleidoscope shards of anger burst in her brain when children mocked Gabe's intense study of the reflective lights on a bicycle. Humiliation painted every cell in her body fluorescent red, when Gabe trumpeted "I have to go poopy!" in the middle of an upscale restaurant.

Fury's orange flames warred with murky brown despair when Lydia told Gabe, "Stop being weird! You're embarrassing me!" Gray loneliness locked her into solitary confinement when she heard about another neighborhood get-together to which they had not been invited.

Today was one of those days, in one of those weeks, during one of those months. She was attempting to pray her way out of the doldrums.

"Hey, Lord, I'm struggling here! I don't want to feel this way, but I do. Hello? Help!"

No answer. God often answered by opening Tori's eyes to hidden humor or a previously unnoticed accomplishment. Like the sherbet incident.

They had been at the dollar store, running an hour behind schedule as usual, when Gabe discovered the new frozen section and recognized an immediate need for sherbet. Tori agreed to buy some.

She then made the mistake of asking, "Lemon or raspberry?"

Five minutes later Gabe had not made a decision.

Breaking Phillip's mandate of only one sugary treat at a time, Tori said, "Look, just get one of each, okay?"

Gabe looked at her in surprise, and then, to Tori's astonishment, said, "All *right,* girlfriend, you da bomb!"

Delighted, Tori touched fists with him. She had heard Gabe parrot jargon before, but had never realized he could use it appropriately. The knowledge propelled her from dejection to celebration.

Unfortunately, today God's answer was not as obvious.

One of Tori's favorite psalms asked, *"Why so downcast, oh, my soul?"*

She addressed her negative emotions by gritting her teeth and saying with the psalmist, "I know I will yet praise Him in the land of the living."

However, several days of frustration had piled up. Tori did not feel relief well up in her heart as she read King David's optimistic psalm.

She was tempted to search out one of David's more militant psalms as a prayer model instead. It would be nice to ask God, as David often had, to rain down poverty, pain, and death on her enemies. People like the karate instructor who would not give Gabe a trial.

Were David in Tori's shoes, she felt sure the shepherd-king, whom God called a man after His own heart, would call down plagues on insurance companies seemingly delighted to deny treatment on the flimsiest of excuses.

Remembering God's dealings with Egypt, she mused that flea infestation would be appropriate for state agencies, which changed rules in midstream. Swarming locusts would be suitable for bureaucrats who created layers of officialdom between children and needed therapies, generating a jungle of red tape that only the most resolute of guardians could hack through.

Tori was content to piously pray the offenders would see the error of their ways, preferably in a manner that overwhelmed them with agonizing remorse. Tori looked out the window at the beautiful day and decided a sun-filled walk might burn away her shadows. Heather, a neighbor, agreed to join her. They set off at a brisk pace.

"I saw your car at school yesterday," Heather said, "but I never ran into you."

Tori explained she had gone to scold Gabe, who had decided urinating in the trashcan during homeroom was amusing.

"It was his second time. After the first incident, the teachers reprimanded Gabe, and then had him pretend to clean it up. I told them to forget pretending. He hates to wear rubber gloves, and can't stand the smell of bleach cleaners, so hopefully he's cured.

Their conversation became labored as they trudged uphill.

"I could never do what you do," Heather huffed. "I mean, I think I'd just suck my thumb and wait for someone to take me away. Weren't you totally embarrassed?"

"Not really. Something worse happened to my friend, Monica. She was in her favorite grocery store with her daughter, Song, who's nine years old. Song walked up to a well-endowed matron, grabbed one breast in each hand, squeezed, and said, 'beep, beep!'"

Heather gasped; eyes wide.

"Monica," Tori mused, "doesn't own a sense of humor. She left a full grocery cart in the middle of the canned goods aisle, made a bee-line for her car, and hasn't shopped there since."

Tori stuffed her hair under her ball cap.

"Whew. Hot."

She glanced at her friend out of the corner of her eye and decided Heather could stand one more story.

"My personal worst was at Phillip's family reunion last year. One of his nephews, Garrett, is obese. We were about to pray before lunch, so everyone was quiet. Gabe looked at Garrett and very loudly asked, 'Is a baby in tummy?' It may have been forgiven in a toddler, but in a boy almost ten, not so much."

Heather snickered.

"Well, all I can say is, Gabe and Lydia are lucky to have you."

Tori blushed, remembered the thoughts she had been wallowing in all morning.

"I'm not unusual. You lost your twin sister to breast cancer three years ago; you yourself just went through a double mastectomy. You know Bill Parker, lives two blocks over in the stone house?"

Heather nodded.

"Yeah. Single dad, great guy; adores his daughter."

"She ran away six months ago with a skuzzy boyfriend. She's only fourteen. No trace of them."

Heather gasped, "Oh, no!"

Tori nodded and continued.

"Then, there's my cousin, Phyllis. She's been widowed fifteen years. Her father-in-law, who's lived with her for twelve of those years, has developed dementia. She adores him, but had to commit him to assisted living. He cries like a baby every time she visits, begging her to take him home. I fight bouts of self-pity, but in my rational moments, I've come to the conclusion that everybody's dealing with something."

Tori wiped sweat from her brow.

"Gabe and Lydia aren't the easiest children in the world, but they're not the hardest, either. They've brought joy and depth to our lives. I wouldn't want to go through what you experienced, but look what you've accomplished through it. How much money did you raise with the Breast Cancer walk?"

"Nineteen thousand dollars."

Tori gave her a high five.

"You rock!"

They finished a two-mile circuit around the neighborhood, ending in front of Tori's garage.

"Here," Tori said, opening the garage refrigerator, "hydrate before you go."

She tossed Heather a bottle of water.

"Thanks. I still think you're the best, though. I know people hurt you sometimes, about Gabe. Cancer didn't make people reject me." Heather took a swig of water. "You always seem to be smiling, though. Don't people make you mad?"

"I was wishing plagues of locusts on some people just a few hours ago." Tori traced a finger through the condensation on her water bottle. "If I had thunderbolts at my fingertips, my initial reactions would atomize some people. Fortunately, for them, what I do have at my finger-tips, most of the time, is a pen. So, I let my ire out by drawing ugly pictures of them."

Heather grinned.

"I saw the picture you drew of that policeman who gave you a speeding ticket. Amazing, the way you made him look like a Gestapo agent."

"I was only going ten miles over!" Tori tilted her water bottle at Heather. "He was obviously trying to fill a quota. Anyway, I've realized most people aren't mean; just un-informed. They're uncertain of how to deal with Gabe's issues."

Tori wiped sweat off her face with her T-shirt.

"The people who've dealt with significant pain in their own lives are usually the ones most willing to show compassion to someone else. Before Gabe, I didn't have any more empathy for special needs than the next person. Plenty of people reach out to us. You and Andy took the kids last month, so Phillip and I could have a date night."

Heather smiled.

"It was fun; I'd like to do it again."

Heather drained her water.

"I'd better go; I have a million errands. Thanks for calling!"

Tori waved as Heather jogged off. She went inside, smiling. She realized her moroseness was vanquished, at least for now.

The negativity demons were riding Monica relentlessly. Tori was making chili when her high-strung friend called. Tori listened and stirred as Monica fumed that Song's yearlong stint of oxygen therapy had not helped.

"Two hours a day, five days a week for a year in a hyperbaric oxygen chamber. Nothing changed; nothing. Waste of money and time."

The sound of Monica's cigarette-rasped voice conjured up the image of her haggard face.

"I'm sorry it didn't work. At least Song's autism is stable. She's no worse."

"Maintaining the status quo is unacceptable, don't you see? If our kids aren't moving forward, they're going backwards. Song's thirteen, Gabe's ten. They need to make progress."

"Or what; we'll turn them in for a new model? Song and Gabe are healthy and seem happy. That's a lot to be thankful for."

"Don't start with the thankfulness routine. Why should I thank God for a daughter who isn't normal, doesn't make progress, and will never live a typical, happy life?"

Goose pimples rose on Tori's arm.

"I know you love Song. Why are you talking like she's unacceptable?"

Without thinking, Tori dumped more chili powder into the pot.

"Song's not unacceptable; her situation is. I'll see she gets better—whatever it takes."

"What'll you try next?"

Gabe had about exhausted all the available treatments, too. "Stem cell replacement. You know—when they harvest healthy stem cells and introduce them into the child. They've seen phenomenal results."

"Whoa! It's not approved here, last I heard. And isn't it amazingly expensive?"

"We're going to Germany. It'll cost about thirty thousand dollars. My parents set up a college account for Song when she was born. I'm using that money. I'll worry about college later."

"But . . . what if it doesn't work? You may need that money for Song when she's an adult."

"If this doesn't work, money won't be an issue."

Tori was puzzled by the comment, but Monica's next question distracted her.

"Do you ever have a normal day?"

"What do you mean?" Tori questioned as she inhaled sizzling chili vapor.

Hot!

"A day where no weird special needs thing happens."

Just then Gabe came in.

"Want ice cream!"

"Not before dinner," Tori said absently.

"Well, I think—ouch! Gabe just pinched me and ran out of the room. He asks for ice cream, I say no. It's tradition. What the heck was he thinking?"

Tori rubbed her thigh and glared at Gabe's retreating back.

"See, that's what I mean. Our kids and, therefore, our lives are unpredictable."

"No one's life is predictable."

"True, but I want predictable unpredictability. Like, surprise, Song is failing math. Not surprise, Song went up to a strange family and took a toddler's ice cream cone."

Monica was always intense, but there was desperation in her voice today. Tori visualized Monica sucking on her cigarette, worry lines rippling across her forehead.

"You seem to become calmer, more balanced every year, Tori. Is it because your life is easier? Are you having normal days; days when you're not fretting about Gabe's future, times when you're relatively, well . . . content?"

"I do have days like that, yes."

"How? My life is a series of one disappointment after another. I want . . . I need for Song and me to have normal lives someday."

"I used to paint, Monica, did you know that?"

"No, but what—?"

"Even when I was in business, averaging sixty hour weeks, I painted watercolors. Nothing special, but they were a creative outlet. I painted because I didn't want my life to be defined by my career. I stopped shortly after the kids got here."

The door slammed. Lydia was home. Tori smiled and pointed to a bowl, which was full of hard, crunchy apples. Lydia bit into one, and left with a wave of her hand.

"The other day I realized I was defining myself by Gabe. If Gabe had a good day, life was good. If a promising therapy failed, even my gardenias smelled like garbage."

Tori stirred her chili and hoped her speech, which she had shared with Seth a few days ago, would encourage Monica like it had Seth.

"I've decided I'm more than Tori St. John—special needs parent, mother, and wife. Those are the most important parts of my life, but they're not *me*. I can't base my level of contentment on how those roles are going."

Over the phone came the sound of something hitting the floor and a burst of profanity.

"Sorry, Tori, knocked over an ashtray. So, you're saying I should take up a hobby?"

"I'm saying life could be normal if you'd stop defining happiness by whether Song's improving or not. Can't you just enjoy yourself and Song as you are in this moment?"

"How is that an answer?"

Tori pretended her chili represented Monica's stubbornness and stirred hard, trying to break down her friend's resistance. Monica inhaled a lungful of smoke, and then continued.

"Normal is . . . well . . . normal. Abnormal isn't. Give me an example of how you can take pleasure in Gabe's abnormality."

"Okay, hold on."

Tori gave her chili a final stir, turned the heat down, and covered it.

"Here goes. When I choose my own standards of what's normal or accept the world's definition of happiness, life is pretty bad. On those days—at best—I miss moments of joy and laughter God has for me. At worst, I'm down-in-the-dumps miserable and have trouble functioning."

"Don't shoot religious sunshine up my derriere."

"It's not sunshine; it's part of who I am. Do you want to hear the example or not?"

"I guess."

"I was in an IEP, no big issues. We were discussing the goal for Gabe to use correct and appropriate language." Tori chuckled. "I asked if Gabe had been using the words 'wee wee penis' at school to express extreme dislike of something."

Monica hooted, "Wee wee penis?"

"Yes, can you believe it? Here's what the speech therapist said: 'We were practicing table manners at breakfast on Monday, in a social group with typical kids. I forgot to tell the regular education kids Gabe despises bread. One sweet, well-mannered young lady offered him a plate of toast.' She asked, 'Gabe, would you care for toast?' He said, 'No. That's wee wee penis toast!'"

Monica gasped, choking back laughter.

"The poor girl! He *didn't* say that!"

"He most certainly did. So, anyway, all of us are dying laughing. After a bit, we got control of ourselves and soberly agreed wee wee penis was an inappropriate phrase and Gabe would be encouraged to express disapproval another way. The meeting dragged on. Finally, I said we really needed to wrap it up."

She continued, "The therapist replied, 'Yes. I need to get home and pay my wee wee penis bills!'"

Monica laughed, and then started coughing.

"You do live the life."

"Wee wee penis isn't normal by the world's standards, but we had fun with it."

"You're a better woman than I am. I'd prefer normality via stem cell replacement."

"Well, I'll be praying it works. When are you going?"

"Not for a few months. I'll keep you posted. Gotta run. Bye."

The conversation with Monica revived Tori's fears. Dread about her beautiful, wonderful, trusting son encountering a pedophile or a murderer someday when she and Phillip were not around to protect him. She agonized about Gabe's uncertain middle and high school options. She panicked as she remembered the price tag for the type of group home they would like an adult Gabe to live in. She experienced troubled projections of a grown up Lydia, who might be unwilling or unable to take the same loving care of Gabe that her parents had.

Impatiently, Tori pushed the thoughts away. Gabe *was* improving. He was only ten and a half. Scientists were bound to discover, if not a cure, at least something to minimize the symptoms. Gabe would be able to live a relatively normal life. It was only a matter of time and perseverance.

Chapter 20
Painful Transitions

The ringing phone jabbed like a knife into Tori's stomach. Gabe had seemed out of sorts this morning, and he'd been aggressive lately.

"Hello."

It was the school. Tammy, the nurse at Creekside Elementary, sounded harassed.

"Hello, Tori? Gabe doesn't feel well and he's upset."

"Does he have a temp?"

"No." Tammy's voice raised three octaves. "He punched Antonio!"

Antonio's his favorite aide. This is bad.

"On my way!"

Phillip looked up as Tori flew by.

"What's up?"

"Trouble . . . I'm headed to school."

Phillip sighed. He was working at home to avoid distractions—like Delia. He had taken off work too often to help with Gabe. He hoped Tori could handle it this time. The Racoby proposal had been submitted, and they were fielding questions. Racoby's consultant, Dick Sniderleigh, was trying every trick in the book to eliminate them. Phillip and Delia were scrambling.

A policeman waited for Tori outside the school. Her heart sank.

Oh, yeah, this is really bad.

The clinic hallway was shut off. Gabe's frantic screams reverberated through the solid oak door. The receptionist hit her intercom.

"Gabe's mom is here."

The principal, Mrs. Knarr, barged through the doors.

"Is Mr. St. John available? Our resource officers are helping, but I'd rather a parent restrain him. I doubt you're strong enough to handle Gabe today. We think Antonio's finger is broken."

Tori called Phillip while she sprinted toward the clinic.

"Come now!"

"Can it wait until I finish this round of questions? I'm approximately 79 percent done. I don't want to lose my train of thought."

"Broken bones and police. Get here!"

The clinic door was locked. Gabe's howls were background noise for what sounded like a dog fight. Something crashed inside. Mrs. Knarr pounded on the door.

"Gabe, your mom is here."

The door unlocked. Tori's boots crunched on shards of glass from a shattered vase, while crushed hyacinths emitted perfume incongruous with the scene that greeted her.

Gabe lay on his stomach, held down by another school policeman, his teacher Maggie, and the nurse. Gabe stopped struggling when he saw Tori.

"Hey, Darlin', what's wrong?" Tori crooned, stroking his head.

"Gabe was crying!" her son sobbed.

Tori rubbed Gabe's back.

"Everything's gonna be alright. Want me to sing?"

"No," he quavered. "He's be sweet boy, want up."

"Are you okay now?"

"Yes."

Gabe breathed rapidly, but lay quietly. Tori nodded to the adults. One-by-one, they loosened their grips.

Gabe sat up and made eye contact with Tori. His lunge knocked her down. Pandemonium ensued. Tori held her arms in front of her face as Gabe attacked again.

He acts possessed!

When Phillip ran in, three adults were holding Gabe's thrashing body, barely containing him. Tori had a hand imprint on her cheek and a bloody nose.

"Gabe, stop that this instant!" Phillip thundered.

Gabe froze.

"This is unacceptable." Phillip was implacable. "We're going home, you're going to bed, and you get *no dessert* for thirty-one days. Understand?"

Silence.

"Answer me! Do you understand?"

"Yes," Gabe spat.

"Yes?"

"Yes, *sir!*"

"Let him go."

Gabe's captors were doubtful, but slowly released him. Gabe was sullen, but passive. Phillip captured his arm.

Tori heaved a sigh of relief, but then Gabe ripped his arm from Phillip's grasp and attacked, his fingers extended like talons. Before anyone could intervene, blood spurted from Phillip's gouged face and Gabe dashed away.

Tearing after him, Phillip caught up, grabbed Gabe's arms, crossed them behind his back, and marched him toward the exit. Gabe was submissive for a few steps, and then stomped on Phillip's foot, and fell backward. Phillip caught him. They struggled, Gabe's head bobbing a few inches from the concrete floor.

"Watch his head, watch his head!" the nurse screamed, echoed by the principal.

Tori circled, looking for an opening to intervene, finding none.

Gabe fought like a cornered animal. His father wrestled him to the floor, but in the melee, Phillip's hand came within range of his son's mouth. Gabe sank crocodile teeth into Phillip's hand and held on with the tenacity of a starving lion. Blood oozed down his fingers as Phillip tried to break free.

Tori darted in, gripped Gabe's jaws, and squeezed until Phillip could wrench his hand free. Oblivious to the scarlet droplets splattering the floor, Phillip shook Gabe.

Bellowing in defiance, Gabe head-butted Phillip's stomach.

"Oof!"

Phillip tumbled backwards. Recovering, he pulled his arm back, fist clenched. The resource officer stepped forward. Tori grabbed Phillip's arm and yanked downward with phenomenal strength.

"Stop Phillip, no!"

Gabe, panting harshly, stopped brawling for a second. He was immediately immobilized by the officers.

Phillip's face drained as he realized how close he had come to punching Gabe. Together he and the policeman hustled Gabe to Phillip's car. Phillip bundled him into the back seat and jumped in behind his belligerent son, who was kicking and hitting.

"There's ammonium carbonate in the glove compartment, grab it!" Phillip screamed.

Tori rushed to the passenger side, dove into Phillip's eclectically-stocked glove box, and rummaged until she found the small bottle of smelling salts. Ripping it open, she leaned into the backseat, waving it under Gabe's nose. He slapped it away.

Small crystals rained throughout the car, but Gabe had gotten a big enough whiff to startle him into a momentary pause. Phillip seized the moment and pinned him.

"You think your husband's got him?" the resource officer asked. "I could follow you home."

Tori looked into the rear view mirror. Gabe was trapped, struggling like a fish in the net of his father's long arms and legs.

"No thank you, officer. We'll be fine."

Tori drove the short distance home listening to occasional scuffling sounds from the back seat. Fifteen minutes later, they sat, stunned, on the couch. Gabe's fit had subsided.

Gabe turned a tear-stained face to Tori.

"Mama!"

Tori tensed as Gabe flung his body at her. Poised for defense she hugged him tentatively, but Gabe's fight was gone. He wailed remorsefully.

"Sorry, you're sorry, not nice to bite and kick and scratch and bite and kick and slap."

As Tori rocked her son and listened to his abject regrets, she met Phillip's eyes.

"Get him another Sixtetra," she mouthed.

"We don't *do* that! That was naughty. He's going to be a *good* boy."

"You are a good boy, son," said Phillip. "We'll figure this out."

He left and came back with a glass of water and a pill, which Gabe swallowed obediently.

"I told Dr. Klein Gabe had gained weight and we needed to increase his dosage," Tori said, grinding her teeth. "She wanted to wait."

After more than an hour, Gabe's tears and piteous self-recriminations stopped.

"How about a little nap?" Tori suggested.

"Ok-a-ay." Gabe sniffled. "Then Gabe goes back to school?"

Their eyes met over Gabe's head.

"Not today, son." Phillip said.

"He *wants* to go school."

"Come on, let's get some rest." Phillip led Gabe up the stairs.

Dazed, Tori listened as Gabe anxiously repeated, "But he *wants* to go school."

She thanked God she had a supportive husband, and then cringed at the memory of Phillip's fist, poised to strike. She wondered if Gabe would be expelled. Her thoughts plunged into a vortex of fear and despair.

Phillip came downstairs. Desolation gloomed from his eyes.

"I'm sorry," he said before she could speak. "It was so intense; I felt like I was defending myself and you, and I couldn't control him and he was hurting everyone . . . he was as strong as a grown man."

He broke off. "I've apologized to him."

Lydia did a double take when she got home and saw them clinging to each other. A grin spread over her face.

"Hey, lovebirds." She noticed the tears. "What's wrong?"

"Your brother."

"What'd he do? Be really disobedient? Cool."

"It's not cool." Phillip stood. "He attacked . . . everybody at school today."

Lydia looked with interest at Phillip's bloody hand and Tori's swollen nose.

"Did Gabe do that? Whoo wee, he's like, majorly busted."

"Don't sound so pleased. I'm afraid he may be expelled."

Lydia spoke with the full authority of vast teen knowledge.

"Naw; he's special needs. He'd have to do something really bad first. Like drugs or a knife or sex in the supply room."

"They had a lock-down in the hallway he was in because they were afraid he'd hurt the other students." Phillip glowered at Lydia. "Is that bad enough for you?"

Lydia's pretty lips formed a round O.

"Is he in jail?"

"He's eleven. Of course he's not in jail," Tori said. "He's upstairs asleep. We're not mad at him—"

"What a surprise!" Lydia said, feigning shock.

"—but he's in major trouble at school. The *reason* we're not angry is this wasn't misbehavior. This was . . ."

Tori looked at Phillip, hunting for a word. Phillip shook his head.

"I don't know what this was."

Lydia shrugged. "Whatever."

She pulled out her cell phone.

"And don't dare text this to any of your friends!"

"Aw, Mom!"

"Or call, email, or anything else!"

Lydia stomped off, muttering under her breath, "Fudgesicle! For once my brother does something interesting, and I can't talk about it."

Late that night, Phillip wandered through dark, silent rooms and wondered what was happening to his family. He had dreams;

Chapter 20 – Painful Transitions

visions of a happy, cohesive family. A laughing son who would throw the football and watch sports with him. He had pictured them sitting together in church, going on camping trips.

He had modified his dreams because he loved his boy. Those adjustments had not equipped him to find himself fighting opposite his son in a war zone. Phillip sank to his knees. He had not prayed in a long time, but maybe God would hear him, for Gabe's sake.

Tori was not sleeping; every hour or so, she checked Gabe. He slept peacefully in the moonlight, which streamed through the bedroom window.

His cherubic looks were belied by the scratches on his face and arms. She tried to pray to the God who had allowed this, but the words bounced back off the ceiling, mocking her.

She sent emails to Dr. Klein, Serena, and Cassie explaining what had happened. Dr. Klein, a night owl, called Tori right away.

"I'm sorry you're going through this. I've forwarded your email to Karen Paulding, an excellent behavior modification therapist."

"Thanks for responding so quickly. I'm dumbfounded. Gabe's had periodic mild aggression, but this was brutal."

"I suspect hormone imbalance. Puberty causes testosterone output, which often makes even neuro-typical boys highly aggressive."

"But Gabe's only eleven," Tori protested, raking her fingers along her scalp.

Please don't tell me those tufts of hair he's sprouting mean incipient manhood.

"Early maturation is common with autism. Gabe's sensory system is already off-balance, so additional hormone surges can be catastrophic."

"What do you recommend?"

"See his pediatrician immediately," Dr. Klein said briskly, "to confirm whether Gabe's begun puberty. He needs vigorous exercise daily before school, followed by calming sensory input. I'd recommend a thirty-minute run followed by a bath or shower. Hold on."

Tori tried to visualize taking Gabe on a pre-dawn jog while Dr. Klein punched keys in the background.

"Let me see . . . can't cancel that one," Dr. Klein muttered. "Ahh! She can wait."

Dr. Klein came back on the line, "I have an opening at two o'clock this afternoon."

Klein hung up without saying goodbye.

Serena knocked on the door at 6:00 a.m., carrying a thermos and a heavenly-smelling, steaming basket. Phillip let her in, and then called softly up the stairs to Tori.

"Hon? You awake?"

"Who slept?" Tori said, coming downstairs in sweats. "Hey, Serena."

"Buenos Dias. I have brought mint chocolate and the limon cakes with poppy seed. Your email said only that Gabriel went rampaging at school. How is he?"

Phillip rubbed a hand over his stubbled chin.

"He's still asleep." He grabbed a muffin. "I've got to get ready for work, but I'll try to get home early. Keep me posted."

He ran lightly up the stairs.

Serena filled two mugs with hot chocolate, and then pushed the basket of bread toward Tori.

"So; tell me."

"After Gabe stopped trying to maim anyone within striking distance, he cried himself sick," Tori replied, "then spent the rest of the afternoon saying he's going to be good and wants to go back to school. There's a meeting today. I'm not looking forward to it."

Tori came to school prepared for Gabe's expulsion. To her surprise, the possibility was not mentioned. Aggressive Behavior Management training was scheduled for the staff. An IEP meeting was planned for two weeks out.

Cassie called. "Hey, what happened at the meeting?"

"Not much," Tori said, twirling hair around her finger. 'They've scheduled aggression response training for everyone. There's a formal IEP meeting in two weeks. However, Gabe's teacher, Maggie, told me, off-the-record, Ledo County wants to transfer him to the individualized interventions program. You know, second tier special education."

"That'd cost the county less."

"Huh? I thought second tier referred to additional levels of support."

"It does. As a result of his meltdown, Gabe will be put on a behavior plan. The aggressive nature of his outburst means Ledo County will have to dedicate an aide to Gabe. That's probably not in the budget. Second tier programs have separate budgets. They're funded for a smaller student-teacher ratio."

"Budget? They want to transfer him because it's cost-effective? Gabe's a child, not a line item!"

Cassie made a shushing noise.

"Settle down. In theory, second tier is good. The staff is specifically trained in autism. In addition to Gabe getting more attention, he'll be dealing with people experienced with his issues. DeepVista's the closest school to you with second tier, right?"

"I think so."

"They have a good reputation. The teacher's supposed to be phenomenal. It may be good for Gabe. They can teach him how to control himself when the hormones rage."

Tori sighed. "Yeah, but it's a step further from normal kids."

Cassie's silence was eloquent. Tori ran her fingers through her hair.

"Look, Cassie. I know this wasn't normal behavior, but Gabe's never been like this before. One incident and we're going to condemn him to second tier?"

"No. Of course not. How do you know second tier is *condemning* him? Have you researched it?"

"I've been a little busy."

"I know. Just check it out."

Tori disconnected and wandered outside to the deck where Amber lay basking in the sunshine. The cat opened one eye, rolled over onto her back, and waved a paw in gracious invitation. Stroking her fingers through Amber's silky fur usually brought temporary stress relief, but today even the offering of a plump, feline belly had no ability to cheer Tori's heart.

Tori leaned against the balustrade and shaded her eyes. Fluffy clouds, ballerinas in white tutus, glided serenely overhead as if nothing untoward were happening below on earth.

"Intellectually, I know You're good, but You don't feel that way right now," Tori told God. "Gabe's autism may be Your will, but a Dr. Jekyll and Mr. Hyde scenario for an innocent little boy is just *wrong*."

Tori squinted skyward through her fingers, half expecting a thunderbolt or instant blindness. Nothing came other than the typical red, yellow, and black sunspots. She rubbed her eyes, dropped a cursory pat on Amber's head, and went inside.

Phillip had been supportive for a few days, but was back to working long hours. Lydia was taking advantage of her mother's distraction to camp out on the computer, building her social networks instead of her grades. Tori, too fatigued, made no more than a token protest.

She could not pray. Waves of anxiety tumbled her petitions like shells on a beach, burying them in futility. She had plenty of things to do, but no desire to do any of them. Summoning all her energy, she sent an email.

To: Serena, Cassie
I'm slogging through a black fog, trying not to smother. I'm mad at God. What did Gabe or I ever do to deserve this?

From: Serena
*God is always loving, but often inscrutable. Something else, also. Americans, they do not much believe in the Evil One. I believe, so I recognize this smog you speak of as Diablo-Sombr, devilmurk. I remind you Satan is the father of lies. Speak truth to yourself.
I preach well, no?
I've got your backside.*

From: Cassie
So, Christians only trust God when things go well?

To: Cassie
          Does your broom get good mileage?

From: Cassie
          Yeah. It's a hybrid.

The three friends met for a quick lunch. Since Cassie could not be away from school long, they sat at a picnic table on one end of the school's deserted playground and ate sandwiches.

"You look like death on a cracker," Cassie told Tori.

"Si, and also you are growing more wrinkles." Serena commented, rubbing her thumb along Tori's forehead.

Tori pushed Serena's hand away and glared at her friends.

"I think I'm entitled to a little worry, thanks very much. I don't know what to do. If Creekside is still the best place for Gabe, I don't want him moved because there isn't enough money—"

"What is this about money?" Serena asked.

Cassie explained.

Serena's chest swelled with indignation.

"This is not as it should be. Every year, yes, every year for many years, I have no school-age children, but I pay again the school taxes."

"As I've told Tori before," Cassie said, tossing sandwich crusts to a bright-eyed squirrel, "the government doesn't allocate enough money for the schools to fully comply with what the law mandates."

Serena bounced around to face Tori, causing the warped boards of the picnic bench to squeal in protest.

"Does not the special needs community have lobbyists, so when the pork barrels are divided, los niños especiales get enough bacon?"

"The parents are usually too busy scrambling to meet their children's needs to do nearly as much lobbying as we need to," said Tori. "About Gabe—"

"And we special needs teachers are too busy documenting that little Sally has met her goal of greeting people appropriately, without prompts, 75 percent of the time. We can't do much either." Cassie's white teeth crunched ferociously into an apple.

Serena leaned across the table and dabbed at the juice running down Cassie's chin.

"Thanks, Mom." Cassie waved her apple at Serena. "There's a rally on the capitol steps next week, with a legislator meet-n-greet afterwards. Want me to sign you up?"

She grinned at Serena. Serena shook her finger.

"Do not smirk at me. You think I will not go; you are wrong. Me, I am arranging a crowd. I will email to all my friends and tell them if they know special needs children they must come with me to adjust this travesty."

Tori tried to interject. "I'm afraid Gabe will—"

Cassie clapped. "You go, Serena! I'll email you the info."

"Um, ladies?" Tori said. "I hate to break up your summit meeting, but Cassie has to get back to class soon; and Serena, don't you have fencing practice today? I thought we were here to talk about *Gabe's future.*"

"We are, sorry. I'm not sure why you're so upset about this," Cassie said. "I don't think this incident is a predictor of Gabe's future."

She threw her apple core to the squirrel, which had approached within a few feet of the table, hoping for further largesse.

"You weren't there," Tori said darkly. "It was *awful.* Gabe's blowups are infrequent, but they've always been his default reaction when things go badly. Dr. Klein says it's hormonal imbalance—he'll always have that to some degree. This outburst included blood, bruises, and a broken finger."

She shuddered.

"I'm afraid for Gabe." She studied a patch of moss on the table and rubbed her finger over it. "Why would God have me go halfway around the world to get our children and let my son end up in an institution?"

Serena clucked disapprovingly.

"My Gabriel is struggling, but I think no one can institutionalize him while Señora St. John is his mother. Besides, this good Dr. Klein, she has given him better medication for his hormones, is it not so?"

"Yes, and he's doing better, but—"
"Institutionalization; what the *heck* are you talking about?" Cassie interrupted.

"A friend asked me if we'd institutionalize him if he became consistently dangerous," Tori said.

Tears spurted to her eyes. Cassie scowled.

"Unless it was Dr. Klein or a state representative, stop borrowing trouble. Throw a glass of water on yourself then concentrate on what needs to be done now."

Cassie smiled and pushed the corner of Tori's lip up.

"It's going to be okay . . . really."

To: Phillip

From: Tori
*We never talk, anymore. Mrs. Knarr worked carpool this morning. She tried to hide it, but she was **not** happy to see our boy. I can't blame her. Gabe's endangering her school.*
We have to acknowledge Gabe has a significant aggression issue. DeepVista may not be able to handle him. The IEP meeting is tomorrow. Wish you could come with me. Say hi to Delia.

From: Phillip
*The Delia dig was petty. You seem to forget I **work** to pay our astronomical bills, so **you** can handle kid stuff.*

To: Phillip
Excuse me while I pop a few bonbons.

Tori entered the IEP flanked by Dr. Klein and Karen, the behavior specialist. One side of a long oval table was packed with Ledo County employees, including Richard Soulder, the head of special education. Plump, rosy cheeks gave him a jovial look belied by his vinegar personality.

Tori pulled a bag of bagels and a tape recorder from her voluminous bag. School personnel smiled at the bagels. Mr. Soulder greeted the tape recorder with a grimace.

"I'm sorry you obviously feel the need to record these proceedings."

Tori tilted her head and looked at the laptops lining his side of the table.

"Oh? Why? It's one of the rights listed in the Parental Rights Notification I get each meeting; frees me to listen better."

Mr. Soulder pursed his lips, and then swept his hand toward Maggie Faust, Gabe's teacher.

"You may begin."

Maggie did introductions and a summary of events.

Mr. Soulder turned to Tori.

"Obviously, you should have Gabe tested for medical and emotional problems."

"Gabe had an exhaustive physical and a psychological exam immediately after this happened. He has premature puberty, which causes hormonal imbalances, which lead to aggression."

"Then obviously," Mr. Soulder said, fixing a stare on Dr. Klein, "Gabe needs more medication."

"I'm adjusting his medicine," Dr. Klein said curtly "but it's an art, not a science. We have to experiment to find what works. What works today may not work six months from now. Furthermore, medication is only one piece of the solution."

"Puberty can last six or more years," Tori interjected. "I've done research and spoken to parents with children at DeepVista. I think the individualized intervention program is better equipped to handle Gabe at this point."

Maggie nodded, "I agree."

Mr. Soulder shook his head, causing a well-oiled strand of hair to fall from its carefully arranged position on his balding pate. He licked a finger and quickly slid the strand back into place.

Then he said, "Now, ladies, don't jump to premature conclusions. Obviously, we need to try modifying his current placement first."

A rustle of surprise met his statement. Maggie opened her mouth as if to protest. A look from Mr. Soulder quelled her.

"I observed Gabe for several days," Karen said. "Dr. Klein and I can develop a behavior modification program."

"Obviously," Mr. Soulder said, "our behavior consultants will need to review it before implementation."

Dr. Klein inclined her head.

"Obviously."

Tori turned a laugh into a cough.

The meeting took on a surreal quality. A discussion of valium as an emergency fallback was followed by a debate on protective gear. Tori felt like Alice in Wonderland without the fun parts.

Six hours later, they had Gabe's behavior plan.

Level One: Normal

Level Two: Agitation. Observe closely.

Level Three: Verbal or gestural threats. Add an aide. Offer sensory options. Encourage self-regulation, praise success.

Level Four: Violence. Relocate to quiet room. If Level Two phase is not achieved within fifteen minutes, call parents.

Meltdowns seemed to have faded into Gabe's past, but school was not going smoothly. In the past, Tori received an incident report (IR) only if Gabe broke a major school rule. Now, she received them daily.

Incident:	Gabe rocked his chair. He became angry when physically restrained.
Parent Comment:	Restlessness comes with autism. Restraint does not help.

Why didn't you have him jump it out on the mini-trampoline, like you usually do?

Incident:	Gabe objected loudly to doing math. We took a walk instead.
Parent Comment:	Gabe hates math. If protesting gets him out of something he does not like, you're going to be hearing a lot of protests. Call me.
Incident:	Gabe wanted to jump off the roof. When told no, his muscles tensed.

We removed him to the quiet room.

Parent Comment:	As you know, if you calmly say no when Gabe asks to do impossible things, he is fine. I *strongly* object to isolating him because you thought you saw his muscles tense. I am documenting our exchanges.

Tori called the principal.

"Mrs. Knarr, these daily incident reports disturb me. They're trivial and cite typical autistic behaviors. Furthermore, the consequences Maggie is implementing are inappropriate.

"I'll share your concerns."

Click.

Incident: Gabe giggled continuously today, disrupting the class.
Parent Comment: Jake hums constantly, off-key. Brenda spouts movie lines incessantly. Jorge cries after recess. It is difficult to believe Gabe's laughter disturbed the class.

The next day Tori approached Maggie at carpool. When Maggie saw her, she turned and flagged another teacher.

"Cover for me, I need to go in."

She retreated without meeting Tori's eyes.

That afternoon, Gabe trudged down the bus steps, dragging his feet.

"Hey, little prince. How was school?"

"Computer after homework?"

"*Hello*, Gabe."

"Hello, Mama. Computer?"

"How was school?"

"First he had circle time, then read, snack, math, and bus home, see Mommy."

Tori frowned. Gabe hadn't mentioned lunch, the highlight of a typical day.

"What about lunch?"

"Naughty. Didn't eat friends."

Tori's adrenalin surged. She forced herself to speak calmly.

"How were you naughty?"

Gabe flourished his fingers, and then clenched them shut.

"We don't wave hands."

"That wasn't naughty. You can stay home tomorrow if you want."

"No! He wants school!" Gabe's lips quivered.

Tori held placating hands out to him.

"Okay. Don't worry. School tomorrow."

Gabe's stress caused him to think deeply and produce a rare grammatically correct sentence.

"Gabe . . . will . . . go . . . to school . . . tomorrow?"

"Yes, you'll go to school."

"Not next week school?"

Tori made a lip-zipping motion.

"Son, I already told you. You're going to school tomorrow."

"Okay. You can have chocolate milk?"

Gabe asked his standard afterschool question.

Tori ruffled his hair.

"Just this once."

Gabe's eyes widened. Tori usually said no to chocolate milk after school. He rushed out before she changed her mind.

Tori pulled out the day's IR, which stated Gabe had waved his fingers frequently. It was accompanied by a small, handwritten note: *Hands tied. Daily IRs mandated.*

Tori dialed Maggie's cell phone.

"Hello?"

"You're not the one making this garbage happen, but you're the one I can reach out and slap. I'm calling an emergency IEP meeting," Tori said, not bothering to keep the anger out of her voice. "Least Restrictive Environment law prohibits you from separating Gabe from his established peer group unless he's misbehaving. Stimming with his fingers doesn't qualify. If it happens again, I will launch a lawsuit against Ledo County and name every single one of you personally. It's reprehensible to make Gabe think he's naughty for being autistic."

"I'm sorry. We all love Gabe."

"Oh, really."

Tori disconnected. She chewed her braid, thumbed through the IRs, and then scanned the reports to Cassie's personal e-mail.

Richard Soulder called.

"Mrs. St. John, we can't hold an emergency IEP meeting without a crisis. Gabe's had a number of disturbing incidents, obviously, but there's a meeting scheduled soon to review progress. There's no need—"

"Arrange a meeting within three days or I hire Basil Rettinger. I hear he's the nastiest special needs attorney on the planet."

Dead silence. Tori let it drag out.

Mr. Soulder cleared his throat.

"I'll check schedules."

"That would obviously be a good idea," Tori replied.

Cassie called that night.

"These aren't typical incident reports. My guess is DeepVista is building an airtight case for second tier."

"I *suggested* we transfer him to DeepVista. Mr. Soulder said no." Tori crumbled up a paper towel and hurled it toward the trashcan. It missed.

"Yes, but Creekside mentioned DeepVista once before after a minor aggressive incident. You didn't want anything to do with it, remember? They're afraid you'll renege."

"They're messing with Gabe's mind!"

Tori sketched a picture of Gabe with enormous, sad eyes.

Cassie sighed. "It's a litigious society. Special needs parents sue."

"Gabe doesn't belong at Creekside anymore. They're tippy-toeing around; not doing anything that may upset him. I understand, they aren't prepared to handle aggression, but in the meantime, he's learning zilch and being isolated."

She flipped the page and drew a picture of Gabe behind bars.

"Are you going to challenge them?" Cassie asked. "Gabe's borderline second tier and they've botched this. You'd probably win."

Tori snorted.

"Define win. If Gabe never misbehaved again, which is unlikely, they'd still be afraid of him because of what has occurred. There's an IEP meeting the day after tomorrow. I'll tell them to process his transfer."

"I'm sorry."

Tori swallowed hot, salty tears.

"Gabe's having challenges. Maybe DeepVista will be good for him. If not, we'll look into private schools."

She swallowed again. "Thanks for calling."

"Anytime. Chin up."

The next morning, the school called Tori to get Gabe. She rushed in expecting injured staff and a raging son. Instead, she was directed to the quiet room, where she found a calm, depressed-looking Gabe with Maggie and Antonio.

When he saw her, Gabe stood, put on his backpack, and said morosely, "Gabe naughty."

"What happened?" Tori asked Maggie.

"He slapped a desktop. He seems fine now, but we thought—" Tori interrupted. "Antonio, was he aggressive or threatening?"

"No, he calmed down after he hit the desk."

"So . . . Gabe got uptight, behaved aggressively toward an inanimate object, recovered, and you're sending him home?"

"We're concerned—"

Tori held one hand up.

"I don't care to discuss this right now."

She turned to Gabe. "Good job of controlling yourself."

She held out her fist to Gabe. Bewildered, Gabe slowly touched her fist with his.

"Gabe didn't lose computer? Not naughty?"

"Nope. I'm proud of you for controlling your anger." Tori put a hand on his shoulder. "Let's get a milkshake to celebrate."

At the doorway, she looked over her shoulder at Maggie.

"This *incident* isn't over," she hissed.

Maggie looked down.

After Gabe went to bed, Tori called Cassie and poured out the story.

"They are so done with Gabe."

Tori slammed a plate into the dishwasher and winced when she heard it crack. Lydia, who was doing homework at the dining room table, came into the kitchen.

"Mom, you okay?"

"Yes, Sweetie, just upset with Gabe's school. I'm talking to Miss Cassie about it."

Lydia gave her mother a quizzical look, and then took a banana out of the fruit bowl and examined it.

"Hey, thanks for getting the greener ones. I hate brown spots."

She sauntered out.

"Sounds like Lydia's being congenial," Cassie said. "I'd expect her to test a few boundaries while you're distracted."

"Oh, she has. She wanted a second ear piercing, but Phillip and I hadn't had time to discuss it. Sunday afternoon Lydia decided she was tired of waiting for a decision. She pierced it herself. No ice."

"Ouch!"

"Normally, I'd have made her let the hole close, but somehow I couldn't get too worked up about it. Phillip hasn't noticed yet. I think Lydia got a little worried by the lack of an eruption. She's being sweet now, almost protective." Tori took a deep breath. "I'm trying to see Creekside's point-of-view. Gabe has a history now. I get that, but what they did today was just *wrong*. They're acting like he's radioactive!"

Cassie exhaled.

"I've snooped around a little. About six years ago, Ledo County had a young woman in second tier who really needed to be in the class for kids with behavior disorders—third tier special education. She had a major aggressive outburst, much worse than Gabe's. The parents didn't want her moved, so the school didn't push it."

"I don't like where this story is headed."

"The girl grabbed a pair of safety scissors one day, and then stabbed a teacher and one of her classmates. They recovered, but the parents of the student who got stabbed sued on the grounds of school negligence. The case was settled out of court for $5.8 million. The teacher was reprimanded; Mr. Soulder's counterpart was downgraded several levels."

"But Gabe's not—"

"They're not taking any chances. Like you said, they're done. He's such a doll in his normal state, but it sounds like when he loses it everyone runs for cover. I'd hate to be in his teacher's shoes."

"I understand they're afraid," Tori said, scrubbing furiously at a meatloaf pan. "Ouch! Fudgesicle! There went a nail."

"Get acrylics. The school's in violation of his IEP. Complain in writing, or I suspect they'll start sending him home when he yawns, saying they saw teeth."

Late that night Tori walked to the back of her closet and pulled out a well-cut navy business suit with classic lines. Her hand hovered over a white shirt with a lace inset, and then settled decisively on a high-necked red silk blouse. She was standing in front of the mirror, studying the effect of knee-high black boots when Phillip walked in.

"Wow, you look fabulous! Gorgeous, but lethal. What's the occasion?" Phillip asked, stretching.

Tori raised an eyebrow. "Gabe's IEP? The meeting likely to determine your son's educational future?"

Oops. Walked right into that one.

"I'm sorry, honey. I forgot. I know you'll do an awesome job, though."

And she will. No one else would spend the time and energy she spends on our family.

He had a sudden vision of Delia with the kids and shook his head. Delia was tough, but not strong enough to handle the things Tori dealt with. On impulse, he walked up to Tori, who had turned back to the mirror, and spun her around.

Holding her by her shoulders, he said, "Listen, Little Love, I meant that. I know I haven't been around much lately—"

"That's for sure."

"—but I really admire the way you've handled all this. I know I can count on you, and that makes all the difference in the world."

He dropped a kiss onto Tori's forehead.

"I'm glad I make it easy for you to be gone all the time while I raise our kids."

Phillip dropped his hands from her shoulders and turned away.

It's like trying to reconcile with a porcupine.

"Carry your red briefcase. It completes your statement."

Tori strode into the IEP meeting late the following afternoon. Her red hair was twisted into an elegant chignon, held in place by a pearl comb. Large pearl earrings glowed at her ears. She positioned a podium at the end of the table, opened her red briefcase, and began passing papers down each side.

Mr. Soulder's eyes bulged like an indignant pig's.

"We have a procedure. You can't just—"

"Watch me," Tori replied.

She nodded at the aide typing notes. "I waive the reading of parental rights."

Stepping behind the podium she picked up a letter.

"Duplicates are coming by certified mail, with copies to your attorney."

Chapter 20 – Painful Transitions

Tori flashed a confident smile and made eye contact with each person.

"Naturally, Gabe's attorney, Mr. Rettinger, already has a copy."

"You're distraught, Mrs. St. John. Yesterday's incident was obviously unfortunate—" Mr. Soulder began.

"It was obviously illegal."

Tori cleared her throat and started reading.

"By slapping a desk yesterday, Gabe entered Level Three of our mutually-developed and agreed upon crisis behavior management plan."

Tori slapped the top of the podium, causing her listeners to jump.

"I've often felt like slapping something, haven't you? Back to the letter: protocol for Level Three is that another aide is called, and Gabe is offered sensory options. If he is able to move back into Level Two, he's to be encouraged and observed closely. If he attains Level One, he receives praise and normal activities resume."

"Tori, we made a mistake," Gabe's teacher said.

Mr. Soulder glared at her.

"That is, *I* made a mistake," Maggie amended.

Tori cocked her head and looked at Maggie with compassion.

"Have they assigned you the scapegoat role? Don't worry. Mr. Rettinger has given us some excellent insight . . ."

Soulder groaned softly.

"I believe if we dig we'll find you're acting under instructions."

Tori adjusted tortoise-shell reading glasses and proceeded.

"Gabe caused no harm and recovered quickly. Yet, instead of receiving the mandated praise, he was punished." Tori tapped a pencil and looked around. "You demonstrated there's no benefit in controlling himself."

"Last meeting's notes will indicate Maggie and I suggested second tier for Gabe and were told no by Mr. Soulder."

Soulder squirmed.

"We were under the erroneous impression Ledo County was sincerely attempting accommodations to keep Gabe at Creekside. It's become clear you're simply creating a paper trail for a decision that has already been made. Your actions in putting

Gabe through an emotional wringer, so you could CYA, were despicable as well as illegal."

Tori stared at Soulder a minute, and then folded the letter.

"I've been assured we have solid grounds for legal action."

She strode back and front of the podium, tapping the document against her open palm. After a few paces, she leaned against the front of the podium, unfolded the letter, and finished reading it.

"Transfer Gabe to the individualized intervention program at DeepVista as quickly as possible. In Gabe's remaining time at Creekside we expect his IEP and behavior plan to be followed as written."

Tori took off her reading glasses and put the letter away. She spoke softly and clearly.

"Gabe's had many good years with Ledo County. You served him well until now. We appreciate that, and understand there are mitigating factors to your actions. I'm hoping we can get back on track without litigation. Handle it."

She picked up the red briefcase and left the room without a backward glance.

CHAPTER 21

Mounting Tensions

Relations with Creekside were politically- and IEP-correct during the ten days it took to get Gabe transferred to DeepVista. The school staff seemed regretful things had turned out as they did. There were no more incident reports.

Gabe had been mainstreamed with an assistant into a typical homeroom class at Creekside. Tori was touched when the class threw him a going-away party on his last day, complete with popsicles, Blazin' Buffalo Doritos, computer games, and homemade cards. Tori became misty-eyed as she and Gabe drove away. It was the end of an era that had been mostly good.

Gabe settled into the second tier program at Deep Vista with minimum fuss. His new teachers were not surprised or intimidated by him. Impassioned protests did not get him out of tasks he disliked.

The new medication dose kept his system fairly under control, and the Deep Vista Staff was well-equipped to recognize and head-off a budding outburst before it bloomed. Gabe was allowed to hang out with other kids again. After a short time in the second tier program, Gabe became his sweet, idiosyncratic self again.

Tori still struggled. Until this upheaval, she had cherished a secret hope Gabe was moving out of the special needs shadows, becoming more normal. He was doing well in his new setting, but she could no longer fool herself into believing her baby was progressing toward typical.

To: Serena
Subject: Touching Base

> Hey lady! How's the vacation? I miss your cheerful smile! Yesterday was Lydia's school talent show. The funniest act was "Yo, Leonardo," by a couple of fifth graders. Mona Lisa sat on a stool holding an empty frame up to her face, while Da Vinci painted, danced, sang, and generally had a blast. Gabe's in the fifth grade, but he's not on the same planet as that boy. Will Gabe ever experience the same pure, unbridled joy this kid did? What about me? Will I ever get to feel the pleasure that comes from knowing my child has done really well?

To: Tori

> Recall when we caught him dropping eggs on the floor? When you asked of him why, he said "Gabe likes smoosh!"
> You gave him the wicked eyeball. He corrected himself, said, "*I* like smoosh" and dropped another egg.
> Me, I tried not to laugh. You looked like his time on earth was short. He grabbed my skirt and tried to hide under it, and then peeked out and said, "It was an accidentally, Mama!"
> You said, "That was no accident, smoosh-boy! Clean it up now!"
> Then, Gabriel called Scotch, "Snack, Scotch, eat smooshies!"
> Scotch, he likes fresh smooshies. He cleaned up without argument. You sent Gabe to his room, and then we laughed till we cried. Gabe came back downstairs, crawled into your lap, kissed you, and asked, "He can smoosh tomorrow?"

We started laughing and he joined with pure pleasure. My Gabriel experiences unbridled joy, but his joy is for him unique.

To: Tori

I am looking, since getting your email, for a saying of Andrew Murray. Every time I read it, I am encouraged. So, if it is again I am sending it you, tough fate. Read it over once more!
Andrew Murray's In Times of Trouble Say[6]:
First – *[He] brought me here; it is by His will I am in this hard[7] place: in that I will rest.*
Next – *[He] will keep me in His love, and give me grace in this trial to behave as His child.*
Then – *[He] will make the trial a blessing, teaching me lessons He intends me to learn, and working in me the grace He means to bestow.*
Last – *In His good time He can bring me out again—how and when He knows.*
Say: I am here—
 a. By God's appointment.
 b. In His keeping.
 c. Under His training.
 d. For His time.
Psalm 50:15

Tori fought a smile at the remembrance of the egg-smooshies. She was not finished being miserable.
If anyone deserves to sulk a while, it's me!

---

[6] "The Baptist Start Page" at: http://www.baptiststart.com/print/time_of_trouble_say.html

[7] Original word is *strait*. The emphasized capitalization of pronoun when speaking of God is mine.

To: Serena
So, just accept whatever God dishes out and like it? Tell myself: I might as well accept it since I can't change it, anyway? That's not working for me.

Tori hit the SEND button before she thought better of it. *Oops. Not good.*

But it seemed like everyone was either singing "Don't Worry, Be Happy" or telling her if they were in her shoes, they would contemplate suicide.

I'm tired of it! Still, I shouldn't have snapped at Serena.

Her cell phone sang out "I Heard It Through the Grapevine," which indicated an incoming text message from Serena.

Who'd have thought the old lady could text so fast?

From: Serena
U kno thts not wat Im syng. Do bst chng stuatn lv rslt 2 God & dnt strss if He has dfrnt pln. Nwsflsh: He's God. Ur not. Enjy pty prty but dnt invit me. Rfus feel sorry 4 U/Gabe. Luv

To: Serena
Luv U 2. Sorry. Come home soon.

Tori put down her phone. Lydia wandered into the room, gnawing an apple core and looking dejected.

"Hey, Princessa, what's up?

Lydia draped herself around Tori's neck and gave a huge sigh.

"I don't fit in, Mom."

Lydia was in middle school and almost fourteen. Hard years, Tori remembered. Girls could be so mean.

"What makes you say don't fit? Are your friends being ugly?"

"No. It's just, I'm not all that interested in boys, makeup—they bore me."

"What about sports? You love basketball."

"Yeah, but I'm too short. The other girls have always been taller, but now they're really taller."

Chapter 21 — Mounting Tensions

Lydia flung her hands up in despair.

"And then, there's the adoption stuff. I'm not really an American girl, but I'm not really Bulgarian. I'm not really anything. Sometimes I don't feel real. I'm like one of those spirit things, like a . . . a . . . wreath?"

"Do you mean you feel like a wraith, Honey? Like a ghost?"

Tori was not aware she was biting her lip until she tasted the salt of blood.

"Yeah, like I'm the ghost of Stolcha past, and only a shadow of Lydia present. Like Lydia St. John isn't real; she's just this make-believe girl the St. Johns pretend is their daughter."

I may have skipped the physical pangs of childbirth, but the worst pain is the hurt you can't fix for someone else. My poor, out-of-place child.

Tori pulled Lydia to her.

"Sweetheart. I'm so sorry you feel this way. But your emotions aren't telling you the whole truth. You *are* real. Stolcha is part of you, but you are Lydia St. John, our precious daughter, our eldest child, Gabe's beloved sister."

"Yeah. I'm Gabe's sister. The normal one. The one who has to be mature and understand everything's about my brother 'cause he needs help and I don't."

Oh . . . My . . . God. Help!

She wasn't equipped to address Lydia's adoption angst. She would have to get online, find someone, who specialized in adoption issues, and convince Lydia to go to counseling.

In the meantime though, she needed to address Lydia's feelings of Gabe-inferiority. Tori held Lydia at arm's length and studied her daughter's downcast face.

"Do you really feel like you take second place to Gabe?"

Lydia scuffed her tennis shoe against the carpet.

"Yeah. Sometimes."

Tori hugged Lydia fiercely and spoke into her hair.

"You're every bit as important as Gabe, you just need different things. Tell you what. I've been thinking about something for just you and me, only I was afraid we couldn't afford it. But we *will* afford it, somehow."

Tori bit her lip. Lydia raised her head.

"Afford what?"

"Our first annual mother-daughter weekend. Where would you like to go?"

Lydia's eyes widened.

"Just us? Go somewhere . . . without Daddy and Gabe?"

"Yep—just you and me—no guys. We're going to do a long weekend every year, starting now."

Lydia clapped her hands.

"Really? Could we go to the beach this week? Monday's a teacher workday."

Tori calculated. Six hours to Destin. She could pull Lydia out of school at noon. They could stay gone until late Monday night. Three and a half days to lavish her daughter with undivided attention.

She decided. "Yes! You get on the Internet and find places for rent in Destin. I'll ask Serena if she'll watch Gabe until Daddy gets home Friday. Daddy's got plenty of vacation time. He can take Monday off."

Lydia looked doubtfully at her mother.

"Daddy's not going to like that."

"Daddy," said Tori, "will deal with it. And honey?"

"Yeah?"

"I think it may be a good idea for you to talk to someone about how you feel about being adopted."

"Like a shrink?" Lydia scowled. "I'm not crazy."

"Of course not. It'd be a psychologist, someone to help you sort through your feelings."

Lydia tilted her head and considered.

"Some of my friends go. They talk about their parents' divorce and stuff. Would you have to come with me, or could I go by myself?"

Tori closed her eyes.

This is part of growing up. She needs to deal with her own emotions and feelings. I'd rather be her anchor, but I know I need to give her wings.

Tori opened her eyes and forced a smile.

"Sure. You can go by yourself."

Chapter 21 — Mounting Tensions

A month or so after Gabe's transfer from Creekside, Tori rushed into Lydia's crowded gymnasium towing Gabe behind her. Her daughter's junior varsity basketball team, Lady Thunder, was playing the undefeated Lady Rattlers. Tori found a spot on the crowded bleachers and gave Gabe his latest helicopter book. He opened it to his favorite page and stared intently. Tori knew he might not turn the page for an hour.

It allows him to escape into his own world: bad. It gives me an undistracted hour: good.

Tori watched as Lydia nailed a three-pointer during warm-up.

"Whoo hoo!" Tori cheered.

Lydia acknowledged Tori by tipping her chin. She glanced around nonchalantly.

Probably looking for Phillip. Hope he's not stuck at the office.

The buzzer sounded. During the first period, the Rattlers and Thunder traded the lead back and forth. The girls raced from one end of the court to the other; rubber soles screeching on the polished gym floor.

Tori wondered how they could hear their coach's hoarse instructions amidst the cacophony of fan participation, but she knew the girls drew energy from their supporters. Tori yelled louder.

In the second period, the Thunder scored seven unanswered points. Lydia had three fouls. The Rattlers sank a three-pointer. Everyone's attention was riveted on the fast-paced game.

Something jabbed Tori's side. She turned and was kicked in the face by Gabe's tennis shoe as he disappeared under the bleachers.

"Gabe!" Tori hissed. "Get back here!"

He crawled out of sight. Jumping up, Tori clumsily navigated the bleachers, apologizing as she peered under fans' seats.

The crowd roared. Tori turned to see players high-fiving Lydia. The red-faced opposing coach called a time out, screaming and gesturing frantically. Lydia scanned the bleachers, frowning. Tori caught Lydia's attention and gave her the thumbs up gesture. Lydia smiled and turned back to the game.

She found Gabe tapping his head against the back wall of the bleachers and giggling. He stopped when he saw Tori glaring down at him though the aluminum risers.

"Come out right now, young man!"

Gabe crawled toward her, looking apprehensive. Tori bent down and yanked him up through the bleachers. She felt a sharp twinge in her low back and scowled.

"Young man . . ."

Gabe looked piteous and shed crocodile tears.

"We don't crawl seats, Mama."

"No, we don't!" Tori snapped.

Her back throbbing with pain, Tori marched Gabe back to their seats. As she sat down, she noticed two acquaintances whispering and shaking their heads. Seeing her look, one of them smiled.

She asked brightly, "Did you see Lydia make that play?"

Fudgesicle.

"No." Tori put her hands to her head, trying to corral errant curls back into her ponytail.

"I was chasing Gabe. What happened?"

"She stole the ball, flew down the court, made a beautiful left-handed layup, and managed to draw a foul on the way down. The Rattler coach almost had apoplexy. He wanted the foul called on Lydia. It's a shame you have to drag Gabe to these games. He can be so disruptive, bless his heart. Don't you ever leave him with a sitter?"

"It's difficult to find someone appropriate. When we do, it's sixteen dollars an hour. We can't afford to do that often, bless our hearts."

Tori focused on Lydia, who was crouched by the officials' table, waiting to tag in. She hoped she didn't miss anything else.

"I need to go potty."

"Please wait. Mommy wants to watch sister. Watch sister. Look, Sister's got the ball." Tori groaned as she heard herself baby-talking. "Yay! Lydia stole the ball. Cheer for your sister, Gabe."

Gabe glanced at Lydia without much interest.

"Yay, sister. I have to go poopy!"

Chapter 21 – Mounting Tensions

Unfortunately, Gabe made his announcement during a momentary lull in the noise. Hands on her hips, Lydia glared at them and sliced her index finger across her throat.

Tori sighed.

"Gabe, you're eleven now. Stop saying you have to go poopy. Say you have to use the bathroom."

"Say you have to use the bathroom," Gabe said.

With exasperation, Tori left the bleachers, apologizing as she and Gabe crawled over disgruntled fans. While she waited for Gabe, Tori called Phillip.

"Hello?" His voice was impatient.

"Hi, honey. Are you on your way? Lydia's having a great game."

"No, it's been crazy here today. Anyway, you're there." He sounded distracted.

Tori rubbed her forehead.

"I know, but Lydia likes us both to be here. Besides, Gabe's embarrassing her. I'd hoped you would be here soon, so I could take him home."

"Half the office is out with the flu. It's a zoo."

"Can you at least be home for dinner?"

"I'll try."

The line went dead. Tori heard splashing and giggling from the men's room. She opened the door.

"Stop playing!"

The open door revealed a startled high school boy.

"Um, sorry," Tori told the blushing young man, "I was talking to my son."

He mumbled, "No problem," as he brushed past her.

Tori slumped against the wall and slid down to the floor.

Just another day in paradise.

Gabe came out sopping wet, looking extremely proud of himself.

"Wash hands!"

"Yes, I see that. Looks like you washed all of you."

Tori meant to be stern, but Gabe looked so cute, standing there staring off into space with an angelic smile on his face.

"What are you thinking?" Tori mused. "I wish I knew."

She scrambled to her feet and took his hand.

"Come on. Let's sit on the far bleachers, where we won't bother anyone."

Phillip was only an hour late for dinner. Tori had thrown a lean pork loin and fresh vegetables in the crock-pot that morning, so dinner could wait. Phillip loved the meat and savory vegetables. The accompanying wheat rolls satisfied Lydia's carb-tooth. Gabe was not enthusiastic about meals bereft of cheese, or sour cream, but the prospect of "pie-apple" and ice cream for dessert motivated him to eat without complaint.

The evening was enjoyable. Lydia was disappointed Phillip had not made her game, but he questioned her avidly about every detail. Lydia's defensive skills had neutralized the Rattler's offense and she had scored ten points.

Her father's genuine regret at missing the game and his enthusiasm about hearing how well she had played consoled Lydia for his absence. Phillip complemented Tori on her latest hairstyle, helped with the dishes, and rough-housed with Gabe until his son howled with laughter.

This is how it used to be. Maybe we've turned a corner.

The next day dispelled that hope. Gabe boarded the bus scowling and unresponsive. Lydia, who had refused to go to bed until late, stomped around, rubbed her eyes, and refused to eat breakfast. Tori's back felt like it was in a vise.

"Short Stuff, where's my cleaning?" Phillip hollered from upstairs.

Tori's responded with a, long, stricken sentence.

"I am so sorry. I meant to pick it up, but the school called saying Gabe wasn't acting right, and strep throat was going around, so would I please come get him; so of course I rushed him to the pediatrician and by the time we'd waited an hour for the doctor to say Gabe was fine, we needed to leave for Lydia's game and it flew right out of my head."

Phillip's voice rose.

"That's the third time you've forgotten it."

Chapter 21 — Mounting Tensions

"I *said* I was sorry. It's not like I was off getting a manicure! I'll pick it up today!"

"Never mind," Phillip said in his misunderstood-martyr voice.

"I need my best blue sport coat today. I'll have to swing by the cleaners on my way to work. When do they open?"

Tori went to the bottom of the stairs.

"Eight o'clock."

Phillip moaned. He looked at his watch.

"By the time I get through traffic, it'll be 9:30! I wanted to get in early today."

"You have tons of clothes. Can't you wear one of your other blue sport jackets?"

Phillip ticked suits off on his fingers.

"One's too heavy for this time of year, the other has a pull. Besides, they're at the cleaners, too, remember? I found a 20 percent off coupon, so you could take everything in at once, save $13.95."

"You have several other sport coats. What's wrong with your tweed, the grey, one of the khakis, or even black?"

Phillip answered with exaggerated patience, speaking as if Tori possessed dubious intelligence and less taste.

"We're taking Racoby for golf after a late lunch at the country club. I need a blue sport coat to wear with a golf shirt and khakis. You surely understand I cannot wear khaki on khaki. None of my golf shirts go well with grey, black is too hot for this time of year, and as for tweed . . . !" He shuddered. "I'll have to get it myself. I'll be late tonight, don't wait up."

"Again? Lydia needs help selling Girl Scout cookies. The deadline's a week from now. I don't have anyone to watch Gabe."

"Sorry, dear, but I *work* for a living. Surely you have time to do it. Take Gabe with you."

Gabe's penchant for investigating the refrigerator of any house he came to made him a poor candidate for door-to-door sales, but before Tori could answer him Phillip ran downstairs, grabbed his laptop, and left.

Tori sank down on the stairs.

Anyone could forget. He refused to sell cookies at work, so the least he could do is . . . what was that crack about him working for a living?

Tori bet she worked Phillip under the table seven days a week and she didn't get perks like hanging out at the country club.

I have a good mind to stop cleaning and handling the bills. I'll sign him up to attend the next school meeting, let him do a little of the research . . .

"Mom! C'mon! I can't be late again!"

Tori grabbed her keys, slurped a sip of lukewarm tea, and dashed out the door.

By the time Phillip picked up the cleaning, traffic was a mess. His cell phone rang as he fumed and shouted insults at the other drivers.

If that's Tori, expecting me to do another errand . . .!

"Hello!"

"Well, well," purred Delia. "A bit grumpy this morning, are we? Where are you?"

"On my way. I had to pick up my cleaning and now I'm sitting on I-285 surrounded by—moron!" he yelled at a woman who was trying to inch in ahead of him.

"Couldn't Teri pick up the cleaning?"

"Tori? She's been busy."

Delia laughed.

What a pretty, musical laugh.

"Awww. Poor man. Get here as soon as you can. The place doesn't run as well without you."

"Ri-ight! It just falls apart without me."

Delia's voice became serious.

"Jokes aside, Phillip. You're creative, energetic . . . everyone respects you. Most men your age couldn't handle your level of responsibility."

Phillip felt gratified by her comment. Tori did not appreciate the load he carried.

Still, Delia is laying it on thick.

"All that, plus good-looking and modest to boot, right?" Phillip asked lightly.

Chapter 21 – Mounting Tensions

"Handsome, yes, and sexy with it. I'm not sure about the modest part, but why should you be? I prefer self-assured men. Oops, there's my other line. See you when you get here."

Phillip was thoughtful. Delia had always been flirty, but she had kicked it up a notch. Surely she remembered he was a happily married man? A renegade reflection surfaced.

Not quite as happy lately.

He ignored the deviant thought.

Handsome and sexy?

Delia's admiration felt good. He didn't get much respect at home these days. His thoughts made the commute seem faster. Still it was 9:45 a.m. by the time he got to the office. The first person he saw was Stuart, his ex-boss.

"So, Phillip, working half days now?"

"Ha, ha, very funny." Phillip's face burned.

He knows I put in insane hours. Stuart would love to make me look bad. Wonder how many opportunities he'll find to mention my late arrival?

Phillip nodded at his administrative assistant, strode into his office, and shut the door. He listened to voicemail as he turned on his computer. He had forty-five new messages.

I was here until seven last night!

Shaking his head, Phillip got to work. He was still immersed two hours later when Delia sauntered in.

When did she stop knocking?

Like him, Delia wore a blue jacket with a golf shirt and khaki, except on her, the outfit looked hot. The khaki pencil skirt skimmed her hips and flat stomach, while the snug golf shirt and fitted jacket did nothing to hide her full bust.

Whoa buddy, you're married.

"I rather thought you'd stop by when you got in." Delia's voice was slightly frigid.

Does she expect me to check in? Maybe it's time for a little distance between Delia and me.

"Sorry, no time. I was deluged the minute I walked in. I can't believe it's time to go already." Phillip glanced at his watch and gathered papers. "I'll meet you there."

Delia arched a perfect eyebrow.

"Why? I come back by here on my way home. We can review strategy on the way over. Besides, you'll save gas."

That was true. As he'd crawled along the highway this morning, Phillip noticed gas had jumped another fifty and nine-tenths of a cent. Some people tended to forgot the nine-tenths. Not Phillip. Delia was right. It made sense to carpool.

"Fine. I'll bring my laptop. I hope we get the opportunity to talk ballpark pricing today. Not likely, though; Sniderleigh will think up more objections."

"Sniderleigh's not coming."

Phillip stared.

"Since when?"

"Since I had a drink with Daryl Racoby last night."

Phillip gave a soundless whistle.

"You had drinks with Racoby's CEO?"

"Mm hmm," she purred proudly. "I mentioned Sniderleigh didn't seem to respect his opinion as much as you and I did—said we wanted to be sure our bid met *his* needs. A drink later, he suggested we have lunch without Sniderleigh."

"And when were you planning on mentioning this to me?"

"Today," Delia said, languidly sweeping down her long eyelashes. "Don't be angry. "Mr. Racoby thinks it was all his idea. I knew we'd close it quicker with Sniderleigh sidelined."

She looked up and widened her eyes in appeal. "You've made it impossible for them to choose anyone, except us. I wanted it to happen faster. Okay?"

"It would have blown up in our faces if Mr. Racoby had said no and told Sniderleigh," Phillip said.

Delia's smile was slyly complacent.

"Trust me. I know how to handle older men."

Phillip shook his head.

Audacious.

In spite of himself and his earlier strictures on distancing himself, he was impressed.

"You're incorrigible."

Delia cocked her head.

"Am I forgiven?"

Chapter 21 – Mounting Tensions

Phillip swung his briefcase against her rear.

"You know you are. Let's go."

Delia flashed a triumphant smile and strolled out ahead of him. Phillip's head brushed the roof of Delia's Porsche. Their elbows brushed and he could smell smoky, sensuous perfume. It bore no resemblance to the eight-dollar-a-bottle vanilla musk Tori wore these days.

Phillip sternly commanded his thoughts to behave.

Tori's sticking to our budget.

He opened his laptop, keeping his demeanor strictly businesslike. Delia's lips curved in a faint smile. Phillip suspected Delia knew he was unsuccessfully trying to distance himself.

At the country club, the maître de ushered them to a choice table overlooking the golf course.

"Mr. Racoby, won't you please choose the wine for us?" asked Delia, fluttering her eyelashes. "I know so little about fine wines. I understand you are quite the connoisseur."

Racoby beamed.

"Please, my dear, call me Daryl. You, too, St. John," he added.

Phillip drank water. Delia and Daryl drank two bottles of wine between them. Phillip noticed although Delia refilled Racoby's glass often, she sipped hers sparingly.

It was nearly three o'clock when they hit the golf course. Delia rode with Daryl while Phillip followed in a second cart. Delia, an excellent golfer, played badly and beseeched Daryl to help her.

I can see his chest swell. If I didn't know we're the best company for their requirements, I'd feel bad.

The few concerns Daryl had were resolved between tee boxes.

"It's clear you're the right company for Racoby," Daryl said. "I'll let Sniderleigh know. Our lawyers can start the paperwork."

Nine holes turned into more drinks and dinner. Phillip could not refuse.

Besides, I don't want to! This is the culmination of over two years of work. I deserve to celebrate.

He arrived home well after midnight, jubilant over the sale. Delia had given him a quick celebratory kiss as their client drove off.

Just a friendly kiss, not passionate.

He *could* have agreed to Delia's suggestion they go by her place for a night cap.

I could've become her lover tonight.

Phillip's desire shocked him. He vowed to hold Delia at arm's length from now on.

The dark house smelled sour. He turned on the kitchen light. A greasy pot sat on the stove. From habit, he lifted the lid.

Ugh.

Tori *knew* he loathed the smell of cabbage! Slamming the cover, he went upstairs.

Their bedroom was quiet. Suddenly, he wanted to tell Tori they had closed the deal. It would generate a huge commission. Maybe he and Tori would hire someone to watch the kids. They hadn't been away in ages.

"You awake, Munchkin?"

Tori did not respond.

Phillip shook her shoulder.

Tori jerked.

"What?" she snarled. "I was sleeping!"

"Sorry. I wanted to tell you we've clinched Racoby."

"That's nice, but could you wait until tomorrow to give me the details? I've been up *working* since five this morning."

Tori turned away and pulled the blankets up around her face. Phillip climbed into bed and lay on his back, looking at the ceiling, trying not to think about the warmth of Delia's approval and the allure of her long, shapely legs.

CHAPTER 22

Two Sides of the Coin

"You look glum," Tori commented. She and Cassie were enjoying girls' breakfast out. Tori thought the smell of buttery pancakes and strong coffee, accompanied by the sound of bacon sizzling on the grill created a cheerful ambiance, but Cassie sat with slumped shoulders.

"I'm fine."

Their waitress, a young girl just out of training and eager to please, hustled over with a coffee-pot.

"You're frowning, ma'am. Is everything okay? Can I get you more—?"

Cassie smoothed out her forehead.

"No, thank you, everything's fine."

Another patron beckoned her and the waitress dashed away. Tori looked after her.

"I think we should name her Sunbeam; unlike you."

"I have eight IEP meetings next week."

Cassie stirred her drink so hard it sloshed over the sides of her tall cup.

"Oops."

Tori slid a pile of napkins across the table and frowned as her sleeve stuck in something gooey. Evidently, Sunbeam had missed a spot of honey when she cleaned the table.

"IEPs, the meetings from Hades. I don't particularly enjoy them myself."

"Hopefully, you don't come in acting like your child's under attack and we're the enemy."

Tori gave her a level look over the top of her teacup.

"Interesting perspective."

"Yes, well, what do you think IEPs are about, denying resources to your child?"

Tori quirked one eyebrow.

"At times, yes, the meetings seem to be more about satisfying school system goals and protocols than getting our children what they need. Remember what happened around Gabe's transfer to DeepVista?"

Tori did not want to fight with Cassie.

She added, "Most of our experiences with the public school system have been positive. Things happen, but most educators seem caring and proficient."

"Because we *are!* We're certainly not in it for the money!"

Cassie's voice was like her physique, robust and voluptuous. Her passionate declaration carried over the hubbub of conversation and the clatter of dishes. After a heartbeat of silence, the noise in the crowded restaurant resumed. Sunbeam appeared at Cassie's elbow and looked at her with a worried expression.

"Ma'am?"

"Everything's fine, miss."

The waitress left, looking back over her shoulder at Cassie.

"She's not sure about you," Tori said with a grin.

Cassie's cheeks were flushed. She pounded the table lightly with her fist. Seeing Sunbeam glance her way, she spoke in a vehement whisper.

"We do try to work with parents, but we *are* the professionals."

Tori pursed her lips.

"You're experts in special needs education, in interventions the school systems approve. *I'm* the subject matter expert on Gabe; I spend hours researching new treatments and interventions, specifically for him.

"True. Nonetheless, you can't be objective about Gabe, where I can. In case you didn't notice, it's not just Gabe out there. We have many children to serve, with a wide range of disabilities."

Cassie crushed a creamer container with her thumb. Tori tried to defuse the mounting tension by shaking her head in mock sadness.

"There you go, perpetuating the rumor that Gabe's needs don't come before everyone else's."

Cassie's knuckles were white against her coffee mug.

"We want our kids to get all the help they need."

Tori's smile vanished and she punched her index finger at her friend.

"Maybe, but I know for a *fact*, from an ex-teacher, you're instructed not to recommend any additional service, regardless of how badly you feel the child needs it, unless the parents request it. You're definitely *not* supposed to recommend anything cutting edge because the parents may expect the county to pay for it."

Cassie raised her cup in a toast.

"Touché. We have an anemic budget, one that doesn't begin to give kids everything they need, much less all their parents want. It's stupid to provide insistent parents with a new, unproven therapy, when we can't even buy communication devices for all the children who need them. Part of our problem is parents with unreasonable demands."

Tori raised her chin. Despite her good intentions, her voice was frosty.

"Oh?"

Cassie held her palm out for Tori to stop.

"Hear me out."

Tori compressed her lips into a thin line and waited.

"Some parents ask us to do things *they* should be doing for their children," Cassie said.

She paused and smirked at Tori.

"We're not the ones responsible for raising their kids. Furthermore, *you* may be joking when you say Gabe's needs should come before everyone else's, but I assure you many parents have no sense of balance or fairness when it comes to their child."

Silverware jumped as she pounded her fist on the table. People stared. Glancing over, Tori met the eyes of an elderly couple. The wife looked frightened. The man patted his wife's hand and frowned at them. Tori shrugged her shoulders apologetically.

"Sorry," she mouthed.

Noticing Sunbeam headed their way again, Tori smiled, shook her head, and waved her off.

"Calm down. I'm too old to be thrown out of a restaurant."

"Sorry," Cassie lowered her voice, "but this is my life we're talking about."

"And you think it isn't mine? I live it 24/7."

"Listen. Most special education instructors[8] love kids. At least, we started out loving them! SPEDs get advanced teaching degrees because we want to make a difference. We spend weekends and vacations getting recertified, planning lessons, etc.," Cassie explained. "The government requires so much documentation now, I average seventy hours a week, but spend more time with paperwork than I do with my students. Yet, I make less than an entry-level manager."

Tori spread her hands and shrugged.

"I help when I can—fill out the forms and anything else the teachers ask me to do."

"Lots of parents are great; they have their noses to the grindstone with us. But all too often, we get parents who are totally unrealistic, don't discipline, or are unwilling to work with their kids at home."

"Give me an example," Tori said.

"Okay. Larry's parents want him to go to college. Barring a miracle, he can't handle college, but he loves to cook. When I suggest vocational training, I'm told not to limit his potential."

Tori chose her words carefully.

"Part of a parent's responsibility is to uncover their child's abilities. Isn't it conceivable sometimes you may under-estimate a child?"

"Possibly, but not to a major degree. We want our kids to succeed."

---

8   Special education instructors (SPEDs)

Sunbeam hovered a few yards away, looking anxious. Tori signaled her over.

"Please bring my friend another soy Frappuccino." Tori grinned at Cassie. "With the mood she's in today, better make it white chocolate."

As the waitress hustled away, Tori leaned over to the table next to them, which had not yet been cleared. She snagged a sprig of parsley from an empty plate and handed it to Cassie.

"Olive branch. Truce?"

Cassie stared at it, and then chuckled. "You can always make me laugh. Sorry 'bout my mood; I shouldn't take it out on you."

"Want to tell me what's really bothering you?"

Cassie sighed. "There's a boy whose parents insisted he be mainstreamed; I had to call his mom yesterday because he spread feces all over his homeroom's toilet. It's the third time he's done it since he joined his typical peers."

Frowning, she went on, "Academically, he's capable of attending typical classes with an assistant, but his social skills are minimal. Since he started regular ed, he's had the bathroom incidents, aggressive outbursts, and a disagreement with the student art teacher that left her in tears. Nothing similar happened when he was in a self-contained class. I think his behavior is a plea to return to a predictable environment, one with a safe routine."

Sunbeam brought Cassie's drink. She drank half in one gulp.

"I told mom her son doesn't yet have the social skills necessary to thrive in a mainstream environment; suggested an IEP meeting to discuss a better placement and a plan to develop those skills.

"What happened?"

"She went ballistic. Said she refused to have her son quarantined because teachers couldn't deal with minor conduct problems. She claimed his behavior is a direct result of my hostility and accused me of prejudicing the other instructors against him."

"Wow."

"Yeah, wow. Mom wrapped up by notifying me she's sent the school board a letter requesting my, um . . . bottom be fired."

Cassie choked back tears. Tori handed her more napkins.

"You know that won't happen. You're teacher of the year."

"Do *you* expect the teachers to work miracles with Gabe?" Cassie drained her coffee and pushed it away. "I can be honest with you because you're my friend, and you're not in my school district. Straight up, what do you parents expect?"

Cassie collapsed against the back of the booth and crossed her arms. Tori doodled on her napkin and prayed for wisdom. She was glad when Sunbeam came to their table, beaming and holding a tray of sweets.

"We're carrying a new line of desserts," she burbled. "Would you like to try one? They're on the house today!"

"Not me," Tori said.

"Is that chocolate cheesecake?" Cassie pointed. "Whatever it is, I'll have one."

"Right away." The waitress leaned in and confided in a giggly whisper, "These yummy looking things are actually papier-mâché!"

Cassie looked at the waitress's retreating back.

"I wonder how long it'll take for her perky to run down. Now, tell me what parents expect. Although, you've grown beyond the maturity level of most of the parents I deal with. You're less self-centered, more sane and logical."

"First, it was wrong of her to attack you personally. You'd be surprised, though, how quickly reason and good judgment vanish when a parent is afraid. You interact with parents in their worst moments."

Cassie snatched away the napkin Tori had been scribbling on.

"Let me see that sketch."

The picture showed Cassie and Tori at opposing podiums with a faceless moderator in between them.

"Clever. Wait. Is that drool you've drawn coming out of my mouth?"

"Of course not, that's a smudge." Tori answered, snatching back her drawing. "Try to step inside the head of the woman who thinks you want to sabotage her son. She craves a normal life for him; for her whole family. Since he's been mainstreamed, he's been around ordinary kids during school. She hopes he's getting better, somehow absorbing the characteristics of normal kids. But you tell Mom about incidents that show her son can't handle even a slice of normality. She's fighting for a dream. You're something tangible to attack."

Tori observed Cassie carefully over the top of her cup, gauging her receptiveness. Cassie's arms were uncrossed. Tori took a deep breath and continued.

"She's like many of us. We don't admit it, but, irrationally, yes, we want you to fix our child. All our own efforts have tanked. The educational system is our last hope."

"But, common sense—"

Tori held up her hand.

"A parent backed into a corner has the common sense of an enraged tigress protecting a threatened cub."

Cassie's grin was reluctant.

"Doesn't make it any easier to deal with." She drummed her fingernails on the table. "Thankfully, all parents aren't like that."

"There'll always be a few, just as there are special needs workers better suited as accountants or prison guards." Tori took a deep breath. "Remember the boy who committed suicide after being put in isolation daily for months?"

Cassie dropped her eyes.

"I cried for hours. We were devastated."

Tori touched Cassie's hand.

"I know, but the knowledge of abuse is another factor that can make a parent appear hyper-sensitive and unreasonable."

Sunbeam materialized at Cassie's elbow.

"I just know you're going to love—"

Cassie, startled, turned as Sunbeam bent over. Her shoulder connected with the dessert tray and sent cheesecake flying into Tori's lap.

"Oh, no! I am so sorry! Sunbeam exclaimed, as she wiped ineffectively at Tori's lap with a napkin.

"Never mind," Tori said. She stood and let the cheesecake fall to the floor.

"I think a wet cloth may work better."

The waitress hustled away, hands to her cheeks.

"Let's re-name her Ubiquitous Sunbeam," Tori said, shaking her head. "She's everywhere we don't expect her to be."

"Don't change the subject. *You're* reasonable. You handled the bit with Gabe's aggression more rationally than I would have expected."

"I've grown some over the years."

"Yes. You have the rep of being logical, for a parent."

"The rep?"

Cassie grinned sheepishly.

"Teachers talk. Word is you're one of the exceptions. Lots of parents walk into IEP meetings wearing combat boots, with a copy of the latest Individual with Disabilities Education Act (IDEA) rulings tucked under one arm and their attorney's number on speed dial. Your friend, Monica, is one of them."

"Monica's memorized IDEA; she doesn't need a copy. As for me, evidently you haven't spoken with Gabe's original third grade teacher. *He* wouldn't describe me as reasonable." Tori gave a lopsided grin. "Overall, I'm a typical special needs mom."

"Yeah, right. I hear you come in with a basket of muffins under one arm."

"The third grade teacher's muffins had ex-lax instead of chocolate chips. But I do try to come in peace. As Serena says, you catch fatter grasshoppers with honey than you do with vinegar. However, on my other arm is my laptop, fully-charged, with IDEA and case law at my fingertips."

Cassie made a face at her.

"See. Even you come in expecting to fight."

"If a parent isn't educated about what their child is entitled to, the school system may not feel compelled to inform them. Present company exempted," Tori said sweetly.

Cassie's mouth drooped.

"Unfortunately, if all parents fully understood what their child was entitled to, states would go bankrupt. The parents who do understand . . . present company exempted—" Cassie fluttered her eyelashes at Tori, "—often have an entitlement mentality. If some doctor develops a treatment using oxygen bottled in Tibet at $750 a bottle, there are parents who expect the school system to pay for it."

"Hey," Tori said with an ingenuous expression, "Phillip read about that yesterday. We were thinking of trying it. Surely, the school will—"

Cassie ignored her.

"Sometimes it's cheaper for schools to give in than to fight, leaving less money for mainstream therapies."

Tori raised a finger.

"Yes, but some of the treatments schools fought against in the past are now validated mainstream therapies. I guess both sides need to fight for funding and keep an open mind."

"*Where* did you develop that attitude? You should teach parenting classes."

Tori grimaced.

"You see my good side. I know how I *should* think and act. I don't always live up to it. Trust me."

"That's what I'm talking about!" Cassie exclaimed. "Your 'how I should think and act?' standards; where did they come from?"

"There are free seminars all over town every Sunday" Tori said. "Open to educators *and* parents."

"Sundays? I haven't heard of . . . oh, no . . . you don't mean . . . are you talking church?"

"Nope. Not *church*. I'm talking about a deep trust that God is good and in control, which means Gabe is in better hands than mine—"

"Yeah, yeah. I know. God will work this all out for good, despite my rancid circumstances," Cassie said, giving Tori a saccharine smile while she twisted her index finger in a fake dimple.

"Sorry, not interested!"

"Well," Tori smiled mischievously, "you asked. Sorry you don't like the answer."

She looked at her menu.

"I'm starving. They have high-fiber, low-fat muffins, sweetened with fruit juice. Wonder if they're even vaguely edible? Do you have room for a snack after that massive hunk of cheesecake you ate?" Tori looked pointedly at Cassie's empty dessert plate.

"There's always room for another snack, Your Reverence. I'll have the sour cream pound cake, toasted with butter, topped with raspberries and ice cream, while you tell me how Lydia's counseling is going. She seems more content lately." Cassie twisted in her seat and looked around. "Where's Sunbeam now that we want her?"

"Have I ever mentioned I wish you and your perfect figure would blossom exponentially?"

Her quip broke the tension and they passed to a discussion of Lydia's emerging acceptance of her adoption. However, occasionally, throughout the next hour, Tori caught Cassie studying her thoughtfully.

CHAPTER 23

Irrevocable Decision

"You couldn't have said *or* done anything to stop me." Tori's voicemail ended.

Monica and Song must be back from Germany.

Tori's shoulders sagged. She wasn't up for another misery-laden discussion with her friend. A conversation with Monica had inspired the nickname: **Moa**nica. Tori had told Monica that listening to her gripe was like drinking a double shot of vinegar. Monica had been a good sport, laughing at the name, and nicknaming Tori *St. Sunshine* in retaliation.

She sounds devastated. Guess the stem cells replacement didn't take.

Tori had warned Monica not to pin all her hopes on the controversial treatment. Monica's defiant message indicated she expected Tori to say, "I told you so."

A friend would call.

Tori squared her shoulders and dialed. No answer. Her forehead puckered. Monica could not resist a ringing phone. She usually answered, if only to snarl and hang up.

Tori groaned. Her friend was capable of working herself into a month-long blue funk if no one re-directed her. Fortunately, she did not live far away.

Feeling noble, Tori decided to sacrifice a batch of fudge on the altar of Monica's depression. Tori packed up some homemade fudge, and then dropped a Clementine Orange in her purse for Song, who followed a special diet.

"Lydia, watch Gabe. I need to see Monica for a few minutes."

"Aw, Mom! I've got homework!"

"You're on Facebook."

"But what if Gabe tries to bite or hit me?"

"I won't be long and Gabe's never attacked you. He's eight months aggression-free since we adjusted his meds. Besides, he's on the computer. He probably won't know I'm gone until dinnertime. You won't have trouble, but if you do, call Serena."

Scooping her keys off the counter, Tori escaped before Lydia could protest further.

Monica did not answer the doorbell. Tori peered through the sidelights. There were suitcases in the entryway. Tori rang again, and then tried the door.

Locked, of course.

Tori breathed a sigh of relief. She'd tried. She would call again later. As she turned to go, she heard a sound like a motor running from the garage.

Maybe they're getting ready to go out.

Tori waited for a minute, but the garage door did not open. Puzzled, she walked to the back of the house. As she peered in through the dirty windowpanes on the door leading from the yard to the garage, she caught a whiff of exhaust.

Inside the garage, Monica's old van was running. Fear sent adrenalin coursing through Tori's veins. She took off a shoe, smashed one of the windows panes. Shards of glass cut her arm as she reached in and unlocked the door.

The smell of exhaust filled her nostrils seconds before the wave of gas hit. Gagging, she scrabbled her fingers along the rough wall, looking for the garage door controls. Her throat was burning by the time her fingertips located the button and punched it.

Fresh air rushed in, ripping into the carbon monoxide shroud. Coughing, Tori wrenched open the door of Monica's 1995 Dodge Caravan.

Monica was frowning. She ignored Tori.

Thank God, she's alive.

Tori pulled at her arm.

"C'mon, you've gotta get out of here!"

Monica tipped to the side and lay rigid; half in, half out of the car. Her glare never shifted. A quick check of Monica's pulse confirmed death. Cringing, Tori leaned in and turned off the ignition, shuddering as she brushed against Monica's body.

Song lay curled in the back seat, an orange mustache on her stiffly smiling face. A bag of Cheetos lay on the floorboard beside an empty package of Oreo cookies. Song's rigid fingers extended a dirty spoon toward a carton of melted ice cream.

Tori forced herself to touch Song's still wrist. Nothing.

Gasping, Tori stumbled outside through the fumes, threw up the iced tea she had drunk a lifetime earlier, and fumbled to extricate her phone from her pocket. She dialed 9-1-1.

"Ledo County 9-1-1. What is the nature of your emergency?"

"They're dead!"

Tori sank to her knees in the grass, retching.

"Ma'am, are you in a safe location?" the dispatch clerk asked urgently.

Tori wiped her mouth with her hand.

"Yes."

"What's the address?"

"Address?" Tori said blankly. "I have no idea."

The clerk's voice was patient.

"Can you look at the mailbox?"

"Oh, yeah, hang on." Tori stumbled to her feet, went to the mailbox and read. "It's 529 Eagle's Overlook in Norcross."

"Thank you. An officer will be there shortly, please wait."

Minutes crept by, or maybe they flew. It must have been a little while because the blood from the cuts on her arm soaked her sleeves and clotted. She noticed two police officers circling the house, guns drawn. She started to call out, decided it was too much effort, and sunk back into a stupor.

Someone shook Tori's shoulder. She became aware of sirens and flashing lights. People were shouting and clusters of neighbors stood in their yards gawking.

"Ma'am, I'm Officer Raeburn. Are you all right? Did you call 9-1-1?"

Tori looked up. It took a few seconds to process his words.

"Yes."

The officer looked young, twenty-two years old at most. Tori noticed he seemed a little pale. He looked at Tori's bloody arm.

"Those are nasty gashes. Let's have the EMT take a look. Hey, Miller," he yelled to his fellow officer, "talk to the neighbors. Witness needs medical attention."

"I broke the window. They were in the van. I thought maybe . . . they were . . . Song just turned thirteen!" Tori wailed.

"I'm sorry, Ma'am." Officer Raeburn helped Tori to her feet and guided her to the ambulance, where the emergency medical technician started working on her arm.

"May I see your ID?" the officer asked.

"In my purse; in my car." Tori tipped her head towards the Miata. "It's unlocked."

The officer went to her car and retrieved her purse. Tori pulled out her driver's license and handed it to him. She thought he stiffened when he read her name.

"Tori St. John?"

"Yes."

The officer spoke into his radio. "Doctor, I have Tori St. John with me."

He listened a moment.

"Affirmative."

He turned to Tori.

"The medical examiner will be here in a few minutes. She'll probably want to ask you some questions."

Tori nodded, looked toward the garage and started shaking. The emergency medical technician draped a blanket around her shoulders. The police officer allowed her to call Serena, but listened carefully.

"Can you watch the kids? I'm at Monica's. She . . . she and Song are dead."

"Madre de Dios!"

Tori held the phone away from her ear as Serena squawked.

"Are you safe? The burglars may still . . ."

"I'm . . . fine. The police are here. I don't think . . . I don't think it was robbers. It looks like . . . oh, Serena, think Monica did it! She left me a message but I didn't think . . . her van was running . . . there was a towel stuffed in the door. They were inside . . . lots of treats for Song . . ."

Tori's teeth started chattering. The youthful cop took the phone from her and spoke softly to Serena. The emergency medical technician brought another blanket.

"Your kids will be fine, Mrs. St. John. Mrs. D'Angelo will take care of them."

A car drove up, and a tall woman in a well-cut blue pants suit emerged. She spoke to Officer Raeburn a moment, and then came over to where Tori sat in the grass. She extended a long, shapely hand.

"Dr. AnnaLee Roche," she said. "I'm the medical examiner."

Her voice was raspy, but not unpleasant.

"Tori St John."

The doctor nodded. She was striking, rather than pretty, with sharply defined cheek-bones. Tori thought she would be attractive when she smiled.

"You knew the victims?"

"They're friends. Her name is Monica Flowers. Her daughter is . . . was . . . Song."

The medical examiner took notes.

"I see. Why were you here?"

"She left a depressed message on my answering system. I couldn't reach her, so I came over . . ."

Tears gushed from Tori's eyes. She swabbed at her face with her shirtsleeve. Roche handed her a tissue.

"What time did Ms. Flowers leave the message?"

"Um, I don't know. I got it when I got home, about four o'clock, I guess. I could call my daughter and ask her to check."

"Never mind. We'll pull a copy if we need it. Did her message threaten suicide?"

"I didn't take it that way. It just said I couldn't have made a difference. I thought she was talking about stem cell replacement therapy. Song had profound autism and Monica was always trying different treatments."

"I see. What time did you leave your home?"

"As soon as I got the message. No later than 4:15 p.m., probably earlier."

"Mrs. St. John, was it typical for you go to Ms. Flowers home if she didn't answer her phone? Were you worried she might do something drastic?"

Tori shifted in the seat.

"Not worried, exactly. She sounded so down, though. I knew she'd been counting on this therapy. I wanted to cheer her up."

The medical examiner studied Tori for a few moments, not without compassion. She then took Tori step-by-step through her actions after getting Monica's message. Each question pounded another nail of irrevocability into the coffin of two wasted lives.

"Please explain again the exact positions of the bodies when you found them."

As Tori started recounting the nightmare, her stomach roiled. She stumbled to the side and started retching again. Roche handed her more tissues.

"Now, about the bodies—"

"*Not* bodies, detective!" Tori screamed. "Monica and Song! They were my friends and they're dead and I can't . . . won't . . . can't describe again how they looked, dead. I've told you everything I know. Monica killed Song, and then killed herself. End of story."

Tori hugged her body and rocked.

"We have to ask these questions when investigating a suspicious death," the detective said soothingly. "You're our only witness. Just a few more questions, and then you can go."

Tori gripped her hair in two handfuls, and then let it fall.

"Okay," she said wearily. "What?"

"Can you explain the food in the back seat with the bod . . . with the teen?"

"Song was on a special diet. She couldn't eat the junk food normal kids love, the kind of food in the back seat. I guess . . . I guess Monica wanted her to die happy."

Tori's thoughts whirled.

This can't be happening. *Song's dead. Monica killed her. Song and Monica are dead.*

Roche's hoarse voice cut through the fog.

"She left a letter for you. You can read it, but please don't take it out of the plastic bag."

She handed Tori a sheet of paper enclosed in a plastic bag. Tori took the letter with trembling hands.

"Thank you."

Dear Tori:

The stem cell didn't work. There's nothing left to try. I can't go on like this, can't condemn Song to a lifetime of misery.

You're my best friend, the only one who'll care much. Try to understand. Song will never go to the prom or homecoming. I'll never listen to "Pomp and Circumstance"[9] and watch my daughter get a diploma. Song won't experience romance, yet I live in fear of her being molested. After all, Song can't tell on anyone. I'll never plan a wedding or hold a grandchild in my arms. Too many won'ts and nevers.

And who will take care of Song when I die? Certainly not Harold and Pop-Tart.

Funny what you think about when you're going to die. You said God was merciful, so I prayed. Told Him I hadn't followed Him and didn't deserve heaven, but would He please take Song? You know what? I felt God smile at us; me and Song.

I almost didn't go through with it. But God won't fix Song's autism. If that were the case, He'd fix Gabe, because you're so good, St. Sunshine.

Keep fighting. I can't.

---

9   Composed by English composer, Sir Edward Elgar (1857–1934)

Love, Moanica

When she finished, Dr. Roche took the letter.

"Does it look like her handwriting?"

"I think so. We mostly emailed, texted, talked on the phone. She talked like the letter's written."

"Do you know who Harold and Pop-Tart are?"

Tori snorted.

"Her jerk of an ex-husband and his new wife."

"Did they have a cordial relationship?"

"Hardly. Harold was behind on child support and treated Song like she didn't exist."

"We'll talk to them."

Tori dropped her head back against the seat.

"I hate autism. I hate it; hate what it made Monica do. Most of all I hate I wasn't there for Monica when she called."

The medical examiner's voice was sympathetic.

"I'm sorry for your loss. You're free to go, but we'd appreciate it if you stay in town in case we need to talk to you further."

"I'm not going anywhere."

Tori dropped her forehead onto her arms and cried for dreams and opportunities lost, for irrevocable decisions.

By the time she had reviewed and signed her statement, Tori was so pale, Officer Raeburn pronounced her unfit to drive. He got Phillip's number, called, and held a low-voiced conversation.

"He's leaving right away," the policeman said.

Tori sighed with relief.

Delia had a problem understanding why Phillip was leaving. Her eyes narrowed as Phillip shut down his laptop.

"You can't possibly leave right now. We need—"

Phillip gave her a startled look.

"Didn't you hear what the policeman said?" He spoke loudly enough. "Tori's friend murdered her daughter then committed suicide. Tori found the bodies. She's been interrogated for over an hour, and now that she's free to go, she's not fit to drive, poor kid."

"Can't you call a taxi for her?"

Phillip frowned at her.

"I just meant," Delia said with a concerned look, "that a taxi would get the poor thing home quicker."

"She doesn't need a taxi right now, she needs her husband. I'll see you tomorrow."

Phillip took the eight flights of stairs two at a time.

I can't believe Delia expected me to stay and work. I know she's business-minded, but that was pure iceberg.

Phillip usually stayed one mile under the exact speed limit, but today he drove fifteen miles over. On the way, he called Frederica, the moderator of the special needs support group. He got voice mail, and, after a moment's hesitation, left a message. Tough way to break the news, but he didn't want Tori to feel like she needed to talk to Freddi tonight.

Phillip grimaced. Tori was going to have a tough time getting over this. He pounded the steering wheel. How could Monica be so stupid, so irresponsible, and so inconsiderate?

Why are stoplights always red when I'm in a hurry?

Phillip looked up special needs suicide on his android. He was appalled to get so many hits.

At every light, Phillip skimmed articles. He was dismayed at the level of stress cited.

Is Tori this stressed, too? She always seems to have it together.

He pulled into Monica's neighborhood, a cluster of tired-looking homes built in the 70s and 80s. Grass grew up between cracks in the pavement, and most of the street signs sagged. Monica's house was surrounded by emergency vehicles and curious onlookers.

Tori sat, forlorn, in the back of a squad car. Phillip got out, greeted the officer, and pulled Tori into a hug.

"Is she free to go, officer?"

"Yes. We'll let you know if there's anything else."

Phillip supported Tori as he walked her to the car.

"I'm so sorry, Munchkin. I hate you were the one to find them. You're shivering; let's get you to the car."

Phillip started the car and turned the heat up.

"Are you going to be okay?"

Tori pounded her fist on the dashboard.

"Why, why, *why* did I have to get my nails done today? If I'd been there when she called, I could have—"

Phillip killed the ignition, reached across the console, and folded Tori into an awkward hug. She burrowed into him.

It's been a long time since Phillip held me. Our marriage hasn't been great lately, but he's here when it counts. Faithful, reliable Phillip.

Phillip stroked Tori's hair. When the deluge subsided, he reached into his glove compartment, pulled out a hand-towel, wiped her face, and then tipped her chin up.

"This wasn't your fault, Ma Petite. You spent hours listening to Monica gripe."

"She could really irritate me. I used to zone out sometimes—cook dinner, pay bills . . ."

Tori gulped. "If I'd listened to her closely, I'd have known she was suicidal."

"Monica was obsessed with fixing Song. Short of curing autism, you couldn't have helped her."

They pulled in the driveway.

"You go upstairs, take a hot bath, drink some wine, and go to bed. I'll take the kids to dinner. I've already called Freddi. Try to rest."

Tori was tormented by relentless nightmares. They started off pleasantly at the nail salon. Tori reclined in a luxurious vibrating chair, her feet soaking in warm, bubbly water, while an attentive young woman massaged her hands with fragrant lotion.

A phone rang in the background. She heard Monica's voice pleading for help. Tori attempted to get up, but found her body immobilized in the chair. Thrashing violently, she broke free and ran for the door.

The door opened into Monica's garage. Monica hung stiffly out of the van door, eyes glaring. Song was still alive! She could be saved if Tori could just turn off the ignition. Gasping, Tori struggled to turn the key, but it would not budge.

She wrenched open the back door to pull Song out, but the teen was happy eating ice cream topped with Cheetos and would not come. Tori pulled at her arm, fell backwards, and ended up in the nail salon, where the entire sequence started over.

The dreams left Tori afraid to go to sleep. She dragged through the days on willpower, energy drinks, and caffeine.

Freddi called a special support group meeting. As the members came in and sat down, they sneaked sideways glances at each other, as if wondering who might be next.

Freddi had asked Tori to speak. Her friends' faces reflected shock and dismay as she read a copy of the suicide note. While Monica had stayed on the fringes of the group, she'd still been one of them. They thought they had known her. Their grief-stricken self-recriminations echoed Tori's own.

Other than that meeting, Tori avoided people. For a week, she got the kids off to school, and then walked the neighborhood, thinking and remembering. She tried to put herself in Monica's shoes, to feel what Monica felt, to somehow rationalize the unexplainable. Tori recalled conversations and analyzed them, looking for some pre-cursor to her friend's reprehensible act.

"Mom, I'm sorry about Miss Monica . . . and Song. You must be really sad."

Tori sat slumped at the kitchen table. Lydia walked over and briefly touched Tori's head.

"I think, when I'm grown up, I'd like to be a psychologist, maybe; to stop people from doing stuff like this."

Lydia bent to kiss Tori's cheek.

"And to help people like you, who blame themselves."

Tori smiled up at her daughter.

"You'd be an awesome psychologist."

Lydia scuffed her foot.

"Thanks. And thanks for making me see the counselor. It's helped. Mom . . ." Lydia seemed reluctant to continue.

"What, Sweetheart?"

"This probably isn't a good time to mention it, but, someday, I really do want to see if I can find some of my biological family. It's not that I don't love you and Gabe and Daddy, but I need to understand my roots."

Tori nodded. "I get that, Princessa. When you're a little older, after high-school, maybe, we'll help you look for them."

"Thanks, Mom, you're the best. Try and have a good day."

The door slammed. Tori stared after her daughter.

She's growing into a caring young lady, despite the time I don't spend with her.

Serena poured iced tea and pushed a plate of fresh baked cookies toward Tori.

"Your favorite, Pobrecita. Toffee-oatmeal with dark chocolate. You have lost too much of weight."

Tori forcibly swallowed a bite. Serena's fabulous cookies tasted like ashes. She took a long draught of tea, gripping the cool glass like a life-preserver.

"I have seen you, Querida, walking your pilgrimage. You walked for your friend's memory?"

"Partly. Monica could be a pain, but we fought the same war."

"You ask yourself, did I abandon her on the battlefield?"

Tori lifted her chin.

"Pretty much; I also thought about how not to become another casualty."

Serena dropped her cookie.

"I know you do not think of suicide! What are you saying?"

Tori smiled for the first time since finding Monica. She patted Serena's hand.

"No, of course not. But there are many types of deaths. Emotional, relational . . ."

Serena swatted Tori's leg.

"Do not scare me like this again. Scotch has eaten my cookie before it hit the floor. Bad perro!"

Scotch put his head between his paws and whined. Serena frowned at the black German shepherd.

"Me, I do not think you look repentant," she scolded. She turned her attention to Tori. "You found answers?"

"Yes." Tori met Serena's eyes squarely. "Monica made her own decision. Maybe I could've helped if I'd listened more carefully. I'll never know. I can't spare the energy to agonize over a past I can't change."

Serena touched Tori's shoulder.

"A wise conclusion." She reached for another cookie. "If you will not eat these so delicious cookies, I will. A lady must maintain her strength. What do you think made Monica give up the fight? You describe her as a warrior most determined."

Tori took a deep breath.

"Monica misidentified the target."

Serena raised a salt-and-pepper eyebrow and studied Tori.

"You interest me. You interest me extremely."

"I was so angry at God . . . about this whole aggression thing with Gabe," Tori said. "Now that his medicine's correct and he's in second tier, Gabe's fine; I wasn't. I felt like we were on a treadmill, running backwards."

Tori swung her foot back and forth.

"Monica's suicide made me re-evaluate. Monica wanted to fix Song, but Song wasn't broken. Monica was. I was, too."

Tori went to the big kitchen window and gazed out. Serena's glass was so clean Tori felt as if she could have put her hand out and touched the butterfly fluttering about the window sill.

"People with special needs are full human beings; irreplaceable in and of themselves. Our children need help, but they don't need to be fixed. There's a difference."

Tori touched her heart.

"I know this . . . with indestructible certainty . . . now."

Serena stood beside Tori.

"This means you will no longer search to cure my Gabriel?"

Tori looked at Serena as if she'd lost her mind. Serena returned the look blandly. Tori glowered at her for a moment, and then started giggling.

"You do go for the jugular, don't you? I'll still do everything possible to help Gabe. I'll work to inform people about autism. I'll lobby for society to treat special needs individuals with respect. I'll hunt tirelessly for answers and relish every incremental improvement that makes Gabe's life better in any way."

Serena crossed her arms.

"And that is different how, Amazona Pequena?"

Tori punched Serena lightly on the shoulder.

"You're right, I'll still be a little Amazon warrior. The difference is I no longer believe Gabe will be miserable if I can't bring him to a certain level of functionality. I won't think I've failed if I can't get him there. Gabe will enjoy life on his own terms."

Serena had tears in her eyes as she hugged Tori.

"Ahh, Victoria. You are dancing out of the shadows."

Monica and Song were buried privately, side-by-side. A small memorial service was attended largely by support group members. Song's teacher spoke movingly about what a sweet, lovable girl Song had been. Then it was Tori's turn to take the podium.

"Monica's greatest wish was to give Song normalcy. We're here today because Monica thought she failed."

Monica falling out the van door rigid and lifeless. Song's stiff fingers reaching for ice cream.

Tori closed her eyes and shivered.

Hold yourself together, Victoria.

She dug her nails into her hand, opened her eyes, and took a deep breath. The grim memory interspersed itself with swirling black dots, and then receded.

Tori lifted up a sheaf of notes.

"I intended to share some uplifting thoughts, but Monica used to call me little St. Sunshine and tell me not to spout delusional cheer. I'd give almost anything to hear Moanica, as I teasingly called her, harass me about being over-optimistic."

Tori sniffed back tears.

"In honor of Monica, I'm not going to attempt fake words of encouragement."

She dropped the papers on the podium, bent her head for a moment, and then looked into the eyes of her listeners.

"I've realized that I, like Monica, sometimes act like autism sentences our children to a life devoid of purpose and meaning. I've felt I couldn't fully enjoy parenthood while my child had this disability. That's wrong."

She took a sip from a glass of water and looked out.

"Autism isn't our enemy."

Tori saw surprise on Phillip's face. Cassie looked uneasy. Tori swallowed and took another sip of water.

I'm probably about to offend someone.

Serena caught her eye and gave Tori an encouraging smile.

"Autism's horrible; absolutely, but it doesn't diminish the value of the individuals who struggle with it. It doesn't have to lessen the quality of life for their families. My attitude toward disability is the real enemy."

Tori thrust two tightly closed fists towards the audience.

"In all the years I knew Monica, this is how she held her dreams for Song. And how I've held mine for Gabe and for myself as his mother."

The audience listened intently. Her friend Seth, sitting stiffly in a coat and tie, nodded and gave her thumbs up.

Tori slowly unfolded her fists until she held them, palms up, to the ceiling.

"This is how we need to hold our dreams: loosely, with room to come true in different ways. Open, to fully celebrate what our children are without mourning what may have been."

Tori gripped the edges of the podium and raised her chin.

"Normal is just a point-of-view."

There was a moment of silence, and then soft applause escorted Tori off the stage.

CHAPTER 24

The Storm Breaks

Tori savored a second cup of tea and scrutinized her to-do list for ways to stretch the available minutes.

"I may be able to finish the grant request during speech therapy," she told Amber.

The phone jangled.

"Hello?"

"This is Seth. Can you meet me at Starbucks in thirty minutes?"

"Half an hour? I just finished working out, I'm rank. Can't we talk on the phone?" Tori circled an item with her pencil.

This can wait.

She really could not fit one more thing into her day.

"This needs to be face-to-face," Seth insisted.

"What's going on? Are you okay?"

"I'm fine, but we need to talk today. It's important."

After Monica's death, Tori had vowed she would always make time for anyone who needed to talk. Forty minutes later, fresh from the shower, sans makeup, she joined Seth at an outdoor table.

"Mind if we go inside? It's a little chilly. My hair's still wet."

"It's more private here." Seth handed her a steaming cup.

"Tea, not coffee, right? Want my hoodie?"

"No." Tori sat and wrapped her fingers around the hot container. "What's up?"

Chapter 24 – The Storm Breaks

Seth looked down and tapped a spoon on the wrought-iron table. The door swung open, ejecting two people, a blast of warmth and the nutty, dark smell of freshly ground coffee. Seth watched them pass, and then turned back to her. He opened his mouth to speak, and then shut it.

"We needed to talk?" Tori prompted.

She glanced at her watch. To Tori's surprise, when she looked up Seth's face was pale.

"Seth? You don't look well. Are you sick?"

"No. Sorry. I don't know how to say this."

Beads of sweat popped out on his forehead.

"Just spit it out."

He looked up, and with a glance of pure misery, said, "Phillip's having an affair."

The table seemed to slip. Tori grabbed the edge. Seth's face swam in and out of a sea surging ocean, his voice muffled by shrieking winds and crashing waves.

Seth jumped up, put a hand on her shoulder, and shook it gently, and then waved his coffee cup under her nose.

"Your face is white. I shouldn't have said anything."

Tori took a gulp of his coffee and held the scalding liquid in her mouth. The pain steadied her.

"Delia?"

Even as she asked, she recognized she already knew.

"Yes. Rumors have been flying. No one wants to say anything."

His lips twisted as if he had swallowed vinegar.

"Everyone was too nice to tell me Karla was running around. I swore if I ever found one of my friends in the same position, I'd tell."

"Are you sure?"

Tori twisted her napkin, dabbed at her lips, and then stuck the napkin in her ice water and wiped her neck.

"They're working on a big project. I asked Phillip once if Delia was more than business. He said no. I've known Phillip for twenty years. If he were lying, I'd know."

Seth looked at Tori with pity.

"I saw them yesterday. I've seen them together before, but this time the looks Delia was giving Phillip were pornographic. He wasn't quite as intense, but if they aren't already lovers, it won't be long."

Seth put his hand over hers and squeezed. "I'm sorry, really, really sorry. If there's anything I can do—"

Tori gripped his hand for a second before she pulled away. "Thanks. You're a good friend." She pushed her chair back. "I have to go."

Tori drove home through a mist of shock. Bile rose in her throat. Once home, she barely made it to the bathroom before she became violently ill. She lay on the bed, curled in a fetal position, and mourned.

After an hour or so, the pain throbbing in her temple turned from hurt to fury. She got up and strode back and forth, smacking her fist into her palm. Amber disappeared under the bed.

"That conniving Jezebel . . . I'm going to wring her anorexic neck. And Phillip! Castration's too good for the randy moron! After all these years!"

Her rage built to a crescendo. Stomping downstairs to the refrigerator, she ripped off every picture that contained her husband and ripped it to shreds. After a few minutes, the floor was dotted with little heaps of Phillip-confetti. Standing in the middle of the kitchen, fists clenched at her side, Tori threw back her head and howled, a primal scream of wrath mixed with fear.

Exhausted, Tori collapsed into a chair.

I love the philandering jerk. How will I go on if I lose him?

She thought, prayed, and then thought some more. Picking up the phone to call Serena, she set it back down. Tori knew what she needed to do. A few phone calls later, her day was clear.

Tori went into the bathroom to don battle gear. Her hair went up into an elegant chignon, with a few wispy curls hanging on each side. She worked on her makeup until it was perfect, and then went to her closet.

She had lost weight and firmed up.

Should I wear her skinny jeans and a tight sweater?

No. She would not try to out-vamp Delia.

Chapter 24 — The Storm Breaks

Instead, Tori chose a flattering blue sheath. The classy dress skimmed over her curves, hinting at hidden fire. She fastened on pearl earrings, strapped on blue heels, and eyed herself in the mirror. Amber came out of concealment and meowed approval.

Tori looked good. As an extra confidence boost, she spritzed with her last bit of Patou's "Joy."

Half an hour later, she arrived at Phillip's office. She took the elevator to his floor and went to what was called *admin mile*, where the support staff worked.

"Oh, hi, Tori. Mr. St. John isn't here—"

Tori bestowed a dazzling smile on Phillip's aide.

"That's fine; I'm here to see Delia."

There was a brief second of alert silence, and then everyone pretended to be busy. The assistant scanned her computer screen.

"Ms. Minton is in. I don't see you on her schedule—"

Tori spoke sweetly.

"Don't worry, this won't take long."

She swept down the hall to Delia's glass-walled office. Excited murmurs rose behind her. Tori opened Delia's closed door, stepped in, and shut it firmly behind her.

Delia looked up. Her irritated expression turned to surprise.

"What are you doing here? Phillip's gone—"

"I know. I'm here to see you."

Tori sat in one of Delia's leather chairs and crossed her legs. Delia seemed at a loss.

"Admin row looks intrigued by our meeting. Wonder why they think I came?" Tori said, as a receptionist passed the office with a furtive glance.

Delia's eyes narrowed.

"Why did you?"

"To slap a HANDS-OFF sticker on Phillip."

Delia smirked.

"You're a little late."

"He's not your lover. You're not quite smug enough."

"Not yet. He will be."

"I wonder." Out of the corner of her eye, Tori saw a matronly lady walk by with a sideways glance. "Tell me, how would upper management feel about you having an affair with an employee two levels below you?"

Delia stiffened. Her eyes became wary.

"Phillip's not a direct report."

"Mmm; still doesn't look good. Makes staff nervous, creates a fearful, hostile environment. I have friends here. They tell me Phillip's old boss, Stuart, has the company embroiled in a major sexual harassment suit. Your CEO's livid. Maybe I should stop by his office, give my imitation of a loose cannon, and talk about my press connections."

"Are you threatening me?" Delia bared her teeth. "You're out of your league, Traci. Tell you what. Maybe if you're a good girl, I'll stop with an affair, instead of marrying Phillip."

Tori looked across the desk and curled her lips.

"As if."

She pulled a family photo out of her large purse and handed it to Delia.

Delia sneered.

"You think showing me your happy family will make me back off?"

"Not at all, Delilah. That would imply you have morals."

Delia's fists clenched.

Tori leaned toward her.

"I'm letting you know what I'm fighting for."

She locked her eyes onto Delia's.

"Phillip and I have been married fifteen years. We balance each other. We . . . fit. It's been rough since we got the kids. I'm not surprised he's tempted by your blatant charms. However, Phillip *does* have morals and discerning taste. I can work with that."

"Why, you—" Delia sputtered.

She half rose from her chair, gripping the arms, her face contorted with rage.

"Ahh, ahh, ahh."

Chapter 24 – The Storm Breaks

Tori wagged her index finger at Delia and tipped her head toward glass wall. A secretary gave them sideways glances as she slowly walked by.

"Don't want them talking any more than they already are, do you?"

Delia ground her teeth, but pasted an unconvincing smile on her face and sank back into the chair. Tori rose.

"I'll do whatever it takes to keep my family intact. Consider yourself warned."

Quietly shutting the door, she left, beaming broadly at the admin pool.

"Game on, ladies."

She winked and marched, head high, to the elevator.

His home was quiet and filled with the fragrant aroma of roasting meat. Phillip's mouth watered as he tossed his briefcase on the couch and shucked off his coat. Following his nose to the kitchen, he kissed Tori on the cheek, lifted the crock-pot lid, and inhaled.

"Yum; pot roast! The kids won't be happy."

The kids hated pot roast, especially the carrots and onions. He glanced at the table. It was set for two. A flask of his favorite homemade vinaigrette sat beside a steaming breadbasket. Phillip was glad he had called to say he was on his way home. He was starving.

"Speaking of kids, where are they?"

"They're at Serena's tonight. Dinner's ready. Would you pour our drinks?"

"Serena has them? What's the occasion?" he asked, as he poured iced tea.

"You look nice, by the way," he added.

Her glossy hair hung down her back over one of his favorite sweaters. Her snug-fitting jeans emphasized her shapely rear.

"You've been doing well on your exercise; I can tell the difference."

Did I imagine it or did Tori's shoulders stiffen?

"Thanks." Tori spoke pleasantly.

Whew. I imagined it.

Tori served their plates, they sat, and Phillip blessed the meal.

"Mmm, this is really good. I've missed your honey-multigrain yeast rolls. Again, what's the occasion?"

"I thought we should do some long-term planning."

"Oh, good idea. We haven't looked at goals and priorities in a while."

As the meal continued, Phillip became a bit uneasy. There was tension in the air, something Phillip couldn't quite put his finger on. Finally, he pushed back his chair.

"Excellent meal, Honey. I'll help clean up later. Let's get that planning out of the way."

Tori led the way to the couch.

"Shouldn't we go into my office? The financial records are there."

"No."

Something is definitely off.

Phillip took a deep breath, sat down and crooked an eyebrow.

"So, what type of planning are we doing?"

"Futures planning. As in, is your future with us or Delia?"

Phillip closed his eyes. He opened them to a green-eyed glare.

"I'm not sleeping with Delia."

"Do you plan to?"

Phillip hesitated. He fingered the crease of his trousers and sighed.

"I don't know."

He hated the stricken look on Tori's face, but he had always been honest with her.

"I've always been a good wife and mother. What are you looking for, a trophy wife? I never thought you were that shallow."

Phillip set his jaw. He was not taking full responsibility.

"Delia *sees* me."

"She sees you? What is that supposed to mean? I've been looking at you for fifteen years."

"No. Delia grasps the essential me. Since we got the kids, you see Gabe and Lydia's father; meal ticket; occasional lover. You don't see Phillip St. John."

Chapter 24 – The Storm Breaks

He jumped to his feet and began pacing. Tori jumped up and blocked his path, her stricken expression replaced by one of cold fury.

"Excuse me if I haven't spent enough time pampering you. I've been a little occupied, raising our children."

Phillip heard glass crack and saw blood trickling over Tori's fingers. She had snapped the fragile stem of her glass.

"I stood by you when you lost your job, never begrudged supporting us for a year while you found the perfect position. You can bet your sweet calculator Delia would never have done that. So, now you're looking for sexier pastures?"

Phillip set his jaw.

Wait a minute. I'm not accepting all the blame.

"Delia respects me. You don't, anymore. And you're bleeding."

Tori wrapped her hand in a napkin.

"This is nothing compared to what your leaving will do to our kids."

"They're more yours than they are mine."

Their voices had become increasingly loud. Phillips words froze them into a stunned silence. Tori stepped back, her hand over her mouth.

Uh oh, rewind.

"Scratch that, Tori. I didn't mean it."

"You said it. Which means it was in your mind, if only subconsciously."

"No, really, I love the kids. It's just that—"

"Just what?"

Tori had crossed her arms, oblivious to the blood seeping through the napkin onto her sweater. Phillip felt a twinge of guilt but her accusing attitude made his hackles rise.

"You were the main one who wanted children. We were doing fine without them."

Phillip raked his fingers through his hair. Years of resentment bubbled to the surface and the words could not be stopped.

"We had all the time and money in the world. You knew me then, cared about where my career was going, what I thought, what I dreamed. Now, all you care about is fixing Gabe."

Tori poked a finger in his chest.

"You said you wanted kids."

"Of course, I did. I didn't want to lose you. I never realized I'd lose you to the kids."

Phillip kicked the leg of the coffee table and glared at her.

"I loved you. I would have said anything to make you happy."

Tori sank to the couch. She looked as if he'd bludgeoned her.

"Past tense, Phillip? You *loved* me?"

Phillip's anger drained away. His stiff shoulders wilted, his head drooped.

"I don't know what I think, anymore. Maybe I should move into the guest room."

"Should we get counseling or a lawyer?"

His head jerked up.

"A lawyer?" he said wrinkling his forehead.

"Of course. I can take care of myself, but I have children to provide for. I'd rather have you, but if Delia gets you, I'll take your money."

Oh my God, what have I done?

"I never said anything about divorce, Tori. In my own way, I love you and the kids. I don't want to lose you."

Tori's face contorted.

"In your own way? I won't play second fiddle. If you run into Delia's open arms and legs, we're done," she snarled.

Phillip considered apologizing, but raised his chin instead and headed toward the basement.

"Do what you need to do."

Afternoon sunlight filtered through the canopy of trees, its hazy beams contrasting with Phillip's dark mood as he meandered through the forest. He had skipped work, started driving, and ended up at Callaway Gardens.

He was one kiss away from an affair with Delia. He'd never been unfaithful. He would not sleep with Delia lightly. It could easily turn into more. Even if it didn't, would Tori ever forgive him?

Chapter 24 – The Storm Breaks

He came to Calloway's serene stone chapel and stepped inside. A fragrant, flower-scented breeze swayed the branches outside, causing fragmented streams of light to illuminate the beautiful stained glass windows.

Other than the soft rustling of pine needles and the occasional burst of birdsong, the sanctuary was silent. Phillip's angst defied its tranquility. Gazing unseeingly at the huge rock altar, he wondered what to do.

He cared for Tori, but she was not the carefree, adoring playmate he had married. Becoming a mother had made her a softer, deeper, more mature person. He admired the woman she had become, but missed his place at the center of her world.

Besides, Delia excites me. Tori doesn't, anymore.

Delia vibrated with life. He had always been drawn to successful professional women. Delia was as good a marketer as Tori had been. Tori never had Delia's take no prisoners attitude, though.

Tori won by putting herself in her clients' shoes, and not giving up until she found the best answer for everyone. She had the moral fiber to walk away when her company was not the best solution.

Delia never walked away from anything she wanted. Like an elegant bulldozer, she razed through opposition with no thought for the rubble left in her wake. She had clawed her way up the ladder in an industry that favored men.

Delia knew what she wanted. It was obvious one of the things she wanted was him. Phillip's heart beat faster as he remembered the provocative clothes she had started wearing.

Or have I just started to notice?

Phillip yanked his thoughts back to PG. Delia's physical beauty was not what made him long to be in her company.

Tori engrossed herself with Gabe and Lydia; Delia was absorbed in him. Delia respected him, looked up to him. To Tori, he was a cog in the family mechanism, a component to be corrected, adjusted, and brought into line with the overall plan. Her love for him was steady but complacent.

Although, there was nothing low-key about her last night.

"What about for better or for worse," a small voice asked. "Tori's diverted by this phase of life, which will pass. She's still

Tori. Don't destroy what you have because you want everything to be about you."

Phillip left the chapel.

God, You don't want me to be unhappy, do You? After all, You made me this way.

Phillip wondered if he still loved Tori, really loved her. If he didn't, wasn't he being unfair to stay in the marriage?

Leaves crunched under his feet, emitting a musty, deep forest smell. A light rain coated his face, leaving a sheen of moisture. Phillip hardly noticed. Choices and options tumbled in his head.

Carefree times and a hot career or hanging out with his family at the neighborhood pool? Sexy, driven Delia, or loyal, mature Tori; spunky Lydia; and . . . Gabe.

His sweet, troubled son—bright, yet unable to process; compliance interspersed with bouts of aggression—loveable, high maintenance Gabe. Lifelong responsibility. Phillip trudged on.

There are no answers.

"None that you want to hear, anyway," the quiet voice whispered.

Chapter 25
Accident

The thermometer read one hundred and three degrees. The afternoon was booked: first, an orthodontist appointment for Lydia then an appointment for Gabe's updated psych-social profile. Tori wanted to have it in time to compare with the school's profile at the next IEP meeting.

Tori's eyes throbbed. Everything ached, even her hair follicles. She called Phillip's cell phone.

"Hi, Tori, what's up?"

"I'm sick. High fever, dizzy . . . can you take the rest of the day off? The kids have back-to-back appointments."

"Let me see."

Tori heard talking in the background. Phillip groaned and came back on the phone.

"I'm sorry, there's a deadline we can't miss. Cancel the appointments and rest."

"Can't. The orthodontist charges for missed appointments and it takes forever to get an appointment with a Deeming Waiver psychologist."

"I'll be home by six o'clock. Promise. You can go straight to bed."

I forgot. No sick days in my Mom-contract.

"Okay." Tori said faintly.

They had been having brunch in a secluded corner booth when Tori called. Delia jumped Phillip the second he hung up.

"Phil-lip! We're working around the clock to get the contracts signed in time to hit this year's results. Tell you what; let's take a little break. Relieve some tension," Delia purred. "My condo's close by. I'm sure we'll concentrate better . . . after."

Phillip's mouth went dry.

"But . . . Tori . . . the deadline . . ."

"I've already finished the cost projections."

Phillip felt a frisson of irritation.

Why hadn't she told me?

Delia stretched, and then flicked her tongue over her lips.

That tongue; like a snake's. Smooth, fast, tempting . . .

Phillip tried hard to fan the small spark of anger he felt.

"Delia, you're telling me there's practically nothing left to do. I could've helped Tori. Why'd you lie to me?"

Delia shrugged. Phillip watched her breasts move under the wispy camisole that barely qualified as public attire. He drew in a sharp breath.

"I told a little fib," Delia placed her thumb and forefinger close together, "because I want you with me this morning."

She placed her hand on Phillip's thigh.

"As for Lori—all I'm talking about . . . for now . . . is raw, *un*-wifely sex between two consenting adults."

Phillip looked nervously around the restaurant. Good thing it was empty. Delia was practically in his lap.

"Tori," he said half-heartedly. "Not Lori."

Delia spoke softly, "If physical attraction is all it is, we'll enjoy and stop when we're bored. If it's more . . . it's fairer to *Tor-ee* if we discover it sooner rather than later, don't you think?"

Phillip was past thinking. He threw two twenties on the table and propelled Delia out of the restaurant.

Tori's head felt like a block of foam rubber. Serena did not answer and everyone else was at work, except Monica, who was dead. Tori shook her head.

Don't go there.

She was out of options. Tori poured a glass of juice, hoping the cool liquid would feel good. Instead, it burned like ground glass down her throat. She staggered to her car.

Phillip followed Delia through an ornate wrought-iron gate fronting expensive high-rise townhomes. In the elevator, Delia molded her body against his as he hungrily kissed her. He barely heard the faint whisper of his conscience.

Leave! Leave now!

As the elevator glided to a stop, Phillip took a shaky step away from Delia.

"I'm not sure—"

Delia shook her head playfully and took his hand. Her mouth seared the inside of his palm. She crooked her finger at him, and then walked—hips swaying—to a stylish door. She punched in a security code. Within moments they were inside.

It was seventy-seven degrees outside, but Tori turned on the heater as she pulled out of the driveway. The blast of heat felt good.

Just until 6:00 p.m. I can do this.

She missed the exit.

"Fudgesicle! How'd I do that?" Tori muttered. "My car practically drives itself to the kids' schools!"

She looped back. She was sure her head would explode any minute, and why was it so hot all the sudden?

Tori turned the heater off then slammed on the brakes, skidding to a stop scant inches from the car in front of her.

"Pay attention, Victoria." Tori wiped the sweat pouring down her face, and then pulled in front of Lydia's high school.

"Hey, Mom! Can I drive?" Lydia asked as she got in.

"We're going downtown. I don't think you're ready—"

"Wow, Mom, what's wrong?" Lydia interrupted. "You look awful."

"Thanks," Tori said dryly. "I think it's the flu."

"My driver's ed coach said we shouldn't drive when we're sick. Why don't you pull over," Lydia wheedled, "and I—" she broke off and studied Tori.

"Seriously, Mom, you look like you're about to hurl. Let's cancel my appointment and go home. I'll fix you some tea and you can go to bed. I'll watch Gabe. I'll even be nice to him."

It sounded like heaven. Tori shook her head.

"Thanks, honey, but Gabe has an appointment, too, so it really doesn't matter."

She broke into a paroxysm of coughing.

"I'm calling Dad."

"Already did. He's busy." Tori's hands trembled on the wheel. "You probably should drive, though. Let me find a good place to pull over."

Phillip stood in the foyer of Delia's townhome.

"Now," she murmured, unbuttoning his shirt, "you were saying?"

Surging desire fought with guilt. Phillip nuzzled her neck and breathed in lust.

"For some reason, I was saying maybe this wasn't a good idea," he said with a ragged sigh.

Delia looked smug.

"I think I trump playing nursemaid to a sick wife."

A memory flashed through Phillip's mind. It was the Fourth of July and he had a bad summer cold. They had plans to join friends on a houseboat and watch the fireworks over Lake Lanier. Tori had been looking forward to it. Serena had the kids, so Phillip told Tori to go on and have a good time, but Tori had insisted on staying home.

She was the proverbial ministering angel: plying Phillip with cool washcloths and her personal cure for the common cold: tall glasses of cool juice and bowls of tomato soup served with buttered Ritz crackers. He could almost taste the tart, sweet juice; feel it as it slid soothingly down his throat. She had waited on him hand and foot for three days.

Sanity hit like a wave of ice water. He dropped his arms and stepped back.

"No!"

"Oh, come on," Delia protested. "You and I will happen. It's inevitable. We have chemistry, common goals; we're good together already. We're going to be fantastic."

"No. No we're not. I'm sorry I led you on."

Delia's eyes flashed bullets, and then suddenly melted.

"You're feeling guilty. Your integrity is one of the things that attracted me from the beginning. I guess it *would* be a little tacky for our first time to happen while Doree's sick. Go home and take care of her, but remember, I'm not a patient woman."

"Her . . . name . . . is . . . Tori!"

Phillip fled. He jumped in the car and started it. He had expected to feel a twinge of regret, but instead, his mind was clearer than it had been in months. A sense of optimism flooded him.

Tori should still be at the orthodontist. He would get Lydia, send Tori home, and then get Gabe's appointment handled before he went home and cooked dinner.

Saved from his folly; henceforth, he intended to be the best husband and father on the planet. Maybe he and Tori could get counseling.

He bet Freddi could give them the name of a psychologist expert in dealing with special needs families. Counseling had certainly helped Lydia.

Humming, he drove to the orthodontist's office. He was anxious to see Tori, but kept his speed one mile under the limit. He still reached the doctor's office in good time.

Tori's car was not there. Lydia's appointment must have finished early. He called Tori's cell phone. It rang repeatedly then went to voicemail. He immediately called again. A second call was their private code to answer regardless. To his surprise a male voice answered on the third ring.

"Mr. St. John?"

"Yes. Who's this?"

"Officer Michaels, Johns Creek Police Department. Your wife and daughter have had an accident. Come to the emergency room at Northside Hospital immediately."

Phillip felt the blood drain from his face.

"What happened?" Horns blared as he made an illegal U-turn. "Are they okay?"

"I don't know, sir. I'm working the accident scene. Mrs. St. John was air-lifted to the hospital. Your daughter went by ambulance."

"Air-lifted? How bad is she? She's alive, right?"

"She was alive when she left. You'll need to talk to the doctors."

"Oh my, God," Phillip whispered in terrified disbelief, "this can't be happening."

He prayed, "Lord, please, I'm so sorry! Don't let anything bad happen to them. I'll be the best husband and father—"

Phillip glanced at his watch.

Gabe's riding home on the bus.

He called Serena and explained. She gasped, but quickly controlled herself and promised to take care of Gabe until further notice.

Thank you, God, for Serena. Gabe adores her and she knows how to handle him.

"I am going to pummel the gates of heaven," Serena said. "Post me!"

Phillip hit every speed bump as he raced around the full emergency room parking lot. He pulled into a handicapped spot and sprinted in.

Running to the desk, he demanded, "Tori and Lydia! St. John! How are they? Can I see them?

"Are you related?" the receptionist asked, pulling up information.

"They're my wife! Or, rather, Tori is and she's my daughter. Lydia, I mean—" he slapped his driver's license on the counter. "How are they?"

Chapter 25 – Accident

"Your daughter is in serious, but stable condition. Your wife is in surgery."

She scribbled on a form and indicated several lines marked with red plastic arrows.

"Now that you're here, we need you to sign these releases. Sign here, and here, and here. Good. I've buzzed Dr. Portland's assistant. After you speak to her, I'll need insurance information."

Seconds later, a woman dressed in green scrubs approached.

"Mr. St. John? I'm Rossa Marquette, physician's assistant to Dr. Michael Portland, your wife's doctor."

"How is she?"

"Mrs. St. John is in emergency surgery. She has a ruptured spleen, internal bleeding, a bad head injury, and numerous broken bones. We're going to relieve the pressure on her brain, remove the spleen, locate the internal bleeding, and try to stop it."

"But she's going to be alright, isn't she? She has to be!"

Phillip grabbed the nurse by the arm. Rossa hesitated.

"Her vital signs are poor. Dr. Portland would've preferred to operate after she stabilized, but we couldn't wait."

With a loud squawk, Rossa's pager went off.

"They need me in OR. The surgery will last at least six hours. We'll page you."

She vanished down the long, sterile looking hallway. The receptionist handed Phillip a pager. He accepted it and took a few faltering steps away from the front desk, feeling like he was losing his only link to Tori.

"Sir?" the receptionist called. "Sir, don't leave yet. I need your insurance card and there are forms to fill out."

Moving on autopilot, Phillip handed the receptionist his insurance card and filled out the forms.

"Your daughter is in Room C149. No visitors, except family. You'll be paged as soon as there's news on your wife."

Phillip followed the signs to C-Ward, checked in at the nurse's station, and then knocked tentatively on C-149's door before going in.

Lydia's eyelashes swept pale, bruised cheeks. She was swathed in bandages and had an oxygen canella under her nose. An IV hung above the bed. Her right leg was in traction, her left arm in plaster to the elbow.

Machinery whirred and beeped quietly, monitoring his daughter's well-being. Phillip fought a wave of nausea as he looked at the results of his dalliance with Delia.

"Princessa?"

Lydia's eyes opened.

"Daddy?" she murmured. "Where's Mama?"

"There's been an accident. Mom's with the doctor."

Lydia's eyes grew wide.

"Mommy!"

She struggled to sit up, groaning with the effort. Phillip pressed her back down and stroked her hand.

"Lay still, Cupcake," he said, slipping into the long-forgotten nickname.

Lydia shuddered.

"The wreck was really bad. Is Mom okay?"

"Shh, she'll be fine."

"Mama's real sick. I don't think she saw the red light 'cuz we ran it. Mama never does that, leastways, she may sometimes, but not while I'm there. Maybe I 'stracted her."

Lydia sounded drunk. Phillip realized she was heavily drugged.

"I'm not s'posed to yammer n'cessantly when she's driving." Her voice rose. "Maybe she couldn't concentrate."

A nurse wafted in, accompanied by the faint smells of disinfectant and alcohol. She injected something into the port in Lydia's IV line.

"Sir, Lydia needs to stay calm. Perhaps you should return later."

"No!" Lydia said. "Don't leave. I promise not t'get upset."

"Five more minutes," the nurse said. "You'll probably be asleep by then."

Phillip took Lydia's hand.

"Don't worry," he soothed. "Mom's used to you talking."

"Wasn't my fault . . . hones-lee?"

"Honestly."

Phillip crossed his heart.

Chapter 25 — Accident

It was my fault. She wouldn't have been driving if I'd acted like a decent husband.

"There was . . . way big truck. Driver tried ta stop." Lydia's eyelids fought the law of gravity. Her slurred words kept coming.

"He looked scared . . . hesalright?"

"I'm sure he's fine. I'll check." Phillip had not even considered the other driver.

"Loud brakes. He hit Mommy's side . . . lotsa blood . . ." Her drooping eyes flew wide open.

"Mama! She's okay? She wassin hel'copter."

"The doctors are taking good care of Mamma, Sweet Pea. She'll be fine."

"At's good." Lydia's eyes drifted shut. "Butsnafair. Mom hel'copter. I wanna ride . . ." her voice trailed off.

Phillip squeezed her hand.

His voice was choked as he promised, "As soon as we get through this, Honey, I'm taking you on a helicopter ride."

He thought Lydia was asleep, but imagined she smiled faintly. The nurse returned, wearing Tweety Bird Scrubs and an air of starchy competence.

"How's my daughter?" Phillip asked.

"Her doctor says she doesn't need oxygen."

She removed it from under Lydia's nose.

"What's in the bag?"

"Fluids and a sedative," the nurse said, "plus a strong painkiller. She may sleep till tomorrow. Her doctor will be in shortly if you'd like to wait."

The nurse took Lydia's temperature and blood pressure, and then kindly said, "I need her hand, sir, to check her pulse."

Phillip surrendered Lydia's limp hand. The nurse checked Lydia's pulse, and then left.

From outside Phillip heard rubber-soled shoes squeak against linoleum, people talking, pagers buzzing, and rattling carts of medicine and meals. Life went on while he sat, helpless.

Phillip stared at Lydia's pale visage, but the face he saw was Tori's. After what seemed five hours, but was only fifteen minutes, a striking looking African-American woman with grey-streaked hair walked in.

"I'm Dr. Maidenhurst," she said, shaking his hand. "You're Dad?"

She picked up Lydia's chart and studied it.

"Yes. How's she doing?"

"She needed a unit of blood when she first came. One laceration on her leg required thirty stitches."

Phillip cringed.

"She has a mild concussion. Her leg's broken in two places. She has three broken ribs, a broken arm, and assorted bruises." She smiled. "She's a strong, healthy girl, though, and I sense she's a fighter."

The doctor gently touched Lydia's chin, which was firm even in repose.

"She should be fine."

"She's so still," Phillip said. "Lydia's never still."

"We're giving her as much painkiller as we can, as well as something for anxiety."

"Anxiety?" Phillip questioned. "About the accident?"

"Yes, but more about her mother. Have you been given a prognosis on Mrs. St. John?"

Phillip stood and paced.

"Just that she's in critical condition. She's still in surgery. The doctor said it would be a while, that I should come see Lydia."

"Stay as long as you like. I'll check on Lydia again later tonight."

Phillip waited. He checked his pager, thinking it might be broken. The light burned steady green. He watched the slight rise and fall of Lydia's chest.

After a while, Phillip transferred his gaze to the fake ivy on the window sill. While the windows sparkled, the plastic foliage was coated with dust. Time crawled on by centimeters, while Phillip, filled with remorse, reviewed the past year.

He had worked late constantly. He hadn't helped around the house, but criticized Tori for the mess. Sinking his head in his hands, Phillip thought about the lectures he had given on the need to economize, while lunching out daily with Delia.

Dismayed, Phillip acknowledged he had broken his marriage vows morally and had come within a hairsbreadth of violating them physically. Phillip had solemnly sworn to be faithful, loving, and honorable. He had failed.

For once, Phillip didn't justify his behavior with a list of Tori's faults. Instead, he prayed, searched his soul, and beat himself up. Time inched on.

Phillip looked at the clock on the wall. Seven hours.

Didn't Dr. Portland's assistant say six?

His pocket came to life, vibrating insistently against his thigh. He jumped up, knocking the chair over with a clatter, and pulled out the flashing pager. Phillip kissed Lydia's ashen cheek, rushed to the surgery waiting room, and approached the receptionist's desk with a mixture of hope and dread.

"My wife . . . you paged me. St. John. How is she?"

She looked at him with a trace of pity.

"No word yet, but you have visitors."

From the far side of the waiting room, Cassie, Brother Mike, his pastor, and his friend, Rick, approached with concerned faces. Brother Mike and Rick wrung his hand. Cassie hugged him, tears running down her face.

"Serena called." Cassie said. "She's also called your families. They're on their way."

Rick squeezed Phillip's shoulder. "How's Lydia? They wouldn't let us see her."

"Not great," Phillip said. "Broken bones, a concussion and some deep cuts. Still, they expect her to recover. But, based on the things they aren't saying . . ."

He broke down, weeping.

"I think Tori may die!"

He was quickly enveloped in a group hug.

"The kids will be lost without her," Phillip hiccupped, "and so will I!"

Brother Mike drew them to a corner of the room and began praying.

It had been nine hours since Dr. Portland left. Phillip refused to leave the waiting room. Cassie went downstairs and brought back sandwiches from the cafeteria, insisting he eat. Phillip ploughed through a fat-laden roast beef sandwich on white bread without tasting it or thinking about fat content.

Rick checked on Lydia and reported she was sleeping deeply. Lydia's track coach volunteered to sit in the C-Ward waiting room and bring news if anything changed. Phillip accepted the offer; grateful to continue his vigil outside surgery.

Eleven hours. Phillip tried not to look at his watch, but could not stop himself. He chewed his fingernails a little lower with every ten minutes that passed. At twelve hours, Phillip went to the reception desk.

"Can you tell me *anything*?" he begged.

The night receptionist looked at him with compassion.

"I'm sorry. I only know your wife is in surgery. As soon as—"

Phillip walked away, shoulders sagging.

There were over thirty people waiting now, mostly Tori's friends.

All around him, people talked about Tori, how great she was, what a good friend she had been, what an impact she had in the community.

Phillip barely restrained himself from yelling, "She's not dead yet!"

Seth arrived.

"I need to talk to you," he told Phillip.

Phillip shrugged.

Why not? I have my ever-silent pager.

He walked down the hall with Tori's friend. To his surprise, Seth led him into an outside stairwell. The second the door swung shut; Seth grabbed Phillip and slammed him against the wall.

"You're despicable! I heard Tori was sick. Why'd you let her drive? Were you busy with your *co-worker*? Tori's worth a thousand of her!"

Red-faced, Seth pulled his fist back. Phillip didn't move.

Chapter 25 – Accident

"Hit me. I deserve it. I'm a prize idiot," Phillip urged him.

Seth glared. The quiet stairwell reeked with the faint stench of urine. Seth dropped his fist.

"Looks like I may never get to tell Tori I love her," he said, and then thundered down the stairs, leaving Phillip to return to the waiting room alone.

Thirteen hours after Dr. Portland left for surgery, the receptionist announced, "St. John friends and family, please approach the desk."

A large group stampeded forward. Consternation crossed the receptionist's face.

"Um, let's make that just family, please!"

Reluctantly, most people stepped back.

"Your wife is in recovery, Mr. St. John. The doctor will talk with you shortly."

"Then she's okay?" Phillip demanded.

"I don't know. Dr. Portland—"

"Don't know, or won't say?" Phillip challenged loudly.

Brother Mike and Rick quickly hustled him away.

Fifteen minutes later, Dr. Portland appeared. He looked exhausted. His expression was grim.

"Mrs. St. John is in intensive care recovery. I'm afraid—"

Phillip interrupted. "She made it through surgery. That's a good sign, right?"

"Mmm. Her vital signs aren't good. We cut a piece of her skull away to ease the pressure on her brain. Swelling cuts off blood flow to the brain. She's in a medically induced coma."

"An induced coma? Why?"

"Your wife's brain is too swollen for us to assess the extent of damage, but we can tell it's extensive. A coma allows the brain to rest, which could help the swelling go down, allowing better blood flow to her brain."

"Thank you, doctor. It seems Tori's in good hands."

"I don't want to mislead you, sir." Dr. Portland took off his glasses and polished them, avoiding Phillip's eyes. "Your wife's prognosis is poor. I'd notify friends and family."

There was a moment of silence as the little group grasped what the doctor was saying. Phillip staggered against a wall and stared, open-mouthed.

"Tori's healthy. Won't that help?" Cassie asked.

"She had a high fever before the accident, which means she was already fighting an infection or a virus. That compromises her body's ability to recover."

Dr. Portland replaced his glasses.

"I wish I had better news. It's possible she may stabilize during the next 24–48 hours. If she does, we can probably keep her alive on life support. Her brain, though . . ." the doctor shook his head, and then walked slowly down the hall.

Chapter 26
Limbo

Tori stabilized and immediately went into a natural coma. She was fed intravenously, and did not breathe on her own. Dr. Portland was pessimistic.

"We still can't determine the full extent of brain damage," Portland said, "but it appears to be substantial. Did she—never mind."

"No, doctor, please go ahead," Phillip said.

"It's just a question I had, but it's pre-mature. We'll talk later."

"I'd rather talk now," Phillip said.

"As you wish." Dr. Portland looked uncomfortable. "Did Mrs. St. John sign a living will?"

The blood drained from Phillip's face.

"We both did, as well as organ donor releases. I have copies in my glove box, but . . ."

He gripped a chair for support. In a flash, Serena stood toe-to-toe with the doctor.

"For shame! Talking to end my Tori's life—"

"I *said* it was pre-mature—"

"—before you have yet begun the fight to save her!"

Dr. Portland's neck flushed.

"That's scarcely fair. I saved her life several times during surgery, once when the rest of the team had given up."

"Si, but what have you done for her newly? The nurses speak of how skilled, how dedicated, is this Dr. Portland. Where is that man? Cease talking of living wills! What about your hypocritical oath?"

Serena glared up at the tall doctor. Phillip watched as if from a distance.

I suppose I should say something. But what does it matter? I'm losing her.

Numbly, he watched Dr. Portland attempt to respond professionally to Serena's diatribe.

"I wouldn't even consider disconnecting life support today," Dr. Portland protested. "I simply wanted to clarify the situation in case she continues in this unresponsive state. I agree it was pre-mature, I said so. But I think you meant to say Hippocratic Oath, not hypocritical."

"I have said what I have said!" Serena stamped her foot. "Many people come out of bad commas."

"The support Mrs. St. John is receiving from family and friends tells me she's a special lady. *If* she comes out of the *coma*, do you want her to simply exist the rest of her life, a shadow of who she was, until all the wonderful memories you have are swamped by that of a vegetable?"

Evidently, Dr. Portland realized he had stepped beyond professional bounds.

"Please excuse my passion, it was inappropriate."

He cleared his throat. "The situation is this: the brain MRI's thus far indicate an extremely low level of functioning. If Mrs. St. John hadn't signed a living will, we'd be dealing with some difficult decisions. Since she did, we can honor her wishes if the time comes."

"It won't," Phillip said. "It can't."

He straightened and threw back his shoulders.

"I hope you're right," Dr. Portland replied, polishing his glasses. "But you don't think so."

Phillip's momentary surge of energy vaporized. He sank into a chair, knowing his legs could not support the weight of Dr. Portland's prognosis.

Chapter 26 – Limbo

"I'm sixty-five years old. I've had twenty-five years of experience with this type case. My gut feeling is Mrs. St. John won't come out of this."

"Maybe you should try some Tums," Serena muttered sotto voce.

Dr. Portland glared. "Surely it's more merciful to let her pass with dignity?"

Serena stomped her foot.

"You think you can determine when a life has value, and when it should end? God only has the right to say who shall live and who shall die!"

"If we take her off the oxygen and stop feeding her intravenously, she'll die. Man's keeping her alive, not God."

Dr. Portland pointedly turned away from Serena to Phillip.

"I apologize if I gave the impression I'm giving up on Mrs. John. I'm not."

"No problem. I'm the one who insisted you continue. Tori and I believe in organ donation. We signed living wills for situations where all hope was gone. We're people of faith, doctor. We'll wait to see what God will do."

"All we can do is wait. How about if you," the doctor said to Serena, "try to disabuse yourself of the notion I'm Jack Kevorkian."

He stalked out of the room.

"I think he likes me," Serena said.

Rossa had walked up during the discussion. She looked after Dr. Portland's retreating back.

"He's one of the top ten neurosurgeons in the nation. Please excuse him. He lost his wife many years ago, after she'd been in a coma for two years. He hates this type of case."

Phillip applied for indefinite family leave. His boss called right away to say it had been approved.

"You've taken only one sick day in seven years and have never taken all your vacation."

His manager's voice was hearty. Phillip winced.

How can he sound so upbeat when Tori may be about to die?

"HR tells me you can stay out with full pay for several months," his boss continued. "Delia's on a month cruise. Thanks mainly to you; the Racoby contracts are signed. You and Delia have already far exceeded all your objectives for this year. We've *all* exceeded our objectives for this year. Take all the time you need. There's a mahogany desk on the executive floor waiting for you when you get back, and there'll be a nice, fat bonus in your next check."

It was what Phillip had dreamed of. Without Tori, he didn't care.

There was an endless stream of visitors. One day Phillip walked into the room to find Tori's dad sitting by her bed, talking to her and sobbing. Phillip stood at the door and listened.

"Your mom told me you knew I originally wanted a boy. I hope you didn't go into this coma thinking that was still true." He pulled out a handkerchief and mopped his face. "I wouldn't trade you for ten football playing sons. I never told you how proud I am of you, of all you've accomplished, of the kind of woman you've become. I hope you knew."

Phillip came to stand beside his father-in-law and put a hand on his shoulder.

"I hope Tori knew I loved her beyond what she did for my ego. Having a beautiful woman pour all her energy and time into me soothed my insecurities. I didn't handle it well when I had to share with the kids. I pray she realizes she was more than a cheerleader."

Side-by-side they prayed, watched, and regretted while the object of their love lay in limbo between this world and the next.

After a month, Lydia came home from the hospital struggling with guilt. She had begged to see her mother before she left. Against Dr. Portland's advice, Phillip took her to Tori's room.

Not a good decision. Lydia went into hysterics when she saw her mother. Phillip took her out quickly, but Lydia was so upset she had to stay in the hospital another night before they would release her.

She asked repeatedly to see Tori again, but Phillip would not allow it. Lydia had to settle for Phillip's promise to tell her every word the doctor said about Tori.

Once home, Lydia went back to school. She got around well with crutches and a wheelchair. She learned to work around her broken arm. Physically, she functioned adequately, but her emotional injuries were not healing. She was convinced the accident was her fault.

Gabe was confused.

He kept asking, "Where's Mama?"

Told she was very sick and in the hospital, he nodded wisely, and then said, "And tomorrow, Mama will come home?"

He repeated his question until Lydia screamed at him.

"Shut up!"

"Lydia!" Phillip said. "Try to be patient with him."

"He is *so* irritating! I think he does it on purpose, just to get me in trouble."

Gabe giggled, which was his typical response when someone expressed anger.

"See?" Lydia demanded.

She spun her wheelchair around with her good arm and left the room.

Phillip was in the kitchen heating one of a never-ending supply of casseroles when he heard Gabe in the playroom.

"Mama! Ma-Ma?"

As Phillip ran toward the playroom, Gabe called from the laundry room.

"Mama! Where's Mama?"

Gabe wandered from room to room searching for Tori. When Phillip caught up with him in the den, he saw Gabe had removed a picture of Tori from their bulletin board and clutched it to his chest.

"Mama! Where's Mama?"

It was too much. Phillip collapsed onto the couch, pulled Gabe into a bear hug, and cried.

I think I've cried more in the last two months than I have my entire life.

Gabe endured the hug for a few seconds then pulled away. He studied Phillip intently. He had never seen Phillip cry before. He giggled. Soon he was belly-laughing.

Lydia erupted into the room.

"Mom's dying and he's laughing! Can't you shut him up?"

She looked at Gabe, saw Tori's picture in his hands, and tore it away from him.

"Mom's not coming back!" she screamed, ripping the picture in two. "Stop laughing! She was worn down and sick because she was so busy taking care of *you*. She glared at her father. "And why did you let her drive when she was sick?"

Gabe's laughter stopped like a faucet had been turned off.

"No more Mama?"

Lydia burst into tears.

Gabe frowned.

"No more, Mama?" he asked again in a bewildered voice.

His lips trembled.

"I'm sorry, Gabe; I didn't mean it. You, too, Daddy. I'm just so scared."

Lydia sobbed.

"We're all scared," Phillip said as he gathered them into his arms. "I'm sorry, baby. We'll get through this, somehow. We have to stick together though, not blame each other. Okay?"

"Okay," Lydia sniffed, brushing her face against her cast.

"Oh-kay," Gabe echoed.

But it's not okay. I'm not sure if it'll ever be okay again.

Another month passed. Dr. Portland was never encouraging; Serena referred to him as: Dr. Doom. They fell into a dismal daily routine. Phillip got the kids off to school, went to the hospital, and stayed until time to get Gabe off the bus.

Dr. Portland had advised Phillip to talk to Tori, so he held her hand and talked. Sometimes he told funny stories, hoping her dormant sense of humor would be engaged.

"You won't believe what happened today, Fun-Size. Delia came to the hospital. I've apologized about Delia, right?"

Phillip paused.

"Right."

Most men wouldn't tell their wives this story, but Tori will enjoy the outcome, and it'll make her see that I really am done with Delia.

"So, anyway . . ."

Delia strode into the waiting room like she owned it, dressed in black. She wore thigh-high boots with a short skirt and carried a huge arrangement of white mums.

"Make sure these get to Mrs. St. John," she instructed the desk nurse. "She okay?"

"Mrs. St. John's condition is unchanged. She—"

"Good."

Delia plopped down the flowers, spilling water over the nurse's papers, and then checked out the waiting area. Her gaze passed over Seth, Cassie, and Serena, and then fastened on Phillip, who waited outside Tori's room while she was being bathed.

"Phillip, dear! How are you, poor man? I've missed you."

She flashed him a sympathetic smile and walked toward him, hips swaying like they could churn butter.

Serena's face grew red. She whispered something to Seth. He nodded. Serena leapt up, grabbed a broom from a startled orderly and swept Delia toward the door.

"How do you dare come here? Out!"

She thrust the broom at Delia.

"Go! Rapidamente!"

"Phillip! Who is this lunatic! Stop her! I need to talk to you!"

"Sorry." Phillip grinned. "Serena likes to clean house."

Serena swiped the broom against Delia's boots, forcing her to jump backwards.

"Nurse!" Delia yelled. "Help! Call security!"

The nurse smothered a laugh.

"Ma'am, you'll have to leave if you can't keep your voice down."

Serena smacked Delia's bottom with the broom.

"The exit, it is this way, Arana Negra."

Delia left.

"What did she call her?" Seth asked Cassie.

"A black spider."

"Astute woman, Serena," Seth said.

Cassie giggled.

Phillip chuckled as he finished the story.

"I think there may be sparks starting between Seth and Cassie."

He looked hopefully at Tori.

Nothing. Tori was a blank presence.

Phillip felt an answering blankness rise in him. Without Tori, his existence would be a shadow-life. He would be a man trying hard for the sake of his children, living a one-dimensional life.

Phillip stopped going to the gym. He spent every free minute with Tori. People offered to take Lydia evenings or weekends.

No one but Serena wanted Gabe.

Even though Gabe's been aggression-free for over a year now, I guess people are afraid.

For the first time, Phillip truly understood the social isolation Gabe and Tori experienced outside the special needs community.

Dr. Doom visited Tori daily. He never said much, but Phillip read resignation in every line of his face. The doctor was there the day Tori's monitors went crazy.

Alarms sounded. Dr. Portland shouted orders. Nurses ran in and out. Phillip stood helplessly as Tori's heart monitor lines fluttered erratically.

They went flat.

No, no, no . . .

Phillip slumped against the wall.

"I need the defibrillator *stat!*" Dr. Portland roared.

He grabbed the unit from a nurse.

Dr. Portland worked while Phillip prayed. Finally, the green line moved, faltered, and then settled back into a weak but steady rhythm.

"What just happened?" Phillip asked.

Dr. Portland placed his hand on Phillip's shoulder.

"I'm afraid her systems are shutting down. It's no longer premature to say you need to decide whether your wife sincerely wanted to be an organ donor."

Chapter 27

The End

Driving home from the hospital, Phillip prayed non-stop.
"Lord, if it's time to release her, You're going to have to help me. I can't let her go."

Phillip didn't remember the drive home. He found the kids watching television. He shut the kitchen door, beckoned Serena, and told her what had happened.

Serena bowed her head.

"I hoped never would I see this day. What will—"

The door exploded open. Lydia hobbled up to Phillip, and spat out her words.

"I wanna see Mom! I haven't seen her since I left the hospital. It's not fair to keep us away."

"But, Princessa, the last time—"

"I won't get upset again. I've matured."

"Doctor Portland doesn't want—"

Lydia stomped her crutch on the floor.

"I have to tell her I'm sorry for arguing; to say . . . to say goodbye."

She burst into tears. Gabe appeared in the kitchen.

"Gabe see Mama!"

He looked expectant. Phillip groaned.

"Mom doesn't look like Mom," he said.

"She'd *smell* like Mom!" Lydia said, chin jutting.

Phillip smiled. Lydia's sense of smell was legendary. She loved Tori's vanilla musk perfume.

"Um, she's not wearing perfume."

"I don't care. We'll take her some."

Serena folded clothes at the kitchen table. Since the accident, she had been doing what she called the Mount St. John laundry. For the first time, she looked old.

"Take them, Phillip. They need to close her. I will come too, if you like."

Phillip chewed the inside of his lip.

"Go see Mama, go see Mama," Gabe chanted.

Lydia joined in. Phillip heaved a sigh.

"We'll go tomorrow after school."

Phillip knew the kids would be devastated.

Then again, how much worse can it get?

Lydia quizzed him non-stop the rest of the evening about Tori's condition and treatments. Phillip answered her questions honestly, including the ramifications of her heart attack.

Lydia dashed tears from her eyes and acted as if she hadn't just heard her mother's life was drawing to a close.

"So, you talk to Mama and hold her hand because maybe she knows, because you're hoping something gets through to her brain."

"That's about it," Phillip agreed. "Now, come on. It's bedtime. Grab your crutches."

He scooped her into his arms, carried her upstairs, deposited her on her bed, and dropped her crutches beside it.

"Gabe was in bed hours ago. Tomorrow's going to be hard."

To Phillip's surprise, Lydia went to bed without protest. The next morning, Gabe was in full spout.

"Going see Mama! Going to see Mama today, Daddy?"

"Yes, after school."

"Not just Daddy and Lydia?"

"No, Gabe. You, too. All three of us and Serena."

"Not just Gabe and Serena?"

Phillip sighed. How had Tori survived Gabe's chatter with such patience? He used to think she blew up too easily, got depressed too quickly. He had thought if she was stronger, she wouldn't need antidepressants. Now, he wondered where she kept the bottle.

"We're all going, son."

"Gabe is not staying home?"

Phillip remembered something Tori used to do. He touched his own chest.

"I am going."

He touched Gabe's chest and paused.

After a few seconds, Gabe touched his chest, and then spoke in a complete sentence; a skill he seldom used.

"I am going to see Mama today."

"Yes, you are."

"Lydia will stay home?"

"No. Lydia and you," he tapped Gabe's chest, "and me."

He pointed to himself.

"And Serena. We're *all* going to the hospital together."

"Not tomorrow, hotpeetal?"

"No! We're going to the hotpeetal . . . hospital, *today*. Now hush."

Phillip made a zipping motion over his mouth.

"Hos-pee-tail!" Gabe chortled. "Maybe Mama will have ice cream."

"No ice cream!" Phillip snapped.

Tori wouldn't have snapped.

"Sorry, Gabe. Mama won't have ice cream."

"Gabe, just *be quiet!*"

Lydia bellowed from upstairs.

"Lydia, be nice!" Phillip yelled. "And get ready. I'll be up in a minute to help you down. I don't want to have to chase your bus again today."

He heard grumbling, the stomp of crutches, and the beep of a bus outdoors.

"Aagh! Gabe, your bus! Get your backpack. Where's your lunch?"

He hustled Gabe to the curb as the bus pulled away.

Phillip yelled. The bus driver stopped. A substitute driver glared at them.

"Been here for five minutes. Honked the horn twice."

"Sorry."

From the bus stairs, Gabe asked, "Not just Daddy? Gabe and Lydia and—"

"Yes, yes, yes! Sit down!"

Gabe sat. The bus roared off.

When he came in, Lydia was sliding down the stairs on her bottom, clutching her crutches.

"I was coming to help you."

"I know; I didn't want to wait. But, Da-ad! Why does Gabe have to go to the hospital?" Lydia whined. "All he wants is ice cream. He doesn't know what's happening. Why can't he just stay home?"

"First of all, he misses your mother, a lot. Gabe depended on her even more than we did. Second of all, we can't leave him home by himself."

"But the retard embarrasses me."

With a snarl, Phillip clapped his hand over Lydia's mouth.

"Gabe's going. Do you understand me?"

Lydia's eyes were wide and scared. She nodded and tried to remove Phillip's hand. He kept her mouth covered in a stern grip.

"Furthermore, your brother is *not* a retard. If I *ever* hear you say that again, you will lose Facebook, your phone, your iPod, your computer, and all friend privileges for a month!"

Phillip dropped his hand. Lydia was shaking.

"I'm sorry, Dad. I didn't really mean he's a retard. It's just a word people use. It doesn't mean anything."

"It's derogatory! And would it *kill* you to be nice to Gabe?"

Phillip dropped his hand.

"I'm sorry. I've been trying to be nicer. It's just . . . without Mom here, Gabe seems more irritating."

"You're not the only one missing your Mom. When she . . . if she . . ."

Phillip's hand trembled.

"The three of us need each other. Treat Gabe like Mom would want you to treat him."

As Lydia used her crutches to maneuver towards the kitchen counter and her backpack, Phillip saw the red mark on her chin where he had grabbed her. Sinking heavily to a chair, he bowed his head on his arms and breathed deeply, wondering what would become of his family. He had never felt so inadequate before.

Lydia was halfway down the sidewalk when Phillip caught up with her.

"I'm sorry, baby."

Tears streamed down Phillip's face.

"I'm sorry, too."

Lydia reached up and wiped Phillip's tears just as he bent down to wipe hers. They hugged. He waited for the bus with her, his hand on her shoulder, wondering if he would ever get this parenting thing right.

The weather that afternoon matched Phillip's outlook on their coming visit: dismal. Dark clouds floated ominously overhead, occasionally spitting out a few hard drops of rain. An icy blast of wind sliced through them as Phillip, Serena and the kids trudged through the marble canyon formed by the two wings of the hospital. Hurrying, they made it to the entrance seconds before the heavens released a sharp, wintry downpour.

Gabe beamed and chanted, "See Mama, he's going to see Mama!"

They rode up to the eighth floor, restraining Gabe, who loved to jump up and down in elevators. Entering Tori's room, they quietly approached the bed. She lay as pale and motionless as a wax figure.

"Hi, Little Bit," Phillip said, leaning over to kiss Tori's forehead.

Lydia looked horrified. Gabe gazed at the woman in the bed.

"Where's Mama?" he asked Phillip,

"That is Mama, son."

Gabe went back to the bed and stared suspiciously at Tori. Lydia put her arm around him.

"That *is* Mom, buddy. She's sick, remember?"

Gabe shrugged out of her embrace, but stayed close to her. He leaned in close and pulled Tori's arm.

"Mama, wake up!" Frustrated, Gabe shook her leg.
"Time get up!"
Tori did not move. Gabe was indignant.
"Mommy sleeping long!" he protested.
"It is okay, Pobrecito," Serena said.
She looked at Phillip and spelled aloud, "I-C-E C-R-E-A-M?"
"Ice cream!" Gabe chortled. "He wants ice cream!"
Strained laughter filled the room.
"Go ahead," Phillip said. "It'll give Lydia and me some alone time."
"Yes!" Gabe said. "Get ice cream with Serena."
Gabe took her hand and they left.
"Dad," Lydia asked, "could I sit . . . alone . . . with Mom for a while?"
Phillip squeezed her arm.
"That's fine, Cupcake. I'll be outside."
As he left, Phillip heard Lydia talking and paused by the door to listen.
"All I really ever wanted to be when I grew up was you, Mom. I'm not nearly there yet, so you need to come back. Please."
Phillip shut the door quietly, leaned his head against the doorpost, and prayed.

Phillip walked back into Tori's room with Dr. Portland. Lydia perched on the bed, waving a perfume bottle under Tori's nose.
"Okay, this is your Vanilla Musk. My science teacher says smell is one of the strongest senses. Smell it?"
Hearing them, Lydia turned, frowned, and laid one finger on her lips. As they watched, she put a set of headphones on Tori's ears, working carefully around the wires and tubes surrounding the hospital bed.
"Here's some music from your Rock Praise playlist."
Dr. Portland said, "Music can be beneficial, but I don't think—"
"Shush!" Lydia snapped. Dr. Portland's eyebrows rose.
"Lydia, that was disrespectful. Apologize." Phillip said.

"I meant it respectfully!"

She hobbled into the hallway, motioning for the men to follow her.

"I'm trying to engage all her senses," Lydia told them. "Mom's eyes twitched!"

Lydia noticed Dr. Portland's dubious look and tossed her head. "Really! Her eyelashes fluttered. It was a teensy, quick flicker, but I saw it. I need more time."

The doctor frowned. "I don't believe you saw anything significant, Miss St. John."

"Will it hurt anything to let her try?" Phillip asked.

"No, but I hate to see the child get her hopes up."

Lydia, who had turned fifteen three months ago, said "I'm not a child! I'm almost sixteen!"

"Her hopes are already up," Phillip said. "Lydia often suggests we do things differently. It's usually about Gabe, but we've been surprised how often her odd ideas work out. Besides, at this point, we've got nothing to lose."

"Very well," Dr. Portland sighed. "Let me look at her first."

Noting Lydia's frown, he dryly added, "I'll do my best not to interfere with your experiment, young lady."

They went back into Tori's room. While Dr. Portland examined Tori, Lydia rooted around in her purse. She pulled out a small jar of fudge sauce.

"Mom loves chocolate."

"She isn't able to eat."

Dr. Portland crossed his arms.

"I'm not planning on feeding her a hot fudge sundae. I'm just going to put a tiny drop of chocolate on her tongue."

"Fine," Dr. Portland sighed. "You're a single-minded young lady. So was I in my youth. But if we're going to experiment, let's create the ideal environment first. Give her some ice. Her tongue is parched."

He placed a sliver of ice into Tori's mouth, and then said, "Okay, try it now, but don't expect too much."

Lydia washed her hands at the sink in the room, then crutched back to the bed. She dipped a plastic coffee stirrer into the fudge sauce, gently pushed her mother's lips apart, and put a tiny amount of chocolate on her tongue.

They waited. Despite his pessimism, Dr. Portland watched closely.

"Look!" Lydia exclaimed. "Her tongue moved!"

Dr. Portland bent close and stared. He laid his hand against Tori's throat, lifted one of her eyelids and checked her pupil with a penlight. He straightened up and ran his hand through his hair until it stood up like ruffled gray feathers.

"Did you see something, doctor?"

"I saw a minute movement, yes. Probably an involuntary spasm. I'll order a brain scan. I wouldn't get my hopes up."

"Of course you wouldn't," muttered Serena, coming into the room with Gabe.

"Ahh, Ms. D'Antonio. My biggest fan," Dr. Portland said.

"For what should I not raise my hopes?" Serena demanded.

Lydia bounced with excitement and almost lost a crutch as she relayed the news.

"Wonderful! But usually when you are listening to your iPot, I hear sound through your ear blossoms," Serena said. "I do not hear music. Are you sure it is loud enough?"

Lydia grinned and increased the volume. "That's the first time a grownup ever asked me to turn my music up!"

Phillip went to Lydia and tilted her chin up.

"You combine creativity, stubbornness, and love into an incredible package. Just like your mother."

Through his hug, he heard Lydia's delighted response

"Really? Me? Like Mom?"

Phillip spoke into Lydia's hair.

"Yes, Princessa. We're always telling you no and stop. Maybe we don't tell you enough that you're awesome, but you are."

Lydia squeezed him.

"Thanks, Dad."

Dr. Portland's pager buzzed. He looked at it and announced he must leave. He asked Rossa, his PA, to stay in the room and observe Tori closely.

Tori didn't move. Phillip continued to move the perfume bottle back and forth under Tori's nostrils, praying with renewed fervor for a miracle. The room reeked of musk and Gabe had polished off all the chocolate sauce when Dr. Portland returned.

"Are you coming back tomorrow?" he asked Lydia.

"Yes. I thought I'd bring one of her favorite candles, some Chick-fil-A sweet tea with lemon, and more of her favorite music. What do you think?"

"I think you're an innovative and caring young lady," Dr. Portland said. "I'm still dubious, but I have hopes you'll succeed. For tonight, though, your mother needs to rest."

"But all she does is rest," protested Lydia.

The adults chuckled.

"We do need to go home," Phillip said, "school tomorrow. Gabe, say goodbye to your mother."

"Don't wanna go!" Gabe said with the rebellious, pre-teen attitude he had been displaying for the past six months.

"Want Mama get up!"

"Hey, Gabe!" Lydia exclaimed. "Remember that game you and Mama used to play? The wake up princess game?"

Gabe looked at her blankly.

"Come on, Gabe, *you* know! When you want Mom to get up? She pretends she's a princess who can't wake up until you give her lots of kisses."

"Querida, I do not think . . ." Serena said.

Lydia held up her hand. Gabe processed the idea, forehead wrinkled. It took a minute, but then he smiled and nodded.

"Gabe is prince!"

Phillip was uneasy. How would Gabe react when Tori didn't respond?

"Son, don't—"

Too late. Gabe leaned over Tori, giggling.

"Mama! Prince is here! Mwah, mwah, mwah!"

He smacked juicy kisses on her wan cheek. Nothing happened. Phillip closed his eyes.

Why did Lydia have to pick now to include her brother?

Gabe grabbed Tori's arm and shook it.

"Time to get *up!*"

He shook his finger in Tori's face then stomped over to Serena. "Mama's being naughty," he informed her. "She needs get up!"

"We will return tomorrow," Serena soothed.

Gabe sank his teeth into his own arm.

Lifting his head he said, "Don't want tomorrow Mama! Want now Mama!"

Phillip enfolded his agitated son in a gentle hug that stopped Gabe from biting himself.

"Stop!" Dr. Portland said.

They all turned at the doctor's peremptory tone. Surprised, Phillip released Gabe. Tori moved her lips. The heart monitor beside her bed showed a stronger beat.

Lydia clapped.

"Look, Gabe!" she told him. "Mama's giving you back kisses!"

Gabe gave Tori a perfunctory kiss on the cheek and told her to get up.

Lydia put her weight on her good leg and rose halfway from her chair to lay her head on Tori's chest. Tears streamed down Phillip's cheeks as he watched Tori's hand feebly stroke Lydia's hair once before falling back to her side.

Dr. Portland's mouth dropped open.

"An extremity movement! Unbelievable!"

Gabe sat on the floor, lacing and unlacing his tennis shoes. As Phillip's glance fell on him, Gabe looked Phillip straight in the eye.

"Gabe wake Mama. Gabe's good boy prince."

His smile was fat with satisfaction. Phillip grabbed Gabe and tussled with him.

"You're a prince, alright! C'mere, Prince. How 'bout giving Daddy a kiss?"

"No more kisses!"

Gabe shrieked with joy as Phillip pinned him and smothered him with kisses. Finally, Phillip messed his hair a last time and released him.

I can't believe this. God used Lydia and Gabe . . . Gabe! . . . to bring Tori out of her coma. All the sensory issues Tori struggled with over the years have come full circle.

Chapter 27 – The End

Dr. Portland was shaken. He took his glasses off and looked through them as if to make sure dirty lenses had not warped his view.

"Ms. Marquette . . . you saw Mrs. St. John, too?"

"Yes, doctor. Her lips moved in a meaningful way, I think," Rossa said.

"Hmm. Yes. Will you please get a message to Dr. Edwards that I'd like to meet him here as soon as he's available? I want a full series of brain scans done first thing tomorrow. We need to know the extent of brain damage, so we can develop a recovery strategy. We'll want to start therapy as soon as possible, if she continues to improve."

"Yes, doctor," Rossa murmured.

She turned to go, but paused at the door.

"Mr. St. John?"

"Yes?"

"I . . . I just wanted to say me and others on the staff, we've been praying for Mrs. St. John, too. You have a lovely family."

"So, doctor, those are involuntary movements?" Serena asked slyly.

Rossa hid a smile as Serena needled Dr. Portland.

"No. Happily, I was wrong. Mrs. St. John appears to be emerging from her coma. We'll try taking her off the respirator tomorrow to see if she can breathe on her own."

"So, there is hope, after all?"

Dr. Portland smiled.

"Ma'am, it appears I can't rule out the power of hope and love to bring a patient back when, medically, no return can be expected."

"It is, most of all, the power of prayer we have seen today."

"Ahh . . . yes . . . prayer. I understand people have prayed extensively for her. I wonder."

He stared, unseeing, at a mass-produced picture on the wall, and then snapped out of his reverie.

"It seems I must also consider the possibility of effective prayer. Although why a loving God would answer some prayers and ignore others . . ." he shook his head. "It's beyond my comprehension."

"Yes," Serena said, "it *is* beyond your comprehension."

Dr. Portland frowned.

"I know you're not fond of me, but I assure you, I'm adequately intelligent."

"I don't dislike you, doctor. Well, maybe a little, when you are spreading the doom and gloom all over the place. Not most of the time. And I know you are not stupid." Serena put her hand on his arm. "I also am incapable of understanding God, why He does what He does and does not do."

"But why—" Dr. Portland asked.

"I need to take the children home," Serena said. "I doubt Phillip will leave tonight. The next time I see you, if you have a few minutes, we could talk more."

Dr. Portland bent at the waist.

"Delighted. Perhaps you would even join me for dinner one night, if Mrs. St. John continues to gain ground?"

Serena glared at him.

"Ahem," the doctor coughed. "Allow me to rephrase. Since Mrs. St. John will undoubtedly improve rapidly now that she is emerging from her coma, will you do me the honor of having dinner with me?"

Serena smiled.

"Certainly. It will be your pleasure."

Serena and the kids left. Dr. Portland came over and shook Phillip's hand.

"Congratulations. Mrs. St. John has a long recovery in front of her, but your wife has one of the strongest support teams I've had the privilege of seeing over the years."

"Will she recover fully?"

"I'm tempted to say it's doubtful. Most with her injuries would have died. But based on what I've seen today, she may surprise me. We'll have to wait and see."

"It's immaterial. We're just glad she's still with us."

"I believe you. Good luck."

He shut the door behind him. Phillip sat down beside the bed and gazed at Tori. She lay still, as she had for months.

Phillip spoke softly, "I don't know how fast you're going to recover, or even if you'll ever recover fully. It doesn't matter. I'm going

Chapter 27 — The End

to be with you, be strong for you, whatever happens. I thought I'd lost you."

He ran his finger down her cheek.

"I was petrified. Without you and the kids, I'd be like a puzzle with key pieces missing."

Tori's eyelids lifted a quarter of an inch, and then sank, as if each weighed several pounds.

"Me, too."

The halting words sent a frisson of joy up Phillip's spine.

"These past four months with the kids have matured me. I'm going to be a better father and husband." He paused as a thought hit him. "You've been growing since the kids got here. I plan to catch up."

Tori feebly pressed his hand.

Phillip's voice was choked with tears. "I love you, Little Bit." Tori sighed, turned her head into the pillow, and slipped into natural, healing sleep.

Epilogue

Three Years Later

"He *tired* shopping!" Gabe said defiantly. Tori understood, but her son's tone was unacceptable. She raised an eyebrow.

Gabe sighed, "I am tired to shop. Can I have frappé?"

"I guess."

They'd been looking for prom dresses for several hours. Gabe looked miserable in the small vintage boutique they had just entered. No airplanes, no food, no pretty girls, nothing of interest. Gabe had naturally honed in on the Starbucks next door.

"I'm taking Gabe next door for a frappé," Tori called. "I'll be right back."

"Okay." Lydia had already plunged deep into the store. "Hurry. I see some cool dresses."

Gabe walked outside. He turned when his mother did not follow. Tori waited patiently inside. The store owner, an elegant older woman, glided over to help. Tori shook her head and tipped her chin toward Gabe, who came back inside, opened the door, and held it.

"Thanks, Sweetheart."

Tori propelled her wheelchair out onto the sidewalk.

"Push?" Gabe asked.

"No thanks, honey, I'm fine."

Tori wanted to get as much exercise as possible. She had resisted a motorized wheelchair. It was frustrating that after three years of therapy, her leg muscles still did not fully comprehend her brain's command to walk. Tori worked fiercely at therapy and vowed to lose the chair someday. No one doubted she would.

Inside Starbucks, Tori went with Gabe to the counter, but remained silent while he gave his order.

"Wannawhite chocolatefrappaccino nowhippedcream."

The clerk looked confused.

"Slower, Gabe," Tori said. "He can't understand you. Remember your manners."

"May I please have whitechocolate frappé?"

"What size?"

"Large."

Tori gave a slight shake of her head. Gabe looked mulish, but changed his order.

"Small. No whippedcream."

"Small white chocolate Frappuccino, no whipped. That'll be $3.46."

Gabe handed the clerk his wallet. Tori shook her head.

"Take the wallet back, Gabe."

Gabe took it.

"Now, the drink is $3.46. That's almost how much?"

Gabe thought.

"Four?"

"That's right," Tori said with an encouraging smile. "You can do this."

Gabe opened his wallet and pulled out a twenty, a five, and three ones. He pondered the bills, counted the clerk three ones, and frowned. He slowly laid the five on the counter and looked at Tori.

"Excellent! Good job of counting! Three ones are not enough for something that costs almost four. The five will work."

Gabe closed his wallet and walked toward the pick-up counter, leaving the three dollars.

"Sir . . . Sir, you left your dollars and your change."

Gabe returned and retrieved the money. Looking to Tori for approval, he dropped the coins in the tip jar. Tori nodded. He started to add the dollar, but at Tori's head shake, stuffed it back in his wallet. Tori gave him thumbs up.

Gabe cupped his drink in reverent hands and they left. There were several small wrought iron tables outside Starbucks. Two could be seen from the dress store. Tori told Gabe to sit at one until he finished his drink, and then wheeled toward the vintage shop door.

There was no handicapped button. Tori grasped the door handle, but she could not open the door far enough to get her chair through. She ground her teeth and looked over her shoulder.

Gabe was engrossed in his drink and she did not want to yell. No one was visible inside the store. She backed her wheelchair up and studied the situation, feeling her irritation rise.

You'd think, in this day and age, wheelchair access would be a given.

A black teenager rolling by on his skateboard turned to look. He flipped his board up into his hands, came back, and opened the door for Tori.

"Thanks so much," Tori told him.

"No problem."

Tori re-entered the store, struggling to suppress her ire.

One of the many good things that have come out of my accident is a better understanding of Gabe. I know, now, why he got frustrated so easily. It's aggravating, not being able to do the things everyone around you is doing.

Lydia was in the dressing room. Several dresses hung over the door.

"How's it going?" Tori called through the door. "Find anything?"

"Mom, look! It's the absolute, perfect prom dress!" A whirlwind of lace and satin erupted from the dressing room and swayed around the mirror.

"I'm gor-geous, I'm gor-geous!"

"Stop prancing, Princessa. Let me see."

Tori's daughter pirouetted to a stand-still. The sapphire blue formal hugged Lydia's slender body to the knees, and then billowed out in a playful, mermaid-like pouf. Every time she moved, the dress's diamante sequins sparkled, creating a vision of moonbeams dancing on a star-lit sea.

"Mama, how did you know to bring me here? I *never* would have stopped in a vintage store if you hadn't made me."

"Older fashions often have a flair you don't find in today's dresses. I wanted to find something as special as you are," Tori said.

The owner gave an approving nod.

"This frock is unique. It was made by Johann Kalida, who never did the same gown twice. He was one of my favorite designers when I was in my twenties," she said with a soft, reminiscent smile.

"You look like an old-time movie star or a torch singer," Tori told Lydia.

The owner tapped her chin thoughtfully with her index finger. "Somewhere, I think, there's a matching stole."

She disappeared into the back of the store.

"It's perfect, Mom. And it's under our budget. Daddy will love it."

"Hmm. It's not money Daddy's most worried about. Move around, sweetheart—let's see if everything stays put."

Although slim, Lydia had generous curves. They had problems finding a dress which passed Phillip's lynx-eyed scrutiny.

Lydia swayed and strutted, two-stepped and twirled in front of her mother and the three-way mirror. Tori watched her eighteen year old daughter with a lump in her throat. The past three years had been rough.

After the accident Lydia had shouldered more responsibility than a typical fifteen-year-old. As a result, she had developed an inner beauty and strength, which, coupled with her good looks and vivacious personality, made her one of the loveliest girls around.

"So far, so good, Princessa. The last dress we brought home for Daddy's approval failed the plunge test. Is this one going to work?"

Lydia threw her body into an almost back-bend, so she was looking at her mother upside-down; her long black hair cascading to the floor.

"That looks fine—"

With a mischievous smile, Lydia straightened, turned, bent over, and did a bosom-bouncing shimmy.

"How's that, Mom?"

"I'd suggest you not try that move again unless you want a ten o'clock curfew and your father super-glued to your side the entire evening."

Lydia's grin was un-repentant.

"Just thought I'd add a little interest. It stayed up. So, can I have it?"

"Yes, it's perfect. About shoes—"

Just then, Gabe came inside, tossing his empty cup into the trash can.

"Hey, Gabe," Lydia said.

She stuck her hip out and curved one arm dramatically overhead.

"Do you think it's pretty?"

Gabe studied his sister and slowly grinned.

In the low, husky voice that had accompanied his burgeoning height, he said, "Oh, yeah!"

He cocked his head. "Gabe prom?"

"It's not your year, my prince," Tori said. "This is Lydia's senior prom. You still have a few years, and then we'll see."

And maybe Gabe *would* go to his senior prom. The regular kids in his school had been good, in recent years, to invite the special education students to school activities. Maybe, with supervision, it would work out.

On the other hand, her handsome teenage son's hormones seemed totally normal. Tori was uneasy with the gleam she had seen in Gabe's eyes when pretty girls were around. Her anxiety increased when she realized a few of the more mature young ladies in Gabe's class tended to cluster around him like kids around an ice cream truck.

Tori shuddered. Like Scarlett, she would think about that later. Today, she had a daughter on the brink of high school graduation. As her graduation present, the entire St. John family was going to Bulgaria this summer. The visit would include a trip to the kids' orphanage and preliminary inquiries about the children's' birth family.

Who knows what we'll find? I'm glad God's in charge of that, not me.

Later that night, Tori and Gabe watched as Lydia, wearing her newly father-sanctioned dress, waltzed around the den with Phillip to the strains of "Blue Velvet." When the music ended, Lydia swept her father a curtsey, and then hurried over to her iPod and started "Get Low."

"C'mon, Gabe, dance with me!"

Phillip stood behind Tori's wheelchair. His hand squeezed her shoulder as they watched Gabe mimic Lydia's moves. His steps were not quite in sync with his sister's, but he moved well and seemed to be enjoying himself.

"Happy, my elfin beauty?" Phillip questioned.

"Very," Tori answered. Gabe skittered to a stop in front of Tori.

"Mama, dance!" Gabe's eyes, for this moment at least, were locked into hers.

Tori leaned forward, took his hand, and moved her torso back and forth in time with the music. She had become pretty adept at handling the wheelchair; she was able to move it rhythmically in all directions, following Gabe's movements.

Lydia squealed in delight and claimed Phillip as her partner. All four danced.

Tori supposed that someone looking in through the window might pity their wheelchair waltz, look with sympathy at the clumsy movements of this family ballet.

Or, they may envy us our hard-won joy. We're moving in steps designed specifically for us by the Master Choreographer. We can dance oblivious to accepted standards. The music ended. Lydia went upstairs to put away her dress and Gabe wandered off in the direction of his computer.

Phillip smiled at Tori and ruffled her hair.

"What're you thinking, Little Love?"

"I'm thinking we've danced out of the shadows."

IF YOU WOULD LIKE TO KNOW MORE ABOUT
THE SOURCE OF TORI'S STRENGTH AND PEACE, PLEASE CALL
1-800-NEEDHIM TO LEARN ABOUT
A SAVING RELATIONSHIP WITH JESUS CHRIST.

For more information about
D'Ann Renner
&
Dancing from the Shadows
please visit:

dannrenner.com
rennerdann@gmail.com
www.facebook.com/dannrennerauthor
@DAnnRenner

For more information about
AMBASSADOR INTERNATIONAL
please visit:

www.ambassador-international.com
@AmbassadorIntl
www.facebook.com/AmbassadorIntl